THE SCIONS OF SHANNARA

Also from Orbit by Terry Brooks:

THE SWORD OF SHANNARA
THE ELFSTONES OF SHANNARA
WISHSONG OF SHANNARA
THE DRUID OF SHANNARA

MAGIC KINGDOM FOR SALE/SOLD!
THE BLACK UNICORN
WIZARD AT LARGE

TERRY BROOKS

The Scions of Shannara

Book One of *The Heritage of Shannara*

ORBIT

An Orbit Book

Copyright © 1989 by Terry Brooks

The right of Terry Brooks to be identified
as author of this work has been asserted.

First published in Great Britain in 1989 by
Macdonald & Co (Publishers) Ltd
London & Sydney

This edition published by Orbit Books in 1990.
Reprinted in 1991 (twice)

ISBN 0 7088 4899 0

Printed and bound in Great Britain by
BPCC Hazell Books
Aylesbury, Bucks, England
Member of BPCC Ltd.

Orbit Books
A Division of
Macdonald & Co (Publishers) Ltd
165 Great Dover Street
London SE1 4YA

A member of Maxwell Macmillan Publishing Corporation

For Judine
who makes all the magic possible

CHAPTER

1

THE OLD MAN SAT ALONE in the shadow of the Dragon's Teeth and watched the coming darkness chase the daylight west. The day had been cool, unusually so for midsummer, and the night promised to be chill. Scattered clouds masked the sky, casting their silhouettes upon the earth, drifting in the manner of aimless beasts between moon and stars. A hush filled the emptiness left by the fading light like a voice waiting to speak.

It was a hush that whispered of magic, the old man thought.

A fire burned before him, small still, just the beginning of what was needed. After all, he would be gone for several hours. He studied the fire with a mixture of expectation and uneasiness before reaching down to add the larger chunks of deadwood that brought the flames up quickly. He poked at it with a stick, then stepped away, driven back by the heat. He stood at the edge of the light, caught between the fire and the growing dark, a creature who might have belonged to neither or both.

His eyes glittered as he looked off into the distance. The peaks of the Dragon's Teeth jutted skyward like bones that the earth could not contain. There was a hush to the mountains, a secrecy that clung like mist on a frosty morning and hid all the dreams of the ages.

The fire sparked sharply and the old man brushed at a

stray bit of glowing ash that threatened to settle on him. He was just a bundle of sticks, loosely tied together, that might crumble into dust if a strong wind were to blow. Gray robes and a forest cloak hung on him as they would have on a scarecrow. His skin was leathery and brown and had shrunken close against his bones. White hair and beard wreathed his head, thin and fine, like wisps of gauze against the firelight. He was so wrinkled and hunched down that he looked to be a hundred years old.

He was, in fact, almost a thousand.

Strange, he thought suddenly, remembering his years. Paranor, the Councils of the Races, even the Druids — gone. Strange that he should have outlasted them all.

He shook his head. It was so long ago, so far back in time that it was a part of his life he only barely recognized. He had thought that part finished, gone forever. He had thought himself free. But he had never been that, he guessed. It wasn't possible to be free of something that, at the very least, was responsible for the fact that he was still alive.

How else, after all, save for the Druid Sleep, could he still be standing there?

He shivered against the descending night, darkness all about him now as the last of the sunlight slipped below the horizon. It was time. The dreams had told him it must be now, and he believed the dreams because he understood them. That, too, was a part of his old life that would not let him go — dreams, visions of worlds beyond worlds, or warnings and truths, of things that could and sometimes must be.

He stepped away from the fire and started up the narrow pathway into the rocks. Shadows closed about him, their touch chill. He walked for a long time, winding through narrow defiles, scrambling past massive boulders, angling along craggy drops and jagged splits in the rock. When he emerged again into the light, he stood within a shallow, rock-strewn valley dominated by a lake whose glassy surface reflected back at him with a harsh, greenish cast.

The lake was the resting place for the shades of Druids come and gone. It was to the Hadeshorn that he had been summoned.

'Might as well get on with it,' he growled softly.

He walked slowly, cautiously downward into the valley, his steps uneasy, his heart pounding in his ears. He had been away a long time. The waters before him did not stir; the shades lay sleeping. It was best that way, he thought. It was best that they not be disturbed.

He reached the lake's edge and stopped. All was silent. He took a deep breath, the air rattling from his chest as he exhaled like dry leaves blown across stone. He fumbled at his waist for a pouch and loosened its drawstrings. Carefully he reached within and drew out a handful of black powder laced with silver sparkle. He hesitated, then threw it into the air over the lake.

The powder exploded skyward with a strange light that brightened the air about him as if it were day again. There was no heat, only light. It shimmered and danced against the nighttime like a living thing. The old man watched, robes and forest cloak pulled close, eyes bright with the reflected glow. He rocked back and forth slightly and for a moment felt young again.

Then a shadow appeared suddenly in the light, lifting out of it like a wraith, a black form that might have been something strayed from the darkness beyond. But the old man knew better. This was nothing strayed; this was something called. The shadow tightened and took shape. It was the shade of a man cloaked all in black, a tall and forbidding apparition that anyone who had ever seen it before would have recognized at once.

'So, Allanon,' the old man whispered.

The hooded face tilted back so that the light revealed the dark, harsh features clearly — the angular bearded face, the long thin nose and mouth, the fierce brow that might have been cast of iron, the eyes beneath that seemed to look directly into the soul. The eyes found the old man and held him fast.

— I need you —

The voice was a whisper in the old man's mind, a hiss of dissatisfaction and urgency. The shade communicated by using thoughts alone. The old man shrank back momentarily, wishing that the thing he had called would instead be gone. Then he recovered himself and stood firm before his fears.

'I am no longer one of you!' he snapped, his own eyes narrowing dangerously, forgetting that it was not necessary to speak aloud. 'You cannot command me!'

— I do not command. I request. Listen to me. You are all that is left, the last that may be until my successor is found. Do you understand —

The old man laughed nervously. 'Understand? Ha! Who understands better than me?'

— A part of you will always be what once you would not have questioned. The magic stays within you. Always. Help me. I send the dreams and the Shannara children do not respond. Someone must go to them. Someone must make them see. You —

'Not me! I have lived apart from the races for years now. I wish nothing more to do with their troubles!' The old man straightened his stick form and frowned. 'I shed myself of such nonsense long ago.'

The shade seemed to rise and broaden suddenly before him, and he felt himself lifted free of the earth. He soared skyward, far into the night. He did not struggle, but held himself firm, though he could feel the other's anger rushing through him like a black river. The shade's voice was the sound of bones grating.

— Watch —

The Four Lands appeared, spread out before him, a panorama of grasslands, mountains, hills, lakes, forests, and rivers, bright swatches of earth colored by sunlight. He caught his breath to see it so clearly and from so far up in the sky, even knowing that it was only a vision. But the sunlight began to fade almost at once, the color to wash. Darkness closed about, filled with dull gray mist and sulfurous ash that rose from burned out craters. The land lost its character and became barren and lifeless. He

felt himself drift closer, repulsed as he descended by the
sights and smells of it. Humans wandered the devastation
in packs, more animals than men. They rent and tore at
each other; they howled and shrieked. Dark shapes flitted
among them, shadows that lacked substance yet had eyes
of fire. The shadows moved through the humans, joining
with them, becoming them, leaving them again. They
moved in a dance that was macabre, yet purposeful. The
shadows were devouring the humans, he saw. The
shadows were feeding on them.

— Watch —

The vision shifted. He saw himself then, a skeletal,
ragged beggar facing a cauldron of strange white fire that
bubbled and swirled and whispered his name. Vapors
lifted from the cauldron and snaked their way down to
where he stood, wrapping about him, caressing him as if
he were their child. Shadows flitted all about, passing by
at first, then entering him as if he were a hollow casing in
which they might play as they chose. He could feel their
touch; he wanted to scream.

— Watch —

The vision shifted once more. There was a huge forest
and in the middle of the forest a great mountain. Atop the
mountain sat a castle, old and weathered, towers and
parapets rising up against the dark of the land. Paranor,
he thought! It was Paranor come again! He felt something
bright and hopeful well up within him, and he wanted to
shout his elation. But the vapors were already coiling
about the castle. The shadows were already flitting close.
The ancient fortress began to crack and crumble, stone
and mortar giving way as if caught in a vise. The earth
shuddered and screams lifted from the humans become
animals. Fire erupted out of the earth, splitting apart the
mountain on which Paranor sat and then the castle itself.
Wailing filled the air, the sound of one bereft of the only
hope that had remained to him. The old man recognized
the wailing as his own.

Then the images were gone. He stood again before the
Hadeshorn, in the shadow of the Dragon's Teeth, alone

5

with the shade of Allanon. In spite of his resolve, he was shaking.

The shade pointed at him.

— It will be as I have shown you if the dreams are ignored. It will be so if you fail to act. You must help. Go to them — the boy, the girl, and the Dark Uncle. Tell them the dreams are real. Tell them to come to me here on the first night of the new moon when the present cycle is complete. I will speak with them then —

The old man frowned and muttered and worried his lower lip. His fingers once more drew tight the drawstrings to the pouch, and he shoved it back into his belt. 'I will do so because there is no one else!' he said finally, spitting out the words in distaste. 'But do not expect . . . !'

— Only go to them. Nothing more is required. Nothing more will be asked. Go —

The shade of Allanon shimmered brightly and disappeared. The light faded, and the valley was empty again. The old man stood looking out over the still waters of the lake for a moment, then turned away.

The fire he had left behind still burned on his return, but it was small now and frail-looking against the night. The old man stared absently at the flames, then hunkered down before them. He stirred at the ashes already forming and listened to the silence of his thoughts.

The boy, the girl, and the Dark Uncle — he knew them. They were the Shannara children, the ones who could save them all, the ones who could bring back the magic. He shook his grizzled head. How was he to convince them? If they would not heed Allanon, what chance that they would heed him?

He saw again in his mind the frightening visions. He had best find a way to make them listen, he thought. Because, as he was fond of reminding himself, he knew something of visions, and there was a truth to these that even one such as he, one who had forsworn the Druids and their magic, could recognize.

If the Shannara children failed to listen, these visions would come to pass.

CHAPTER

2

PAR OHMSFORD STOOD in the rear doorway of the Blue Whisker Ale House and stared down the darkened tunnel of the narrow street that ran between the adjoining buildings into the glimmer of Varfleet's lights. The Blue Whisker was a ramshackle, sprawling old building with weathered board walls and a wood shingle roof and looked for all the world as if once it had been someone's barn. It had sleeping rooms upstairs over the serving hall and storerooms in the back. It sat at the base of a block of buildings that formed a somewhat lopsided U, situated on a hill at the western edge of the city.

Par breathed deeply the night air, savoring its flavors. City smells, smells of life, stews with meats and vegetables laced with spice, sharp-flavored liquors and pungent ales, perfumes that scented rooms and bodies, leather harness, iron from forges still red with coals kept perpetually bright, the sweat of animals and men in close quarters, the taste of stone and wood and dust, mingling and mixing, each occasionally breaking free — they were all there. Down the alleyway, beyond the slat-boarded, graffiti-marked backs of the shops and businesses, the hill dropped away to where the central part of the city lay east. An ugly, colorless gathering of buildings in daylight, a maze of stone walls and streets, wooden siding and pitch-sealed roofs, the city took on a different look at night. The buildings faded into the darkness and the lights appeared, thousands of them, stretching away as far as the eye could see like a swarm of fireflies. They dotted the masked landscape, flickering in the black, trailing lines of gold across the liquid skin of the Mermidon as it passed south. Varfleet was beautiful now, the scrubwoman became a fairy queen, transformed as if by magic.

Par liked the idea of the city being magic. He liked the city in any case, liked its sprawl and its meld of people and things, its rich mix of life. It was far different from his home of Shady Vale, nothing like the forested hamlet that he had grown up in. It lacked the purity of the trees and streams, the solitude, the sense of timeless ease that graced life in the Vale. It knew nothing of that life and couldn't have cared less. But that didn't matter to Par. He liked the city anyway. There was nothing to say that he had to choose between the two, after all. There wasn't any reason he couldn't appreciate both.

Coll, of course, didn't agree. Coll saw it quite differently. He saw Varfleet as nothing more than an outlaw city at the edge of Federation rule, a den of miscreants, a place where one could get away with anything. In all of Callahorn, in all of the entire Southland for that matter, there was no place worse. Coll hated the city.

Voices and the clink of glasses drifted out of the darkness behind him, the sounds of the ale house breaking free of the front room momentarily as a door was opened, then disappearing again as it was closed. Par turned. His brother moved carefully down the hallway, nearly faceless in the gloom.

'It's almost time,' Coll said when he reached him.

Par nodded. He looked small and slender next to Coll, who was a big, strong youth with blunt features and mud-colored hair. A stranger would not have thought them brothers. Coll looked a typical Valeman, tanned and rough, with enormous hands and feet. The feet were an ongoing joke. Par was fond of comparing them to a duck's. Par was slight and fair, his own features un-

8

mistakably Elven from the sharply pointed ears and brows to the high, narrow bones of his face. There was a time when the Elven blood had been all but bred out of the line, the result of generations of Ohmsfords living in the Vale. But four generations back (so his father had told him) his great-great grandfather had returned to the Westland and the Elves, married an Elven girl, and produced a son and a daughter. The son had married another Elven girl, and for reasons never made clear the young couple who would become Par's great-grand-parents had returned to the Vale, thereby infusing a fresh supply of Elven blood into the Ohmsford line. Ever then, many members of the family showed nothing of their mixed heritage; Coll and his parents Jaralan and Mirianna were examples. Par's bloodlines, on the other hand, were immediately evident.

Being recognizable in this way, unfortunately, was not necessarily desirable. While in Varfleet, Par disguised his features, plucking his brows, wearing his hair long to hide his ears, shading his face with darkener. He didn't have much choice. It wasn't wise to draw attention to one's Elven lineage these days.

'She has her gown nicely in place tonight, doesn't she?' Coll said, glancing off down the alleyway to the city beyond. 'Black velvet and sparkles, not a thread left hanging. Clever girl, this city. Even the sky is her friend.'

Par smiled. My brother, the poet. The sky was clear and filled with the brightness of a tiny crescent moon and stars. 'You might come to like her if you gave her half a chance.'

'Me?' Coll snorted. 'Not likely. I'm here because you're here. I wouldn't stay another minute if I didn't have to.'

'You could go if you wanted.'

Coll bristled. 'Let's not start again, Par. We've been all through that. You were the one who thought we ought to come north to the cities. I didn't like the idea then, and I don't like it any better now. But that doesn't change the fact that we agreed to do this together, you and me. A fine brother I'd be if I left you here and went back to the

9

Vale now! In any case, I don't think you could manage without me.'

'All right, all right, I was just . . .' Par tried to interrupt.

'Attempting to have a little fun at my expense!' Coll finished heatedly. 'You have done that on more than one occasion of late. You seem to take some delight in it.'

'That is not so.'

Coll ignored him, gazing off into the dark.

'I would never pick on anyone with duck feet.'

Coll grinned in spite of himself. 'Fine talk from a little fellow with pointed ears. You should be grateful I choose to stay and look after you!'

Par shoved him playfully, and they both laughed. Then they went quiet, staring at each other in the dark, listening to the sounds of the ale house and the streets beyond. Par sighed. It was a warm, lazy midsummer night that made the cool, sharp days of the past few weeks seem a distant memory. It was the kind of night when troubles scatter and dreams come out to play.

'There are rumors of Seekers in the city,' Coll informed him suddenly, spoiling his contentment.

'There are always rumors,' he replied.

'And the rumors are often true. Talk has it that they plan to snatch up all the magic-makers, put them out of business and close down the ale houses.' Coll was staring intently at him. 'Seekers, Par. Not simple soldiers. Seekers.'

Par knew what they were. Seekers — Federation secret police, the enforcement arm of the Coalition Council's Lawmakers. He knew.

They had arrived in Varfleet two weeks earlier, Coll and he. They journeyed north from Shady Vale, left the security and familiarity and protective confines of their family home and came into the Borderlands of Callahorn. They did so because Par had decided they must, that it was time for them to tell their stories elsewhere, that it was necessary to see to it that others besides the Vale people knew. They came to Varfleet because Varfleet was an open city, free of Federation rule, a haven for outlaws and refugees but also for ideas, a place where people still listened with open minds, a place where magic was still tolerated — even courted. He had the magic and, with Coll in tow, he took it to Varfleet to share its wonder. There was already magic aplenty being practiced by others, but his was of a far different sort. His was real.

They found the Blue Whisker the first day they arrived, one of the biggest and best known ale houses in the city. Par persuaded the owner to hire them in the first sitting. He had expected as much. After all, he could persuade anyone to do just about anything with the wishsong.

Real magic. He mouthed the words without speaking them.

There wasn't much real magic left in the Four Lands, not outside the remote wilderness areas where Federation rule did not yet extend. The wishsong was the last of the Ohmsford magic. It had been passed down through ten generations to reach him, the gift skipping some members of his family altogether, picking and choosing on a whim. Coll didn't have it. His parents didn't. In fact, no one in the Ohmsford family had had it since his great-grandparents had returned from the Westland. But the magic of the wishsong had been his from the time he was born, the same magic that had come into existence almost three hundred years ago with his ancestor Jair. The stories told him this, the legends. Wish for it, sing for it. He could create images so lifelike in the minds of his listeners that they appeared to be real. He could create substance out of air.

That was what had brought him to Varfleet. For three centuries the Ohmsford family had handed down stories of the Elven house of Shannara. The practice had begun with Jair. In truth, it had begun long before that, when the stories were not of the magic because it had not yet been discovered but of the old world before its destruction in the Great Wars and the tellers were the few who had survived that frightening holocaust. But Jair was the first to have use of the wishsong to aid in the telling, to give substance to the images created from his words, to

11

make his tales come alive in the minds of those who heard them. The tales were of the old days: of the legends of the Elven house of Shannara; of the Druids and their Keep at Paranor; of Elves and Dwarves; and of the magic that ruled their lives. The tales were of Shea Ohmsford and his brother Flick and their search to find the Sword of Shannara; of Wil Ohmsford and the beautiful, tragic Elven girl Amberle and their struggle to banish the Demon hordes back into the Forbidding; of Jair Ohmsford and his sister Brin and their journey into the fortress of Graymark and confrontation with the Mord Wraiths and the Ildatch; of the Druids Allanon and Bremen; of the Elven King Eventine Elessedil; of warriors such as Balinor Buckhannah and Stee Jans; of heroes many and varied. Those who had command of the wishsong made use of its magic. Those who did not relied on simple words. Ohmsfords had come and gone, many carrying the stories with them to distant lands. Yet for three generations now, no member of the family had told the stories outside the Vale. No one had wanted to risk being caught.

It was a considerable risk. The practice of magic in any form was outlawed in the Four Lands — or at least anywhere the Federation governed, which was practically the same thing. It had been so for the past hundred years. In all that time no Ohmsford had left the Vale. Par was the first. He had grown tired of telling the same stories to the same few listeners over and over. Others needed to hear the stories as well, to know the truth about the Druids and the magic, about the struggle that preceded the age in which they now lived. His fear of being caught was outweighed by the calling he felt. He made his decision despite the objections of his parents and Coll. Coll, ultimately, decided to come with him — just as he always did whenever he thought Par needed looking after. Varfleet was to be the beginning, a city where magic was still practiced in minor forms, an open secret defying intervention by the Federation. Such magic as was found in Varfleet was small stuff really and scarcely worth the trouble. Callahorn was only a protectorate of the Federation, and Varfleet so distant as to be almost into the free territories. It was not yet army-occupied. The Federation so far had disdained to bother with it.

But Seekers? Par shook his head. Seekers were another matter altogether. Seekers only appeared when there was a serious intent on the part of the Federation to stamp out a practice of magic. No one wanted any part of them.

'It grows too dangerous for us here,' Coll said, as if reading Par's mind. 'We will be discovered.'

Par shook his head. 'We are but one of a hundred practicing the art,' he replied. 'Just one in a city of many.'

Coll looked at him. 'One of a hundred, yes. But the only one using real magic.'

Par looked back. It was good money the ale house paid them, the best they had ever seen. They needed it to help with the taxes the Federation demanded. They needed it for their family and the Vale. He hated to give up because of a rumor.

His jaw tightened. He hated to give up even more because it meant the stories must be returned to the Vale and kept hidden there, untold to those who needed to hear. It meant that the repression of ideas and practices that clamped down about the Four Lands like a vise had tightened one turn more.

'We have to go,' Coll said, interrupting his thoughts.

Par felt a sudden rush of anger before realizing his brother was not saying they must go from the city, but from the doorway of the ale house to the performing stage inside. The crowd would be waiting. He let his anger slip away and felt a sadness take its place.

'I wish we lived in another age,' he said softly. He paused, watching the way Coll tensed. 'I wish there were Elves and Druids again. And heroes. I wish there could be heroes again — even one.'

He trailed off, thinking suddenly of something else.

Coll shoved away from the doorjamb, clapped one big hand to his brother's shoulder, turned him about and started him back down the darkened hallway. 'If you keep singing about it, who knows? Maybe there will be.'

13

Par let himself be led away like a child. He was no longer thinking about heroes though, or Elves or Druids, or even about Seekers.

He was thinking about the dreams.

They told the story of the Elven stand at Halys Cut, how Eventine Elessedil and the Elves and Stee Jans and the Legion Free Corps fought to hold the Breakline against the onslaught of the Demon hordes. It was one of Par's favorite stories, the first of the great Elven battles in that terrible Westland war. They stood on a low platform at one end of the main serving room, Par in the forefront, Coll a step back and aside, the lights dimmed against a sea of tightly packed bodies and watchful eyes. While Coll narrated the story, Par sang to provide the accompanying images, and the ale house came alive with the magic of his voice. He invoked in the hundred or more gathered the feelings of fear, anger and determination that had infused the defenders of the Cut. He let them see the fury of the Demons; he let them hear their battle cries. He drew them in and would not let them go. They stood in the pathway of the Demon assault. They saw the wounding of Eventine and the emergence of his son Ander as leader of the Elves. They watched the Druid Allanon stand virtually alone against the Demon magic and turn it aside. They experienced life and death with an intimacy that was almost terrifying.

When Coll and he were finished, there was stunned silence, then a wild thumping of ale glasses and cheers and shouts of elation unmatched in any performance that had gone before. It seemed for a moment that those gathered might bring the rafters of the ale house down about their ears, so vehement were they in their appreciation. Par was damp with his own sweat, aware for the first time how much he had given to the telling. Yet his mind was curiously detached as they left the platform for the brief rest they were permitted between tellings, thinking still of the dreams.

Coll stopped for a glass of ale by an open storage room and Par continued down the hallway a short distance before coming to an empty barrel turned upright by the cellar doors. He slumped down wearily, his thoughts tight.

He had been having the dreams for almost a month now, and he still didn't know why.

The dreams occurred with a frequency that was unsettling. They always began with a black-cloaked figure that rose from a lake, a figure that might be Allanon, a lake that might be the Hadeshorn. There was a shimmering of images in his dreams, an ethereal quality to the visions that made them difficult to decipher. The figure always spoke to him, always with the same words. 'Come to me; you are needed. The Four Lands are in gravest danger; the magic is almost lost. Come now, Shannara child.'

There was more, although the rest varied. Sometimes there were images of a world born of some unspeakable nightmare. Sometimes there were images of the lost talismans — the Sword of Shannara and the Elfstones. Sometimes there was a call for Wren as well, little Wren, and sometimes a call for his uncle Walker Boh. They were to come as well. They were needed, too.

He had decided quite deliberately after the first night that the dreams were a side effect of his prolonged use of the wishsong. He sang the old stories of the Warlock Lord and the Skull Bearers, of Demons and Mord Wraiths, of Allanon and a world threatened by evil, and it was natural that something of those stories and their images would carry over into his sleep. He had tried to combat the effect by using the wishsong on lighter tellings, but it hadn't helped. The dreams persisted. He had refrained from telling Coll, who would have simply used that as a new excuse to advise him to stop invoking the magic of the wishsong and return to the Vale.

Then, three nights ago, the dreams had stopped coming as suddenly as they had started. Now he was wondering why. He was wondering if perhaps he had mistaken their origin. He was considering the possibility that instead of being self-induced, they might have been sent.

But who would have sent them?

Allanon? Truly Allanon, who was three hundred years dead?

Someone else?

Some*thing* else? Something that had a reason of its own and meant him no good?

He shivered at the prospect, brushed the matter from his mind, and went quickly back up the hallway to find Coll.

The crowd was even larger for the second telling, the walls lined with standing men who could not find chairs or benches to sit upon. The Blue Whisker was a large house, the front serving room over a hundred feet across and open to the rafters above a stringing of oil lamps and fish netting that lent a sort of veiled appearance that was apparently designed to suggest intimacy. Par couldn't have tolerated much more intimacy, so close were the patrons of the ale house as they pressed up against the platform, some actually sitting on it now as they drank. This was a different group from earlier, although the Valeman was hard pressed to say why. It had a different feel to it, as if there was something foreign in its makeup. Coll must have felt it, too. He glanced over at Par several times as they prepared to perform, and there was uneasiness mirrored in his dark eyes.

A tall, black-bearded man wrapped in a dun-colored forest cloak waded through the crowd to the platform's edge and eased himself down between two other men. The two looked up as if they intended to say something, then caught a close glimpse of the other's face and apparently thought better of it. Par watched momentarily and looked away. Everything felt wrong.

Coll leaned over as a rhythmic clapping began. The crowd was growing restless. 'Par, I don't like this. There's something . . .'

He didn't finish. The owner of the ale house came up and told them in no uncertain terms to begin before the crowd got out of hand and started breaking things. Coll stepped away wordlessly. The lights dimmed, and Par started to sing. The story was the one about Allanon and the battle with the Jachyra. Coll began to speak, setting the stage, telling those gathered what sort of day it was, what the glen was like into which the Druid came with Brin Ohmsford and Rone Leah, how everything suddenly grew hushed. Par created the images in the minds of his listeners, instilling in them a sense of anxiety and expectation, trying unsuccessfully not to experience the same feelings himself.

At the rear of the room, men were moving to block the doors and windows, men suddenly shed of cloaks and dressed all in black. Weapons glittered. There were patches of white on sleeves and breasts, insignia of some sort. Par squinted, Elven vision sharp.

A wolf's head.

The men in black were Seekers.

Par's voice faltered and the images shimmered and lost their hold. Men began to grumble and look about. Coll stopped his narration. There was movement everywhere. There was someone in the darkness behind them. There was someone all about.

Coll edged closer protectively.

Then the lights rose again, and a wedge of the black-garbed Seekers pushed forward from the front door. There were shouts and groans of protest, but the men making them were quick to move out of the way. The owner of the Blue Whisker tried to intervene, but was shoved aside.

The wedge of men came to a stop directly in front of the platform. Another group blocked the exits. They wore black from head to toe, their faces covered above their mouths, their wolf head insignia gleaming. They were armed with short swords, daggers, and truncheons, and their weapons were held ready. They were a mixed bunch, big and small, stiff and bent, but there was a feral

look to all of them, as much in the way they held themselves as in their eyes.

Their leader was a huge, rangy man with tremendously
long arms and a powerful frame. There was a craggy cast
to his face where the mask ended, and a half-beard of
coarse reddish hair covered his chin. His left arm was
gloved to the elbow.

'Your names?' he asked. His voice was soft, almost a
whisper.

Par hesitated. 'What is it that we have done?'

'Is your name Ohmsford?' The speaker was studying
him intently.

Par nodded. 'Yes. But we haven't ...'

'You are under arrest for violating Federation Supreme
Law,' the soft voice announced. There was a grumbling
sound from the patrons. 'You have used magic in defiance
of ...'

'They was just telling stories!' a man called out from a
few feet away. One of the Seekers lashed out swiftly with
his truncheon and the man collapsed in a heap.

'You have used magic in defiance of Federation
dictates and thereby endangered the public.' The speaker
did not even bother to glance at the fallen man. 'You will
be taken ...'

He never finished. An oil lamp dropped suddenly from
the center of the ceiling to the crowded ale house floor
and exploded in a shower of flames. Men sprang to their
feet, howling. The speaker and his companions turned in
surprise. At the same moment the tall, bearded man who
had taken a seat on the platform's edge earlier came to his
feet with a lunge, vaulted several other astonished
patrons, and slammed into the knot of Seekers, spilling
them to the floor. The tall man leaped onto the stage in
front of Par and Coll and threw off his shabby cloak to
reveal a fully armed hunter dressed in forest green. One
arm lifted, the hand clenched in a fist.

'Free-born!' he shouted into the confusion.

It seemed that everything happened at once after that.
The decorative netting, somehow loosened, followed the

oil lamp to the floor, and practically everyone gathered at the Blue Whisker was suddenly entangled. Yells and curses rose from those trapped. At the doors, green-clad men pounced on the bewildered Seekers and hammered them to the floor. Oil lamps were smashed, and the room was plunged into darkness.

The tall man moved past Par and Coll with a quickness they would not have believed possible. He caught the first of the Seekers blocking the back entrance with a sweep of one boot, snapping the man's head back. A short sword and dagger appeared, and the remaining two went down as well.

'This way, quick now!' he called back to Par and Coll.

They came at once. A dark shape clawed at them as they rushed past, but Coll knocked the man from his feet into the mass of struggling bodies. He reached back to be certain he had not lost his brother, his big hand closing on Par's slender shoulder. Par yelled in spite of himself. Coll always forgot how strong he was.

They cleared the stage and reached the back hallway, the tall stranger several paces ahead. Someone tried to stop them, but the stranger ran right over him. The din from the room behind them was deafening, and flames were scattered everywhere now, licking hungrily at the flooring and walls. The stranger led them quickly down the hall and through the rear door into the alleyway. Two more of the green-clad men waited. Wordlessly, they surrounded the brothers and rushed them clear of the ale house. Par glanced back. The flames were already leaping from the windows and crawling up toward the roof. The Blue Whisker had seen its last night.

They slipped down the alleyway past startled faces and wide eyes, turned into a passageway Par would have sworn he had never seen before despite his many excursions out that way, passed through a scattering of doors and anterooms and finally emerged into a new street entirely. No one spoke. When at last they were beyond the sound of the shouting and the glow of the fire, the stranger slowed, motioned his two companions to take up watch and pulled Par and Coll into a shadowed alcove.

All were breathing heavily from the run. The stranger looked at them in turn, grinning. 'A little exercise is good for the digestion, they say. What do you think? Are you all right?'

The brothers both nodded. 'Who are you?' asked Par.

The grin broadened. 'Why, practically one of the family, lad. Don't you recognize me? Ah, you don't, do you? But, then, why should you? After all, you and I have never met. But the songs should remind you.' He closed his left hand into a fist, then thrust a single finger sharply at Par's nose. 'Remember now?'

Mystified, Par looked at Coll, but his brother appeared as confused as he was. 'I don't think . . .' he started.

'Well, well, it doesn't matter just at the moment. All in good time.' He bent close. 'This is no longer safe country for you, lad. Certainly not here in Varfleet and probably not in all of Callahorn. Maybe not anywhere. Do you know who that was back there? The ugly one with the whisper?'

Par tried to place the rangy speaker with the soft voice. He couldn't. He shook his head slowly.

'Rimmer Dall,' the stranger said, the smile gone now. 'First Seeker, the high mucky-muck himself. Sits on the Coalition Council when he's not out swatting flies. But you, he's taken a special interest if he's come all the way to Varfleet to arrest you. That's not part of his ordinary fly-swatting. That's hunting bear. He thinks you are dangerous, lad — very dangerous, indeed, or he wouldn't have bothered coming all the way here. Good thing I was looking out for you. I was, you know. Heard Rimmer Dall was going to come for you and came to make sure he didn't get the job done. Mind now, he won't give up. You slipped his grasp this time, but that will make him just that much more determined. He'll keep coming for you.'

He paused, gauging the effect of what he was saying. Par was staring at him speechlessly, so he went on. 'That magic of yours, the singing, that's real magic, isn't it? I've seen enough of the other kind to know. You could put that magic to good use, lad, if you had a mind to. It's wasted in these ale houses and backstreets.'

'What do you mean?' Coll asked, suddenly suspicious.

The stranger smiled, charming and guileless. 'The Movement has need of such magic,' he said softly.

Coll snorted. 'You're one of the outlaws!'

The stranger executed a quick bow. 'Yes, lad, I am proud to say I am. More important, I am free-born and I do not accept Federation rule. No right thinking man does.' He bent close. 'You don't accept it yourself now, do you? Admit it.'

'Hardly,' Coll answered defensively. 'But I question whether the outlaws are any better.'

'Harsh words, lad!' the other exclaimed. 'A good thing for you I do not take offense easily.' He grinned roguishly.

'What is it you want?' Par interrupted quickly, his mind clear again. He had been thinking of Rimmer Dall. He knew the man's reputation and he was frightened of the prospect of being hunted by him. 'You want us to join you, is that it?'

The stranger nodded. 'You would find it worth your time, I think.'

But Par shook his head. It was one thing to accept the stranger's help in fleeing the Seekers. It was another to join the Movement. The matter needed a great deal more thought. 'I think we had better decline for now,' he said evenly. 'That is, if we're being given a choice.'

'Of course you are being given a choice!' The stranger seemed offended.

'Then we have to say no. But we thank you for the offer and especially for your help back there.'

The stranger studied him a moment, solemn again. 'You are quite welcome, believe me. I wish only the best for you, Par Ohmsford. Here, take this.' He removed from one hand a ring that was cast in silver and bore the insigne of a hawk. 'My friends know me by this. If you need a favor — or if you change your mind — take this to Kiltan Forge at Reaver's End at the north edge of the city

21

and ask for the Archer. Can you remember that?'

Par hesitated, then took the ring, nodding. 'But why . . .?'

'Because there is much between us, lad,' the other said softly, anticipating his question. One hand reached out to rest on his shoulder. The eyes took in Coll as well. 'There is history that binds us, a bond of such strength that it requires I be there for you if I can. More, it requires that we stand together against what is threatening this land. Remember that, too. One day, we will do so, I think — if we all manage to stay alive until then.'

He grinned at the brothers and they stared back silently. The stranger's hand dropped away. 'Time to go now. Quickly, too. The street runs east to the river. You can go where you wish from there. But watch yourselves. Keep your backs well guarded. This matter isn't finished.'

'I know,' Par said and extended his hand. 'Are you certain you will not tell us your name?'

The stranger hesitated. 'Another day,' he said.

He gripped Par's hand tightly, then Coll's, then whistled his companions to him. He waved once, then melted into the shadows and was gone.

Par stared down momentarily at the ring, then glanced questioningly at Coll. Somewhere close at hand, the sound of shouting started up.

'I think the questions will have to wait,' said Coll.

Par jammed the ring into his pocket. Wordlessly, they disappeared into the night.

CHAPTER

3

T WAS NEARING MIDNIGHT by the time Par and Coll reached the waterfront section of Varfleet, and it was there that they first realized how ill-prepared they were to make their escape from Rimmer Dall and his Federation Seekers. Neither had expected that flight would prove necessary, so neither had brought anything that a lengthy journey might require. They had no food, no blankets, no weapons save for the standard long knives all Valemen wore, no camping gear or foul-weather equipment, and worst of all no money. The ale house keeper hadn't paid them in a month. What money they had managed to save from the month before had been lost in the fire along with everything else they owned. They had only the clothes on their backs and a growing fear that perhaps they should have stuck with the nameless stranger a bit longer.

The waterfront was a ramshackle mass of boathouses, piers, mending shops, and storage sheds. Lights burned along its length, and dockworkers and fishermen drank and joked in the light of oil lamps and pipes. Smoke rose out of tin stoves and barrels, and the smell of fish hung over everything.

'Maybe they've given up on us for the night,' Par suggested at one point. 'The Seekers, I mean. Maybe they won't bother looking anymore until morning — or maybe not at all.'

Coll glanced at him and arched one eyebrow meaningfully. 'Maybe cows can fly, too.' He looked away. 'We should have insisted we be paid more promptly for our work. Then we wouldn't be in this fix.'

Par shrugged. 'It wouldn't have made any difference.'

'It wouldn't? We'd at least have some money!'

'Only if we'd thought to carry it with us to the performance. How likely is that?'

Coll hunched his shoulders and screwed up his face. 'That ale house keeper owes us.'

They walked all the way to the south end of the docks without speaking further, stopping finally as the lighted waterfront gave way to darkness, and stood looking at each other. The night was cooler now and their clothes were too thin to protect them. They were shivering, their hands jammed down in their pockets, their arms clamped tightly against their sides. Insects buzzed about them annoyingly.

Coll sighed. 'Do you have any idea where we're going, Par? Do you have some kind of plan in mind?'

Par took out his hands and rubbed them briskly. 'I do. But it requires a boat to get there.'

'South, then — down the Mermidon?'

'All the way.'

Coll smiled, misunderstanding. He thought they were headed back to Shady Vale. Par decided it was best to leave him with that impression.

'Wait here,' Coll said suddenly and disappeared before Par could object.

Par stood alone in the dark at the end of the docks for what seemed like an hour, but was probably closer to half that. He walked over to a bench by a fishing shack and sat down, hunched up against the night air. He was feeling a mix of things. He was angry, mostly — at the stranger for spiriting them away and then abandoning them — all right, so Par had asked to have it that way, that didn't make him feel any better — at the Federation for chasing them out from the city like common thieves, and at himself for being stupid enough to think he could get away with using real magic when it was absolutely forbidden to do so. It was one thing to play around with the magics of sleight of hand and quick change; it was another altogether to employ the magic of the wishsong. It was too obviously the real thing, and he should have known that sooner or later word of its use would get back to the authorities.

He put his legs out in front of him and crossed his boots. Well, there was nothing to be done about it now. Coll and he would simply have to start over again. It never occurred to him to quit. The stories were too important for that; it was his responsibility to see to it that they were not forgotten. He was convinced that the magic was a gift he had received expressly for that purpose. It didn't matter what the Federation said — that magic was outlawed and that it was a source of great harm to the land and its people. What did the Federation know of magic? Those on the Coalition Council lacked any practical experience. They had simply decided that something needed to be done to address the concerns of those who claimed parts of the Four Lands were sickening and men were being turned into something like the dark creatures of Jair Ohmsford's time, creatures from some nether existence that defied understanding, beings that drew their power from the night and from magics lost since the time of the Druids.

They even had names, these creatures. They were called Shadowen.

Suddenly, unpleasantly, Par thought again of the dreams and of the dark thing within them that had summoned him.

He was aware then that the night had gone still; the voices of the fishermen and dockworkers, the buzz of the insects, and even the rustle of the night wind had disappeared. He could hear the sound of his own pulse in his ears, and a whisper of something else . . .

Then a splash of water brought him to his feet with a start. Coll appeared, clambering out of the Mermidon at the river's edge a dozen feet away, shedding water as he came. He was naked. Par recovered his composure and stared at him in disbelief.

'Shades, you frightened me! What were you doing?'

'What does it look like I was doing?' Coll grinned. 'I was out swimming!'

What he was really doing, Par discovered after applying a bit more pressure, was appropriating a fishing skiff owned by the keeper of the Blue Whisker. The keeper had mentioned it to Coll once or twice when bragging about his fishing skills. Coll had remembered it when Par had mentioned needing a boat, remembered as well the description of the boat shed where the man said it was kept, and gone off to find it. He'd simply swum up to where it was stored, snapped the lock on the shed, slipped the mooring lines and towed it away.

'It's the least he owes us after the kind of business we brought in,' he said defensively as he brushed himself dry and dressed.

Par didn't argue the point. They needed a boat worse than the ale house keeper, and this was probably their only chance to find one. Assuming the Seekers were still scouring the city for them, their only other alternative was to strike out on foot into the Runne Mountains — an undertaking that would require more than a week. A ride down the Mermidon was a journey of only a few days. It wasn't as if they were stealing the boat, after all. He caught himself. Well, maybe it was. But they would return it or provide proper compensation when they could.

The skiff was only a dozen feet in length, but it was equipped with oars, fishing gear, some cooking and camping equipment, a pair of blankets, and a canvas tarp. They boarded and pushed off into the night, letting the current carry them out from the shore and sweep them away.

They rode the river south for the remainder of the night, using the oars to keep it in mid-channel, listening to the night sounds, watching the shoreline, and trying to stay awake. As they traveled, Coll offered his theory on what they should do next. It was impossible, of course, to go back into Callahorn any time in the immediate future. The Federation would be looking for them. It would be dangerous, in fact, to travel to any of the major Southland cities because the Federation authorities stationed there would be alerted as well. It was best that they simply return to the Vale. They could still tell the stories — not right away perhaps, but in a month or so after the Federation had stopped looking for them. Then, later, they could travel to some of the smaller hamlets, the more isolated communities, places the Federation seldom visited. It would all work out fine.

Par let him ramble. He was willing to bet that Coll didn't believe a word of it; and even if he did, there was no point in arguing about it now.

They pulled into shore at sunrise and made camp in a grove of shade trees at the base of a windswept bluff, sleeping until noon, then rising to catch and eat fish. They were back on the river by early afternoon and continued on until well after sunset. Again they pulled into shore and made camp. It was starting to rain, and they put up the canvas to provide shelter. They made a small fire, pulled the blankets about them and sat silently facing the river, watching the raindrops swell its flow and form intricate patterns on its shimmering surface.

They spoke then for a while about how things had changed in the Four Lands since the time of Jair Ohmsford.

Three hundred years ago, the Federation governed only the deep Southland cities, adopting a strict policy of isolationism. The Coalition Council provided its leadership even then, a body of men selected by the cities as representatives to its government. But it was the Federation armies that gradually came to dominate the Council, and in time the policy of isolationism gave way to one of expansion. It was time to extend its sphere of influence, the Federation determined — to push back its frontiers and offer a choice of leadership to the remainder of the Southland. It was logical that the Southland should be

27

united under a single government, and who better to do that than the Federation?

That was the way it started. The Federation began a push north, gobbling up bits and pieces of the Southland as it went. A hundred years after the death of Jair Ohmsford, everything south of Callahorn was Federation governed. The other races, the Elves, the Trolls, the Dwarves, and even the Gnomes cast nervous glances south. Before long, Callahorn agreed to become a protectorate, its Kings long dead, its cities feuding and divided, and the last buffer between the Federation and the other lands disappeared.

It was about this same time that the rumors of the Shadowen began to surface. It was said that the magic of the old days was at fault, magic that had taken seed in the earth and nurtured there for decades and was now coming to life. The magic took many forms, sometimes as nothing more than a cold wind, sometimes as something vaguely human. It was labeled, in any case, as Shadowen. The Shadowen sickened the land and its life, turning pockets of it into quagmires of decay and lifelessness. They attacked mortal creatures, man or beast, and, when they were sufficiently weakened, took them over completely, stealing into their bodies and residing there, hidden wraiths. They needed the life of others for their own sustenance. That was how they survived.

The Federation lent credibility to those rumors by proclaiming that such creatures might indeed exist and only it was strong enough to protect against them.

No one argued that the magic might not be at fault or that the Shadowen or whatever it was that was causing the problem had nothing to do with magic at all. It was easier simply to accept the explanation offered. After all, there hadn't been any magic in the land since the passing of the Druids. The Ohmsfords told their stories, of course, but only a few heard and fewer still believed. Most thought the Druids just a legend. When Callahorn agreed to become a protectorate and the city of Tyrsis was occupied, the Sword of Shannara disappeared. No one

28

thought much of it. No one knew how it happened, and no one much cared. The Sword hadn't ever been seen for over two hundred years. There was only the vault that was said to contain it, the blade set in a block of Tre-Stone, there in the center of the People's Park — and then one day that was gone as well.

The Elfstones disappeared not long after. There was no record of what became of them. Not even the Ohmsfords knew.

Then the Elves began to disappear as well, entire communities, whole cities at a time, until even Arborlon was gone. Finally, there were no more Elves at all; it was as if they had never been. The Westland was deserted, save for a few hunters and trappers from the other lands and the wandering bands of Rovers. The Rovers, unwelcome any place else, had always been there, but even the Rovers claimed to know nothing of what had become of the Elves. The Federation quickly took advantage of the situation. The Westland, it declared, was the seeding ground for the magic that was at the root of the problems in the Four Lands. It was the Elves, after all, who introduced magic into the Lands years earlier. It was the Elves who first practiced it. The magic had consumed them — an object lesson on what would happen to all those who tried to do likewise.

The Federation emphasized the point by forbidding the practice of magic in any form. The Westland was made a protectorate, albeit an unoccupied one since the Federation lacked enough soldiers to patrol so vast a territory unaided, but one that would be cleansed eventually, it was promised, of the ill effects of any lingering magic.

Shortly after that, the Federation declared war on the Dwarves. It did so ostensibly because the Dwarves had provoked it, although it was never made clear in what way. The result was practically a foregone conclusion. The Federation had the largest, most thoroughly equipped and best trained army in the Four Lands by this time, and the Dwarves had no standing army at all. The Dwarves no longer had the Elves as allies, as they had all those years previous, and the Gnomes and Trolls had never been friends. Nevertheless, the war lasted nearly five years. The Dwarves knew the mountainous Eastland far better than the Federation, and even though Culhaven fell almost immediately, the Dwarves continued to fight in the high country until eventually they were starved into submission. They were brought down out of the mountains and sent south to the Federation mines. Most died there. After seeing what happened to the Dwarves, the Gnome tribes fell quickly into line. The Federation declared the Eastland a protectorate as well.

There remained a few pockets of isolated resistance. There were still a handful of Dwarves and a scattering of Gnome tribes that refused to recognize Federation rule and continued to fight from the deep wilderness areas north and east. But they were too few to make any difference.

To mark its unification of the greater portion of the Four Lands and to honor those who had worked to achieve it, the Federation constructed a monument at the north edge of the Rainbow Lake where the Mermidon poured through the Runne. The monument was constructed entirely of black granite, broad and square at its base, curved inward as it rose over two hundred feet above the cliffs, a monolithic tower that could be seen for miles in all directions. The tower was called Southwatch.

That was almost a hundred years ago, and now only the Trolls remained a free people, still entrenched deep within the mountains of the Northland, the Charnals, and the Kershalt. That was dangerous, hostile country, a natural fortress, and no one from the Federation wanted much to do with it. The decision was made to leave it alone as long as the Trolls did not interfere with the other lands. The Trolls, very much a reclusive people for the whole of their history, were happy to oblige.

'It's all so different now,' Par concluded wistfully as they continued to sit within their shelter and watch the rain fall into the Mermidon. 'No more Druids, no Paranor, no magic — except the fake kind and the little we know.

No Elves. Whatever happened to them do you think?' He paused, but Coll didn't have anything to say. 'No monarchies, no Leah, no Buckhannahs, no Legion Free Corps, no Callahorn for all intents and purposes.'

'No freedom,' Coll finished darkly.

'No freedom,' Par echoed.

He rocked back, drawing his legs tight against his chest. 'I wish I knew how the Elfstones disappeared. And the Sword. What happened to the Sword of Shannara?'

Coll shrugged. 'Same thing that happens to everything eventually. It got lost.'

'What do you mean? How could they let it get lost?'

'No one was taking care of it.'

Par thought about that. It made sense. No one bothered much with the magic after Allanon died, after the Druids were gone. The magic was simply ignored, a relic from another time, a thing feared and misunderstood for the most part. It was easier to forget about it, and so they did. They all did. He had to include the Ohmsfords as well — otherwise they would still have the Elfstones. All that was left of their magic was the wishsong.

'We know the stories, the tales of what it was like, we have all that history, and we still don't know anything,' he said softly.

'We know the Federation doesn't want us talking about it,' Coll offered archly. 'We know that.'

'There are times that I wonder what difference it makes anyway.' Par's face twisted into a grimace. 'After all, people come to hear us and the day after, who remembers? Anyone besides us? And what if they do? It's all ancient history — not even that to some. To some, it's legend and myth, a lot of nonsense.'

'Not to everyone,' Coll said quietly.

'What's the use of having the wishsong, if the telling of the stories isn't going to make any difference? Maybe the stranger was right. Maybe there are better uses for the magic.'

'Like aiding the outlaws in their fight against the Federation? Like getting yourself killed?' Coll shook his

31

head. 'That's as pointless as not using it at all.'

There was a sudden splash from somewhere out in the river, and the brothers turned as one to seek out its source. But there was only the churning of rain-swollen waters and nothing else.

'Everything seems pointless.' Par kicked at the earth in front of him. 'What are we doing, Coll? Chased out of Varfleet as much as if we were outlaws ourselves, forced to take that boat like thieves, made to run for home like dogs with our tails between our legs.' He paused, looking over at his brother. 'Why do you think we still have use of the magic?'

Coll's blocky face shifted slightly toward Par's. 'What do you mean?'

'Why do we have it? Why hasn't it disappeared along with everything else? Do you think there's a reason?'

There was a long silence. 'I don't know,' Coll said finally. He hesitated. 'I don't know what it's like to have the magic.'

Par stared at him, realizing suddenly what he had asked and ashamed he had done so.

'Not that I'd want it, you understand,' Coll added hastily, aware of his brother's discomfort. 'One of us with the magic is enough.' He grinned.

Par grinned back. 'I expect so.' He looked at Coll appreciatively for a moment, then yawned. 'You want to go to sleep?'

Coll shook his head and eased his big frame back into the shadows a bit. 'No, I want to talk some more. It's a good night for talking.'

Nevertheless, he was silent then, as if he had nothing to say after all. Par studied him for a few moments, then they both looked back out over the Mermidon, watching as a massive tree limb washed past, apparently knocked down by the storm. The wind, which had blown hard at first, was quiet now, and the rain was falling straight down, a steady, gentle sound as it passed through the trees.

Par found himself thinking about the stranger who had

rescued them from the Federation Seekers. He had puzzled over the man's identity for the better part of the day, and he still hadn't a clue as to who he was. There was something familiar about him, though — something in the way he talked, an assurance, a confidence. It reminded him of someone from one of the stories he told, but he couldn't decide who. There were so many tales and many of them were about men like that one, heroes in the days of magic and Druids, heroes Par had thought were missing from this age. Maybe he had been wrong. The stranger at the Blue Whisker had been impressive in his rescue of them. He seemed prepared to stand up to the Federation. Perhaps there was hope for the Four Lands yet.

He leaned forward and fed another few sticks of dead-wood into the little fire, watching the smoke curl out from beneath the canvas shelter into the night. Lightning flashed suddenly farther east, and a long peal of thunder followed.

'Some dry clothes would be good right now,' he muttered. 'Mine are damp just from the air.'

Coll nodded. 'Some hot stew and bread, too.'

'A bath and a warm bed.'

'Maybe the smell of fresh spices.'

'And rose water.'

Coll sighed. 'At this point, I'd just settle for an end to this confounded rain.' He glanced out into the dark. 'I could almost believe in Shadowen on a night like this, I think.'

Par decided suddenly to tell Coll about the dreams. He wanted to talk about them, and there no longer seemed to be any reason not to. He debated only a moment, then said, 'I haven't said anything before, but I've been having these dreams, the same dream actually, over and over.' Quickly he described it, focusing on his confusion about the dark-robed figure who spoke to him. 'I don't see him clearly enough to be certain who he is,' he explained carefully. 'But he might be Allanon.'

Coll shrugged. 'He might be anybody. It's a dream, Par. Dreams are always murky.'

'But I've had this same dream a dozen, maybe two dozen times. I thought at first it was just the magic working on me, but ...' He stopped, biting his lip. 'What if ...?' He stopped again.

'What if what?'

'What if it isn't just the magic? What if it's an attempt by Allanon — or someone — to send me a message of some sort?'

'A message to do what? To go traipsing off to the Hadeshorn or somewhere equally dangerous?' Coll shook his head. 'I wouldn't worry about it if I were you. And I certainly wouldn't consider going.' He frowned. 'You aren't, are you? Considering going?'

'No,' Par answered at once. *Not until I think about it, at least,* he amended silently, surprised at the admission.

'That's a relief. We have enough problems as it is without going off in search of dead Druids.' Coll obviously considered the matter settled.

Par didn't reply, choosing instead to poke at the fire with a stray stick, nudging the embers this way and that. He was indeed thinking about going, he realized. He hadn't considered it seriously before, but all of a sudden he had a need to know what the dreams meant. It didn't matter if they came from Allanon or not. Some small voice inside him, some tiny bit of recognition, hinted that finding the source of the dreams might allow him to discover something about himself and his use of the magic. It bothered him that he was thinking like this, that he was suddenly contemplating doing exactly what he had told himself he must not do right from the time the dreams had first come to him. But that was no longer enough to deter him. There was a history of dreams in the Ohmsford family and almost always the dreams had a message.

'I just wish I was sure,' he murmured.

Coll was stretched out on his back now, eyes closed against the firelight. 'Sure about what?'

'The dreams,' he hedged. 'About whether or not they were sent.'

34

Coll snorted. 'I'm sure enough for the both of us. There aren't any Druids. There aren't any Shadowen either. There aren't any dark wraiths trying to send you messages in your sleep. There's just you, overworked and under-rested, dreaming bits and pieces of the stories you sing about.'

Par lay back as well, pulling his blanket up about him. 'I suppose so,' he agreed, inwardly not agreeing at all.

Coll rolled over on his side, yawning. 'Tonight, you'll probably dream about floods and fishes, damp as it is.'

Par said nothing. He listened for a time to the sound of the rain, staring up at the dark expanse of the canvas, catching the flicker of the firelight against its damp surface.

'Maybe I'll choose my own dream,' he said softly.

Then he was asleep.

He did dream that night, the first time in almost two weeks. It was the dream he wanted, the dream of the dark-robed figure, and it was as if he were able to reach out and bring it to him. It seemed to come at once, to slip from the depths of his subconscious the moment sleep came. He was shocked at its suddenness, but didn't wake. He saw the dark figure rise from the lake, watched it come for him, vague yet, faceless, so menacing that he would have fled if he could. But the dream was master now and would not let him. He heard himself asking why the dream had been absent for so long, but there was no answer given. The dark figure simply approached in silence, not speaking, not giving any indication of its purpose.

Then it came to a stop directly before him, a being that could have been anything or anyone, good or evil, life or death.

Speak to me, he thought, frightened.

But the figure merely stood there, draped in shadow, silent and immobile. It seemed to be waiting.

Then Par stepped forward and pushed back the cowl

that hid the other, emboldened by some inner strength he did not know he possessed. He drew the cowl free and the face beneath was as sharp as if etched in bright sunlight. He knew it instantly. He had sung of it a thousand times. It was as familiar to him as his own.

The face was Allanon's.

CHAPTER

4

HEN HE CAME AWAKE the next morning, Par decided not to say anything to Coll about his dream. In the first place, he didn't know what to say. He couldn't be sure if the dream had occurred on its own or because he had been thinking so hard about having it — and even then he had no way of knowing if it was the real thing. In the second place, telling Coll would just start him off again on how foolish it was for Par to keep thinking about something he obviously wasn't going to do anything about. Was he? Then, if Par was honest with him, they would fight about the advisability of going off into the Dragon's Teeth in search of the Hadeshorn and a three-hundred-year-dead Druid. Better just to let the matter rest.

They ate a cold breakfast of wild berries and some stream water, lucky to have that. The rains had stopped, but the sky was overcast, and the day was gray and threatening. The wind had returned, rather strong out of the northwest, and tree limbs bent and leaves rustled wildly against its thrust. They packed up their gear, boarded the skiff, and pushed off onto the river.

The Mermidon was heavily swollen and the skiff tossed and twisted roughly as it carried them south. Debris choked the waters, and they kept the oars at hand to push off any large pieces that threatened damage to the boat. The cliffs of the Runne loomed darkly on either side, wrapped in trailers of mist and low-hanging clouds. It was cold in their shadow, and the brothers felt their hands and feet grow quickly numb.

They pulled into shore and rested when they could, but it accomplished little. There was nothing to eat and no way to get warm without taking time to build a fire. By early afternoon, it was raining again. It grew quickly colder in the rainfall, the wind picked up, and it became dangerous to continue on the river. When they found a small cove in the shelter of a stand of old pine, they quickly maneuvered the skiff ashore and set camp for the night.

They managed a fire, ate the fish Coll caught and tried their best to dry out beneath the canvas with rain blowing in from every side. They slept poorly, cold and uncomfortable, the wind howling down the canyon of the mountains and the river churning up against its banks. That night, Par didn't dream at all.

Morning brought a much needed change in the weather. The storm moved east, the skies cleared and filled with bright sunlight, and the air warmed once more. The brothers dried out their clothing as their craft bore them south, and by midday it was balmy enough to strip off tunics and boots and enjoy the feel of the sun on their skin.

'As the saying goes, things always get better after a storm,' Coll declared in satisfaction. 'There'll be good weather now, Par — you watch. Another three days and we'll be home.'

Par smiled and said nothing.

The day wore on, turning lazy, and the summer smells of trees and flowers began to fill the air again.

They sailed beneath Southwatch, its black granite bulk jutting skyward out of the mountain rock at the edge of the river, silent and inscrutable. Even from as far away as it was, the tower looked forbidding, its stone grainy and opaque, so dark that it seemed to absorb the light. There were all sorts of rumors about Southwatch. Some said it was alive, that it fed upon the earth in order to live. Some said it could move. Almost everyone agreed that it seemed to keep getting bigger through some form of ongoing construction. It appeared to be deserted. It always appeared that way. An elite unit of Federation soldiers was supposed to be in service to the tower, but no one ever saw them. Just as well, Par thought as they drifted past undisturbed.

By late afternoon, they reached the mouth of the river where it opened into the Rainbow Lake. The lake spread away before them, a broad expanse of silver-tipped blue water turned golden at its western edge by the sun as it slipped toward the horizon. The rainbow from which it took its name arched overhead, faint now in the blaze of sunlight, the blues and purples almost invisible, the reds and yellows washed of their color. Cranes glided silently in the distance, long graceful bodies extended against the light.

The Ohmsfords pulled their boat to the shore's edge and beached it where a stand of shade trees fronted a low bluff. They set their camp, hanging the canvas in the event of a change back in the weather, and Coll fished while Par went off to gather wood for an evening fire.

Par wandered the shoreline east for a ways, enjoying the bright glaze of the lake's waters and the colors in the air. After a time, he moved into the trees and began picking up pieces of dry wood. He had gone only a short distance when the woods turned dank and filled with a decaying smell. He noticed that many of the trees seemed to be dying here, leaves wilted and brown, limbs broken off, bark peeling. The ground cover looked unwell, too. He poked and scraped at it with his boot and looked about curiously. There didn't appear to be anything living here; there were no small animals scurrying about and no birds calling from the trees. The forest was deserted.

He decided to give up looking for firewood in this direction and was working his way back toward the shoreline when he caught sight of the house. It was a cottage, really, and scarcely that. It was badly overgrown with weeds, vines and scrub. Boards hung loosely from its walls, shutters lay on the ground and the roof was caving in. The glass in the windows was broken out, and the front door stood open. It sat at the edge of a cove that ran far back into the trees from the lake, and the water of the cove was still and greenish with stagnation. The smell that it gave off was sickening.

Par would have thought it deserted if not for the tiny column of smoke that curled up from the crumbling chimney.

He hesitated, wondering why anyone would live in such surroundings. He wondered if there really was someone there or if the smoke was merely a residue. Then he wondered if whoever was there needed help.

He almost went over to see, but there was something so odious about the cottage and its surroundings that he could not make himself do so. Instead, he called out, asking if anyone was home. He waited a moment, then called out again. When there was no reply, he turned away almost gratefully and continued on his way.

Coll was waiting with the fish by the time that he returned, so they hastily built a fire and cooked dinner. They were both a little tired of fish, but it was better than nothing and they were more hungry than either would have imagined. When the dinner was consumed, they sat watching as the sun dipped into the horizon and the Rainbow Lake turned to silver. The skies darkened and filled with stars, and the sounds of the night rose out of dusk's stillness. Shadows from the forest trees lengthened and joined and became dark pools that enveloped the last of the daylight.

Par was in the process of trying to figure out a way to tell Coll that he didn't think they should return to Shady Vale when the woodswoman appeared.

She came out of the trees behind them, shambling from the dark as if one of its shadows, all bent over and hunched down against the fire's faint light. She was clothed in rags, layers of them, all of which appeared to have been wrapped about her at some time in the distant past and left there. Her head was bare, and her rough, hard face peered out through long wisps of dense colorless hair. She might have been any age, Par thought; she was so gnarled it was impossible to tell.

She edged out of the forest cautiously and stopped just beyond the circle of the fire's yellow light, leaning heavily on a walking stick worn with sweat and handling. One rough arm raised as she pointed at Par. 'You the one called me?' she asked, her voice cracking like brittle wood.

Par stared at her in spite of himself. She looked like something brought out of the earth, something that had no right to be alive and walking about. There was dirt and debris hanging from her as if it had settled on her and taken root while she slept.

'Was it?' she pressed.

He finally figured out what she was talking about. 'At the cottage? Yes, that was me.'

The woodswoman smiled, her face twisting with the effort, her mouth nearly empty of teeth. 'You ought to have come in, not just stood out there,' she whined. 'Door was open.'

'I didn't want . . .'

'Keep it that way to be certain no one goes past without a welcome. Fire's always on.'

'I saw your smoke, but . . .'

'Gathering wood, were you? Come down out of Callahorn?' Her eyes shifted as she glanced past them to where the boat sat beached. 'Come a long way, have you?' The eyes shifted back. 'Running from something, maybe?'

Par went instantly still. He exchanged a quick look with Coll.

The woman approached, the walking stick probing the ground in front of her. 'Lots run this way. All sorts. Come down out of the outlaw country looking for something or other.' She stopped. 'That you? Oh, there's those who'd have no part of you, but I'm not one. No, not me!'

'We're not running,' Coll spoke up suddenly.

'No? That why you're so well fitted out?' She swept

the air with the walking stick. 'What's your names?'

'What do you want?' Par asked abruptly. He was liking this less and less.

The woodswoman edged forward another step. There was something wrong with her, something that Par hadn't seen before. She didn't seem to be quite solid, shimmering a bit as if she were walking through smoke or out of a mass of heated air. Her body didn't move right either, and it was more than her age. It was as if she were fastened together like one of those marionettes they used in shows at the fairs, pinned at the joints and pulled by strings.

The smell of the cove and the crumbling cottage clung to the woodswoman even here. She sniffed the air suddenly as if aware of it. 'What's that?' She fixed her eyes on Par. 'Do I smell magic?'

Par went suddenly cold. Whoever this woman was, she was no one they wanted anything to do with.

'Magic! Yes! Clean and pure and strong with life!' The woodswoman's tongue licked out at the night air experimentally. 'Sweet as blood to wolves!'

That was enough for Coll. 'You had better find your way back to wherever you came from,' he told her, not bothering to disguise his antagonism. 'You have no business here. Move along.'

But the woodswoman stayed where she was. Her mouth curled into a snarl and her eyes suddenly turned as red as the fire's coals.

'Come over here to me!' she whispered with a hiss. 'You, boy!' She pointed at Par. 'Come over to me!'

She reached out with one hand. Par and Coll both moved back guardedly, away from the fire. The woman came forward several steps more, edging past the light, backing them further toward the dark.

'Sweet boy!' she muttered, half to herself. 'Let me taste you, boy!'

The brothers held their ground against her now, refusing to move any further from the light. The woodswoman saw the determination in their eyes, and her smile was wicked. She came forward, one step, another step . . .

Coll launched himself at her while she was watching Par, trying to grasp her and pin her arms. But she was much quicker than he, the walking stick slashing at him and catching him alongside the head with a vicious whack that sent him sprawling to the earth. Instantly, she was after him, howling like a maddened beast. But Par was quicker. He used the wishsong, almost without thinking, sending forth a string of terrifying images. She fell back, surprised, trying to fend the images off with her hands and the stick. Par used the opportunity to reach Coll and haul him to his feet. Hastily he pulled his brother back from where his attacker clawed at the air.

The woodswoman stopped suddenly, letting the images play about her, turning toward Par with a smile that froze his blood. Par sent an image of a Demon wraith to frighten her, but this time the woman reached out for the image, opened her mouth and sucked in the air about her. The image evaporated. The woman licked her lips and whined.

Par sent an armored warrior. The woodswoman devoured it greedily. She was edging closer again, no longer slowed by the images, actually anxious that he send more. She seemed to relish the taste of the magic; she seemed eager to consume it. Par tried to steady Coll, but his brother was sagging in his arms, still stunned. 'Coll, wake up!' he whispered urgently.

'Come, boy,' the woodswoman repeated softly. She beckoned and moved closer. 'Come feed me!'

Then the fire exploded in a flash of light, and the clearing was turned as bright as day. The woodswoman shrank away from the brightness, and her sudden cry ended in a snarl of rage. Par blinked and peered through the glow.

An old man emerged from the trees, white-haired and gray-robed, with skin as brown as seasoned wood. He stepped from the darkness into the light like a ghost come into being. There was a fierce smile on his mouth and a strange brightness in his eyes. Par wheeled about

43

guardedly, fumbling for the long knife at his belt. Two of them, he thought desperately, and again he shook Coll in an effort to rouse him.

But the old man paid him no notice. He concentrated instead on the woodswoman. 'I know you,' he said softly. 'You frighten no one. Begone from here or you shall deal with me!'

The woodswoman hissed at him like a snake and crouched as if to spring. But she saw something in the old man's face that kept her from attacking. Slowly, she began to edge back around the fire.

'Go back into the dark,' whispered the old man.

The woodswoman hissed a final time, then turned and disappeared into the trees without a sound. Her smell lingered on a moment longer, then faded. The old man waved almost absently at the fire, and it returned to normal. The night filled again with comforting sounds, and everything was as before.

The old man snorted and came forward into the firelight. 'Bah. One of nighttime's little horrors come out to play,' he muttered in disgust. He looked at Par quizzically. 'You all right, young Ohmsford? And this one? Coll, is it? That was a nasty blow he took.'

Par eased Coll to the ground, nodding. 'Yes, thanks. Could you hand me that cloth and a little water?'

The old man did as he was asked, and Par wiped the side of Coll's head where an ugly bruise was already beginning to form. Coll winced, sat forward, and put his head down between his legs, waiting for the throbbing to ease off. Par looked up. It dawned on him suddenly that the old man had used Coll's name.

'How do you know who we are?' he asked, his tone guarded.

The old man kept his gaze steady. 'Well, now. I know who you are because I've come looking for you. But I'm not your enemy, if that's what you're thinking.'

Par shook his head. 'Not really. Not after helping us the way you did. Thank you.'

'No need for thanks.'

44

Par nodded again. 'That woman, or whatever she was — she seemed frightened of you.' He didn't make it a question, he made it a statement of fact.

The old man shrugged. 'Perhaps.'

'Do you know her?'

'I know of her.'

Par hesitated, uncertain whether to press the matter or not. He decided to let it drop. 'So. Why are you looking for us?'

'Oh, that's rather a long story. I'm afraid,' the old man answered, sounding very much as if the effort required to tell it was entirely beyond him. 'I don't suppose we might sit down while we talk about it? The fire's warmth provides some relief for these ageing bones. And you wouldn't happen to have a touch of ale, would you? No? Pity. Well, I suppose there was no chance to procure such amenities, the way you were hustled out of Varfleet. Lucky to escape with your skins under the circumstances.'

He ambled in close and lowered himself gingerly to the grass, folding his legs before him, draping his gray robes carefully about. 'Thought I'd catch up with you there, you know. But then that disruption by the Federation occurred, and you were on your way south before I could stop you.'

He reached for a cup and dipped it into the water bucket, drinking deeply. Coll was sitting up now, watching, the damp cloth still held to the side of his head. Par sat down next to him.

The old man finished his water and wiped his mouth on his sleeve. 'Allanon sent me,' he declared perfunctorily.

There was a long silence as the Ohmsford brothers stared first at him, then at each other, then back again at him.

'Allanon?' Par repeated.

'Allanon has been dead for three hundred years,' Coll interjected bluntly.

The old man nodded. 'Indeed. I misspoke. It was

45

actually Allanon's ghost, his shade — but Allanon, still, for all intents and purposes.'

'Allanon's shade?' Coll took the cloth from the side of his head, his injury forgotten. He did not bother to hide his disbelief.

The old man rubbed his bearded chin. 'Now, now, you will have to be patient for a moment or two until I've had a chance to explain. Much of what I am going to tell you will be hard for you to accept, but you must try. Believe me when I tell you that it is very important.'

He rubbed his hands briskly in the direction of the fire. 'Think of me as a messenger for the moment, will you? Think of me as a messenger sent by Allanon, for that's all I am to you just now. You, Par. Why have you been ignoring the dreams?'

Par stiffened. 'You know about that?'

'The dreams were sent by Allanon to bring you to him. Don't you understand? That was his voice speaking to you, his shade come to address you. He summons you to the Hadeshorn — you, your cousin Wren and . . .'

'Wren?' Coll interrupted, incredulous.

The old man looked perturbed. 'That's what I said, didn't I? Am I going to have to repeat everything? Your cousin, Wren Ohmsford. And Walker Boh as well.'

'Uncle Walker,' Par said softly. 'I remember.'

Coll glanced at his brother, then shook his head in disgust. 'This is ridiculous. No one knows where either of them is!' he snapped. 'Wren lives somewhere in the Westland with the Rovers. She lives out of the back of a wagon! And Walker Boh hasn't been seen by anyone for almost ten years. He might be dead, for all we know!'

'He might, but he isn't,' the old man said testily. He gave Coll a meaningful stare, then returned his gaze to Par. 'All of you are to come to the Hadeshorn by the close of the present moon's cycle. On the first night of the new moon, Allanon will speak with you there.'

Par felt a chill go through him. 'About magic?'

Coll seized his brother's shoulders. 'About Shadowen?' he mimicked, widening his eyes.

46

The old man bent forward suddenly, his face gone hard. 'About what he chooses! Yes, about magic! And about Shadowen! About creatures like the one that knocked you aside just now as if you were a baby! But mostly, I think, young Coll, about this!'

He threw a dash of dark powder into the fire with a suddenness that caused Par and Coll to jerk back sharply. The fire flared as it had when the old man had first appeared, but this time the light was drawn out of the air and everything went dark.

Then an image formed in the blackness, growing in size until it seemed to be all around them. It was an image of the Four Lands, the countryside barren and empty, stripped of life and left ruined. Darkness and a haze of ash-filled smoke hung over everything. Rivers were filled with debris, the waters poisoned. Trees were bent and blasted, shorn of life. Nothing but scrub grew anywhere. Men crept about like animals, and animals fled at their coming. There were shadows with strange red eyes circling everywhere, dipping and playing within those humans who crept, twisting and turning them until they lost their shape and became unrecognizable.

It was a nightmare of such fury and terror that it seemed to Par and Coll Ohmsford as if it were happening to them, and that the screams emanating from the mouths of the tortured humans were their own.

Then the image was gone, and they were back again about the fire, the old man sitting there, watching them with hawk's eyes.

'That was a part of my dream,' Par whispered.

'That was the future,' the old man said.

'Or a trick,' a shaken Coll muttered, stiffening against his own fear.

The old man glared. 'The future is an ever-shifting maze of possibilities until it becomes the present. The future I have shown you tonight is not yet fixed. But it is more likely to become so with the passing of every day because nothing is being done to turn it aside. If you would change it, do as I have told you. Go to Allanon!

47

Listen to what he will say!'

Coll said nothing, his dark eyes uneasy with doubt.

'Tell us who you are,' Par said softly.

The old man turned to him, studied him for a moment, then looked away from them both, staring out into the darkness as if there were worlds and lives hidden there that only he could see. Finally, he looked back again, nodding.

'Very well, though I can't see what difference it makes. I have a name, a name you should both recognize quickly enough. My name is Cogline.'

For an instant, neither Par nor Coll said anything. Then both began speaking at once.

'Cogline, the same Cogline who lived in the Eastland with . . .?'

'You mean the same man Kimber Boh . . .?'

He cut them short irritably. 'Yes, yes! How many Coglines can there possibly be!' He frowned as he saw the looks on their faces. 'You don't believe me, do you?'

Par took a deep breath. 'Cogline was an old man in the time of Brin Ohmsford. That was three hundred years ago.'

Unexpectedly, the other laughed. 'An old man! Ha! And what do you know of old men, Par Ohmsford? Fact is, you don't know a whisker's worth!' He laughed, then shook his head helplessly. 'Listen. Allanon was alive five hundred years before he died! You don't question that, do you? I think not, since you tell the story so readily! Is it so astonishing then that I have been alive for a mere three hundred years?' He paused, and there was a surprisingly mischievous look in his eyes. 'Goodness, what would you have said if I had told you I had been alive longer even than that?'

Then he waved his hand dismissively. 'No, no, don't bother to answer. Answer me this instead. What do you know about me? About the Cogline of your stories? Tell me.'

Par shook his head, confused. 'That he was a hermit, living off in the Wilderun with his granddaughter, Kimber

48

Boh. That my ancestor, Brin Ohmsford, and her companion, Rone Leah, found him there when they . . .'

'Yes, yes, but what about the *man*? Think now of what you've seen of me!'

Par shrugged. 'That he . . .' He stopped. 'That he used powders that exploded. That he knew something of the old sciences, that he'd studied them somewhere.' He was remembering the specifics of the tales of Cogline now, and in remembering found himself thinking that maybe this old man's claim wasn't so farfetched. 'He employed different forms of power, the sorts that the Druids had discarded in their rebuilding of the old world. Shades! If you are Cogline, you must still have such power. Do you? Is it magic like my own?'

Coll looked suddenly worried 'Par!'

'Like your own?' the old man asked quickly. 'Magic like the wishsong? Hah! Never! Never so unpredictable as that! That was always the trouble with the Druids and their Elven magics — too unpredictable! The power I wield is grounded in sciences proven and tested through the years by reliable study! It doesn't act of its own accord; it doesn't evolve like something alive!' He stopped, a fierce smile creasing his aged face. 'But then, too, Par Ohmsford, my power doesn't sing either!'

'Are you really Cogline?' Par asked softly, his amazement at it being possible apparent in his voice.

'Yes,' the old man whispered back. 'Yes, Par.' He swung quickly then to face Coll, who was about to interrupt, placing a narrow, bony finger to his lips. 'Shhhh, young Ohmsford, I know you still disbelieve, and your brother as well, but just listen for a moment. You are children of the Elven house of Shannara. There have not been many and always much has been expected of them. It will be so with you as well, I think. More so, perhaps. I am not permitted to see. I am just a messenger, as I have told you — a poor messenger at best. An unwilling messenger, truth is. But I am all that Allanon has.'

'But why you?' Par managed to interject, his lean face troubled now and intense.

The old man paused, his gnarled, wrinkled face tightening even further as if the question demanded too much of him. When he spoke finally, it was in a stillness that was palpable.

'Because I was a Druid once, so long ago I can scarcely remember what it felt like. I studied the ways of the magic and the ways of the discarded sciences and chose the latter, forsaking thereby any claim to the former and the right to continue with the others. Allanon knew me, or if you prefer, he knew about me, and he remembered what I was. But, wait. I embellish a bit by claiming I actually was a Druid. I wasn't; I was simply a student of the ways. But Allanon remembered in any case. When he came to me, it was as one Druid to another, though he did not say as much. He lacks anyone but myself to do what is needed now, to come after you and the others, to advise them of the legitimacy of their dreams. All have had them by now, you understand — Wren and Walker Boh as well as you. All have been given a vision of the danger the future holds. No one responds. So he sends me.'

The sharp eyes blinked away the memory. 'I was a Druid once, in spirit if not in practice, and I practice still many of the Druid ways. No one knew. Not my grandchild Kimber, not your ancestors, no one. I have lived many different lives, you see. When I went with Brin Ohmsford into the country of the Maelmord, it was as Cogline the hermit, half-crazed, half-able, filled with magic powers and strange notions. That was who I was then. That was the person I had become. It took me years afterward, long after Kimber was gone, to recover myself, to act and talk like myself again.'

He sighed. 'It was the Druid Sleep that kept me alive for so long. I knew its secret; I had carried it with me when I left them. I thought many times not to bother, to give myself over to death and not cling so. But something kept me from giving way, and I think now that perhaps it was Allanon, reaching back from his death to assure that the Druids might have at least one spokesman after he was gone.'

He saw the beginning of the question in Par's eyes, anticipated its wording, and quickly shook his head. 'No, no, not me! I am not the spokesman he needs! I barely have time enough left me to carry the message I have been given. Allanon knows that. He knew better than to come to me to ask that I accept a life I once rejected. He must ask that of someone else.'

'Me?' asked Par at once.

The old man paused. 'Perhaps. Why don't you ask him yourself?'

No one said anything, hunched forward toward the firelight as the darkness pressed close all about. The cries of night birds echoed faintly across the waters of the Rainbow Lake, a haunting sound that somehow seemed to measure the depth of the uncertainty Par felt.

'I want to ask him,' he said finally. 'I need to, I think.'

The old man pursed his thin lips. 'Then you must.'

Coll started to say something, then thought better of it. 'This whole business needs some careful thought,' he said finally.

'There is little time for that,' the old man grumbled.

'Then we shouldn't squander what we have,' Coll replied simply. He was no longer abrasive as he spoke, merely insistent.

Par looked at his brother a moment, then nodded. 'Coll is right. I will have to think about this.'

The old man shrugged as if to indicate that he realized there was nothing more he could do and came to his feet. 'I have given you the message I was sent to give, so I must be on my way. There are others to be visited.'

Par and Coll rose with him, surprised. 'You're leaving now, tonight?' Par asked quickly. Somehow he had expected the old man to stay on, to keep trying to persuade him of the purpose of the dreams.

'Seems best. The quicker I get on with my journey, the quicker it ends. I told you, I came first to you.'

'But how will you find Wren or Walker?' Coll wanted to know.

'Same way I found you.' The old man snapped his

fingers and there was a brief flash of silver light. He grinned, his face skeletal in the firelight. 'Magic!'

He reached out his bony hand. Par took it first and found the old man's grip like iron. Coll found the same. They glanced at each other.

'Let me offer you some advice,' the old man said abruptly. 'Not that you'll necessarily take it, of course — but maybe. You tell these stories, these tales of Druids and magic and your ancestors, all of it a kind of litany of what's been and gone. That's fine, but you don't want to lose sight of the fact that what's happening here and now is what counts. All the telling in the world won't mean a whisker if that vision I showed you comes to pass. You have to live in this world — not in some other. Magic serves a lot of purposes, but you don't use it any way but one. You have to see what else it can do. And you can't do that until you understand it. I suggest you don't understand it at all, either one of you.'

He studied them a moment, then turned and shambled off into the dark. 'Don't forget, first night of the new moon!' He stopped when he was just a shadow and glanced back. 'Something else you'd better remember and that's to watch yourselves.' His voice had a new edge to it. 'The Shadowen aren't just rumors and old wives' tales. They're as real as you and I. You may not have thought so before tonight, but now you know different. They'll be out there, everywhere you're likely to go. That woman, she was one of them. She came sniffing around because she could sense you have the magic. Others will do the same.'

He started moving away again. 'Lots of things are going to be hunting you,' he warned softly.

He mumbled something further to himself that neither of them could hear as he disappeared slowly into the darkness.

Then he was gone.

CHAPTER

5

PAR AND COLL OHMSFORD did not get much sleep that night. They stayed awake long after the old man was gone, talking and sometimes arguing, worrying without always saying as much, eyes constantly scanning the darkness against the promise that *things*, Shadowen or otherwise, were likely to be hunting them. Even after that, when there was nothing left to say, when they had rolled themselves wearily into their blankets and closed their eyes against their fears, they did not sleep well. They rolled and tossed in their slumber, waking themselves and each other with distressing regularity until dawn.

They rose then, dragged themselves from the warmth of their coverings, washed in the chilling waters of the lake, and promptly began talking and arguing all over again. They continued through breakfast, which was just as well because once again there wasn't much to eat and it took their minds off their stomachs. The talk, and more often now the arguments, centered around the old man who claimed to be Cogline and the dreams that might or might not have been sent and if sent might or might not have been sent by Allanon, but included such peripheral topics as Shadowen, Federation Seekers, the stranger who had rescued them in Varfleet, and whether there was sense to the world anymore or not. They had established their positions on these subjects fairly well by this time, positions that, for the most part, weren't within a week's walk of each other. That being the case, they were reduced to communicating with each other across vast stretches of intractability.

Before their day was even an hour old, they were already thoroughly fed up with each other.

'You cannot deny that the possibility exists that the old man really is Cogline!' Par insisted for what must have been the hundredth time as they carried the canvas tarp down to the skiff for stowing.

Coll managed a quick shrug. 'I'm not denying it.'

'And if he really is Cogline, then you cannot deny the possibility that everything he told us is the truth!'

'I'm not denying that either.'

'What about the woodswoman? What was she if not a Shadowen, a night thing with magic stronger than our own?'

'Your own.'

Par fumed. 'Sorry. My own. The point is, she *was* a Shadowen! She had to be! That makes at least part of what the old man told us the truth, no matter how you view it!'

'Wait a minute.' Coll dropped his end of the tarp and stood there with his hands on his hips, regarding his brother with studied dismay. 'You do this all the time when we argue. You make these ridiculous leaps in logic and act as if they make perfect sense. How does it follow that, if that woman was a Shadowen, the old man was telling the truth?'

'Well, because if . . .'

'I won't even question your assumption that she *was* a Shadowen,' Coll interrupted pointedly. 'Even though we haven't the faintest idea what a Shadowen is. Even though she might just as easily have been something else altogether.'

'Something else? What sort of . . .?'

'Like a companion to the old man, for instance. Like a decoy to give his tale validity.'

Par was incensed. 'That's ridiculous! What would be

the purpose of that?'

Coll pursed his lips thoughtfully. 'To persuade you to go with him to the Hadeshorn, naturally. To bring you back into Callahorn. Think about it. Maybe the old man is interested in the magic, too — just like the Federation.'

Par shook his head vehemently. 'I don't believe it.'

'That's because you never like to believe anything that you haven't thought of first,' Coll declared pointedly, picking up his end of the tarp again. 'You decide something and that's the end of it. Well, this time you had better not make your decision too quickly. There are other possibilities to consider, and I've just given you one of them.'

They walked down to the shoreline in silence and deposited the tarp in the bottom of the skiff. The sun was barely above the eastern horizon, and already the day was beginning to feel warm. The Rainbow Lake was smooth, the air windless and filled with the scent of wildflowers and long grass.

Coll turned. 'You know, it's not that I mind you being decisive about things It's just that you then assume I ought simply to agree. I shouldn't argue, I should acquiesce. Well, I am not going to do that If you want to strike out for Callahorn and the Dragon's Teeth — fine, you go right ahead. But quit acting as if I ought to jump at the chance to go along.'

Par didn't say anything back right away. Instead, he thought about what it had been like for them growing up. Par was the older by two years and while physically smaller than Coll, he had always been the leader. He had the magic, after all, and that had always set him apart. It was true, he was decisive; it had been necessary to be decisive when faced with the temptation to use the magic to solve every situation. He had not been as even-tempered as he should have; he wasn't any better now. Coll had always been the more controlled of the two — slower to anger, thoughtful and deliberate, a born peace-maker in the neighborhood fights and squabbles because no one else had the physical and emotional presence. Or was as well liked, he added — because Coll was always that, the sort of fellow that everyone takes to instantly. He spent his time looking after everyone, smoothing over hard feelings, restoring injured pride. Par was always charging around, oblivious to such things, busy searching for new places to explore, new challenges to engage, new ideas to develop. He was visionary, but he lacked Coll's sensitivity. He foresaw so clearly life's possibilities, but Coll was the one who understood best its sacrifices.

There had been a good many times when they had covered for each other's mistakes. But Par had the magic to fall back on and covering up for Coll had seldom cost him anything. It hadn't been like that for Coll. Covering up for Par had sometimes cost him a great deal. Yet Par was his brother, whom he loved, and he never complained. Sometimes, thinking back on those days, Par was ashamed of how much he had let his brother do for him.

He brushed the memories aside. Coll was looking at him, waiting for his response. Par shifted his feet impatiently and thought about what that response ought to be. Then he said simply, 'All right. What do you think we should do?'

'Shades, I don't know what we should do!' Coll said at once. 'I just know that there are a lot of unanswered questions, and I don't think we should commit ourselves to anything until we've had a chance to answer some of them!'

Par nodded stoically. 'Before the time of the new moon, you mean.'

'That's better than three weeks away and you know it!'

Par's jaw tightened. 'That's not as much time as you make it seem! How are we supposed to answer all the questions we have before then?'

Coll stared at him. 'You are impossible, you know that?'

He turned and walked back from the shoreline to where the blankets and cooking gear were stacked and began carrying them down to the skiff. He didn't look at

Par. Par stood where he was and watched his brother in silence. He was remembering how Coll had pulled him half-drowned from the Rappahalladran when he had fallen in the rapids on a camping trip. He had gone under and Coll had been forced to dive down for him. He became sick afterward and Coll had carried him home on his back, shaking with fever and half-delirious. Col was always looking out for him, it seemed. Why was that, he wondered suddenly, when he was the one with the magic?

Coll finished packing the skiff, and Par walked over to him. 'I'm sorry,' he said and waited.

Coll looked down at him solemnly a moment, then grinned. 'No, you're not. You're just saying that.'

Par grinned back in spite of himself. 'I am not!'

'Yes, you are. You just want to put me off my guard so you can start in again with your confounded decision-making once we're out in the middle of that lake where I can't walk away from you!' His brother was laughing openly now.

Par did his best to look mortified. 'Okay, it's true. I'm not sorry.'

'I knew it!' Coll was triumphant.

'But you're wrong about the reason for the apology. It has nothing to do with getting you out in the middle of the lake. I'm just trying to shed the burden of guilt I've always felt at being the older brother.'

'Don't worry!' Coll was doubled over 'You've always been a terrible older brother!'

Par shoved him, Coll shoved back, and for the moment their differences were forgotten. They laughed, took a final look about the campsite and pushed the skiff out onto the lake, clambering aboard as it reached deeper water. Coll took up the oars without asking and began to row.

They followed the shoreline west, listening contentedly as the distant sounds of birds rose out of the trees and rushes, letting the day grow pleasantly warm about them. They didn't talk for a while, satisfied with the renewed feeling of closeness they had found on setting out, anxious to avoid arguing again right away.

Nevertheless, Par found himself rehashing matters in his mind — much the same as he was certain Coll was doing. His brother was right about one thing — there were a lot of unanswered questions. Reflecting on the events of the previous evening, Par found himself wishing he had thought to ask the old man for a bit more information. Did the old man know, for instance, who the stranger was who had rescued them in Varfleet? The old man had known about their trouble there and must have had some idea how they escaped. The old man had managed to track them, first to Varfleet, then down the Mermidon, and he had frightened off the woodswoman — Shadowen or whatever — without much effort. He had some form of power at his command, possibly Druid magic, possibly old world science — but he had never said what it was or what it did. Exactly what was his relationship with Allanon? Or was that simply a claim without any basis in fact? And why was it that he had given up on Par so easily when Par had said he must think over the matter of going off to the Hadeshorn for a meeting with Allanon? Shouldn't he have worked harder at persuading Par to go?

But the most disturbing question was one that Par could not bring himself to discuss with Coll at all — because it concerned Coll himself. The dreams had told Par that he was needed and that his cousin Wren and his uncle Walker Boh were needed as well. The old man had said the same — that Par, Wren, and Walker had been called.

Why was there no mention of Coll?

It was a question for which he had no answer at all. He had thought at first that it was because he had the magic and Coll didn't, that the summons had something to do with the wishsong. But then why was Wren needed? Wren had no magic either. Walker Boh was different, of course, since it had always been rumored that he knew something of magic that none of the others did. But not

Wren. And not Coll. Yet Wren had been specifically named and Coll hadn't.

It was this more than anything that made him question what he should do. He wanted to know the reason for the dreams; if the old man was right about Allanon, Par wanted to know what the Druid had to say. But he did not want to know any of it if it meant separating from Coll. Coll was more than his brother; he was his closest friend, his most trusted companion, practically his other self. Par did not intend to become involved in something where both were not wanted. He simply wasn't going to do it.

Yet the old man had not forbidden Coll to come. Nor had the dreams. Neither had warned against it.

They had simply ignored him

Why would that be?

The morning lengthened, and a wind came up. The brothers rigged a sail and mast using the canvas tarp and one of the oars, and soon they were speeding across the Rainbow Lake, the waters slapping and foaming about them. Several times they almost went over, but they stayed alert to sudden shifts in the wind and used their body weight to avoid capsizing. They set a southwest course and by early afternoon had reached the mouth of the Rappahalladran.

There they beached the skiff in a small cove, covered it with rushes and boughs, left everything within but the blankets and cooking gear, and began hiking upriver toward the Duln forests. It soon became expedient to cut across country to save time, and they left the river, moving up into the Highlands of Leah. They hadn't spoken about where they were going since the previous evening, when the tacit understanding had been that they would debate the matter later. They hadn't, of course. Neither had brought the subject up again, Coll because they were moving in the direction he wanted to go anyway, and Par because he had decided that Coll was right that some thinking needed to be done before any trip back north into Callahorn was undertaken. Shady

Vale was as good a place as any to complete that thinking.

Oddly enough, though they hadn't talked about the dreams or the old man or any of the rest of it since early that morning, they had begun separately to rethink their respective positions and to move closer together — each inwardly conceding that maybe the other made some sense after all.

By the time they began discussing matters again, they were no longer arguing. It was midafternoon, the summer day hot and sticky now, the sun a blinding white sphere before them as they walked, forcing them to shield their eyes protectively. The country was a mass of rolling hills, a carpet of grasses and wildflowers dotted with stands of broad-leafed trees and patches of scrub and rock. The mists that blanketed the Highlands year-round had retreated to the higher elevations in the face of the sun's brightness and clung to the tips of the ridgelines and bluffs like scattered strips of linen.

'I think that woodswoman was genuinely afraid of the old man,' Par was saying as they climbed a long, gradual slope into a stand of ash. 'I don't think she was pretending. No one's that good an actor.'

Coll nodded. 'I think you're right. I just said all that earlier about the two of them being in league to make you think. I can't help wondering, though, if the old man is telling us everything he knows. What I mostly remember about Allanon in the stories is that he was decidedly circumspect in his dealings with the Ohmsfords.'

'He never told them everything, that's true.'

'So maybe the old man is the same way.'

They crested the hill, moved into the shade of the ash trees, dropped their rolled up blankets wearily and stood looking out at the Highlands. Both were sweating freely, their tunics damp against their backs.

'We won't make Shady Vale tonight,' Par said, settling to the ground against one of the trees.

'No, it doesn't look like it.' Coll joined him, stretching until his bones cracked.

'I was thinking.'

'Good for you.'

'I was thinking about where we might spend the night. It would be nice to sleep in a bed for a change.'

Coll laughed. 'You won't get any argument out of me. Got any idea where we can find a bed out here in the middle of nowhere?'

Par turned slowly and looked at him. 'Matter-of-fact, I do. Morgan's hunting lodge is just a few miles south. I bet we could borrow it for the night.'

Coll frowned thoughtfully. 'Yes, I bet we could.'

Morgan Leah was the eldest son in a family whose ancestors had once been Kings of Leah. But the monarchy had been overthrown almost two hundred years ago when the Federation had expanded northward and simply consumed the Highlands in a single bite. There had been no Leah Kings since, and the family had survived as gentlemen farmers and craftsmen over the years. The current head of the family, Kyle Leah, was a landholder living south of the city who bred beef cattle. Morgan, his oldest son, Par and Coll's closest friend, bred mostly mischief.

'You don't think Morgan will be around, do you?' Coll asked, grinning at the possibility.

Par grinned back. The hunting lodge was really a family possession, but Morgan was the one who used it the most. The last time the Ohmsford brothers had come into the Highlands they had stayed for a week at the lodge as Morgan's guests. They had camped, hunted and fished, but mostly they had spent their time recounting tales of Morgan's ongoing efforts to cause distress to the members of the Federation government-in-residence at Leah. Morgan Leah had the quickest mind and the fastest pair of hands in the Southland, and he harbored an abiding dislike for the army that occupied his land. Unlike Shady Vale, Leah was a major city and required watching. The Federation, after abolishing the monarchy, had installed a provisional governor and cabinet and stationed a garrison of soldiers to insure order. Morgan regarded that as a personal challenge. He took every opportunity that presented itself, and a few that didn't, to make life miserable for the officials that now lodged comfortably and without regard for proper right of ownership in his ancestral home. It was never a contest. Morgan was a positive genius at disruption and much too sharp to allow the Federation officials to suspect he was the thorn in their collective sides that they could not even find, let alone remove. On the last go around, Morgan had trapped the governor and vice-governor in a private bathing court with a herd of carefully muddied pigs and jammed all the locks on the doors. It was a very small court and a whole lot of pigs. It took two hours to free them all, and Morgan insisted solemnly that by then it was hard to tell who was who.

The brothers regained their feet, hoisted their packs in place, and set off once more. The afternoon slipped away as the sun followed its path westward, but the air stayed quiet and the heat grew even more oppressive. The land at this elevation at midsummer was so arid that the grass crackled where they walked, the once-green blades dried to a brownish gray crust. Dust curled up in small puffs beneath their boots, and their mouths grew dry.

It was nearing sunset by the time they caught sight of the hunting lodge, a stone-and-timber building set back in a grouping of pines on a rise that overlooked the country west. Hot and sweating, they dumped their gear by the front door and went directly to the bathing springs nestled in the trees a hundred yards back. When they reached the springs, a cluster of clear blue pools that filled from beneath and emptied out into a sluggish little stream, they began stripping off their clothes immediately, heedless of anything but their by now overwhelming need to sink down into the inviting water.

Which was why they didn't see the mud creature until it was almost on top of them.

It rose up from the bushes next to them, vaguely manlike, encrusted in mud and roaring with a ferocity that shattered the stillness like glass. Coll gave a howl, sprang backward, lost his balance and tumbled headfirst into the springs. Par jerked away, tripped and rolled, and the creature was on top of him.

'Ahhhh! A tasty Valeman!' the creature rasped in a voice that was suddenly very familiar.

'Shades, Morgan!' Par twisted and turned and shoved the other away. 'You scared me to death, confound it!'

Coll pulled himself out of the springs, still wearing boots and pants halfway off, and said calmly, 'I thought it was only the Federation you intended to drive out of Leah, not your friends.' He heaved himself up and brushed the water from his eyes.

Morgan Leah was laughing merrily from within his mud cocoon. 'I apologize, I really do. But it was an opportunity no man could resist. Surely you can understand that!'

Par tried to wipe the mud from his clothes and finally gave up, stripping bare and carrying everything into the springs with him. He gave a sigh of relief, then glanced back at Morgan. 'What in the world are you doing anyway?'

'Oh, the mud? Good for your skin.' Morgan walked to the springs and lowered himself into the water gingerly. 'There are mud baths about a mile back. I found them the other day quite by accident. Never knew they were here. I can tell you honestly that there is nothing like mud on your body on a hot day to cool you down. Better even than the springs. So I rolled about quite piglike, then hiked back here to wash off. That was when I heard you coming and decided to give you a proper Highlands greeting.'

He ducked down beneath the water; when he surfaced, the mud monster had been replaced by a lean, sinewy youth approximately their own age with skin so sun-browned it was almost the color of chocolate, shoulder-length reddish hair, and clear gray eyes that looked out of a face that was at once both clever and guileless. 'Behold!' he exclaimed and grinned.

'Marvelous,' Par replied tonelessly.

63

'Oh, come now! Not every trick can be earth-shattering. Which reminds me.' Morgan bent forward questioningly. He spent much of his time wearing an expression that suggested he was secretly amused about something, and he showed it to them now. 'Aren't you two supposed to be up in Callahorn somewhere dazzling the natives? Wasn't that the last I heard of your plans? What are you doing here?'

'What are *you* doing here?' Coll shot back.

'Me? Oh, just another little misunderstanding involving the governor — or more accurately, I'm afraid, the governor's wife. They don't suspect me, of course — they never do. Still, it seemed a good time for a vacation.' Morgan's grin widened. 'But come on now, I asked you first. What's going on?'

He was not to be put off and there had never been any unshared secrets among the three in any case, so Par, with considerable help from Coll, told him what had happened to them since that night in Varfleet when Rimmer Dall and the Federation Seekers had come looking for them. He told him of the dreams that might have been sent by Allanon, of their encounter with the frightening woodswoman who might have been one of the Shadowen, and of the old man who had saved them and might have been Cogline.

'There are a good number of "might have beens" in that story,' the Highlander observed archly when they were finished. 'Are you certain you're not making this all up? It would be a fine joke at my expense.'

'I just wish we were,' Coll replied ruefully.

'Anyway, we thought we'd spend the night here in a bed, then go on to the Vale tomorrow,' Par explained.

Morgan trailed one finger through the water in front of him and shook his head. 'I don't think I'd do that if I were you.'

Par and Coll looked at each other.

'If the Federation wanted you badly enough to send Rimmer Dall all the way to Varfleet,' Morgan continued, his eyes coming up suddenly to meet their own, 'then don't you think it likely they might send him to Shady Vale as well?'

There was a long silence before Par finally said, 'I admit, I hadn't thought of that.'

Morgan stroked over to the edge of the springs, heaved himself out, and began wiping the water from his body. 'Well, thinking has never been your strong point, my boy. Good thing you've got me for a friend. Let's walk back up to the lodge and I'll fix you something to eat — something besides fish for a change — and we'll talk about it.'

They dried, washed out their clothes and returned to the lodge where Morgan set about preparing dinner. He cooked a wonderful stew filled with meat, carrots, potatoes, onions, and broth, and served it with hot bread and cold ale. They sat out under the pines at a table and benches and consumed the better part of their food and drink, the day finally beginning to cool as night approached and an evening breeze rustled down out of the hills. Morgan brought out pears and cheese for dessert, and they nibbled contentedly as the sky turned red, then deep purple and finally darkened and filled with stars.

'I love the Highlands,' Morgan said after they had been silent for a time. They were seated on the stone steps of the lodge now. 'I could learn to love the city as well, I expect, but not while it belongs to the Federation. I sometimes find myself wondering what it would have been like to live in the old home, before they took it from us. That was a long time ago, of course — six generations ago. No one remembers what it was like anymore. My father won't even talk about it. But here — well, this is still ours, this land. The Federation hasn't been able to take that away yet. There's just too much of it. Maybe that's why I love it so much — because it's the last thing my family has left from the old days.'

'Besides the sword,' Par reminded.

'Do you still carry that battered old relic?' Coll asked. 'I keep thinking you will discard it in favor of something newer and better made.'

Morgan glanced over. 'Do you remember the stories that said the Sword of Leah was once magic?'

'Allanon himself was supposed to have made it so,' Par confirmed.

'Yes, in the time of Rone Leah.' Morgan furrowed his brow. 'Sometimes I think it still is magic. Not as it once was, not as a weapon that could withstand Mord Wraiths and such, but in a different way. The scabbard has been replaced half-a-dozen times over the years, the hilt once or twice at least, and both are worn again. But the blade — ah, that blade! It is still as sharp and true as ever, almost as if it cannot age. Doesn't that require magic of a sort?'

The brothers nodded solemnly. 'Magic sometimes changes in the way it works,' Par said. 'It grows and evolves. Perhaps that has happened with the Sword of Leah.' He was thinking as he said it how the old man had told him he did not understand the magic at all and wondered if that were true.

'Well, truth is, no one wants the weapon in any case, not anymore.' Morgan stretched like a cat and sighed. 'No one wants anything that belongs to the old days, it seems. The reminders are too painful, I think. My father didn't say a word when I asked for the blade. He just gave it to me.'

Coll reached over and gave the other a friendly shove. 'Well, your father ought to be more careful to whom he hands out his weapons.'

Morgan managed to look put upon. 'Am I the one being asked to join the Movement?' he demanded. They laughed. 'By the way. You mentioned the stranger gave you a ring. Mind if I take a look?'

Par reached into his tunic, fished out the ring with the hawk insigne and passed it over. Morgan took it and examined it carefully, then shrugged and handed it back. 'I don't recognize it. But that doesn't necessarily mean anything. I hear there are a dozen outlaw bands within the Movement and they all change their markings regularly to confuse the Federation.'

He took a long drink from his ale glass and leaned back

again. 'Sometimes I think I ought to go north and join them — quit wasting time here playing games with those fools who live in my house and govern my land and don't even know the history.' He shook his head sadly and for a moment looked old.

Then he brightened. 'But now about you.' He swung his legs around and sat forward. 'You can't risk going back until you're certain it's safe. So you'll stay here for a day or so and let me go ahead. I'll make certain the Federation hasn't gotten there before you. Fair enough?'

'More than fair,' Par said at once. 'Thanks, Morgan. But you have to promise to be careful.'

'Careful? Of those Federation fools? Ha!' The Highlander grinned ear to ear. 'I could step up and spit in their collective eye and it would still take them days to work it out! I haven't anything to fear from them!'

Par wasn't laughing. 'Not in Leah, perhaps. But there may be Seekers in Shady Vale.'

Morgan quit grinning. 'Your point is well taken. I'll be careful.'

He drained the last of his ale and stood up. 'Time for bed. I'll want to leave early.'

Par and Coll stood up with him. Coll said, 'What was it exactly that you did to the governor's wife?'

Morgan shrugged. 'Oh, that? Nothing much. Someone said she didn't care for the Highlands air, that it made her queasy. So I sent her a perfume to sweeten her sense of smell. It was contained in a small vial of very delicate glass. I had it placed in her bed, a surprise for her. She accidentally broke it when she lay on it.

His eyes twinkled. 'Unfortunately, I somehow got the perfume mixed up with skunk oil.'

The three of them looked at each other in the darkness and grinned like fools.

The Ohmsfords slept well that night, wrapped in the comfort and warmth of real beds with clean blankets and pillows. They could easily have slept until noon, but

Morgan had them awake at dawn as he prepared to set out for Shady Vale. He brought out the Sword of Leah and showed it to them, its hilt and scabbard badly worn, but its blade as bright and new as the Highlander had claimed. Grinning in satisfaction at the looks on their faces, he strapped the weapon across one shoulder, stuck a long knife in the top of one boot, a hunting knife in his belt and strapped an ash bow to his back.

He winked. 'Never hurts to be prepared.'

They saw him out the door and down the hill west for a short distance where he bade them goodbye. They were still sleepy eyed and their own goodbyes were mixed with yawns.

'Go on back to bed,' Morgan advised. 'Sleep as long as you like. Relax and don't worry. I'll be back in a couple of days.' He waved as he moved off, a tall, lean figure silhouetted against the still-dark horizon, brimming with his usual self-confidence.

'Be careful!' Par called after him.

Morgan laughed. 'Be careful yourself!'

The brothers took the Highlander's advice and went back to bed, slept until afternoon, then wasted the remainder of the day just lying about. They did better the second day, rising early, bathing in the springs, exploring the countryside in a futile effort to find the mud baths, cleaning out the hunting lodge, and preparing and eating a dinner of wild fowl and rice. They talked a long time that night about the old man and the dreams, the magic and the Seekers, and what they should do with their immediate future. They did not argue, but they did not reach any decisions either.

The third day turned cloudy and by nightfall it was raining. They sat before the fire they had built in the great stone hearth and practiced the storytelling for a long time, working on some of the more obscure tales, trying to make the images of Par's song and the words of Coll's story mesh. There was no sign of Morgan Leah. In spite of their unspoken mutual resolve not to do so, they began to worry.

On the fourth day, Morgan returned. It was late afternoon when he appeared, and the brothers were seated on the floor in front of the fire repairing the bindings on one of the dinner table chairs when the door opened suddenly and he was there. It had been raining steadily all day, and the Highlander was soaked through, dripping water everywhere as he lowered his backpack and weapons to the floor and shoved the door closed behind him.

'Bad news,' he said at once. His rust-colored hair was plastered against his head, and the bones of his chiseled features glistened with rainwater. He seemed heedless of his condition as he crossed the room to confront them.

Par and Coll rose slowly from where they had been working. 'You can't go back to the Vale,' Morgan said quietly. 'There are Federation soldiers everywhere. I can't be certain if there are Seekers as well, but I wouldn't be surprised. The village is under "Federation Protection" — that's the euphemism they use for armed occupation. They're definitely waiting for you. I asked a few questions and found out right away; no one's making any secret of it. Your parents are under house arrest. I think they're okay, but I couldn't risk trying to talk to them. I'm sorry. There would have been too many questions.'

He took a deep breath. 'Someone wants you very badly, my friends.'

Par and Coll looked at each other, and there was no attempt by either to disguise the fear. 'What are we going to do?' Par asked softly.

'I've been thinking about that the whole way back,' Morgan said. He reached over and put a hand on his friend's slim shoulder. 'So I'll tell you what we're going to do — and I do mean "we" because I figure I'm in this thing with you now.'

His hand tightened. 'We're going east to look for Walker Boh.'

CHAPTER

6

ORGAN LEAH COULD BE VERY PERSUASIVE when he chose, and he proved it that night in the rain-shrouded Highlands to Par and Coll.

He obviously had given the matter a great deal of thought, just as he claimed he had, and his reasoning was quite thorough. Simply stated, it was all a matter of choices. He took just enough time to strip away his wet clothing and dry off before seating the brothers cross-legged before the warmth of the fireplace with glasses of ale and hot bread in hand to hear his explanation.

He started with what they knew. They knew they could not go back to Shady Vale — not now and maybe not for a long time. They could not go back to Callahorn either. Matter-of-fact, they could not go much of anywhere they might be expected to go because, if the Federation had expended this much time and effort to find them so far, they were hardly likely to stop now. Rimmer Dall was known to be a tenacious enforcer. He had personally involved himself in this hunt, and he would not give it up easily. The Seekers would be looking for the brothers everywhere Federation rule extended — and that was a long, long way. Par and Coll could consider themselves, for all intents and purposes, to be outlaws.

So what were they to do? Since they could not go any

place where they were expected, they must go someplace they were not expected. The trick, of course, was not to go just anywhere, but to go where they might accomplish something useful.

'After all, you could stay here if you chose, and you might not be discovered for who-knows-how-long because the Federation wouldn't know enough to look for you in the Highlands.' He shrugged. 'It might even be fun for a while. But what would it accomplish? Two months, four months, whatever, you would still be outlaws, you would still be unable to go home, and nothing would have changed. Doesn't make sense, does it? What you need to do is to take control of things. Don't wait for events to catch up with you; go out and meet them head-on!'

What he meant was that they should attempt to solve the riddle of the dreams. There was nothing they could do about the fact that the Federation was hunting them, that soldiers occupied Shady Vale, or that they were now outlaws. One day, all that might change — but not in the immediate future. The dreams, on the other hand, were something with which they might be able to come to grips. If the dreams were the real thing, they were worth knowing more about. The old man had told them to come to the Hadeshorn on the first night of the new moon. They hadn't wanted to do that before for two very sound reasons. First, they didn't know enough about the dreams to be certain they were real, and second, there were only the two of them and they might be placing themselves in real danger by going.

'So why not do something that might ease those concerns,' the Highlander finished. 'Why not go east and find Walker. You said the old man told you the dreams had been sent to Walker as well. Doesn't it make sense to find out what he thinks about all this? Is he planning on going? The old man was going to talk to him, too. Whether that's happened or not, Walker is certain to have an opinion on whether the dreams are real or not. I always thought your uncle was a strange bird, I'll admit,

71

but I never thought he was stupid. And we all know the stories about him. If he had the use of any part of the Shannara magic, now might be a good time to find out.'

He took a long drink and leaned forward, jabbing his finger at them. 'If Walker believes in the dreams and decides to go to the Hadeshorn, then you might be more inclined to go as well. There would be four of us then. Anything out there that might cause trouble would have to think twice.'

He shrugged. 'Even if you decide not to go, you'll have satisfied yourselves better than you would have by just hiding out here or somewhere like here. Shades, the Federation won't think to look for you in the Anar! That's just about the last place they'll think to look for you!'

He took another drink, bit off a piece of fresh bread and sat back, eyes questioning. He had that look on his face again, that expression that suggested he knew something they didn't and it amused him no end. 'Well?' he said finally.

The brothers were silent. Par was thinking about his uncle, remembering the whispered stories about Walker Boh. His uncle was a self-professed student of life who claimed he had visions; he insisted he could see and feel things others could not. There were rumors that he practiced magic of a sort different from any known. Eventually, he had gone away from them, leaving the Vale for the Eastland. That had been almost ten years ago. Par and Coll had been very young, but Par still remembered.

Coll cleared his throat suddenly, eased himself forward and shook his head. Par was certain his brother was going to tell Morgan how ridiculous his idea was, but instead he asked, 'How do we go about finding Walker?'

Par looked at Morgan and Morgan looked at Par, and there was an instant of shared astonishment. Both had anticipated that Coll would prove intractable, that he would set himself squarely in the path of such an outrageous plan, and that he would dismiss it as foolhardy. Neither had expected this.

Coll caught the look that passed between them and said, 'I wouldn't say what I was thinking, if I were you. Neither of you knows me as well as he thinks. Now how about an answer to my question?'

Morgan quickly masked the flicker of guilt that passed across his eyes. 'We'll go first to Culhaven. I have a friend there who will know where Walker is.'

'Culhaven?' Coll frowned. 'Culhaven is Federation-occupied.'

'But safe enough for us,' Morgan insisted. 'The Federation won't be looking for you there, and we need only stay a day or two. Anyway, we won't be out in the open much.'

'And our families? Won't they wonder what's happened to us?'

'Not mine. My father is used to not seeing me for weeks at a time. He's already made up his mind that I'm undependable. And Jaralan and Mirianna are better off not knowing what you're about. They're undoubtedly worried enough as it is.'

'What about Wren?' Par asked.

Morgan shook his head. 'I don't know how to find Wren. If she's still with the Rovers, she could be anywhere.' He paused. 'Besides, I don't know how much help Wren would be to us. She was only a girl when she left the Vale, Par. We don't have time to find both. Walker Boh seems a better bet.'

Par nodded slowly. He looked uncertainly at Coll and Coll looked back. 'What do you think?' he asked.

Coll sighed. 'I think we should have stayed in Shady Vale in the first place. I think we should have stayed in bed.'

'Oh, come now, Coll Ohmsford!' Morgan exclaimed cheerfully. 'Think of the adventure! I'll look out for you, I promise!'

Coll glanced at Par 'Should I feel comforted by that?'

Par took a deep breath. 'I say we go.'

Coll studied him intently, then nodded. 'I say what have we got to lose?'

So the issue was decided. Thinking it over later, Par guessed he was not surprised. After all, it was indeed a matter of choices, and any way you looked at it the other choices available had little to recommend them.

They slept that night at the lodge and spent the following morning outfitting themselves with foodstuffs stored in the cold lockers and provisions from the closets. There were weapons, blankets, travel cloaks, and extra clothing (some of it not a bad fit) for the brothers. There were cured meats, vegetables and fruits, and cheeses and nuts. There were cooking implements, water pouches and medications. They took what they needed, since the lodge was well-stocked, and by noon they were ready to set out.

The day was gray and clouded when they stepped through the front door and secured it behind them, the rain had turned to drizzle, the ground beneath their feet was no longer hard and dusty, but as damp and yielding as a sponge. They made their way north again toward the Rainbow Lake, intent on reaching its shores by nightfall. Morgan's plan for making the first leg of their journey was simple. They would retrieve the skiff the brothers had concealed earlier at the mouth of the Rappahalladran and this time follow the southern shoreline, staying well clear of the Lowlands of Clete, the Black Oaks, and the Mist Marsh, all of which were filled with dangers best avoided. When they reached the far shore, they would locate the Silver River and follow it east to Culhaven.

It was a good plan, but not without its problems. Morgan would have preferred to navigate the Rainbow Lake at night when they would be less conspicuous, using the moon and stars to guide them. But it quickly became apparent as the day drew to a close and the lake came in sight that there would be no moon or stars that night and as a result no light at all to show them the way. If they tried to cross in this weather, there was a very real possibility of them drifting too far south and becoming entangled in the dangers they had hoped to avoid.

So, after relocating the skiff and assuring themselves

that she was still seaworthy, they spent their first night out in a chill, sodden campsite set close back against the shoreline of the lake, dreaming of warmer, more agreeable times. Morning brought a slight change in the weather. It stopped raining entirely and grew warm, but the clouds lingered, mixing with a mist that shrouded everything from one end of the lake to the other.

Par and Coll studied the morass dubiously.

'It will burn off,' Morgan assured them, anxious to be off.

They shoved the skiff out onto the water, rowed until they found a breeze, and hoisted their makeshift sail. The clouds lifted a few feet and the skies brightened a shade, but the mist continued to cling to the surface of the lake like sheep's wool and blanketed everything in an impenetrable haze. Noon came and went with little change, and finally even Morgan admitted he had no idea where they were.

By nightfall, they were still on the lake and the light was gone completely. The wind died and they sat unmoving in the stillness. They ate a little food, mostly because it was necessary and not so much because anyone was particularly hungry, then they took turns trying to sleep.

'Remember the stories about Shea Ohmsford and a thing that lived in the Mist Marsh?' Coll whispered to Par at one point. 'I fully expect to discover firsthand whether or not they were true!'

The night crept by, filled with silence, blackness, and a sense of impending doom. But morning arrived without incident, the mist lifted, the skies brightened, and the friends found that they were safely in the middle of the lake pointing north. Relaxed now, they joked about their own and the others' fears, turned the boat east again, and took turns rowing while they waited for a breeze to come up. After a time, the mist burned away altogether, the clouds broke up, and they caught sight of the south shore. A northeasterly breeze sprang up around noon, and they stowed the oars and set sail.

Time drifted, and the skiff sped east. Daylight was

disappearing into nightfall when they finally reached the far shore and beached their craft in a wooded cove close to the mouth of the Silver River. They shoved the skiff into a reed-choked inlet, carefully secured it with stays, and began their walk inland. It was nearing sunset by now, and the skies turned a peculiar pinkish color as the fading light reflected off a new mix of low-hanging clouds and trailers of mist. It was still quiet in the forest, the night sounds waiting expectantly for the day to end before beginning their symphony. The river churned beside them sluggishly as they walked, choked with rain-water and debris. Shadows reached out to them, the trees seemed to draw closer together and the light faded. Before long, they were enveloped in darkness.

They talked briefly of the King of the Silver River.

'Gone like all the rest of the magic,' Par declared, picking his way carefully along the rain-slicked trail. They could see better this night, though not as well as they might have liked; the moon and stars were playing hide-and-seek with the clouds. 'Gone like the Druids, the Elves — everything but the stories.'

'Maybe, maybe not,' Morgan philosophized. 'Travelers still claim they see him from time to time, an old man with a lantern, lending guidance and protection. They admit his reach is not what it was, though. He claims only the river and a small part of the land about it. The rest belongs to us.'

'The rest belongs to the Federation, like everything else!' Coll snorted.

Morgan kicked at a piece of deadwood and sent it spinning into the dark. 'I know a man who claims to have spoken to the King of the Silver River — a drummer who sells fancy goods between the Highlands and the Anar. He comes through this country all the time, and he said that once he lost his way in the Battlemound and this old man appeared with his lantern and took him clear.' Morgan shook his head. 'I never knew whether to believe the man or not. Drummers make better storytellers than truth-sayers.'

'I think he's gone,' Par said, filled with a sense of sadness at his own certainty. 'The magic doesn't last when it isn't practiced or believed in. The King of the Silver River hasn't had the benefit of either. He's just a story now, just another legend that no one but you and I and Coll and maybe a handful of others believe was ever real.'

'We Ohmsfords always believe,' Coll finished softly.

They walked on in silence, listening to the night sounds, following the trail as it wound eastward. They would not reach Culhaven that night, but they were not yet ready to stop either, so they simply kept on without bothering to discuss it. The woods thickened as they moved farther inland, deeper into the lower Anar, and the pathway narrowed as scrub began to inch closer from the darkness. The river turned angry as it passed through a series of rapids, and the land grew rough, a maze of gullies and hillocks peppered with stray boulders and stumps.

'The road to Culhaven isn't what it once was,' Morgan muttered at one point. Par and Coll had no idea if that was so or not since neither had ever been to the Anar. They glanced at each other, but gave no reply.

Then the trail ended abruptly, blocked by a series of fallen trees. A secondary pathway swung away from the river and ran off into the deep woods. Morgan hesitated, then took it. The trees closed about overhead, their branches shutting out all but a trickle of moonlight, and the three friends were forced to grope their way ahead. Morgan was muttering again, inaudibly this time, although the tone of his voice was unmistakable. Vines and overhanging brush were slapping at them as they passed, and they were forced to duck their heads. The woods began to smell oddly fetid, as if the undergrowth was decaying. Par tried to hold his breath against the stench, irritated by its pervasiveness. He wanted to move faster, but Morgan was in the lead and already moving as fast as he could.

'It's as if something died in here,' Coll whispered from behind him.

Something triggered in Par's memory. He remembered the smell that had emanated from the cottage of the woodswoman the old man had warned them was a Shadowen. The smell here was exactly the same.

In the next instant, they emerged from the tangle of the forest into a clearing that was ringed by the lifeless husks of trees and carpeted with mulch, deadwood and scattered bones. A single stagnant pool of water bubbled at its center in the fashion of a cauldron heated by fire. Gimlet-eyed scavengers peered out at them from the shadows.

The companions came to an uncertain halt. 'Morgan, this is just like it was ...' Par began and then stopped.

The Shadowen stepped noiselessly from the trees and faced them. Par never questioned what it was; he knew instinctively. Skepticism and disbelief were erased in an instant's time, the discarded trappings of years of certainty that Shadowen were what practical men said they were — rumors and fireside tales. Perhaps it was the old man's warning whispering in his ear that triggered his conversion. Perhaps it was simply the look of the thing. Whatever it was, the truth that was left him was chilling and unforgettable.

This Shadowen was entirely different than the last. It was a huge, shambling thing, manlike but twice the size of a normal man, its body covered in coarse, shaggy hair, its massive limbs ending in paws that were splayed and clawed, its body hunched over at the shoulders like a gorilla. There was a face amid all that hair, but it could scarcely be called human. It was wrinkled and twisted about a mouth from which teeth protruded like stunted bones, and it hid within leathery folds eyes that peered out with insistent dislike and burned like fire. It stood looking at them, studying them in the manner of a slow-witted brute.

'Oh-oh,' Morgan said softly.

The Shadowen came forward a step, a hitching movement that suggested a stalking cat. 'Why are you here?' it rasped from some deep, empty well within.

'We took a wrong ...' Morgan began.

'You trespass on what is mine!' the other cut him short, teeth snapping wickedly. 'You cause me to be angered!'

Morgan glanced back at Par and the Valeman quickly mouthed the word 'Shadowen' and glanced in turn at Coll. Coll was pale and tense. Like Par, he was no longer questioning.

'I will have one of you in payment!' the Shadowen growled. 'Give me one of you! Give me!'

The three friends looked at each other once more. They knew there was only one way out of this. There was no old man to come to their aid this time. There was no one but themselves.

Morgan reached back and slid the Sword of Leah from its scabbard. The blade reflected brightly in the eyes of the monster. 'Either you let us pass safely ...' he began.

He never finished. The Shadowen launched itself at him with a shriek, bounding across the little clearing with frightening swiftness. He was on top of Morgan almost at once, claws ripping. Even so, the Highlander managed to bring the flat of the blade about in time to deflect the blow and knock the creature off-balance, driving it sideways so that its attack missed. Coll slashed at it with the short sword he was carrying as he leaped past toward the pool, and Par struck at it with the magic of the wishsong, clouding its vision with a swarm of buzzing insects.

The Shadowen surged back to its feet with a roar of anger, flailed madly at the air, then rushed them once more. It caught Morgan a stinging blow as the Highlander jumped aside and knocked him sprawling. The Shadowen turned, and Coll struck it so hard with the short sword that he severed one arm above the elbow. The Shadowen reeled away, then darted back, snatched up its severed limb and retreated again. Carefully, it placed its arm back against its shoulder There was sudden movement, an entwining of sinew and muscle and bone, like snakes moving. The limb had reattached itself.

The Shadowen hissed in delight.

'Then it came at them. Par tried to slow it with images of wolves, but the Shadowen barely saw them. It slammed into Morgan, shoving past the blade of his sword, throwing the Highlander back. He might have been lost then if not for the Ohmsfords, who flung themselves on the beast and bore it to the ground. They held it there for only an instant. It heaved upward, freed itself, and sent them flying. One great arm caught Par across the face, snapping his head back, causing flashes to cloud his vision as he tumbled away. He could hear the thing coming for him, and he threw out every image he could muster, rolling and crawling to regain his feet. He could hear Coll's cry of warning and a series of grunts. He pushed himself upright, forcing his vision to clear.

The Shadowen was right in front of him, clawed forelimbs spread wide to embrace him. Coll lay slumped against a tree a dozen paces to his left. There was no sign of Morgan. Par backed away slowly, searching for an escape. There was no time for the magic now. The creature was too close. He felt the rough bark of a tree trunk jammed against his back.

Then Morgan was there, launching himself from the darkness, crying out 'Leah, Leah' as he hammered into the Shadowen. There was blood on his face and clothing, and his eyes were bright with anger and determination. Down came the Sword of Leah, an arc of glittering metal — and something wondrous happened. The sword struck the Shadowen full on and burst into fire.

Par flinched and threw one arm across his face protectively. No, he thought in amazement, it wasn't fire he was seeing, it was magic!

The magic happened all at once, without warning, and it seemed to freeze the combatants in the circle of its light. The Shadowen stiffened and screamed, a shriek of agony and disbelief. The magic spread from the Sword of Leah into the creature's body, ripping through it like a razor through cloth. The Shadowen shuddered, seemed to sag inward against itself, lost definition, and began to disintegrate. Quickly Par dropped under the thing and rolled

80

free. He saw it heave upward desperately, then flare as brightly as the weapon that was killing it and disappear into ash.

The Sword of Leah winked instantly into darkness. The air was a blanket of sudden silence. Smoke floated in a cloud across the little clearing, its smell thick and pungent. The stagnant pool bubbled once and went still.

Morgan Leah dropped to one knee, the sword falling to the ground before him, striking the little mound of ash and flaring once. He flinched and then shuddered. 'Shades!' he whispered, his voice choked with astonishment. 'The power I felt, it was ... I never thought it possible ...'

Par came to him at once, knelt beside him and saw the other's face, cut and bruised and drained of blood. He took the Highlander in his arms and held him.

'It still has the magic, Morgan!' he whispered, excited that such a thing could be. 'All these years, and no one has known it, but it still has the magic!' Morgan looked at him uncomprehendingly. 'Don't you see? The magic has been sleeping since the time of Allanon! There's been no need for it! It took another magic to bring it awake! It took a creature like the Shadowen! That's why nothing happened until the magics touched ...'

He trailed off as Coll stumbled over to them and dropped down as well. One arm hung limply. 'Think I broke it,' he muttered.

He hadn't, but he had bruised it severely enough that Par felt it wise to bind it against his body in a cradle for a day or so. They used their drinking water to wash themselves, bandaged their cuts and scrapes, picked up their weapons, and stood looking at each other. 'The old man said there would be lots of things hunting us,' Par whispered.

'I don't know if that thing was hunting us or if we were just unlucky enough to stumble on it.' Coll's voice was ragged. 'I do know I don't want to run across any more like it.'

'But if we do,' Morgan Leah said quietly and stopped.

'If we do, we have the means now to deal with them.' And he fingered the blade of the Sword of Leah as he might have the soft curve of a woman's face.

Par would never forget what he felt at that moment. The memory of it would overshadow even that of their battle with the Shadowen, a tiny piece of time preserved in perfect still life. What he felt was jealousy. Before, he had been the one who had possessed real magic. Now it was Morgan Leah. He still had the wishsong, of course, but its magic paled in comparison to that of the High-lander's sword. It was the sword that had destroyed the Shadowen. Par's best images had proven to be little more than an irritation.

It made him wonder if the wishsong had any real use at all.

CHAPTER

7

PAR REMEMBERED SOMETHING LATER that night that forced him to come to grips with what he was feeling toward Morgan. They had continued on to Culhaven, anxious to complete their journey, willing to walk all night and another day if need be rather than attempt one moment's sleep in those woods. They had worked their way back to the main pathway where it ran parallel to the Silver River and pushed eastward. As they trudged on, nudged forward by apprehension one step, dragged backward by weariness the next, buffeted and tossed, their thoughts strayed like grazing cattle to sweeter pastures, and Par Ohmsford found himself thinking of the songs.

That was when he remembered that the legends had it that the power of the Sword of Leah was literally two-edged. The sword had been made magic by Allanon in the time of Brin Ohmsford while the Druid was journeying east with the Valegirl and her would-be protector, Morgan's ancestor, Rone Leah. The Druid had dipped the sword's blade into the forbidden waters of the Hadeshorn and changed forever its character. It became more than a simple blade; it became a talisman that could withstand even the Mord Wraiths. But the magic was like all the magics of old; it was both blessing and curse. Its power was addictive, causing the user to become increasingly dependent. Brin Ohmsford had recognized the danger, but her warnings to Rone Leah had gone unheeded. In their final confrontation with the dark magic, it was her own power and Jair's that had saved them and put an end to further need for the magic of the sword. There was no record of what had become of the weapon after — only that it was not required and therefore not used again.

Until now. And now it seemed it might be Par's obligation to warn Morgan of the danger of further use of the sword's magic. But how was he to do that? Shades, Morgan Leah was his best friend next to Coll, and this newfound magic Par envied so had just saved their lives! He was knotted up with guilt and frustration at the jealousy he was feeling. How was he supposed to tell Morgan that he shouldn't use it? It didn't matter that there might be good reason to do so; it still sounded impossibly grudging. Besides, they would need the magic of the Sword of Leah if they encountered any further Shadowen. And there was every reason to expect that they might.

He struggled with his dilemma only briefly. He simply could not ignore his discomfort and the vivid memory of that creature breathing over him. He decided to keep quiet. Perhaps there would be no need to speak out. If there was, he would do so then. He put the matter aside.

They talked little that night, and when they did it was mostly about the Shadowen. There was no longer any doubt in their minds that these beings were real. Even Coll did not equivocate when speaking of what it was that had attacked them. But acceptance did not bring enlightenment. The Shadowen remained a mystery to them. They did not know where they had come from or why. They did not even know what they were. They had no idea as to the source of their power, though it seemed it must derive from some form of magic. If these creatures were hunting them, they did not know what they could do about it. They knew only that the old man had been right when he had warned them to be careful.

It was just after dawn when they reached Culhaven, emerging aching and sleepy-eyed from the fading night

shadows of the forest into the half-light of the new day.
Clouds hung across the Eastland skies, scraping the treetops as they eased past, lending the Dwarf village
beneath a gray and wintry cast. The companions
stumbled to a halt, stretched, yawned, and looked about.
The trees had thinned before them and there was a
gathering of cottages with smoke curling out of stone
chimneys, sheds filled with tools and wagons, and small
yards with animals staked and penned. Vegetable gardens
the size of thumbprints fought to control tiny patches of
earth as weeds attacked from everywhere. Everything
seemed crammed together, the cottages and sheds, the
animals, the gardens and the forest, each on top of the
other. Nothing looked cared for; paint was peeling and
chipped, mortar and stone were cracked, fences broken
and sagging, animals shaggy and unkempt, and gardens
and the weeds grown so much into each other as to be
almost indistinguishable.

Women drifted through doors and past windows, old
mostly, some with laundry to hang, some with cooking to
tend, all with the same ragged, untended look. Children
played in the yards, on the pathways, and in the roads, as
shabby and wild as mountain sheep.

Morgan caught Par and Coll staring and said, 'I forgot
— the Culhaven you're familiar with is the one you tell
about in your stories. Well, all that's in the past. I know
you're tired, but, now that you're here, there are things
you need to see.'

He took them down a pathway that led into the village.
The housing grew quickly worse, the cottages replaced by
shacks, the gardens and animals disappearing entirely.
The path became a roadway, rutted and pocked from lack
of repair, filled with refuse and stones. There were more
children here, playing as the others had, and there were
more women working at household chores, exchanging a
few words now and then with each other and the children, but withdrawn mostly into themselves. They
watched guardedly as the three strangers walked past,
suspicion and fear mirrored in their eyes.

'Culhaven, the most beautiful city in the Eastland, the heart and soul of the Dwarf nation,' Morgan mused quietly. He didn't look at them. 'I know the stories. It was a sanctuary, an oasis, a haven of gentle souls, a monument to what pride and hard work could accomplish.' He shook his head. 'Well, this is the way it is now.'

A few of the children came up to them and begged for coins. Morgan shook his head gently, patted one or two, and moved past.

They turned off into a lane that led down to a stream clogged with trash and sewage. Children walked the banks, poking idly at what floated past. A walkway took them across to the far bank. The air was fetid with the smell of rotting things.

'Where are all the men?' Par asked.

Morgan looked over. 'The lucky ones are dead. The rest are in the mines or in work camps. That's why everything looks the way it does. There's no one left in this city but children, old people, and a few women.' He stopped walking. 'That's how it has been for fifty years. That's how the Federation wants it. Come this way.'

He led them down a narrow pathway behind a series of cottages that seemed better tended. These homes were freshly painted, the stone scrubbed, the mortar intact, the gardens and lawns immaculate. Dwarves worked the yards and rooms here as well, younger women mostly, the tasks the same, but the results as different from before as night is to day. Everything here was bright and new and clean.

Morgan took them up a rise to a small park, easing carefully into a stand of fir. 'See those?' He pointed to the well-tended cottages. Par and Coll nodded. 'That's where the Federation soldiers and officials garrisoned here live. The younger, stronger Dwarf women are forced to work for them. Most are forced to live with them as well.' He glanced at them meaningfully.

They walked from the park down a hillside that led toward the center of the community. Shops and businesses replaced homes, and the foot traffic grew thick.

The Dwarves they saw here were engaged in selling and buying, but again they were mostly old and few in number. The streets were clogged with outlanders come to trade. Federation soldiers patrolled everywhere.

Morgan steered the brothers down byways where they wouldn't be noticed, pointing out this, indicating that, his voice at once both bitter and ironic. 'Over there. That's the silver exchange. The Dwarves are forced to extract the silver from the mines, kept underground most of the time — you know what that means — then compelled to sell it at Federation prices and turn the better part of the proceeds over to their keepers in the form of taxes. And the animals belong to the Federation as well — on loan, supposedly. The Dwarves are strictly rationed. Down there, that's the market. All the vegetables and fruits are grown and sold by the Dwarves, and the profits of sale disposed of in the same manner as everything else That's what it's like here now. That's what being a "protectorate" means for these people.'

He stopped them at the far end of the street, well back from a ring of onlookers crowded about a platform on which young Dwarf men and women chained and bound were being offered for sale. They stood looking for a moment and Morgan said, 'They sell off the ones they don't need to do the work.'

He took them from the business district to a hillside that rose above the city in a broad sweep. The hillside was blackened and stripped of life, a vast smudge against a treeless skyline. It had been terraced once, and what was left of the buttressing poked out of the earth like gravestones.

'Do you know what this is?' he asked them softly. They shook their heads. 'This is what is left of the Meade Gardens. You know the story. The Dwarves built the Gardens with special earth hauled in from the farmlands, earth as black as coal. Every flower known to the races was planted and tended. My father said it was the most beautiful thing he had ever seen. He was here once, when he was a boy.'

Morgan was quiet a moment as they surveyed the ruin, then said, 'The Federation burned the Gardens when the city fell. They burn them anew every year so that nothing will ever grow again.'

As they walked away, veering back toward the outskirts of the village, Par asked, 'How do you know all this, Morgan? Your father?'

Morgan shook his head. 'My father hasn't been back since that first visit. I think he prefers not to see what it looks like now, but to remember it as it was. No, I have friends here who tell me what life for the Dwarves is like — that part of life I can't see for myself whenever I come over. I haven't told you much about that, have I? Well, it's only been recently, the last half year or so. I'll tell you about it later.'

They retraced their steps to the poorer section of the village, following a new roadway that was nevertheless as worn and rutted as the others. After a short walk, they turned into a walkway that led up to a rambling stone-and-wood structure that looked as if once it might have been an inn of some sort. It rose three stories and was wrapped by a covered porch filled with swings and rockers. The yard was bare, but clear of debris and filled with children playing.

'A school?' Par guessed aloud.

Morgan shook his head. 'An orphanage.'

He led them through the groups of children, onto the porch and around to a side door set well back in the shadows of an alcove. He knocked on the door and waited. When the door opened a crack, he said, 'Can you spare a poor man some food?'

'Morgan!' The door flew open. An elderly Dwarf woman stood in the opening, gray-haired and aproned, her face bluff and squarish, her smile working its way past lines of weariness and disappointment. 'Morgan Leah, what a pleasant surprise! How are you, youngster?'

'I am my father's pride and joy, as always,' Morgan replied with a grin. 'May we come in?'

'Of course. Since when have you needed to ask?' The

woman stepped aside and ushered them past, hugging
Morgan and beaming at Par and Coll who smiled back
uncertainly. She shut the door behind them and said, 'So
you would like something to eat, would you?'

'We would gladly give our lives for the opportunity,'
Morgan declared with a laugh. 'Granny Elise, these are
my friends, Par and Coll Ohmsford of Shady Vale. They
are temporarily ... homeless,' he finished.

'Aren't we all,' Granny Elise replied gruffly. She
extended a callused hand to the brothers, who each
gripped it in his own. She examined them critically. 'Been
wrestling with bears, have you, Morgan?'

Morgan touched his face experimentally, tracing the
cuts and scrapes. 'Something worse than that, I'm afraid.
The road to Culhaven is not what it once was.'

'Nor is Culhaven. Have a seat, child — you and your
friends. I'll bring you a plate of muffins and fruit.'

There were several long tables with benches in the
center of the rather considerable kitchen and the three
friends chose the nearest and sat. The kitchen was large
but rather dark, and the furnishings were poor. Granny
Elise bustled about industriously, providing the promised
breakfast and glasses of some sort of extracted juice. 'I'd
offer you milk, but I have to ration what I have for the
children,' she apologized.

They were eating hungrily when a second woman
appeared, a Dwarf as well and older still, small and
wizened, with a sharp face and quick, birdlike movements
that never seemed to cease. She crossed the room matter-
of-factly on seeing Morgan, who rose at once and gave
her a small peck on the cheek.

'Auntie Jilt,' Morgan introduced her.

'Most pleased,' she announced in a way that suggested
they might need convincing. She seated herself next to
Granny Elise and immediately began work on some
needlepoint she had brought with her into the room,
fingers flying.

'These ladies are mothers to the world,' Morgan
explained as he returned to his meal. 'Me included,

though I'm not an orphan like their other charges. They adopted me because I'm irresistibly charming.'

'You begged like the rest of them the first time we saw you, Morgan Leah!' Auntie Jilt snapped, never looking up from her work. 'That is the only reason we took you in — the only reason we take any of them in.'

'Sisters, though you'd never know it,' Morgan quickly went on. 'Granny Elise is like a goose down comforter, all soft and warm. But Auntie Jilt — well, Auntie Jilt is more like a stone pallet!'

Auntie Jilt sniffed. 'Stone lasts a good deal longer than goose down in these times. And both longer still than Highland syrup!'

Morgan and Granny Elise laughed, Auntie Jilt joined in after a moment, and Par and Coll found themselves smiling as well. It seemed odd to do so, their thoughts still filled with images of the village and its people, the sounds of the orphaned children playing outside a pointed reminder of how things really stood. But there was something indomitable about these old women, something that transcended the misery and poverty, something that whispered of promise and hope.

When breakfast was finished, Granny Elise busied herself at the sink and Auntie Jilt departed to check on the children. Morgan whispered, 'These ladies have been operating the orphanage for almost thirty years. The Federation lets them alone because they help keep the children out from underfoot. Nice, huh? There are hundreds of children with no parents, so the orphanage is always full. When the children are old enough, they are smuggled out. If they are allowed to stay too long, the Federation sends them to the work camps or sells them. Every so often, the ladies guess wrong.' He shook his head. 'I don't know how they stand it. I would have gone mad long ago.'

Granny Elise came back and sat with them. 'Has Morgan told you how we met?' she asked the Ohmsfords. 'Oh, well, it was quite something. He brought us food and clothes for the children, he gave us money to buy what we could, and he helped guide a dozen children north to be placed with families in the free territories.'

'Oh, for goodness sake, Granny!' Morgan interjected, embarrassed.

'Exactly! And he works around the house now and then when he visits, too,' she added, ignoring him. 'We have become his own private little charity, haven't we, Morgan?'

'That reminds me — here.' Morgan reached into his tunic and extracted a small pouch. The contents jingled as he passed it over. 'I won a wager a week or so back about some perfume.' He winked at the Valemen.

'Bless you, Morgan.' Granny Elise rose and came round to kiss him on the cheek. 'You seem quite exhausted — all of you. There are spare beds in the back and plenty of blankets. You can sleep until dinner time.'

She ushered them from the kitchen to a small room at the rear of the big house where there were several beds, a wash basin, blankets, and towels. Par glanced around, noticing at once that the windows were shuttered and the curtains carefully drawn.

Granny Elise noticed the look that the Valeman exchanged with his brother. 'Sometimes my guests don't wish to draw attention to themselves,' she said quietly. Her eyes were sharp. 'Isn't that the case with you?'

Morgan went over and kissed her gently. 'Perceptive as always, old mother. We'll need a meeting with Steff. Can you take care of it?'

Granny Elise looked at him a moment, then nodded wordlessly, kissed him back and slipped from the room.

It was twilight when they woke, the shuttered room filled with shadows and silence. Granny Elise appeared, her bluff face gentle and reassuring, slipping through the room on cat's feet as she touched each and whispered that it was time, before disappearing back the way she had come. Morgan Leah and the Ohmsfords rose to find their clothes clean and fresh-smelling again. Granny Elise had been busy while they slept.

While they were dressing, Morgan said, 'We'll meet with Steff tonight. He's part of the Dwarf Resistance, and the Resistance has eyes and ears everywhere. If Walker Boh still lives in the Eastland, even in the deepest part of the Anar, Steff will know.'

He finished pulling on his boots and stood up. 'Steff was one of the orphans Granny took in. He's like a son to her. Other than Auntie Jilt, he's the only family she has left.'

They went out from the sleeping room and down the hall to the kitchen. The children had already finished dinner and retired to their rooms on the upper two stories, save for a handful of tiny ones that Auntie Jilt was in the process of feeding, patiently spooning soup to first one mouth, then the next and so on until it was time to begin the cycle all over again. She looked up as they entered and nodded wordlessly.

Granny Elise sat them down at one of the long tables and brought them plates of food and glasses of harsh ale. From overhead came the sounds of thumping and yelling as the children played. 'It is hard to supervise so many when there is only the two of us,' she apologized, serving Coll a second helping of meat stew. 'But the women we hire to help out never seem to stay very long.'

'Were you able to get a message to Steff?' Morgan asked quietly.

Granny Elise nodded, her smile suddenly sad. 'I wish I could see more of that child, Morgan. I worry so about him.'

They finished their meal and sat quietly in the evening shadows as Granny Elise and Auntie Jilt finished with the children and saw them all off to bed. A pair of candles burned on the table where the three sat, but the remainder of the room was left dark. The voices upstairs faded away one by one, and the silence deepened.

Auntie Jilt came back into the kitchen after a time and sat with them. She didn't speak, her sharp face lowered as she concentrated on her needlepoint, her head bobbing slightly. Outside, somewhere, a bell rang three times and went still. Auntie Jilt looked up briefly. 'Federation curfew,' she muttered. 'No one is allowed out after it sounds.'

The room went silent again. Granny Elise appeared and worked quietly at the sink. One of the children upstairs began to cry and she went out again. The Ohmsfords and Morgan Leah looked at each other and the room and waited.

Then, suddenly, there was a soft tapping at the kitchen door. Three taps. Auntie Jilt looked up, her fingers stilled, and waited. The seconds slipped away. Then the tapping came again, three times, a pause, three times again.

Auntie Jilt rose quickly, walked to the door, unlatched it and peeked out. Then she opened the door wide for an instant and a shadowy figure slipped into the room. Auntie Jilt pushed the door closed again. Granny Elise appeared at the same instant from the hall, motioned Morgan and the Ohmsford brothers to their feet and led them over to where the stranger stood.

'This is Teel,' said Granny Elise. 'She will take you to Steff.'

It was hard to tell much of anything about Teel. She was a Dwarf, but smaller than most, rather slight, clothed in dark, nondescript forest clothing including a short cloak and hood. Her features were hidden by a strange leather mask that wrapped the whole of her face, save for her right jaw and her mouth. A glimmer of dusky blond hair was visible within the covering of the hood.

Granny Elise reached up and hugged Morgan. 'Be careful, youngster,' she cautioned. She smiled, patted Par and Coll gently on the shoulder, and hastened to the door. She peeked through the curtains for a moment, then nodded. Teel went out through the door without a word. The Ohmsfords and Morgan Leah went with her.

Outside, they slipped silently along the side of the old house and through a back fence onto a narrow pathway. They followed the pathway to an empty road, then turned right. The mix of cottages and shacks that lined the roadway were dark, their silhouettes ragged and broken against the sky. Teel moved them down the road quickly and into a patch of fir. She stopped then and dropped into a crouch, motioning them down with her. Moments later, a Federation patrol of five appeared. They joked and talked among themselves as they passed, unconcerned with any who might hear them. Then their voices faded and they were gone. Teel stood up, and they were off again.

They stayed on the road for another hundred yards, then turned into the forest. They were on the very edge of the village now, almost due north, and the sounds of insects began to break through the stillness. They slipped along silently through the trees, Teel pausing now and then to listen before continuing on. The smell of wildflowers filled the air, sweet and strong against the reek of garbage.

Then Teel stopped at a line of thick brush, pushed the branches aside, reached down to grip a hidden iron ring and pulled. A trapdoor lifted clear of the earth to reveal a stairway. They felt their way along its walls until they were completely inside and crouched there in the dark. Teel secured the trapdoor behind them, lit a candle and took the lead once more. The company started down.

It was a short descent. The stairs ended after two dozen steps and became a tunnel, the walls and ceiling shored by thick wooden beams and pinned by iron bolts. Teel offered no explanation for the tunnel, but simply moved ahead into it. Twice the tunnel branched in several directions, and each time she made her choice without hesitating. It occurred to Par that if they had to find their way out again without Teel, they probably couldn't do it.

The tunnel ended minutes later at an iron door. Teel struck the door sharply with the hilt of her dagger, paused, then struck it twice more. The locks on the other side snapped free and the door swung open.

The Dwarf who stood there was no older than they, a stout, muscular fellow with a shading of beard and long hair the color of cinnamon, a face that was scarred all over, and the biggest mace Par had ever seen strapped across his back. He had the top half of one ear missing and a gold ring dangling from the remainder.

'Morgan!' he greeted and embraced the Highlander warmly. His smile brightened his fierce countenance as he pulled the other inside and looked past him to where Par and Coll stood nervously waiting. 'Friends?'

'The best,' Morgan answered at once. 'Steff, this is Par and Coll Ohmsford from Shady Vale.'

The Dwarf nodded. 'You are welcome here, Valemen.' He broke away from Morgan and reached out to grip their hands. 'Come take a seat, tell me what brought you.'

They were in an underground room filled with stores, boxed, crated and wrapped, that surrounded a long table with benches. Steff motioned them onto the benches, then poured each a cup of ale and joined them. Teel took up a position by the door, settling carefully onto a small stool.

'Is this where you live now?' Morgan asked, glancing about. 'It needs work.'

Steff's smile wrinkled his rough face. 'I live in a lot of places, Morgan, and they all need work. This one is better than most. Underground, though, like the others. We Dwarves all live underground these days, either here or in the mines or in our graves. Sad.'

He hoisted his mug. 'Good health to us and misfortune to our enemies,' he toasted. They all drank but Teel, who sat watching. Steff placed his mug back on the table. 'Is your father well?' he asked Morgan.

The Highlander nodded. 'I brought Granny Elise a little something to buy bread with. She worries about you. How long since you've been to see her?'

The Dwarf's smile dropped away. 'It's too dangerous to go just now. See my face?' He pointed, tracing the scars with his finger. 'The Federation caught me three months back.' He glanced at Par and Coll conspiratorially. 'Morgan wouldn't know, you see. He hasn't been to see me of late. When he comes to Culhaven, he prefers the company of old ladies and children.'

95

Morgan ignored him. 'What happened, Steff?'

The Dwarf shrugged. 'I got away — parts of me, at least.' He held up his left hand. The last two fingers were missing, sheared off. 'Enough of that, Highlander. Leave off. Instead, tell me what brings you east.'

Morgan started to speak, then took a long look at Teel and stopped. Steff saw the direction his gaze had taken, glanced briefly over his shoulder and said, 'Oh, yes. Teel. Guess I'll have to talk about it after all.'

He looked back at Morgan. 'I was taken by the Federation while raiding their weapons stores in the main compound in Culhaven. They put me in their prisons to discover what I could tell them. That was where they did this.' He touched his face. 'Teel was a prisoner in the cell next to mine. What they did to me is nothing compared to what they did to her. They destroyed most of her face and much of her back punishing her for killing the favorite dog of one of the members of the provisional government quartered in Culhaven. She killed the dog for food. We talked through the walls and came to know each other. One night, less than two weeks after I was taken, when it became apparent that the Federation had no further interest in me and I was to be killed, Teel managed to lure the jailor on watch into her cell. She killed him, stole his keys, freed me, and we escaped. We have been together ever since.'

He paused, his eyes as hard as flint. 'Highlander, I think much of you, and you must make your own decision in this matter. But Teel and I share everything.'

There was a long silence. Morgan glanced briefly at Par and Coll. Par had been watching Teel closely during Steff's narration. She never moved. There was no expression on her face, nothing mirrored in her eyes. She might have been made of stone.

'I think we must rely on Steff's judgment in this matter,' Par said quietly, looking to Coll for approval. Coll nodded wordlessly.

Morgan stretched his legs beneath the table, reached for his ale mug and took a long drink. He was clearly making up his own mind. 'Very well,' he said finally. 'But nothing I say must leave this room.'

'You haven't said anything as yet worth taking out,' Steff declared pointedly and waited.

Morgan smiled, then placed the ale mug carefully back on the table. 'Steff, we need you to help us find someone, a man we think is living somewhere in the deep Anar. His name is Walker Boh.'

Steff blinked. 'Walker Boh,' he repeated quietly, and the way he spoke the name indicated he recognized it.

'My friends, Par and Coll, are his nephews.'

Steff looked at the Valemen as if he were seeing them for the first time. 'Well, now. Tell me the rest of it.'

Quickly, Morgan related the story of the journey that had brought them to Culhaven, beginning with the Ohmsford brothers' flight from Varfleet and ending with their battle with the Shadowen at the edge of the Anar. He told of the old man and his warnings, of the dreams that had come to Par that summoned him to the Hadeshorn, and of his own discovery of the dormant magic of the Sword of Leah. Steff listened to it all without comment. He sat unmoving, his ale forgotten, his face an expressionless mask.

When Morgan was finished, Steff grunted and shook his head. 'Druids and magic and creatures of the night. Highlander, you constantly surprise me.' He rose, walked around the table, and stood looking at Teel momentarily, his rough face creased in thought. Then he said, 'I know of Walker Boh.' He shook his head.

'And?' Morgan pressed.

He wheeled back slowly. 'And the man scares me.' He looked at Par and Coll. 'Your uncle, is he? And how long since you've seen him — ten years? Well, listen close to me, then. The Walker Boh I know may not be the uncle you remember. This Walker Boh is more whispered rumor than truth, and very real all the same — someone that even the things that live out in the darker parts of the land and prey off travelers, wayfarers, strays, and such are said to avoid.'

97

He sat down again, took up the ale mug and drank. Morgan Leah and the Ohmsfords looked at one another in silence. At last, Par said, 'I think we are decided on the matter. Whoever or whatever Walker Boh is now, we share a common bond beyond our kinship — our dreams of Allanon. I have to know what my uncle intends to do. Will you help us find him?'

Steff smiled faintly, unexpectedly. 'Direct. I like that.' He looked at Morgan. 'I assume he speaks for his brother. Does he speak for you as well?' Morgan nodded. 'I see.' He studied them for long moments, lost in thought. 'Then I will help,' he said finally. He paused, judging their reaction. 'I will take you to Walker Boh — if he can be found. But I will do so for reasons of my own, and you'd best know what they are.'

His face lowered momentarily into shadow, and the scars seemed like strands of iron mesh pressed against his skin. 'The Federation has taken your homes from you, from all of you, taken them and made them their own. Well, the Federation has taken more than that from me. It has taken everything — my home, my family, my past, even my present. The Federation has destroyed everything that was and is and left me only what might be. It is the enemy of my life, and I would do anything to see it destroyed. Nothing I do here will accomplish that end in my lifetime. What I do here merely serves to keep me alive and to give me some small reason to stay that way. I have had enough of that. I want something more.'

His face lifted, and his eyes were fierce. 'If there is magic that can be freed from time's chains, if there are Druids yet, ghosts or otherwise, able to wield it, then perhaps there are ways of freeing my homeland and my people — ways that have been kept from us all. If we discover those ways, if the knowledge of them passes into our hands, they must be used to help my people and my homeland.' He paused. 'I'll want your promise on this.'

There was a long moment of silence as his listeners looked at one another.

Then Par said softly, 'I am ashamed for the Southland

when I see what has happened here. I don't begin to understand it. There is nothing that could justify it. If we discover anything that will give the Dwarves back their freedom, we will put it to use.'

'We will,' Coll echoed, and Morgan Leah nodded his agreement as well.

Steff took a deep breath. 'The possibility of being free — just the possibility — is more than the Dwarves dare hope for in these times.' He placed his thick hands firmly on the table. 'Then we have a bargain. I will take you to find Walker Boh — Teel and I, for she goes where I go.' He glanced at each of them quickly for any sign of disapproval and found none. 'It will take a day or so to gather up what we need and to make an inquiry or two. I need not remind you, but I will anyway, how difficult and dangerous this journey is likely to be. Go back to Granny's and rest. Teel will take you. When all is in place, I will send word.'

They rose, and the Dwarf embraced Morgan, then smiled unexpectedly and slapped him on the back. 'You and I, Highlander — let the worst that's out there be wary!' He laughed and the room rang with the sound of it.

Teel stood apart from them and watched with eyes like chips of ice.

CHAPTER

8

WO DAYS PASSED, and they did not hear from Steff. Par and Coll Ohmsford and Morgan Leah passed the time at the orphanage completing some much needed repairs on the old home and helping Granny Elise and Auntie Jilt with the children. The days were warm, lazy ones, filled with the sounds of small voices at play. It was a different world within the confines of the rambling house and the shaded grounds, a world quite apart from the one that crouched begging a dozen yards in any direction beyond the enclosing fence. There was food here, warm beds, comfort and love. There was a sense of security and future. There wasn't a lot of anything, but there was some of everything. The remainder of the city faded into a series of unpleasant memories — the shacks, the broken old people, the ragged children, the missing mothers and fathers, the grime and the wear, the desperate and defeated looks, and the sense that there was no hope. Several times, Par thought to leave the orphanage and walk again through the city of Culhaven, unwilling to leave without seeing once more sights he felt he should never forget. But the old ladies discouraged it. It was dangerous for him to walk about. He might unwittingly draw attention to himself. Better to stay where he was, let the world outside stay where it was, and the both of them get on the best they could.

'There is nothing to be done for the misery of the Dwarves,' Auntie Jilt declared bitterly. 'It's a misery that's put down deep roots.'

Par did as he was told, feeling at once both unhappy and relieved. The ambiguity bothered him. He couldn't pretend he didn't know what was happening to the people of the city — didn't want to, in fact — but at the same time it was a difficult knowledge to face. He could do as the old ladies said and let the world without get along as best it could, but he couldn't forget that it was there, pressed up against the gate like some starving beast waiting for food.

On the third day of waiting, the beast snapped at them. It was early morning, and a squad of Federation soldiers marched up the roadway and into the yard. A Seeker was leading them. Granny Elise sent the Valemen and the Highlander to the attic and with Auntie Jilt in tow went out to confront their visitors. From the attic, the three in hiding watched what happened next. The children were forced to line up in front of the porch. They were all too small to be of any use, but three were selected anyway. The old women argued, but there was nothing they could do. In the end, they were forced to stand there helplessly while the three were led away.

Everyone was subdued after that, even the most active among the children. Auntie Jilt retired to a windowseat overlooking the front yard where she could sit and watch the children and work on her needlepoint, and she didn't say a word to anyone. Granny Elise spent most of her time in the kitchen baking. Her words were few, and she hardly smiled at all. The Ohmsfords and Morgan went about their work as unobtrusively as they could, feeling as if they should be somewhere else, secretly wishing that they were.

Late that afternoon, Par could stand his discomfort no longer and went down to the kitchen to talk to Granny Elise. He found her sitting at one of the long tables, sipping absently at a cup of amber tea, and he asked her quite directly why it was that the Dwarves were being treated so badly, why it was that soldiers of the Federation — Southlanders like himself, after all — could be a part of such cruelty.

Granny Elise smiled sadly, took his hand and pulled him down next to her. 'Par,' she said, speaking his name softly. She had begun using his name the past day or so, a clear indication that she now considered him another of her children. 'Par, there are some things that cannot ever be explained — not properly, not so as we might understand them the way we need to. I think sometimes that there must be a reason for what's happening and other times that there cannot be because it lacks any semblance of logic. It has been so long since it all started, you see. The war was fought over a hundred years ago. I don't know that anyone can remember the beginning of it anymore, and if you cannot remember how it began, how can you determine *why* it began?'

She shook her squarish head and hugged him impulsively. 'I'm sorry, Par, but I don't have any better answer to give you. I suppose I gave up trying to find one a long time ago. All my energy these days is given over to caring for the children. I guess I don't believe questions are important anymore, so I don't look for answers. Someone else will have to do that. All that matters to me is saving the life of one more child, and one more after that, and another, and another, until the need to save them doesn't exist anymore.'

Par nodded silently and hugged her back, but the answer didn't satisfy him. There was a reason for everything that happened, even if the reason wasn't immediately apparent. The Dwarves had lost the war to the Federation; they were a threat to no one. Why, then, were they being systematically ground down? It would have made better sense to heal the wounds that the war had opened than to throw salt into them. It almost seemed as if the Dwarves were being intentionally provoked, as if a cause for them to resist were being deliberately provided. Why would that be?

'Perhaps the Federation wants an excuse to exterminate them altogether,' Coll suggested blackly when Par asked his opinion that night after dinner.

'You mean you think the Federation believes the Dwarves are of no further use, even in the mines?' Par was incredulous. 'Or that they're too much trouble to supervise or too dangerous, so they ought to simply be done away with? The entire nation?'

Coll's blocky face was impassive. 'I mean, I know what I've seen here — what we've both seen. It seems pretty clear to me what's happening!'

Par wasn't so sure. He let the matter drop because for the moment he didn't have any better answer. But he promised himself that one day he would.

He slept poorly that night and was already awake when Granny Elise slipped into the sleeping room at dawn to whisper that Teel had come for them. He rose quickly and dragged the covers from Coll and Morgan. They dressed, strapped on their weapons and went down the hall to the kitchen where Teel was waiting, a shadow by the door, masked and wrapped in a drab forest cloak that gave her the look of a beggar. Granny Elise gave them hot tea and cakes and kissed each of them, Auntie Jilt warned them sternly to keep safe from whatever dangers might lie in wait for them, and Teel led them out into the night.

It was dark still, the dawn not yet even a small glimmer in the distant trees, and they slipped silently through the sleeping village, four ghosts in search of a haunt. The morning air was chill, and they could see their breath cloud the air before them in small puffs. Teel took them down back pathways and through dense groves of trees and gatherings of brush, keeping to the shadows, staying away from the roads and lights. They moved north out of the village without seeing anyone. When they reached the Silver River, Teel took them downstream to a shallows, avoiding the bridges. They crossed water like ice as it lapped at their legs. They were barely into the trees again when Steff appeared out of the shadows to join them. He wore a brace of long knives at his waist, and the giant mace was slung across his back. He said nothing, taking the lead from Teel and guiding them ahead. A few faint streaks of daylight appeared in the east, and the sky began to brighten. The stars winked out and the moon disappeared. Frost glimmered on leaves and grasses like scattered bits of crystal.

A bit farther on, they reached a clearing dominated by a massive old willow, and Steff brought them to a halt. Backpacks, rolled blankets, foul-weather gear, cooking implements, water bags, and forest cloaks for each of them were concealed in an old hollow tree trunk that had fallen into the brush. They strapped everything in place without speaking and were off again.

They walked the remainder of the day at a leisurely pace, bearing directly north. There was little discussion, none whatsoever as to where they were going. Steff offered no explanation, and neither the Valemen nor the Highlander were inclined to ask. When the Dwarf was ready to tell them, he would. The day passed quickly and by midafternoon they had reached the foothills south of the Wolfsktaag. They continued on for what was perhaps another hour, following the forestline upward to where it began to thin before the wall of the mountains, then Steff called a halt in a pine-sheltered clearing close to a small stream that trickled down out of the rocks. He led them over to a fallen log and seated himself comfortably, facing them.

'If the rumors are to be believed — and in this case, rumors are all we have — Walker Boh will be found in Darklin Reach. To get there, we will travel north through the Wolfsktaag — in through the Pass of Noose, out through the Pass of Jade, and from there east into the Reach.'

He paused, considering what he saw in their faces. 'There are other ways, of course — safer ways, some might argue — but I disagree. We could skirt the Wolfsktaag to the east or west, but either way we risk an almost certain encounter with Federation soldiers or Gnomes. There will be neither in the Wolfsktaag. Too many spirits and things of old magic live in the mountains; the Gnomes are superstitious about such and stay away. The Federation used to send patrols in, but most of them never came out. Truth is, most of them just got lost up there because they didn't know the way. I do.'

His listeners remained silent. Finally Coll said, 'I seem to remember that a couple of our ancestors got into a good bit of trouble when they took this same route some years back.'

Steff shrugged. 'I wouldn't know about that. I do know that I have been through these mountains dozens of times and know what to look for. The trick is to stay on the ridgelines and out of the deep forests. What lives in the Wolfsktaag prefers the dark. And there's nothing magic about most of it.'

Coll shook his head and looked at Par. 'I don't like it.'

'Well, the choice is between the devil we know and the one we suspect,' Steff declared bluntly. 'Federation soldiers and their Gnome allies, which we know are out there, or spirits and wraiths, which we don't.'

'Shadowen,' Par said softly.

There was a moment of silence. Steff smiled grimly. 'Haven't you heard, Valeman — there aren't any Shadowen. That's all a rumor. Besides, you have the magic to protect us, don't you? You and the Highlander here? What would dare challenge that?'

He looked about, sharp eyes darting from one face to the next. 'Come, now. No one ever suggested that this journey would be a safe one. Let us have a decision. I won't make you go into the Wolfsktaag if you think it too dangerous. But you have heard my warning about the choices left us if we forgo the mountains. Pay heed.'

There wasn't much any of them could say after that, and they left it to the Dwarf's best judgment. This was his country after all, not theirs, and he was the one who knew it. They were relying on him to find Walker Boh, and it seemed foolish to second guess the way he thought best to go about it.

They spent the night in the clearing of pines, smelling

105

needles and wildflowers and the crispness of the air, slept undisturbed and dreamless in a silence that stretched far beyond where they could see. At dawn, Steff took them up into the Wolfsktaag. They slipped into the Pass of Noose, where Gnomes had once tried to trap Shea and Flick Ohmsford, crossed the rope walkway that bridged the chasm at its center, wound their way steadily upward through the ragged, blunted peaks of slab-sided stone and forested slopes, and watched the sun work its way across the cloudless summer sky. Morning passed into afternoon, and they reached the ridgelines running north and began following their twist and bend. Travel was easy, the sun warm and reassuring, and the fears and doubts of the night before began to fade. They watched for movement in the shadows of rock and wood, but saw nothing. Birds sang in the trees, small animals scampered through the brush, and the forests here seemed very much the same as forests everywhere in the Four Lands. The Valemen and the Highlander found themselves smiling at one another; Staff hummed tonelessly to himself, and only Teel showed nothing of what she was feeling.

When nightfall approached, they made camp in a small meadow nestled between two ridgelines cropped with fir and cedar. There was little wind, and the day's warmth lingered in the sheltered valley long after the sun was gone. Stars glimmered faintly in the darkening skies, and the moon hung full against the western horizon. Par recalled again the old man's admonition to them — that they were to be at the Hadeshorn on the first day of the new moon. Time was slipping past.

But it wasn't of the old man or Allanon that Par found himself thinking that night as the little company gathered around the fire Steff had permitted them and washed down their dinner with long draughts of spring water. It was of Walker Boh. Par hadn't seen his uncle in almost ten years, but what he remembered of him was strangely clear. He had been just a boy then, and his uncle had seemed rather mysterious — a tall, lean man with dark features and eyes that could see right through you. The eyes — that was what Par remembered most, though he remembered them more for how remarkable they had seemed than for any discomfort they might have caused him. In fact, his uncle had been very kind to him, but always rather introspective or perhaps just withdrawn, sort of there but at the same time somewhere else.

There were stories about Walker Boh even then, but Par could recall few of them. It was said he used magic, although it was never made clear exactly what sort of magic. He was a direct descendant of Brin Ohmsford, but he had not had use of the wishsong. No one on his side of the family had, not in ten generations. The magic had died with Brin. It had worked differently for her than for her brother Jair, of course. Where Jair had only been able to use the wishsong to create images, his sister had been able to use it to create reality. Her magic had been by far the stronger of the two. Nevertheless, hers had disappeared with her passing, and only Jair's had survived.

Yet there had always been stories of Walker Boh and the magic. Par remembered how sometimes his uncle could tell him things that were happening at other places, things he could not possibly have known yet somehow did. There were times when his uncle could make things move by looking at them, even people. He could tell what you were thinking, too. Sometimes. He would look at you and tell you not to worry, that this or that would happen, and it would turn out that it was exactly what you were thinking about.

Of course, it was possible that his uncle had simply been astute enough to reason out what he was thinking, and that it had simply appeared that the older man could read his thoughts.

But there was the way he could turn aside trouble, too — make it disappear almost as fast as it came. Anything threatening always seemed to give way when it encountered him. That seemed a sort of magic.

And he was always encouraging to Par when he saw the boy attempting to use the wishsong. He had warned

Par to learn to control the images, to be cautious about their use, to be selective in the ways in which he exposed the magic to others. Walker Boh had been one of the few people in his life who had not been afraid of its power.

So as he sat there with the others in the silence of the mountain night, the memories of his uncle skipping through his mind, his curiosity to know more was piqued anew, and finally he gave in to it and asked Steff what tales the other had heard of Walker Boh.

Steff looked thoughtful. 'Most of them come from woodsmen, hunters, trackers and such — a few from Dwarves who fight in the Resistance like myself and who pass far enough north to hear of the man. They say the Gnome tribes are scared to death of him. They say they think of Walker Boh in the same way they think of spirits. Some of them believe that he's been alive for hundreds of years, that he's the same as the Druids of legend.' He winked. 'Guess that's just talk, though, if he's your uncle.'

Par nodded. 'I don't remember anyone ever suggesting he hadn't lived the same number of years as any normal man.'

'One fellow swore to me that your uncle talked with animals and that the animals understood. He said he saw it happen, that he watched your uncle walk right up to a moor cat the size of a plains bull and speak with it the same way I'm speaking with you.'

'It was said that Cogline could do that,' Coll interjected, suddenly interested. 'He had a cat called Whisper that followed him. The cat protected his niece, Kimber. Her name was Boh as well, wasn't it, Par?'

Par nodded, remembering that his uncle had taken the name Boh from his mother's side of the family. Strange, now that he thought about it, but he could never remember his uncle using the Ohmsford name.

'There was one story,' Steff said, pausing then to mull the details over in his mind. 'I heard it from a tracker who knew the deep Anar better than most and, I think, knew Walker Boh as well, though he'd never admit to it. He

108

told me that something born in the days of the old magic wandered down out of the Ravenshorn into Darklin Reach two years back and started living off the life it found there. Walker Boh went out to find it, confronted it, and the creature turned around and went back to wherever it had come from — just like that.' Steff shook his head and rubbed his chin slowly. 'It makes you think, doesn't it?'

He stretched his hands toward the fire. 'That's why he scares me — because there doesn't appear to be much of anything that scares him. He comes and goes like a ghost, they say — here one minute, gone the next, just a shadow out of night. I wonder if even the Shadowen frighten him. I'd guess not.'

'Maybe we should ask him,' Coll offered with a sly grin.

Steff brightened. 'Well, now, maybe we should,' he agreed. 'I suggest you be the one to do it!' He laughed. 'That reminds me, has the Highlander told you yet how we happened on each other that first time?'

The Ohmsford brothers shook their heads no, and despite some loud grumbling from Morgan, Steff proceeded to tell the tale. Morgan was fishing the eastern end of the Rainbow Lake at the mouth of the Silver River some ten months earlier when a squall capsized his craft, washed away his gear, and left him to make his way ashore as best he could. He was drenched and freezing and trying without success to start a fire when Steff came across him and dried him out.

'He would have died of exposure, I expect, if I hadn't taken pity on him,' Steff finished. 'We talked, exchanged information. Before you know it, he was on his way to Culhaven to see whether life in the homeland of the Dwarves was as grim as I had described it.' Steff cast an amused look at the chagrined Highlander. 'He kept coming back after that — each time with a little something to help out Granny and Auntie and the Resistance as well. His conscience won't allow him to stay away, I suppose.'

'Oh, for goodness sake!' Morgan huffed, embarrassed.

Steff laughed, his voice booming out through the stillness, filling up the night. 'Enough, then, proud Highland Prince! We will talk of someone else!' He shifted his weight and looked at Par. 'That stranger, the one who gave you the ring — let's talk about him. I know something of the outlaw bands that serve in the Movement. A rather worthless bunch, for the most part; they lack leadership and discipline. The Dwarves have offered to work with them, but the offer hasn't been accepted as yet. The problem is that the whole Movement has been too fragmented. In any case, that ring you were given — does it bear the emblem of a hawk?'

Par sat bolt upright. 'It does, Steff. Do you know whose it is?'

Steff smiled. 'I do and I don't, Valeman. As I said, the Southland outlaws have been a fragmented bunch in the past — but that may be changing. There are rumors of one among them who seems to be taking control, uniting the bands together, giving them the leadership they have been lacking. He doesn't use his name to identify himself; he uses the symbol of a hawk.'

'It must be the same man,' Par declared firmly. 'He was reluctant to give his name to us as well.'

Steff shrugged. 'Names are often kept secret in these times. But the way in which he managed your escape from the Seekers — well, that sounds like the man I have been hearing about. They say he would dare anything where the Federation is concerned.'

'He was certainly bold enough that night,' Par agreed, smiling.

They talked a bit longer of the stranger, the outlaw bands in both Southland and Eastland, and the way in which the Four Lands festered like an open sore under Federation rule. They never did get back to the subject of Walker Boh, but Par was content with where they had left it. He had his mind made up where his uncle was concerned. It did not matter how frightening Walker Boh appeared to others, to Steff or anyone else; he would remain for Par the same man he had been when the Valeman was a boy until something happened to change his mind — and he had a curious feeling that nothing would.

Their talk dwindled finally, interrupted by frequent yawns and distracted looks, and one by one they began to roll into their blankets. Par offered to build the fire up one final time before they went to sleep and walked to the edge of the trees in search of deadwood. He was in the process of gathering some pieces of an old cedar that had been blown down by the winds last winter when he suddenly found himself face to face with Teel. She seemed to materialize right in front of him, her masked face intent, her eyes quite steady as she looked at him.

'Can you make the magic for me?' she asked quietly.

Par stared. He had never heard her speak, not once, not a single time since he had encountered her that first night in Granny Elise's kitchen. As far as he had been able to determine, she couldn't. She had traveled with them as if she were Steff's faithful dog, obedient to him, watchful of them, unquestioning and aloof. She had sat there all evening listening and not speaking, keeping what she knew and what she thought carefully to herself. Now, this.

'Can you make the images?' she pressed. Her voice was low and rough. 'Just one or two, so I can see them? I would like it very much if you could.'

He saw her eyes then, where he hadn't seen them before. They were a curious azure, the way the sky had been that day so high up in the mountains, clear and depthless. He was startled by how bright they were, and he remembered suddenly that her hair was a honey color beneath the covering hood, behind the concealing mask. She had seemed rather unpleasant before in the way in which she chose to distance herself from them, but now, standing here amid the silence and shadows, she just seemed small.

'What images would you like to see? he asked her.

She thought for a moment. 'I would like to see what

111

Culhaven was like in the days of Allanon.'

He started to tell her he wasn't sure what Culhaven had been like that long ago, then caught himself and nodded. 'I can try,' he said.

He sang softly to her, alone in the trees, reaching out with the magic of the wishsong to fill her mind with images of the village as it might have looked three hundred years ago. He sang of the Silver River, of the Meade Gardens, of the cottages and homes all carefully tended and kept, of life in the home city of the Dwarves before the war with the Federation. When he was finished, she studied him expressionlessly for a moment, then turned without a word and disappeared back into the night.

Par stared after her in confusion for a moment, then shrugged, finished picking up deadwood and went off to sleep.

They struck out again at dawn, working their way along the upper stretches of the Wolfsktaag where the forests thinned and the sky hovered close. It was another warm, bright day filled with good smells and a sense of endless possibilities. Breezes blew gently against their faces, the woods and rocks were filled with tiny creatures that darted and flew, and the mountains were at peace.

Despite all that, Par was uneasy. He hadn't felt that way the previous two days, but he did so on this one. He tried to dispel the uneasiness, telling himself it lacked any discernible cause, that it was probably the result of needing something to worry about when it appeared that Steff had been right about this being the safest way after all. He tried studying the faces of the others to see if they were experiencing any discomfort, but the others seemed quite content. Even Teel, who seldom showed anything, walked with an air of total unconcern.

The morning slipped away into afternoon, and the uneasiness grew into a certainty that something was following them. Par found himself glancing back on any number of occasions, not knowing what it was he was looking for, but knowing nevertheless that it was back there. He hunted through the distant trees and across the rocks and there was nothing to be seen. Above, to their right, the ridgelines rose into the cliffs and defiles where the rock was too barren and dangerous to traverse. Below, to their left, the forest was thick with shadows that gathered in pools amid a tangle of heavy brush and close-set black trunks.

Several times, the trail branched downward into the murk. Steff, who was in the lead with Teel, motioned that way once and said, 'That is what might have happened to those missing Federation parties. You don't want to wander into the dark places in these mountains.'

It was Par's hope that this was the source of his discomfort. Identifying the source should allow him to dismiss it, he told himself. But just as he was prepared to believe that the matter had resolved itself, he glanced over his shoulder one final time and saw something move in the rocks.

He stopped where he was. The others walked on a few steps, then turned and looked at him. 'What is it?' Steff asked at once.

'There's something back there,' Par said quietly, not shifting his eyes from where he had last seen the movement.

Steff walked back to him. 'There, in the rocks,' Par said and pointed.

They stood together and looked for a long time and saw nothing. The afternoon was waning, and the shadows were lengthening in the mountains as the sun dropped low against the western horizon, so it was difficult to discern much of anything in the mix of half-light. Par shook his head finally, frustrated. 'Maybe I was mistaken,' he admitted.

'Maybe you weren't,' Steff said.

Ignoring the surprised look Par gave him, he started them walking again with Teel in the lead and himself trailing with Par. Once or twice, he told Par to glance back, and once or twice he did so himself. Par never saw anything, although he still had a sense of something being back there. They crossed a ridgeline that ran from east to west and started down. The far side was cloaked in shadow, the sun's fading light blocked away entirely, and the trail below wound its way through a maze of rocks and scrub that were clustered on the mountainside like huddled sheep. The wind was at their backs now, and the sound of Steff's voice, when he spoke, carried ahead to them.

'Whatever's back there is tracking us, waiting for dark or at least twilight before showing itself. I don't know what it is, but it's big. We have to find a place where we can defend ourselves.'

No one said anything. Par experienced a sudden chill. Coll glanced at him, then at Morgan. Teel never turned.

They were through the maze of rocks and brush and back on an open trail leading up again when the thing finally emerged from the shadows and let them see what it was. Steff saw it first, called out sharply and brought them all about. The creature was still more than a hundred yards back, crouched on a flat rock where a narrow shaft of sunlight sliced across its blunted face like a lance. It looked like some sort of monstrous dog or wolf with a massive chest and neck thick with fur and a face that was all misshapen. It had oddly fat legs, a barrel body, small ears and tail, and the look of something that had no friends. Its jaws parted once, the biggest jaws Par had ever seen on anything, and spittle drooled out. The jaws snapped shut, and it started toward them in a slow amble.

'Keep moving,' Steff said quietly, and they did. They walked ahead steadily, following the weave of the trail, trying not to look back.

'What is it?' Morgan asked, his voice low.

'They call it a Gnawl,' Steff answered calmly. 'It lives east in the deepest part of the Anar, beyond the Ravenshorn. Very dangerous.' He paused. 'I never heard of one being seen in the central Anar, though — let alone in the Wolfsktaag.'

114

'Until now, you mean,' muttered Coll.

They made their way through a broad split in the mountains where the trail began to dip sharply downward into a hollows. The sun was gone, and gray twilight hung over everything like a shroud. It was getting hard to see. The thing behind them appeared and disappeared in fits and starts, causing Par to wonder what would happen when they lost sight of it altogether.

'I never heard of one stalking men either,' Steff declared suddenly from just behind him.

The strange hunt continued, the Gnawl trailing them at a distance of about a hundred yards, apparently content to wait for darkness to descend completely. Steff urged them on, searching for a spot where they could make a stand.

'Why don't you simply let me go after it!' Morgan snapped back at him at one point.

'Because you would be dead quicker than I could say your name, Highlander,' the Dwarf answered, his voice cold. 'Don't be fooled. This creature is more than a match for the five of us if it catches us unprepared. All the magic in the world won't make a difference if that happens!'

Par froze, wondering suddenly if the magic in Morgan's sword was of any use against this beast. Wasn't the sword's magic triggered only by an encounter with similar magic? Wasn't it simply a common sword when otherwise employed? Wasn't that what Allanon had intended when he had given the blade its power? He struggled to remember the particulars of the story and failed. But the other magics, those of the Sword of Shannara and of the Elfstones, had been effective only against things of magic — he remembered that well enough. It was very likely the same with ...

'Ahead, down by that hollows,' Steff said abruptly, ending his speculation. 'That's where we will ...'

He never finished. The Gnawl came at them, hurtling through the darkness, a huge, black shape bounding across the broken rock and scrub with a speed that was astonishing. 'Go!' Steff shouted at them, pointed hurriedly down the trail and turned to face the beast.

They went without thinking, all but Morgan who wrenched free the Sword of Leah and rushed to stand with his friend. Teel, Coll and Par dashed ahead, glancing back just as the Gnawl reached their companions. The creature lunged at Steff, but the Dwarf was waiting, the huge mace held ready. He caught the beast full against the side of its head with a blow that would have dropped anything else. But the Gnawl shrugged the blow aside and came at the Dwarf again. Steff hammered it a second time, then broke past it, pulling the Highlander after him. They came down the trail in a sprint, quickly catching the fleeing Valemen and Teel.

'Down the slope!' Steff yelled, literally shoving them off the trail. They rushed into the scrub and rocks, skidding and sliding. Par went down, tumbled head-over-heels, and came back to his feet all in the same motion. He was disoriented, and there was blood in his eyes. Steff jerked him about and dragged him forward, down the slide, the sound of labored breathing and shouting all about him.

Then he was aware of the Gnawl. He heard it before he saw it, its heavy body churning up the ground behind them, scattering rocks and dirt as it came, its cry an ugly whine of hunger. The magic, Par thought, distracted — I have to use the magic. The wishsong will work, confuse it, at least . . .

Steff pulled him onto a flat rock, and he felt the others bunched around him. 'Stay together!' the Dwarf ordered. 'Don't leave the rock!'

He stepped out to meet the Gnawl's rush.

Par would never forget what happened next. Steff took the Gnawl's charge on the slope just to the left of the rock. He let the creature come right up against him, then suddenly fell back, mace jamming upward into the Gnawl's throat, booted feet thrusting against its massive chest. Steff went down, and the Gnawl went right over him, the momentum of its lunge carrying it past. The Gnawl could not catch itself. It tumbled past Steff, rolled

116

wildly down the slope into the hollows below, right up against the fringe of the trees. It came to its feet instantly, growling and snarling. But then something huge shot out of the trees, snapped up the Gnawl in a single bite and pulled back again into the murk. There was a sharp cry, a crunching of bones, and silence.

Steff came to his feet, put a finger to his lips, and beckoned them to follow. Silently, or as nearly so as they could keep it, they climbed back up to the trail and stood looking downward into the impenetrable dark.

'In the Wolfsktaag, you have to learn what to look out for,' Steff whispered with a grim smile. 'Even if you're a Gnawl.'

They brushed themselves off and straightened their packs. Their cuts and bruises were slight. The Pass of Jade, which would take them clear of the mountains, was no more than another hour or two ahead, Steff advised.

They decided to keep walking.

CHAPTER

9

I T TOOK LONGER than Steff had estimated to reach the Pass of Jade, and it was almost midnight when the little company finally broke clear of the Wolfsktaag. They slept in a narrow canyon screened by a tangle of fir and ancient spruce, so exhausted that they did not bother with either food or fire, but simply rolled into their blankets and dropped off to sleep. Par dreamed that night, but not about Allanon or the Hadeshorn. He dreamed instead of the Gnawl. It tracked him relentlessly through the landscape of his mind, chasing him from one dark corner to the next, a vaguely distinguishable shadow whose identity was nevertheless as certain as his own. It came for him and he ran from it, and the terror he felt was palpable. Finally it cornered him, backing him into a shadowed niche of rock and forest, and just as he was about to attempt to spring past it, something monstrous lunged from the dark behind him and took him into its maw, dragging him from sight as he screamed for the help that wouldn't come.

He came awake with a start.

It was dark, though the sky was beginning to lighten in the east, and his companions still slept. The scream was only in his mind, it seemed. There was sweat on his face and body, and his breathing was quick and ragged. He lay back quietly, but did not sleep again.

They walked east that morning into the central Anar, winding through a maze of forested hills and ravines, five pairs of eyes searching the shadows and dark places about them as they went. There was little talking, the encounter of the previous day having left them uneasy and watchful. The day was clouded and gray, and the forests about them seemed more secretive somehow. By noon, they came upon the falls of the Chard Rush, and they followed the river in until nightfall.

It rained the next day, and the land was washed in mist and damp. Travel slowed, and the warmth and brightness of the previous few days faded into memory. They passed the Rooker Line Trading Center, a tiny waystation for hunters and trappers in the days of Jair Ohmsford that had built itself into a thriving fur exchange until the war between the Dwarves and the Federation disrupted and finally put an end altogether to Eastland commerce north of Culhaven. Now it stood empty, its doors and windows gone, its roof rotted and sagging, its shadows filled with ghosts from another time.

At lunch, huddled beneath the canopy of a massive old willow that overhung the banks of the river, Steff talked uneasily of the Gnawl, insisting again that one had never before been seen west of the Ravenshorn. Where did this one come from? How did it happen to be here? Why had it chosen to track them? There were answers to his questions, of course, but none that any of them cared to explore. Chance, they all agreed outwardly, and inwardly thought just the opposite.

The rain slowed with the approach of nightfall, but continued in a steady drizzle until morning, when it changed to a heavy mist. The company pushed on, following the Chard Rush as it wound its way down into Darklin Reach. Travel grew increasingly difficult, the forests thick with brush and fallen timber, the pathways almost nonexistent. When they left the river at midday, the terrain transformed itself into a series of gullies and ravines, and it became almost impossible to determine their direction. They slogged through the mud and debris,

Steff in the lead, grunting and huffing rhythmically. The Dwarf was like a tireless machine when he traveled, tough and seemingly inexhaustible. Only Teel was his equal, smaller than Steff but more agile, never slowing or complaining, always keeping pace. It was the Valemen and the Highlander who grew tired, their muscles stiffened, their wind spent. They welcomed every chance to rest that the Dwarf offered them, and when it was time to start up again it was all they could do to comply. The dreariness of their travel was beginning to affect them as well, especially the Valemen. Par and Coll had been running either from or toward something for weeks now, had spent much of that time in hiding, and had endured three very frightening encounters with creatures best left to one's imagination. They were tired of keeping constant watch, and the darkness, mist, and damp just served to exhaust them further. Neither said anything to the other, and neither would have admitted it if the other had asked, but both were starting to wonder if they really knew what they were doing.

It was late afternoon when the rain finally stopped, and the clouds suddenly broke apart to let through a smattering of sunlight. They crested a ridge and came upon a shallow, forested valley dominated by a strange rock formation shaped like a chimney. It rose out of the trees as if a sentinel set at watch, black and still against the distant skyline. Steff brought the others to a halt and pointed down.

'There,' he said quietly. 'If Walker Boh's to be found, this is the place he's said to be.'

Par shoved aside his exhaustion and despondency, staring in disbelief. 'I know this place!' he exclaimed. 'This is Hearthstone! I recognize it from the stories! This is Cogline's home!'

'Was,' Coll corrected wearily.

'Was, is, what's the difference?' Par was animated as he confronted them. 'The point is, what is Walker Boh doing here? I mean, it makes sense that he would be here because this was once the home of the Bohs, but it was

Cogline's home as well. If Walker lives here, then why didn't the old man tell us? Unless maybe the old man isn't Cogline after all or unless for some reason he doesn't know Walker is here, or unless Walker ...' He stopped suddenly, confused to the point of distraction. 'Are you sure this is where my uncle is supposed to live?' he demanded of Steff.

The Dwarf had been watching him during all this the same way he might have watched a three-headed dog. Now he simply shrugged. 'Valeman, I am sure of very little and admit to less. I was told this was where the man makes his home. So if you're all done talking about it, why don't we simply go down there and see?'

Par shut his mouth, and they began their descent. When they reached the valley floor, they found the forest surprisingly clear of scrub and deadwood. The trees opened into clearings that were crisscrossed with streams and laced with tiny wildflowers colored white, blue, and deep violet. The day grew still, the wind calmed, and the lengthening shadows that draped the way forward seemed soft and unthreatening. Par forgot about the dangers and hardships of his journey, put aside his weariness and discomfort, and concentrated instead on thinking further about the man he had come to find. He was admittedly confused, but at least he understood the reason. When Brin Ohmsford had come into Darklin Reach three hundred years earlier, Hearthstone had been the home of Cogline and the child he claimed as his granddaughter, Kimber Boh. The old man and the little girl had guided Brin into the Maelmord where she had confronted the Ildatch. They had remained friends afterward, and that friendship had endured for ten generations. Walker Boh's father had been an Ohmsford and his mother a Boh. He could trace his father's side of the family directly back to Brin and his mother's side to Kimber. It was logical that he would choose to come back here — yet illogical that the old man, the man who claimed to be Cogline, the very same Cogline of three hundred years earlier, would know nothing about it.

121

Or say nothing, if in fact he knew.

Par frowned. What *had* the old man said about Walker Boh when they had talked with him? His frown deepened. Only that he knew Walker was alive, he answered himself. That and nothing else.

But was there more between them than what the old man had revealed? Par was certain of it. And he meant to discover what it was.

The brief flurry of late sunlight faded and twilight cloaked the valley in darkening shades of gray. The sky remained clear and began to fill with stars, and the three-quarter moon, waning now toward the end of its cycle, bathed the forest in milky light. The little company walked cautiously ahead, working its way steadily in the direction of the chimney-shaped rock formation, crossing the dozens of little streams and weaving through the maze of clearings. The forest was still, but its silence did not feel ominous. Coll nudged Par at one point when he caught sight of a gray squirrel sitting up on its hindlegs and regarding them solemnly. There were night sounds, but they seemed distant and far removed from the valley.

'It feels sort of ... protected here, don't you think?' Par asked his brother quietly, and Coll nodded.

They continued on for almost an hour without encountering anyone. They had reached the approximate center of the valley when a sudden glimmer of light winked at them through the forest trees. Steff slowed, signalled for caution, then led them forward. The light drew closer, flickering brightly through the dark, changing from a single pinprick of brightness to a cluster. *Lamps*, Par thought. He pushed ahead to reach Steff, his sharp Elven senses picking out the source. 'It's a cottage,' he whispered to the Dwarf.

They broke clear of the trees and stepped into a broad, grassy clearing. There was indeed a cottage. It stood before them, precisely at the center of the clearing, a well-kept stone-and-timber structure with front and rear porches, stone walkways, gardens, and flowering shrubs. Spruce and pine clustered about it like miniature watch-towers. Light streamed forth from its windows and mingled with moonglow to brighten the clearing as if it were midday.

The front door stood open.

Par started forward at once, but Steff quickly yanked him back. 'A little caution might be in order, Valeman,' he lectured.

He said something to Teel, then left them all to go on alone, sprinting across the open spaces between the spruce and pine, keeping carefully to the shadows between, eyes fixed on the open door. The others watched him make his way forward, crouched now at Teel's insistence at the edge of the forest. Steff reached the porch, hunkered close to it for a long time, then darted up the steps and through the front door. There was a moment of silence, then he reappeared and waved them forward.

When they reached him, he said, 'No one is here. But it appears we are expected.'

They discovered his meaning when they went inside. A pair of chimneys bracketed the central room, one for a seating area in which chairs and benches were drawn up, the other for a cooking grill and oven. Fires burned brightly in both. A kettle of stew simmered over the grill and hot bread cooled on a cutting board. A long trestle table was carefully set with plates and cups for five. Par stepped forward for a closer look. Cold ale had been poured into all five cups.

The members of the little company looked at each other silently for a moment, then glanced once more about the room. The wood of the walls and beams was polished and waxed. Silver, crystal, carved wooden pieces and clothwork hangings gleamed in the light of oil lamps and hearth flames. There was a vase of fresh flowers on the trestle table, others in the sitting area. A hall led back into the sleeping rooms. The cottage was bright and cheerful and very empty.

'Is this Walker's?' Morgan asked doubtfully of Par. Somehow it didn't fit the image he had formed of the man.

Par shook his head. 'I don't know. There isn't anything here I recognize.'

Morgan moved silently to the back hall, disappeared from sight for a moment and returned. 'Nothing,' he reported, sounding disappointed.

Coll walked over to stand with Par, sniffed the stew experimentally, and shrugged. 'Well, obviously our coming here isn't such a surprise after all. I don't know about the rest of you, but that stew smells awfully good. Since someone has gone to the trouble of making it — Walker Boh or whoever — I think the least we can do is sit down and eat it.'

Par and Morgan quickly agreed, and even Teel seemed interested. Steff was again inclined to be cautious, but since it was apparent Coll was probably right in his analysis of the situation he gave in. Nevertheless, he insisted on checking first to make certain neither food nor drink was tainted in any way. When he had pronounced the meal fit, they seated themselves and eagerly consumed it.

When dinner was over, they cleared and washed the dishes and put them carefully away in a cabinet built to contain them. Then they searched the cottage a second time, the grounds around it, and finally everything for a quarter-mile in every direction. They found nothing.

They sat around the fire after that until midnight, waiting. No one came. There were two small bedrooms in back with two beds in each. The beds were turned down and the linens and blankets fresh. They took turns sleeping, one keeping watch for the others. They slept the night undisturbed, the forest and the valley at peace about them. Dawn brought them awake feeling much refreshed. Still no one came.

That day, they searched the entire valley from one end to the other, from the cottage to the odd, chimney-shaped rock, from north wall to south, from east to west. The day was warm and bright, filled with sunshine and gentle breezes and the smell of growing things. They took their time, wandering along the streams, following the pathways, exploring the few dens that burrowed the valley slopes like pockets. They found scattered prints, all of them made by animals, and nothing else. Birds flew overhead, sudden flashes of color in the trees, tiny woods creatures watched with darting eyes, and insects buzzed and hummed. Once a badger lumbered into view as Par and Coll hunted the west wall by the rock tower, refusing to give way to them. Other than that, none of them saw anything.

They had to fix their own meal that night, but there was fresh meat and cheese in a cold locker, day old bread from the previous evening, and vegetables in the garden. The Valemen helped themselves, forcing the others to partake as well despite Steff's continued misgivings, convinced that this was what was expected of them. The day faded into a warm and pleasant night, and they began to grow comfortable with their surroundings. Steff sat with Teel before the gathering fire and smoked a long-stemmed pipe, Par worked in the kitchen with Coll cleaning the dishes, and Morgan took up watch on the front steps.

'Someone has put a lot of effort into keeping up this cottage,' Par observed to his brother as they finished their task. 'It doesn't seem reasonable that they would just go off and leave it.'

'Especially after taking time to make us that stew,' Coll added. His broad face furrowed. 'Do you think it belongs to Walker?'

'I don't know. I wish I did.'

'None of this really seems like him though, does it? Not like the Walker I remember. Certainly not like the one Steff tells us about.'

Par wiped the last few droplets of dishwater from a dinner plate and carefully put it away. 'Maybe that's how he wants it to appear,' he said softly.

It was several hours after midnight when he took the watch from Teel, yawning and stretching as he came out onto the front porch to look for her. The Dwarf was nowhere to be seen at first, and it wasn't until he had come thoroughly awake that she appeared from behind a spruce some several dozen yards out. She slipped noiselessly through the shadows to reach him and disappeared into the cottage without a word. Par glanced after her curiously, then sat down on the front steps, propped his chin in his hands, and stared off into the dark.

He had been sitting there for almost an hour when he heard the sound.

It was a strange sound, a sort of buzzing like a swarm of bees might make, but deep and rough. It was there and then just as quickly gone again. He thought at first he must have made it up, that he had heard it only in his mind. But then it came again, for just an instant, before disappearing once more.

He stood up, looked around tentatively, then walked out onto the pathway. The night was brilliantly clear and the sky filled with stars and bright. The woods about him were empty. He felt reassured and walked slowly around the house and out back. There was an old willow tree there, far back in the shadows, and beneath it a pair of worn benches. Par walked over to them and stopped, listening once again for the noise and hearing nothing. He sat down on the nearest bench. The bench had been carved to the shape of his body, and he felt cradled by it. He sat there for a time, staring out through the veil of the willow's drooping branches, daydreaming in the darkness, listening to the night's silence. He wondered about his parents — if they were well, if they worried for him. Shady Vale was a distant memory.

He closed his eyes momentarily to rest them against the weariness he was feeling. When he opened them again, the moor cat was standing there.

Par's shock was so great that at first he couldn't move. The cat was right in front of him, its whiskered face level with his own, its eyes a luminous gold in the night. It was the biggest animal that Par had ever seen, bigger even than the Gnawl. It was solid black from head to tail except for the eyes which stared at him unblinkingly.

Then the cat began to purr, and he recognized it as the sound he had heard earlier. The cat turned and walked away a few paces and looked back, waiting. When Par continued to stare at it, it returned momentarily, started away again, stopped and waited.

It wanted him to follow, Par realized.

He rose mechanically, unable to make his body respond in the way he wanted it to, trying to decide if he should do as the cat expected or attempt to break away. He discarded any thought of the latter almost immediately. This was no time to be trying anything foolish. Besides, if the cat wanted to harm him, it could have done so earlier.

He took a few steps forward, and the cat turned away again, moving off into the trees.

They wound through the darkened forest for long minutes, moving silently, steadily into the night. Moonlight flooded the open spaces, and Par had little trouble following. He watched the cat move effortlessly ahead of him, barely disturbing the forest about him, a creature that seemed to have the substance of a shadow. His shock was fading now, replaced by curiosity. Someone had sent the cat to him, and he thought he knew who.

Finally, they reached a clearing in which several streams emptied through a series of tiny rapids into a wide, moonlit pool. The trees here were very old and broad, and their limbs cast an intricate pattern of shadows over everything. The cat walked over to the pool, drank deeply for a moment, then sat back and looked at him. Par came forward a few steps and stopped.

'Hello, Par,' someone greeted.

The Valeman searched the clearing for a moment before finding the speaker who sat well back in the dark on a burled stump barely distinguishable from the shadows about him. When Par hesitated, he rose and stepped into the light.

'Hello, Walker,' Par replied softly.

His uncle was very much as he remembered him — and at the same time completely different. He was still tall and slight, his Elven features apparent though not as pronounced as Par's, his skin a shocking white hue that provided a marked contrast to the shoulder-length black hair and close-cropped beard. His eyes hadn't changed either; they still looked right through you, even when shadowed as they were now. What was different was more difficult to define. It was mostly in the way Walker Boh carried himself and the way he made Par feel when he spoke, even though he had said almost nothing. It was as if there were an invisible wall about him that nothing could penetrate.

Walker Boh came forward and took Par's hands in his own. He was dressed in loose-fitting forest clothing — pants, tunic, a short cloak, and soft boots, all colored like the earth and trees. 'Have you been comfortable at the cottage?' he asked.

Par seemed to remember himself then. 'Walker, I don't understand. What are you doing out here? Why didn't you meet us when we arrived? Obviously, you knew we were coming.'

His uncle released his hands and stepped away. 'Come sit with me, Par,' he invited, and moved back again into the shadows without waiting for his nephew's response. Par followed, and the two seated themselves on the stump from which Walker had first risen.

Walker looked him over carefully. 'I will only be speaking with you,' he said quietly. 'And only this once.'

Par waited, saying nothing. 'There have been many changes in my life,' his uncle went on after a moment. 'I expect you remember little of me from your childhood, and most of what you remember no longer has much to do with who I am now in any case. I gave up my Vale life, any claim to being a Southlander, and came here to begin again. I left behind me the madness of men whose lives are governed by the baser instincts. I separated myself from men of all races, from their greed and their prejudice, their wars and their politics, and their monstrous conception of betterment. I came here, Par, so that I could live alone. I was always alone, of course; I was made to feel alone. The difference now is that I am alone, not because others choose it for me, but because I choose it

128

for myself. I am free to be exactly what I am — and not to feel strange because of it.'

He smiled faintly. 'It is the time we live in and who we are that makes it difficult for both of us, you know. Do you understand me, Par? You have the magic, too — a very tangible magic in your case. It will not win you friends; it will set you apart. We are not permitted to be Ohmsfords these days because Ohmsfords have the magic of their Elven forebears and neither magic nor Elves are appreciated or understood. I grew tired of finding it so, of being set apart, of being constantly looked at with suspicion and mistrust. I grew tired of being thought different. It will happen to you as well, if it hasn't done so already. It is the nature of things.'

'I don't let it bother me,' Par said defensively. 'The magic is a gift.'

'Oh? Is it now? How so? A gift is not something you hide as you would a loathsome disease. It is not something of which you are ashamed or cautious or even frightened. It is not something that might kill you.'

The words were spoken with such bitterness that Par felt chilled. Then his uncle's mood seemed to change instantly; he grew calm again, quiet. He shook his head in self-reproach. 'I forget myself sometimes when speaking of the past. I apologize. I brought you here to talk with you of other things. But only with you, Par. I leave the cottage for your companions to use during their stay. But I will not come there to be with them. I am only interested in you.'

'But what about Coll?' Par asked, confused. 'Why speak with me and not with him?'

His uncle's smile was ironic. 'Think, Par. I was never close with him the way I was with you.'

Par stared at him silently. That was true, he supposed. It was the magic that had drawn Walker to him, and Coll had never been able to share in that. The time he had spent with his uncle, the time that had made him feel close to the man, had always been time away from Coll.

'Besides,' the other continued softly 'what we need to

129

talk about concerns only us.'

Par understood then. 'The dreams.' His uncle nodded. 'Then you have experienced them as well — the figure in black, the one who appears to be Allanon, standing before the Hadeshorn, warning us, telling us to come?' Par was breathless. 'What about the old man? Has he come to you also?' Again, his uncle nodded. 'Then you do know him, don't you? Is it true, Walker? Is he really Cogline?'

Walker Boh's face emptied of expression. 'Yes, Par, he is.'

Par flushed with excitement, and rubbed his hands together briskly. 'I cannot believe it! How old is he? Hundreds of years, I suppose — just as he claimed. And once a Druid. I knew I was right! Does he live here still, Walker — with you?'

'He visits, sometimes. And sometimes stays a bit. The cat was his before he gave it to me. You remember that there was always a moor cat. The one before was called Whisper. That was in the time of Brin Ohmsford. This one is called Rumor. The old man named it. He said it was a good name for a cat — especially one who would belong to me.'

He stopped, and something Par couldn't read crossed his face briefly and was gone. The Valeman glanced over to where the cat had been resting, but it had disappeared.

'Rumor comes and goes in the manner of all moor cats,' Walker Boh said as if reading his thoughts.

Par nodded absently, then looked back at him. 'What are you going to do, Walker?'

'About the dreams?' The strange eyes went flat. 'Nothing.'

Par hesitated. 'But the old man must have . . .'

'Listen to me,' the other said, cutting him short. 'I am decided on this. I know what the dreams have asked of me; I know who sent them. The old man has come to me, and we have talked. He left not a week past. None of that matters. I am no longer an Ohmsford; I am a Boh. If I could strip away my past, with all its legacy of magic and all its glorious Elven history, I would do so in an instant. I want none of it. I came into the Eastland to find this valley, to live as my ancestors once lived, to be just once where everything is fresh and clean and untroubled by the presence of others. I have learned to keep my life in perfect order and to order the life around me. You have seen this valley; my mother's people made it that way and I have learned to keep it. I have Rumor for company and occasionally the old man. Once in a while, I even visit with those from the outside. Darklin Reach has become a haven for me and Hearthstone my home.'

He bent forward, his face intense. 'I have the magic, Par — different from yours, but real nevertheless. I can tell what others are thinking sometimes, even when they are far away. I can communicate with life in ways that others cannot. All forms of life. I can disappear sometimes, just like the moor cat. I can even summon power!' He snapped his fingers suddenly, and a brief spurt of blue fire appeared on his fingers. He snuffed it out. 'I lack the magic of the wishsong, but apparently some of its power has taken root inside me. Some of what I know is innate; some is self-taught; some was taught to me by others. But I have all I need, and I wish no more. I am comfortable here and will never leave. Let the world get on as best it can without me. It always did so before.'

Par struggled to respond. 'But what if the dream is right, Walker?' he asked finally.

Walker Boh laughed derisively. 'Par! The dreams are never right! Have you not paid heed to your own stories? Whether they manifest themselves as they have this time or as they did when Allanon was alive, one fact remains unchanged — the Ohmsfords are never told anything, only what the Druids deem necessary!'

'You think that we are being used.' Par made it a statement of fact.

'I think I would be a fool to believe anything else! I do not trust what I am being told.' The other's eyes were as hard as stone. 'The magic you insist on regarding as a gift has always been little more than a useful tool to the

Druids. I do not intend to let myself be put to whatever new task they have discovered. If the world needs saving as these dreams suggest, let Allanon or the old man go out and save it!'

There was a long moment of silence as the two measured each other. Par shook his head slowly. 'You surprise me, Walker. I don't remember the bitterness or the anger from before.'

Walker Boh smiled sadly. 'It was there, Par. It was always there. You just didn't bother to look for it.'

'Shouldn't it be gone by now?'

His uncle kept silent.

'So you are decided on this matter, are you?'

'Yes, Par. I am.'

Par took a deep breath. 'What will you do, Walker, if the things in the dream come to pass? What will become of your home then? What will happen if the evil the dream showed us decides to come looking for you?'

His uncle said nothing, but the steady gaze never wavered. Par nodded slowly. 'I have a different view of matters from yours, Walker,' he said softly. 'I have always believed that the magic was a gift, and that it was given to me for a reason. It appeared for a long time that it was meant to be used to tell the stories, to keep them from being forgotten completely. I have changed my mind about that. I think now that the magic is meant for something more.'

He shifted, straightening himself because he was feeling suddenly small in the presence of the other. 'Coll and I cannot go back to the Vale because the Federation has found out about the magic and is hunting for us. The old man, Cogline, says there may be other things hunting us as well — perhaps even Shadowen. Have you seen the Shadowen? I have. Coll and I are scared to death, Walker, though we don't talk about it much. The funny thing is, I think the things hunting us are scared, too. It's the magic that scares them.' He paused. 'I don't know why that is, but I mean to find out.'

There was a flicker of surprise in Walker Boh's eyes.

132

Par nodded. 'Yes, Walker, I have decided to do as the dreams have asked. I believe they were sent by Allanon, and I believe they should be heeded. I will go to the Hadeshorn. I think I made the decision just now; I think listening to you helped me decide. I haven't told Coll. I don't really know what he will do. Maybe I will end up going alone. But I will go. If for no other reason, I will go because I think Allanon can tell me what the magic is intended to do.'

He shook his head sadly. 'I can't be like you, Walker. I can't live apart from the rest of the world. I want to be able to go back to Shady Vale. I don't want to go away and start life over. I came this way through Culhaven. The Dwarves who brought us are from there. All of the prejudice and greed, the politics and wars, all of the madness you speak about is very much in evidence there. But unlike you I don't want to escape it; I want to find a way to end it! How can that happen if I simply pretend it doesn't exist!'

His hands tightened into fists. 'You see, I keep thinking, what if Allanon knows something that can change the way things are? What if he can tell me something that will put an end to the madness?'

They faced each other in the dark for a long time without speaking, and Par thought he saw things in his uncle's dark eyes that he hadn't seen since his childhood — things that whispered of caring and need and sacrifice. Then the eyes were flat again, expressionless, empty. Walker Boh came to his feet.

'Will you reconsider?' Par asked him quietly.

Walker regarded him silently, then walked to the pool at the center of the clearing and stood looking down. When his fingers snapped, Rumor materialized from out of nowhere and came over to him.

He turned momentarily and looked back. 'Good luck, Par,' was all he said.

Then he turned, the cat beside him, and disappeared into the night.

CHAPTER

10

PAR WAITED UNTIL MORNING to tell the others of his meeting with Walker Boh. There did not seem to be any reason to hurry it. Walker had made clear his intentions, and there was nothing any of them could do about it in any case. So Par made his way back to the cottage, surprising himself at how easily he was able to retrace his steps, resumed his watch without disturbing the others, lost himself in his thoughts, and waited for dawn.

Reactions were mixed when he finally related his story. There was some initial doubt as to whether he was mistaken about what happened, but that dissipated almost at once. They made him tell the story twice more after that, interjecting comments and questions in equal measure as he went. Morgan was outraged that Walker should treat them like this, declaring that they deserved at the very least the courtesy of a direct confrontation. He insisted that they search the valley again, convinced that the man must be close by and should be found and made to face them all. Steff was more pragmatic. He was of the opinion that Walker Boh was no different from most, preferring to stay out of trouble when he could, avoiding situations in which trouble would most probably result.

'It seems to me that his behavior, however irritating you might find it, is certainly not out of character,' the Dwarf declared with a shrug. 'After all, you said yourselves that he came here to escape involvement with the Races. By refusing to go to the Hadeshorn, he is simply doing what he said he would do.'

Teel, as usual, had nothing to say. Coll only said, 'I wish I could have spoken with him,' and dropped the matter.

There was no reason now to stay longer at Hearthstone, but they decided to postpone leaving for at least another day. The moon was still more than half full, and they had at least another ten days left to them before they were required to be at the Hadeshorn — if, indeed, they were going at all. The subject of what was to happen next was being carefully avoided. Par had made up his own mind, but had not yet told the others. They, of course, were waiting to hear from him. While they played at this game of cat-and-mouse, they finished breakfast and decided to go along with Morgan's suggestion and scout the valley one more time. It gave them something to do while they considered the implications of Walker Boh's decision. Tomorrow morning would be time enough to make any decisions of their own.

So they went back to the clearing where Par had met with Walker and the moor cat the previous night and began a second search, agreeing to meet back at the cottage by late afternoon. Steff and Teel formed one group, Par and Coll a second, and Morgan went alone. The day was warm and filled with sunshine, and a light breeze blew down out of the distant mountains. Steff scoured the clearing for signs of any sort and found nothing — not even the tracks of the cat. Par had a feeling that it was going to be a long day.

He walked east with Coll after parting from the others, his mind crowding with thoughts of what he should say to his brother. A mix of emotions worked their way through him, and he found it difficult to sort them out. He ambled along halfheartedly, conscious of Coll watching him from time to time, but avoiding his gaze. After they had wandered through several dozen clearings and forded half that many streams without coming on

135

even a trace of Walker Boh, Par called a halt.

'This is a waste of time,' he announced, a hint of exasperation creeping into his voice. 'We're not going to find anything.'

'I don't imagine we are,' Coll replied.

Par turned to him, and they faced each other silently for a moment. 'I have decided to go on to the Hadeshorn, Coll. It doesn't matter what Walker does; it only matters what I do. I have to go.'

Coll nodded. 'I know.' Then he smiled. 'Par, I haven't been your brother all these years without learning something about the way you think. The moment you told me that Walker had said he would have nothing to do with the matter, I knew you'd decided you would. That's the way it is with you. You're like a dog with a bone in its teeth — you can't let go.'

'I suppose that's the way it seems sometimes, doesn't it?' Par shook his head wearily and moved over to a patch of shade beneath an old hickory. He turned his back to the trunk and slid to the ground. Coll joined him. They sat staring out at the empty woodlands. 'I admit I made the decision pretty much the way you describe it. I just couldn't accept Walker's position. Truth is, Coll, I couldn't even understand it. I was so upset, I didn't even think to ask him whether he believed the dreams were real or not.'

'Not consciously, perhaps — but you thought about it. And you decided at some point it wasn't necessary. Walker said that he'd had the same dreams as you. He told you the old man had come to him just as he did to us. He admitted the old man was Cogline. He didn't dispute any of it. He simply said he didn't want to become involved. The implication is that he believes the dreams are real — otherwise, there wouldn't be anything to get involved with.'

Par's jaw tightened. 'I don't understand it, Coll. That was Walker I spoke with last night; I know it was. But he didn't talk like Walker. All that business about not becoming involved, about his decision to separate himself from the Races, and to live out here like a hermit. Something's not right; I can feel it! He wasn't telling me everything. He kept talking about how the Druids kept secrets from the Ohmsfords, but he was doing the same thing with me! He was hiding something!'

Coll looked unconvinced. 'Why would he do that?'

Par shook his head. 'I don't know. I just sense it.' He looked at his brother sharply. 'Walker never backed down from anything in his entire life; we both know that. He was never afraid to stand up and be counted when he was needed. Now he talks as if he can scarcely bear the thought of getting up in the morning! He talks as if the only important thing in life is to look out for himself!' The Valeman leaned back wearily against the hickory trunk. 'He made me feel embarrassed for him. He made me feel ashamed!'

'I think you might be reading too much into this.' Coll scuffed the ground with the heel of his boot. 'It may be just the way he says it is. He's lived alone out here for a long time, Par. Maybe he simply isn't comfortable with people anymore.'

'Even you?' Par was incensed. 'For goodness sake, Coll — he wouldn't even speak with you!'

Coll shook his head and held his gaze steady. 'The truth is, Par, we never spoke much as it was. You were the one he cared about, because you were the one with the magic.'

Par looked at him and said nothing. Walker's exact words, he thought. He was just fooling himself when he tried to equate Coll's relationship with their uncle to his own. It had never been the same.

He frowned. 'There is still the matter of the dreams. Why doesn't he share my curiosity about them? Doesn't he want to know what Allanon has to say?'

Coll shrugged. 'Maybe he already knows. He seems to know what everyone is thinking most of the time.'

Par hesitated. He hadn't considered that. Was it possible his uncle had already determined what the Druid would tell them at the Hadeshorn? Could he read the mind of a shade, a man three hundred years dead?

He shook his head. 'No, I don't think so. He would have said something more than he did about the reason for the dreams. He spent all of his time dismissing the matter as one more instance when the Ohmsfords would be used by the Druids; he didn't care what the reason was.'

'Then perhaps he is relying on you to tell him.'

Par nodded slowly. 'That makes better sense. I told him I was going; maybe he thinks that one of us going is enough.'

Coll stretched his big frame full length on the ground and stared up into the trees. 'But you don't believe that either, do you?'

His brother smiled faintly. 'No.'

'You still think that it's something else.'

'Yes.'

They didn't speak for a time, staring off into the woods, thinking their separate thoughts. Slender streams of sunlight played along their bodies through chinks in the limbs canopied overhead, and the songs of birds filtered through the stillness. 'I like it here,' Par said finally.

Coll had his eyes closed. 'Where do you think he's hiding?'

'Walker? I don't know. Under a rock, I suppose.'

'You're too quick to judge him, Par. You don't have the right to do that.'

Par bit off what he was going to say next and contented himself with watching a ray of sunlight work its way across Coll's face until it was in his eyes, causing him to blink and shift his body. He sat up, his squarish face a mask of contentment. Not much of anything ruffled Coll; he always managed to keep his sense of balance. Par admired him for that. Coll always understood the relative importance of events in the greater scheme of things.

Par was aware suddenly of how much he loved his brother.

'Are you coming with me, Coll?' he asked then. 'To the Hadeshorn?'

Coll looked at him and blinked. 'Isn't it odd,' he replied, 'that you and Walker and even Wren have the dreams and I don't, that all of you are mentioned in them, but never me, and that all of you are called, but not me?' There was no rancor in his voice, only puzzlement. 'Why do you think that is? We've never talked about it, you and I, have we? Not once. I think we have both been very careful to avoid talking about it.'

Par stared at him and didn't know what to say. Coll saw his discomfort and smiled. 'Awkward, isn't it? Don't look so miserable, Par. It isn't as if the matter is any fault of yours.' He leaned close. 'Maybe it has something to do with the magic — something none of us knows yet. Maybe that's it.'

Par shook his head and sighed. 'I'd be lying if I said that the whole business of me having the dreams and you not having them doesn't make me very uncomfortable. I don't know what to say. I keep expecting you to involve yourself in something that doesn't really concern you. I shouldn't even ask — but I guess I can't help it. You're my brother, and I want you with me.'

Coll reached out and put a hand on Par's shoulder. His smile was warm. 'Now and then, Par, you do manage to say the right thing.' He tightened his grip. 'I go where you go. That's the way it is with us. I'm not saying I always agree with the way you reason things out, but that doesn't change how I feel about you. So if you believe you must go to the Hadeshorn to resolve this matter of the dreams, then I am going with you.'

Par put his arms around his brother and hugged him, thinking of all the times Coll had stood by him when he was asked, warmed by the feeling it gave him to know that Coll would be with him again now. 'I knew I could depend on you,' was all he said.

It was late afternoon by the time they started back.

139

They had intended to return earlier, but had become preoccupied with talking about the dreams and Allanon and had wandered all the way to the east wall of the valley before realizing how late it had become. Now, with the sun already inching toward the rim of the western horizon, they began to retrace their steps.

'It looks as if we might get our feet wet,' Coll announced as they worked their way back through the trees.

Par glanced skyward. A mass of heavy rain clouds had appeared at the northern edge of the valley, darkening the whole of the skyline. The sun was already beginning to disappear, enveloped in the growing darkness. The air was warm and sticky, and the forest was hushed.

They made their way more quickly now, anxious to avoid a drenching. A stiff breeze sprang up, heralding the approach of the storm, whipping the leafy branches of the trees about them in frantic dances. The temperature began to drop, and the forest grew dark and shadowed.

Par muttered to himself as he felt a flurry of scattered raindrops strike his face. It was bad enough that they were out there looking for someone who wasn't about to be found in the first place. Now they were going to get soaked for their efforts.

Then he saw something move in the trees.

He blinked and looked again. This time he didn't see anything. He slowed without realizing it, and Coll, who was trailing a step or so behind, asked what was wrong. Par shook his head and picked up the pace again.

The wind whipped into his face, forcing him to lower his head against its sting. He glanced right, then left. There were flashes of movement to either side.

Something was tracking them.

Par felt the hair on the back of his neck prickle, but he forced himself to keep moving. Whatever was out there didn't have the look or the movement of either Walker Boh or the cat. Too quick, too agile. He tried to gather his thoughts. How far were they from the cottage — a mile, maybe less? He kept his head up as he walked, trying to follow the movement out of the corner of his eye. Movements, he corrected himself. There was clearly more than one of them.

'Par!' Coll said as they brushed close passing through a narrow winding of trees. 'There's something ...'

'I know!' Par cut him short. 'Keep moving!'

They made their way through a broad stand of fir, and the rain began to fall in earnest. The sun, the walls of the valley, even the dark pinnacle of Hearthstone had disappeared. Par felt his breathing quicken. Their pursuers were all around them now, shadows that had taken on vaguely human form as they flitted through the trees.

They're closing in on us, Par thought frantically. How much farther was the cottage?

Coll cried out suddenly as they pushed through a stand of red maple into a small, empty clearing. 'Par, run for it! They're too close ...!'

He grunted sharply and pitched forward. Par wheeled instinctively and caught him. There was blood on Coll's forehead, and he was unconscious.

Par never had time to figure out what had happened. He looked up, and the shadows were on top of him. They broke from the concealment of the trees all around him, bounding into view in a flurry of motion. Par caught a brief glimpse of bent, crooked forms covered with coarse, black hair and of glinting, ferret eyes, and then they were all over him. He flung them away as he struggled to escape, feeling tough, wiry limbs grapple at him. For a moment, he kept his feet. He cried out frantically, summoning the magic of the wishsong, sending forth a scattering of frightful images in an effort to protect himself. There were howls of fear, and his attackers shrank from him.

This time, he got a good look at them. He saw the strange, insectlike forms with their vaguely human faces, all twisted and hairy.

Spider Gnomes, he thought in disbelief!

Then they were on him once more, bearing him down by the sheer weight of their numbers. He was enveloped in a mass of sinew and hair and thrown to the ground. He could no longer summon the magic. His arms were being forced back, and he was being choked. He struggled desperately, but there were too many.

He had only a moment more to try to call out for help, and then everything went dark.

CHAPTER

11

WHEN HE CAME AWAKE AGAIN, Par Ohmsford found himself in the middle of a nightmare. He was bound hand and foot and hanging from a pole. He was being carried through a forest thick with mist and shadows, the dark crease of a deep ravine visible to his left, the jagged edge of a ridgeline sharp against the night sky to his right. Scrub and the dense tangle of grasses and weeds slapped at his back and head as he swung helplessly from the pole, and the air was thick, humid, and still.

There were Spider Gnomes all around him, creeping soundlessly through the half-light on crooked legs.

Par closed his eyes momentarily to shut out the images, then opened them again. The skies were dark and overcast, but a scattering of stars shone through creases in the clouds and there was a faint hint of brightness beyond the drop of the ravine. Night had come and gone, he realized. It was almost morning.

He remembered then what had happened to him, how the Spider Gnomes had chased him, seized him, and taken him away. Coll! What had happened to Coll? He craned his neck in an effort to see if his brother had been brought as well, but there was no sign of him. He clenched his jaw in rage, remembering Coll falling, then sprawled on the ground with blood on his face....

He wiped the image quickly from his mind. It was

useless to dwell on it. He must find a way to get free and return for his brother. He worked momentarily against the ropes that bound him, testing their strength, but there was no give. Hanging as he was, he could not find the leverage necessary to loosen them. He would have to wait. He wondered then where he was being taken — why he had been taken in the first place, for that matter. What did the Spider Gnomes want of him?

Insects buzzed in his face, flying at his eyes and mouth. He buried his face into his arms and left it there.

When he brought it out again, he tried to determine where he was. The light was to his left, the beginnings of the new day. East, then, he decided — the Spider Gnomes were traveling north. That made sense. The Spider Gnomes had made their home on Toffer Ridge in Brin Ohmsford's time. That was probably where he was. He swallowed against the dryness in his mouth and throat. Thirst and fear, he thought. He tried to recall what he could of Spider Gnomes from the stories of the old days, but he was unable to focus his thoughts. Brin had encountered them when she, Rone Leah, Cogline, Kimber Boh, and the moor cat Whisper had gone after the missing Sword of Leah. There was something else, something about a wasteland and the terrifying creatures that lived within it. . . .

Then he remembered. *Werebeasts.* The name whispered in his mind like a curse.

The Spider Gnomes turned down a narrow defile, filling it with their hairy forms like a dark stain, chittering now in what appeared to be anticipation. The brightness in the east disappeared, and shadows and mist closed about them like a wall. His wrists and ankles ached, and his body felt stretched beyond help. The Gnomes were small and carried him close to the ground so that he bumped and scraped himself at every turn. He watched from his upside down position as the defile broadened into a shelf that opened out over a vast, mist-shrouded stretch of emptiness that seemed to run on forever. The shelf became a corridor through a series of boulders that

dotted the side of Toffer Ridge like knots on the back of a
boar. Firelight flickered in the distance, pinpricks of
brightness playing hide-and-seek among the rocks. A
handful of Spider Gnomes bounded ahead, skittering
effortlessly over the rocks.

Par took a deep breath. Wherever it was they were
going, they were almost there.

A moment later, they emerged from the rocks and
came to a halt on a low bluff that ran back to a series of
burrows and caves tunneled into the side of the ridge.
Fires burned all about, and hundreds of Spider Gnomes
shoved into view. Par was dumped unceremoniously, the
bonds that secured him cut and the pole removed. He lay
there on his back for a moment, rubbing his wrists and
ankles, finding creases so deep that he bled, conscious all
the time of the eyes watching him. Then he was hauled to
his feet and dragged toward the caves and burrows. They
bypassed the latter in favor of the former, the gnarled
hands of the Gnomes fastened on him at every conceiv-
able point, the stink of their bodies filling his nostrils.
They chittered at each other in their own language, their
talk incessant now and meaningless to him. He did not
resist; he could barely stand upright. They took him
through the largest of the cave openings, propelled him
past a small fire that burned at its mouth and stopped.
There was some discussion, a few moments' worth at
best, and then he was thrust forward. He saw they were
in a smallish cave that ran back only twenty yards or so
and was no more than eight feet at its highest point. A
pair of iron rings had been hammered into the rock wall
at the cave's deepest point, and the Spider Gnomes
lashed him to those. Then they left him, all but two who
remained behind to take up watch by the fire at the cave
entrance.

Par let his mind clear, listening to the silence, waiting
to see what would happen next. When nothing did, he
took a careful look about. He had been left spread-eagle
against the rock wall, one arm secured to each of the iron
rings. He was forced to remain standing because the rings

were fastened too high up on the rock to allow him to sit. He tested his bonds. They were leather and secured so tightly that his wrists could not slip within them even the smallest amount.

He sagged back momentarily in despair, forcing down the panic that threatened to overwhelm him. The others would be looking for him by now — Morgan, Steff, Teel. They would already have found Coll. They would track the Spider Gnomes and come for him. They would find him and rescue him.

He shook his head. He was just kidding himself, he knew. It was almost dark when the Gnomes had taken him and the rain had been a hard one. There would have been no time for a search and no real chance of finding a trail. The best he could hope for was that Coll had been found or revived himself and gone to the others to tell them what had happened.

He swallowed again against the dryness. He was so thirsty!

Time slipped away, turning seconds to minutes, minutes to hours. The darkness outside brightened minimally, bringing a barely penetrable daylight, choked with heat and mist. The faint sounds of the Spider Gnomes disappeared altogether, and he would have thought them gone completely if not for the two who sat hunkered down by the cave's entrance. The fire went out, smoking for a time, then turning to ash. The day slipped away. Once, one of the guards rose and brought him a cup of water. He drank it greedily from the hands that held it up to his mouth, spilling most of it, soaking his shirt front. He grew hungry as well, but no food was offered.

When the day began to fade to darkness again, the guards rebuilt the fire at the mouth of the cave, then disappeared.

Par waited expectantly, forgetting for the first time the ache of his body, the hunger and the fear. Something was going to happen now. He could feel it.

What happened was altogether unexpected. He was

working again at his bonds, his sweat loosening them now, mingling with traces of his blood from the cuts the ties had made, when a figure appeared from the shadows. It came past the fire and into the light and stopped.

It was a child.

Par blinked. The child was a girl, perhaps a dozen years of age, rather tall and skinny with dark, lank hair and deepset eyes. She was not a Gnome but of the Race of Man, a Southlander, with a tattered dress, worn boots, and a small silver locket about her neck. She looked at him curiously, studied him as she might a stray dog or cat, then came slowly forward. She stopped when she reached him, then lifted one hand to brush back his hair and touch his ear.

'Elf,' she said quietly, fingering the ear's tip.

Par stared. What was a child doing out here among the Spider Gnomes? He wet his lips. 'Untie me,' he begged.

She looked at him some more, saying nothing. 'Untie me!' Par said again, more insistent this time. He waited, but the child just looked at him. He felt the beginnings of doubt creep through him. Something was not right.

'Hug you,' the child said suddenly.

She came to him almost anxiously, wrapping her arms about him, fastening herself to him like a leech. She clung to him, burying herself in his body, murmuring over and over again something he could not understand. What was the matter with this child, he wondered in dismay? She seemed lost, frightened perhaps, needing to hold him as much as he. . . .

The thought died away as he felt her stirring against him, moving within her clothes, against his clothes, then against his skin. Her fingers had tightened into him, and he could feel her pressing, pressing. Shock flooded through him. She was right against him, against his skin, as if they wore no clothes at all, as if all their garments had been shed. She was burrowing, coming against him, then coming into him, merging somehow with him, making herself a part of him.

Shades! What was happening?

147

Repulsion filled him with a suddenness that was terrifying. He screamed, shook himself in horror, kicked out desperately and at last flung her away. She fell in a crouch, her child's face transformed into something hideous, smiling like a beast at feeding, eyes sharp and glinting with pinpricks of red light.

'Give me the magic, boy!' she rasped in a voice that sounded nothing of a child's.

Then he knew. 'Oh, no, oh, no,' he whispered over and over, bracing himself as she came slowly back to her feet.

This child was a Shadowen!

'Give it to me!' she repeated, her voice demanding. 'Let me come into you and taste it!'

She came toward him, a spindly little thing, a bit of nothing, if her face had not betrayed her. She reached for him and he kicked out at her desperately. She smiled wickedly and stepped back.

'You are mine,' she said softly. 'The Gnomes have given you to me. I will have your magic, boy. Give yourself to me. See what I can feel like!'

She came at him like a cat at its prey, avoiding his kick, fastening herself to him with a howl. He could feel her moving almost immediately — not the child herself, but something within the child. He forced himself to look down and could see the faintest whisper of a dark outline shimmering within the child's body, trying to move into his own. He could feel its presence, like a chill on a summer's day, like fly's feet against his skin. The Shadowen was touching, seeking. He threw back his head, clenched his jaw, made his body as rigid as iron, and fought it. The thing, the Shadowen, was trying to come into him. It was trying to merge with him. Oh, Shades! He must not let it! He must not!

Then, unexpectedly, he cried out, releasing the magic of the wishsong in a howl of mingled rage and anguish. It took no form, for he had already determined that even his most frightening images were of no use against these creatures. It came of its own volition, breaking free from some dark corner of his being to take on a shape he did not recognize. It was a dark, unidentifiable thing, and it whipped about him like webbing from a spider about its prey. The Shadowen hissed and tore itself away, spitting and clawing at the air. It dropped again into a crouch, the child's body contorted and shivering from something unseen. Par's cry died into silence at the sight of it, and he sagged back weakly against the cave wall.

'Stay back from me!' he warned, gasping for breath. 'Don't touch me again!'

He didn't know what he had done or how he had done it, but the Shadowen hunched down against the firelight and glared at him in defeat. The hint of the being within the child's body shimmered briefly and was gone. The glint of red in the eyes disappeared. The child rose slowly and straightened, a child in truth once more, frail and lost. Dark eyes studied him for long moments and she said faintly once more, 'Hug me.'

Then she called into the gathering darkness without, and the Spider Gnomes reappeared, several dozen strong, bowing and scraping to the child as they entered. She spoke to them in their own language while they knelt before her, and Par remembered how superstitious these creatures were, believing in gods and spirits of all sorts. And now they were in the thrall of a Shadowen. He wanted to scream.

The Spider Gnomes came for him, loosened the bonds that secured him, seized his arms and legs, and pulled him forward. The child blocked their way. 'Hug me?' She looked almost forlorn.

He shook his head, trying to break free of the dozens of hands that held him. He was dragged outside in the twilight haze where the smoke of the fires and the mist of the lowlands mingled and swirled like dreams in sleep. He was stopped at the bluff's edge, staring down into a pit of emptiness.

The child was beside him, her voice soft, insidious. 'Olden Moor,' she whispered. 'Werebeasts live there. Do you know Werebeasts, Elf-boy?' He stiffened. 'They shall have you now if you do not hug me. Feed on you despite your magic.'

He broke free then, flinging his captors from him. The Shadowen hissed and shrank away, and the Spider Gnomes scattered. He lunged, trying to break through, but they blocked his way and bore him back. He whirled, buffeted first this way, then that. Hands reached for him, gnarled and hairy and grasping. He lost himself in a whirl of coarse bodies and chittering voices, hearing only his own voice screaming from somewhere inside not to be taken again, not to be held.

He was suddenly at the edge of the bluff. He summoned the magic of the wishsong, striking out with images at the Spider Gnomes who beset him, desperately trying to force a path through their midst. The Shadowen had disappeared, lost somewhere in the smoke and shadows.

Then he felt his feet go out from under him, the edge of the bluff giving way beneath the weight of his attackers. He grappled for them, for a handhold anywhere, and found nothing. He toppled clear of the bluff, falling into the abyss, tumbling into the swirl of mist. The Shadowen, the Spider Gnomes, the fires, caves, and burrows all disappeared behind him. Down he fell, head-over-heels, tumbling through scrub brush and grasses, across slides and between boulders. Miraculously, he missed the rocks that might have killed or crippled him, falling clear finally in a long, agonizing drop that ended in jarring blackness.

He was unconscious for a time; he didn't know how long. When he came awake again, he found himself in a crushed bed of damp marsh grasses. The grasses, he realized, must have broken his fall and probably saved his life. He lay there, the breath knocked from his body, listening to the sound of his heart pumping in his breast. When his strength returned and his vision cleared, he climbed gingerly to his feet and checked himself. His entire body was a mass of cuts and bruises, but there appeared to be nothing broken. He stood without moving then and listened. From somewhere far above, he could hear the voices of the Spider Gnomes.

They would be coming for him, he knew. He had to get out of there.

He looked about. Mist and shadows chased each other through a twilight world of gathering darkness, night descending quickly now. Small, almost invisible things skipped and jumped through the tall grasses. Ooze sucked and bubbled all about, hidden quagmires surrounding islands of solid earth. Stunted trees and brush defined the landscape, frozen in grotesque poses. Sounds were distant and directionless. Everything seemed and looked the same, a maze without end.

Par took a deep breath to steady himself. He could guess where he was. He had been on Toffer Ridge. His fall had taken him down off the ridge and right into Olden Moor. In his efforts to escape his fate, he had only managed to find it sooner. He had put himself exactly where the Shadowen had threatened to send him — into the domain of the Werebeasts.

He set his jaw and started moving. He was only at the edge of the moor, he told himself — not fully into it yet, not lost. He still had the ridge behind him to serve as a guide. If he could follow it far enough south, he could escape. But he had to be quick.

He could almost feel the Werebeasts watching him.

The stories of the Werebeasts came back to him now, jarred free by the realization of where he was and sharpened by his fear. They were an old magic, monsters who preyed off strayed and lost creatures who wandered into the moor or were sent there, stealing away their strength and spirit and feeding on their lives. The Spider Gnomes were their principal food; the Spider Gnomes believed the Werebeasts were spirits that required appeasement, and they sacrificed themselves accordingly. Par went cold at the thought. That was what the Shadowen had intended for him.

Fatigue slowed him and made him unsteady. He

151

stumbled several times, and once he stepped hip-deep into a quagmire before quickly pulling free. His vision was blurred, and sweat ran down his back. The moor's heat was stultifying, even at night. He glanced skyward and realized that the last of the light was fading. Soon it would be completely black.

Then he would not be able to see at all.

A massive pool of sludge barred his passage, the wall of the ridge eaten away so that it was impossible to climb past. His only choice was to go around, deeper into the moor. He moved quickly, following the line of the swamp, listening for sounds of pursuit. There were none. The moor was still and empty. He swung back toward the bluff, encountered a maze of gullies with masses of things moving through them, and swung wide again. Steadily, he went on, exhausted, but unable to rest. The darkness deepened. He found the end of the maze and started back again toward the bluff. He walked a long way, circling quagmires and sinkholes, peering expectantly through the gloom.

He could not find Toffer Ridge.

He walked more quickly now, anxious, fighting down the fear that threatened to overwhelm him. He was lost, he realized — but he refused to accept it. He kept searching, unable to believe that he could have mistaken his direction so completely. The base of the ridge had been right there! How could he have become so turned about?

At last he stopped, unable to continue with the charade. There was no point in going on, because the truth of the matter was he had no idea where he was going. He would simply continue to wander about endlessly until either the swamp or the Werebeasts claimed him. It was better that he stand and fight.

It was an odd decision, one brought about less by sound reasoning than by fatigue. After all, what hope was there for him if he didn't escape the moor and how could he escape the moor if he stopped moving? But he was tired and he didn't like the idea of running about blindly. And he kept thinking of that child, that Shadowen —

shrinking from him, driven back by some shading of his magic that he hadn't even known existed. He still didn't understand what it was, but if he could somehow summon it again and master it in even the smallest way, then he had a chance against the Werebeasts and anything else the swamp might send against him.

He glanced about momentarily, then walked to a broad hillock with quagmire on two sides, jutting rocks on a third, and only one way in. Only one way out, as well, he reminded himself as he ascended the rise, but then he wasn't going anywhere, was he? He found a flat rock and seated himself, facing out into the mist and night. Until it grew light again, this was where he would make his stand.

The minutes slipped away. Night descended, the mist thickened, but there was still light, a sort of curious phosphorescence given off by the sparse vegetation. Its glow was faint and deceptive, but it gave Par the means to distinguish what lay about him and the belief that he could catch sight of anything sneaking up on him.

Nevertheless, he didn't see the Shadowen until it was almost on top of him It was the child again, tall, thin, wasted. She appeared seemingly out of nowhere, no more than a few yards in front of him, and he started with the suddenness of her coming.

'Get back from me!' he warned, coming quickly to his feet. 'If you try to touch me ... '

The Shadowen shimmered into mist and disappeared.

Par took a deep breath. It hadn't been a Shadowen after all, he thought, but a Werebeast — and not so tough, if he could send it packing with just a threat!

He wanted to laugh. He was near exhaustion, both physically and emotionally, and he knew he was no longer entirely rational. He hadn't chased anything away. That Werebeast had simply come in for a look. They were toying with him, the way they did with their prey — taking on familiar forms, waiting for the right opportunity, for fatigue or fright or foolishness to give them an opening. He thought again about the stories, about the inevitability of the stalking, then pushed it all from his mind.

Somewhere in the distance, far from where he sat, something cried out once, a quick shriek of dismay. Then everything was still again.

He stared into the mist, watching. He found himself thinking of the circumstances that had brought him here — of his flight from the Federation, of his dreams, his meeting with the old man, and his search for Walker Boh. He had come a long way because of those circumstances and he still wasn't anywhere. He felt a pang of disappointment that he hadn't accomplished more, that he hadn't learned anything useful. He thought again of his conversation with Walker. Walker had told him the wishsong's magic was not a gift, despite his insistence that it was, and that there wasn't anything worthwhile to discover about its use. He shook his head. Well, perhaps there wasn't. Perhaps he had just been kidding himself all along.

But something about it had frightened that Shadowen. Something.

Yet only that child, not any of the others that he had encountered.

What had been different?

There was movement again at the edge of the mists, and a figure detached itself and moved toward him. It was the second Shadowen, the great, shambling creature they had encountered at the edge of the Anar. It slouched toward him, grunting, carrying a monstrous club. For a moment, he forgot what he was facing. He panicked, remembering that the wishsong had been ineffective against this Shadowen, that he had been helpless. He started to back away, then caught himself, thrust away his confusion and shook clear his mind. Impulsively, he used the wishsong, its magic creating an identical image of the creature facing him, an image that he used to cloak himself. Shadowen faced Shadowen. Then the Werebeast shimmered and faded back into the mist.

Par went still and let the image concealing him

dissolve. He sat down again. How long could he keep this up?

He wondered if Coll was all right. He saw his brother stretched upon the earth bleeding and he remembered how helpless he had felt at that moment. He thought about how much he depended on his brother.

Coll.

His mind wandered, shifted. There was a use for his magic, he told himself sternly. It was not as Walker had said. There was purpose in his having it; it was indeed a gift. He would find the answers at the Hadeshorn. He would find them when he spoke to Allanon. He must simply get free of this moor and....

A gathering of shadowy forms emerged from the mists before him, dark and forbidding bits of ethereal motion in the night. The Werebeasts had decided to wait no longer. He jerked to his feet, facing them. They eased gradually closer, first one, then another, none with any discernible shape, all shifting and changing as rapidly as the mists.

Then he saw Coll, pulled from the darkness behind the shadows, gripped in substanceless hands, his face ashen and bloodied. Par went cold. *Help me*, he heard his brother call out, though the sound of the voice was only in his mind. *Help me, Par.*

Par screamed something with the magic of the wishsong, but it dissipated into the dank air of Olden Moor in a scattering of broken sounds. Par shook as if chilled. Shades! That really was Coll! His brother struggled, fighting to break free, calling out repeatedly, Par, Par!

He went to his brother's aid almost without thinking. He attacked the Werebeasts with a fury that was entirely unexpected. He cried out, the wishsong's magic thrusting at the creatures, hammering them back. He reached Coll and seized him, pulling him free. Hands groped for him, touching. He felt pain, freezing and burning both at once. Coll gripped him, and the pain intensified. Poison flooded into him, bitter and harsh. His strength almost gave out, but he managed to keep his feet, hauling his brother clear of the shadows, pulling him onto the rise.

Below, the shadows clustered and shifted watchfully. Par howled down at them, knowing he was infected, feeling the poison work its way through his body. Coll stood next to him, not speaking. Par's thoughts scattered, and his sense of what he was about drifted away.

The Werebeasts began to close.

Then there was fresh movement on the rocks to his right, and something huge appeared. Par tried to move away, but the effort brought him to his knees. Great, luminous yellow eyes blinked in the night, and a massive black shadow bounded to his side.

'Rumor!' he whispered in disbelief.

The moor cat edged carefully past him to face Coll. The huge cat growled, a low, dangerous warning cough that seemed to break through the mist and fill the darkness with shards of sound. 'Coll?' Par called out to his brother and started forward, but the moor cat quickly blocked his way, shoving him back. The shadows were moving closer, taking on form now, becoming lumbering things, bodies covered with scales and hair, faces that showed demon eyes and jaws split wide in hunger. Rumor spat at them and lunged, bringing them up short to hiss back at him.

Then he whirled with claws and teeth bared and tore Coll to pieces.

Coll — what had appeared to be Coll — turned into a thing of indescribable horror, bloodied and shredded, then shimmered and disappeared — another deception. Par cried out in anguish and fury. Tricked! Ignoring the pain and the sudden nausea, he sent the magic of the wishsong hurtling at the Werebeasts, daggers and arrows of fury, images of things that could rend and tear. The Werebeasts shimmered and the magic passed harmlessly by.

Reforming, the Werebeasts attacked.

Rumor caught the closest a dozen paces off, hammering it away with a single breathtaking swipe of one great paw. Another lunged, but the cat caught it as well and sent it spinning. Others were appearing now from the shadows and mist behind those already creeping forward. Too many, thought Par frantically! He was too weak to stand, the poison from the Werebeasts' touch seeping through him rapidly now, threatening to drop him into that familiar black abyss that had begun to open within

Then he felt a hand on his shoulder, firm and instantly comforting, reassuring him and at the same time holding him in place, and he heard a voice call sharply, 'Rumor!'

The moor cat edged back, never turning to look, responding to the sound of the voice alone. Par lifted his face. Walker Boh was beside him, wrapped in black robes and mist, his narrow, chiseled face set in a look that turned Par cold, his skin so white it might have been drawn in chalk.

'Keep still, Par,' he said.

He moved forward to face the Werebeasts. There were more than a dozen now, crouched down at the edge of the rise, drifting in and out of the mist and night. They hesitated at Walker Boh's approach, almost as if they knew him. Par's uncle came directly down to them, stopping when he was less than a dozen yards from the nearest.

'Leave,' he said simply and pointed off into the night. The Werebeasts held their ground. Walker came forward another step, and this time his voice was so hard that it seemed to shiver the air. 'Leave!'

One of them lunged at him, a monstrous thing, jaws snapping as it reached for the black-robed figure. Walker Boh's hand shot out, dust scattering into the beast. Fire erupted into the night with an explosion that rocked the bottomland, and the Werebeast simply disappeared.

Walker's extended hand swept the circle of those that remained, threatening. An instant later, the Werebeasts had faded back into the night and were gone.

Walker turned and came back up the rise, kneeling next to Par. 'This is my fault,' he said quietly.

Par struggled to speak and felt his strength give out. He was sick. Consciousness slipped away. For the third time in less than two days, he tumbled into the abyss. He remembered thinking as he fell that this time he was not sure he would be able to climb out again.

CHAPTER

12

AR OHMSFORD DRIFTED through a landscape of dreams.

He was both within himself and without as he journeyed, a participant and a viewer. There was constant motion, sometimes as charged as a voyage across a stormy sea, sometimes as gentle as the summer wind through the trees. He spoke to himself alternately in the dark silence of his mind and from within a mirrored self-image. His voice was a disembodied whisper and a thunderous shout. Colors appeared and faded to black and white. Sounds came and departed. He was all things on his journey, and he was none.

The dreams were his reality.

He dreamed in the beginning that he was falling, tumbling downward into a pit as black as night and as endless as the cycle of the seasons. There were pain and fear in him; he could not find himself. Sometimes there were voices, calling to him in warning, in comfort, or in horror. He convulsed within himself. He knew somehow that if he did not stop falling, he would be forever lost.

He did stop finally. He slowed and leveled, and his convulsions ceased. He was in a field of wildflowers as wondrous as a rainbow. Birds and butterflies scattered at his approach, filling the air with new brightness, and the smells of the field were soft and fragrant. There was no sound. He tried to speak so that there might be, but found himself voiceless. Nor did he have touch. He could feel nothing of himself, nothing of the world about him. There was warmth, soothing and extended, but that was all.

He drifted and a voice somewhere deep within him whispered that he was dead.

The voice, he thought, belonged to Walker Boh.

Then the world of sweet smells and sights disappeared, and he was in a world of darkness and stench. Fire erupted from the earth and spat at an angry, smudge-colored sky. Shadowen flitted and leaped, red eyes glinting as they whipped about him, hovering one moment, ducking away the next. Clouds rolled overhead, filled with lightning, borne on a wind that howled in fury. He felt himself buffeted and tossed, thrown like a dried leaf across the earth, and he sensed it was the end of all things. Touch and voice returned, and he felt his pain once more and cried out with it.

'Par?'

The voice came once and was gone again — Coll's voice. But he saw Coll in his dream then, stretched against a gathering of rocks, lifeless and bloodied, eyes open in accusation. 'You left me. You abandoned me.' He screamed and the magic of the wishsong threw images everywhere. But the images turned into monsters that wheeled back to devour him. He could feel their teeth and claws. He could feel their touch . . .

He came awake.

Rain fell into his face, and his eyes opened. There was darkness all about, the sense of others close at hand, a feeling of motion, and the coppery taste of blood. There was shouting, voices that called to one another against the fury of a storm. He rose up, choking, spitting. Hands bore him back again, slipping against his body and face.

'. . . awake again, hold him . . . '

'. . . too strong, like he's ten instead of . . . '

'Walker! Hurry!'

Trees thrashed in the background, long-limbed giants lifting into the roiling black, the wind howling all about them. They threw shadows against cliffs that blocked their passage and threatened to pen them up. Par heard himself scream.

Lightning crashed and thunder rolled, filling the dark with echoes of madness. A wash of red screened his vision.

Then Allanon was there — Allanon! He came from nowhere, all in black robes, a figure out of legend and time. He bent close to Par, his voice a whisper that somehow managed to rise above the chaos. Sleep, Par, he soothed. One weathered hand reached out and touched the Valeman, and the chaos dissipated and was replaced by a profound sense of peace.

Par drifted away again, far down into himself, fighting now because he sensed that he would live if he could just will it to be so. Some part of him remembered what had happened — that the Werebeasts had seized him, that their touch had poisoned him, that the poison had made him sick, and that the sickness had dropped him into that black abyss. Walker had come for him, found him somehow, and saved him from those creatures. He saw Rumor's yellow lamp eyes, blinking in warning, lidding and going out. He saw Coll and Morgan. He saw Steff, his smile sardonic, and Teel, enigmatic and silent.

He saw the Shadowen girl-child, begging again to be hugged, trying to enter his body. He felt himself resist, saw her thrown back, watched as she disappeared. Shades! She had tried to enter him, to come into him, to put herself within his skin and become him! That was what they were, he thought in a burst of understanding — shadows that lacked substance of their own and took the bodies of men. And women. And children.

But can shadows have life?

His thoughts jumbled around unanswerable questions, and he slipped from reason to confusion. His mind slept, and his journey through the land of dreams wore on. He climbed mountains filled with creatures like the Gnawl, crossed rivers and lakes of mist and hidden dangers, traversed forests where daylight never penetrated, and swept on into moors where mist stirred in an airless, empty cauldron of silence.

Help me, he begged. But there was no one to hear.

Time suspended then. The journey ended and the dreams faded into nothingness. There was a moment's pause at their end, and then waking. He knew he had slept, but not for how long. He knew only that there had been a passage of time when the dreams had ended and dreamless sleep had begun.

More important, he knew that he was alive.

He stirred gingerly, barely more than a twitch, feeling the softness of sheets and a bed beneath him, aware that he was stretched out full-length and that he was warm and snug. He did not want to move yet, frightened that he might still be dreaming. He let the feel of the sheets soak through him. He listened to the sound of his own breathing in his ears. He tasted the dryness of the air.

Then he let his eyes slip open. He was in a small, sparsely furnished room lit by a single lamp set on a table at his bedside. The walls of the room were bare, the ceiling beams uncovered. A comforter wrapped him and pillows cradled his head. A break in the curtains that covered the windows opposite where he lay told him it was night.

Morgan Leah dozed in a chair just inside the circle of light given off by the lamp, his chin resting on his chest, his arms folded loosely. 'Morgan?' he called, his voice sounding fuzzy.

The Highlander's eyes snapped open, his hawk face instantly alert. He blinked, then jumped to his feet. 'Par! Par, are you awake? Good heavens, we've been worried sick!' He rushed over as if to hug his friend, then thought better of it. He ran the fingers of one hand through his rust-colored hair distractedly. 'How do you feel? Are you all right?'

Par grinned weakly. 'I don't know yet. I'm still waking up. What happened?'

'What *didn't* happen is more like it!' the other replied heatedly. 'You almost died, do you realize that?'

Par nodded. 'I guessed it. What about Coll, Morgan?'

162

'Sleeping, waiting for you to come around. I packed him off several hours ago when he fell out of his chair. You know Coll. Wait here, I'll get him.' He grinned. 'Wait here, I tell you — as if you were going anywhere. Pretty funny.'

Par had a dozen things he wanted to say, questions he wanted to ask, but the Highlander was already out the door and gone. It didn't matter, he guessed. He lay back quietly, flooded with relief. All that mattered was that Coll was all right.

Morgan returned almost immediately Coll beside him, and Coll, unlike Morgan, did not hesitate as he reached down and practically squeezed the life out of Par in his enthusiasm at finding him awake. Par hugged him back, albeit weakly, and the three laughed as if they had just enjoyed the biggest joke of their lives.

'Shades, we thought we'd lost you!' Coll exclaimed softly. He wore a bandage taped to his forehead, and his face seemed pale. 'You were very sick, Par.'

Par smiled and nodded. He'd heard enough of that. 'Will someone tell me what happened? His eyes shifted from one face to the other. 'Where are we anyway?'

'Storlock,' Morgan announced. One eyebrow arched. 'Walker Boh brought you here.'

'Walker?'

Morgan grinned with satisfaction. 'Thought you'd be surprised to learn that — Walker Boh coming out of the Wilderun, Walker Boh appearing in the first place for that matter.' He sighed. 'Well, it's a long story, so I guess we'd better start at the beginning.'

He did, telling the story with considerable help from Coll, the two of them stepping on each other's words in their eagerness to make certain that nothing was overlooked. Par listened in growing surprise as the tale unfolded.

Coll, it seemed had been felled by a Gnome sling when the Spider Gnomes attacked them in that clearing at the eastern end of the valley at Hearthstone. He had only been stunned, but, by the time he had recovered consciousness, Par and their attackers were gone. It was raining buckets by then, the trail disappearing back into the earth as quickly as it was made, and Coll was too weak to give chase in any case. So he stumbled back to the cottage where he found the others and told them what had occurred. It was already dark by then and still raining, but Coll demanded they go back out anyway and search for his brother. They did, Morgan, Steff, Teel, and himself, groping about blindly for hours and finding nothing. When it became impossible to see anything, Steff insisted they give it up for the night, get some rest and start out again fresh in the morning. That was what they did, and that was how Coll encountered Walker Boh.

'We split up, trying to cover as much ground as possible, working the north valley, because I knew from the stories of Brin and Jair Ohmsford that the Spider Gnomes made their home on Toffer Ridge and it was likely they had come from there. At least, I hoped so, because that was all we had to go on. We agreed that if we didn't find you right away we would just keep on going until we reached the Ridge.' He shook his head. 'We were pretty desperate.'

'We were,' Morgan agreed.

'Anyway, I was all the way to the northeast edge of the valley when, all of a sudden, there was Walker and that giant cat, big as a house! He said that he'd sensed something. He asked me what had happened, what was wrong. I was so surprised to see him that I didn't even think to ask what he was doing there or why he had decided to appear after hiding all that time. I just told him what he wanted to know.'

'Do you know what he said then?' Morgan interrupted, gray eyes finding Par's, a hint of the mischievousness in them.

'He said,' Coll took control again of the conversation, '"Wait here, this is no task for you; I will bring him back" — as if we were children playing at a grown-up's game!'

'But he was as good as his word,' Morgan noted.

164

Coll sighed. 'Well, true enough,' he admitted grudgingly.

Walker Boh was gone a full day and night, but when he returned to Hearthstone, where Coll and his companions were indeed waiting, he had Par with him. Par had been infected by the touch of the Werebeasts and was near death. The only hope for him, Walker insisted, lay at Storlock, the community of Gnome healers. The Stors had experience in dealing with afflictions of the mind and spirit and could combat the Werebeast's poison.

They set out at once, the five of them less the cat, who had been left behind. They pushed west out of Hearthstone and the Wilderun, following the Chard Rush upriver to the Wolfsktaag, crossing through the Pass of Jade, and finally reaching the village of the Stors. It had taken them two days, traveling almost constantly. Par would have died if not for Walker, who had used an odd sort of magic that none of them had understood to prevent the poison from spreading and to keep Par sleeping and calm. At times, Par had thrashed and cried out, waking feverish and spitting blood — once in the middle of a ferocious storm they had encountered in the Pass of Jade — but Walker had been there to soothe him, to touch him, to say something that let him sleep once more.

'Even so, we've been in Storlock for almost three days and this is the first time you've been awake,' Coll finished. He paused, eyes lowering. 'It was very close, Par.'

Par nodded, saying nothing. Even without being able to remember anything clearly, he had a definite sense of just how close it had been. 'Where is Walker?' he asked finally.

'We don't know,' Morgan answered with a shrug. 'We haven't seen him since we arrived. He just disappeared.'

'Gone back to the Wilderun, I suppose,' Coll added, a touch of bitterness in his voice.

'Now, Coll,' Morgan soothed.

Coll held up his hands. 'I know, Morgan — I shouldn't judge. He was there to help when we needed him. He saved Par's life. I'm grateful for that.'

'Besides, I think he's still around,' Morgan said quietly. When the other two looked inquiringly at him, he simply shrugged.

Par told them then what had befallen him after his capture by the Spider Gnomes. He was still reasoning out a good part of it, so he hesitated from time to time in his telling. He was convinced that the Spider Gnomes had been sent specifically to find him, otherwise they would have taken Coll as well. The Shadowen had sent them, that girl-child. Yet how had it known who he was or where he could be found?

The little room was silent as they thought. 'The magic,' Morgan suggested finally. 'They all seem interested in the magic. This one must have sensed it as well.'

'All the way from Toffer Ridge?' Par shook his head doubtfully.

'And why not go after Morgan as well?' Coll asked suddenly. 'After all, he commands the magic of the Sword of Leah.'

'No, no, that's not the sort of magic they care about,' Morgan replied quickly. 'It's Par's sort of magic that interests them, draws them — magic that's a part of the body or spirit.'

'Or maybe it's simply Par,' Coll finished darkly.

They let the thought hang a moment in the silence. 'The Shadowen tried to come into me,' Par said finally, then explained it to them in more detail. 'It wanted to merge with me, to be a part of me. It kept saying, "hug me, hug me" — as if it were a lost child or something.'

'Hardly that,' Coll disputed quickly.

'More leech than lost child,' Morgan agreed.

'But what are they?' Par pressed, bits and pieces of his dreams coming back to him, flashes of insight that lacked meaning. 'Where is it that they come from and what is it that they want?'

'Us,' Morgan said quietly.

'You,' Coll said.

They talked a bit longer, mulling over what little they

knew of Shadowen and their interest in magic, then Coll and Morgan rose. Time for Par to rest again, they insisted. He was still sick, still weak, and he needed to get his strength back.

The Hadeshorn, Par remembered suddenly! How much time did they have before the new moon?

Coll sighed. 'Four days — if you still insist on going.'

Morgan grinned from behind him. 'We'll be close by if you need us. Good to see you well again, Par.'

He slipped out the door. 'It is good,' Coll agreed and gripped his brother's hand tightly.

When they were gone, Par lay with his eyes open for a time, letting his thoughts nudge and push one another. Questions whispered at him, asking for answers he didn't have. He had been chased and harried from Varfleet to the Rainbow Lake, from Culhaven to Hearthstone, by the Federation and the Shadowen, by things that he had only heard about and some he hadn't even known existed. He was tired and confused; he had almost lost his life. Everything centered on his magic, and yet his magic had been virtually useless to him. He was constantly running from one thing and toward another without really understanding much of either. He felt helpless.

And despite the presence of his brother and his friends, he felt oddly alone.

His last thought before he fell asleep was that, in a way he didn't yet comprehend, he was.

He slept fitfully, but without dreaming, waking often amid stirrings of dissatisfaction and wariness that darted through the corridors of his mind like harried rats. Each time he came awake it was still night, until the last time when it was almost dawn, the sky beyond the curtained window brightening faintly, the room in which he lay still and gauzy. A white-robed Stor passed briefly through the room, appearing from out of the shadows like a ghost to pause at his bedside and touch his wrist and forehead with hands that were surprisingly warm before turning and disappearing back the way he had come. Par slept soundly after that, drifting far down within himself and floating undisturbed in a sea of black warmth.

When he woke again, it was raining. His eyes blinked open and he stared fixedly into the grayness of his room. He could hear the sound of the raindrops beating on the windows and roof, a steady drip and splash in the stillness. There was daylight yet; he could see it through the part in the curtains. Thunder rolled in the distance, echoing in long, uneven peals.

Gingerly, he hoisted himself up on one elbow. He saw a fire burning in a small stove that he hadn't even noticed the previous night, tucked back in the shadows. It gave a solid warmth to the room that wrapped and cradled him and made him feel secure. There was tea by his bedside and tiny cakes. He pushed himself up the rest of the way, propping himself against the headboard of his bed with his pillows and pulling the cakes and tea to him. He was famished, and he devoured the cakes in seconds. Then he drank a small portion of the tea, which had gone cold in the sitting, but was wonderful in any case.

He was midway through his third cup when the door opened soundlessly and Walker Boh appeared. His uncle paused momentarily on seeing him awake, then closed the door softly and came over the stand at his bedside. He was dressed in forest green — tunic and pants belted tight, soft leather boots unlaced and muddied, long travel cloak spotted with rain. There was rain on his bearded face as well, and his dark hair was damp against his skin.

He pushed the travel cloak back across his shoulders. 'Feeling better?' he asked quietly.

Par nodded. 'Much.' He set his cup aside. 'I understand I have you to thank for that. You saved me from the Werebeasts. You brought me back to Hearthstone. It was your idea to bring me to Storlock. Coll and Morgan tell me that you even used magic to see to it that I stayed alive long enough to complete the journey.'

'Magic.' Walker repeated the word softly, his voice distracted. 'Words and touching in combination, a sort of

168

variation on the workings of the wishsong. My legacy from Brin Ohmsford. I haven't the curse of the fullness of her powers — only the annoyance of its shadings. Still, now and again, it does become the gift you insist it must be. I can interact with another living thing, feel its life force, sometimes find a way to strengthen it.' He paused. 'I don't know if I would call it magic, though.'

'And what you did to the Werebeasts in Olden Moor when you stood up for me — was that not magic?'

His uncle's eyes shifted away from him. 'I was taught that,' he said finally.

Par waited a moment, but when nothing more was forthcoming he said, 'I'm grateful for all of it in any case. Thank you.'

The other man shook his head slowly. 'I don't deserve your thanks. It was my fault that it happened in the first place.'

Par readjusted himself carefully against his pillows. 'I seem to remember you saying that before.'

Walker moved to the far end of the bed and sat down on its edge. 'If I had watched over you the way I should have, the Spider Gnomes would never have even gotten into the valley. Because I chose to distance myself from you, they did. You risked a fair amount in coming to find me in the first place; the least I could have done was to make certain that once you reached me, you would be safe. I failed to do that.'

'I don't blame you for what happened,' Par said quickly.

'But I do.' Walker rose, as restless as a cat, stalking to the windows and peering out into the rain. 'I live apart because I choose to. Other men in other times made me decide that it was best. But I forget sometimes that there is a difference between disassociating and hiding. There are limits to the distances we can place between ourselves and others — because the dictates of our world don't allow for absolutes.' He looked back, his skin pale against the grayness of the day. 'I was hiding myself when you came to find me. That was why you went unprotected.'

Par did not fully understand what Walker was trying to say, but he chose not to interrupt, anxious to hear more. Walker turned from the window after a moment and came back. 'I haven't been to see you since you were brought here,' he said, coming to a stop again at Par's bedside. 'Did you know that?'

Par nodded, again keeping silent. 'It wasn't that I was ignoring you. But I knew you were safe, that you would be well, and I wanted time to think. I went out into the woodlands by myself. I returned for the first time this morning. The Stors told me that you were awake, that the poison was dispelled, and I decided to come to see you.'

He broke off, his gaze shifting. When he spoke again, he chose his words carefully. 'I have been thinking about the dreams.'

There was another brief silence. Par shifted uncomfortably in the bed, already beginning to feel tired. His strength would be awhile returning. Walker seemed to recognize the problem and said, 'I won't be staying much longer.'

He sat down again slowly. 'I anticipated that you might come to me after the dreams began. You were always impulsive. I thought about the possibility, about what I would say to you.' He paused. 'We are close in ways you do not entirely understand, Par. We share the legacy of the magic; but more than that, we share a pre-ordained future that may preclude our right to any meaningful form of self-determination.' He paused again, smiling faintly. 'What I mean, Par, is that we are the children of Brin and Jair Ohmsford, heirs to the magic of the Elven house of Shannara, keepers of a trust. Remember now? It was Allanon who gave us that trust, who said to Brin when he lay dying that the Ohmsfords would safeguard the magic for generations to come until it was again needed.'

Par nodded slowly, beginning to understand now. 'You believe we might be the ones for whom the trust was intended.'

'I believe it — and I am frightened by the possibility as

170

I have never been frightened of anything in my life!' Walker's voice was a low hiss. 'I am terrified of it! I want no part of the Druids and their mysteries! I want nothing to do with the Elven magic, with its demands and its treacheries! I wish only to be left alone, to live out my life in a way I believe useful and fulfilling — and that is all I wish!'

Par let his eyes drop protectively against the fury of the other man's words. Then he smiled sadly. 'Sometimes the choice isn't ours, Walker.'

Walker Boh's reply was unexpected. 'That was what I decided.' His lean face was hard as Par looked up again. 'While I waited for you to wake, while I kept myself apart from the others, out there in the forests beyond Storlock, that was what I decided.' He shook his head. 'Events and circumstances sometimes conspire against us; if we insist on inflexibility for the purpose of maintaining our beliefs, we end up compromising ourselves, nevertheless. We salvage one set of principles only to forsake another. My staying hidden within the Wilderun almost cost you your life once. It could do so again. And what would that, in turn, cost me?'

Par shook his head. 'You cannot hold yourself responsible for the risks I choose to take, Walker. No man can hold himself up to that standard of responsibility.'

'Oh, but he can, Par. And he must when he has the means to do so. Don't you see? If I have the means, I have the responsibility to employ them.' He shook his head sadly. 'I might wish it otherwise, but it doesn't change the fact of its being.'

He straightened. 'Well, I came to tell you something, and I still haven't done so. Best that I get it over with so you can rest.' He rose, pulling the damp forest cloak back about him as if to ward off a chill. 'I am going with you,' he said simply.

Par stiffened in surprise. 'To the Hadeshorn?'

Walker Boh nodded. 'To meet with Allanon's shade — if indeed it is Allanon's shade who summons us — and to hear what it will say. I make no promises beyond that,

Par. Nor do I make any further concessions to your view of matters — other than to say that I think you were right in one respect. We cannot pretend that the world begins and ends at the boundaries we might make for it. Sometimes, we must acknowledge that it extends itself into our lives in ways we might prefer it wouldn't, and we must face up to the challenges it offers.'

His face was lined with emotions Par could only begin to imagine. 'I, too, would like to know something of what is intended for me,' he whispered.

He reached down, his pale, lean hand fastening briefly on one of Par's. 'Rest now. We have another journey ahead and only a day or two to prepare for it. Let that preparation be my responsibility. I will tell the others and come for you all when it is time to depart.'

He started away, then hesitated and smiled. 'Try to think better of me after this.'

Then he was out the door and gone, and the smile belonged now to Par.

Walker Boh proved as good as his word. Two days later he was back, appearing shortly after sunrise with horses and provisions. Par had been out of bed and walking about for the past day and a half now, and he was much recovered from his experience in Olden Moor. He was dressed and waiting on the porch of his compound with Steff and Teel when his uncle walked out of the forest shadows with his pack train in tow into a morning clouded by mist and half-light.

'There's a strange one,' Steff murmured. 'Haven't seen him for more than five minutes for the entire time we've been here. Now, back he comes, just like that. More ghost than man.' His smile was rueful and his eyes sharp.

'Walker Boh is real enough,' Par replied without looking at the Dwarf. 'And haunted by ghosts of his own.'

'Brave ghosts, I am inclined to think.'

Par glanced over now. 'He still frightens you, doesn't he?'

'Frightens me?' Steff's voice was gruff as he laughed. 'Hear him, Teel? He probes my armor for chinks!' He turned his scarred face briefly. 'No, Valeman, he doesn't frighten me anymore. He only makes me wonder.'

Coll and Morgan appeared, and the little company prepared to depart. Stars came out to see them off, ghosts of another sort, dressed in white robes and cloaked in self-imposed silence, a perpetually anxious look on their pale faces. They gathered in groups, watchful, curious, a few coming forward to help as the members of the company mounted. Walker spoke with one or two of them, his words so quiet they could be heard by no one else. Then he was aboard with the others and facing briefly back to them.

'Good fortune to us, my friends,' he said and turned his horse west toward the plains.

Good fortune, indeed, Par Ohmsford prayed silently.

CHAPTER

13

SUNLIGHT SPRAYED THE STILL SURFACE of the Myrian Lake through breaks in the distant trees, coloring the water a brilliant red-gold and causing Wren Ohmsford to squint against its glare. Farther west, the Irrybis Mountains were a jagged black tear across the horizon that separated earth and sky and cast the first of night's shadows across the vast sprawl of the Tirfing.

Another hour, maybe a bit more, and it would be dark, she thought.

She paused at the edge of the lake and, for just a moment, let the solitude of the approaching dusk settle through her. All about, the Westland stretched away into the shimmering heat of the dying summer's day with the lazy complacency of a sleeping cat, endlessly patient as it waited for the coming of night and the cool it would bring.

She was running out of time.

She cast about momentarily for the signs she had lost some hundred yards back and found nothing. He might as well have vanished into thin air. He was working hard at this cat-and-mouse game, she decided. Perhaps she was the cause.

The thought buoyed her as she pressed ahead, slipping silently through the trees along the lake front, scanning the foliage and the earth with renewed determination.

She was small and slight of build, but wiry and strong. Her skin was nut brown from weather and sun, and her ash-blond hair was almost boyish, cut short and tightly curled against her head. Her features were Elven, sharply so, the eyebrows full and deeply slanted, the ears small and pointed, the bones of her face lending it a narrow and high-cheeked look. She had hazel eyes, and they shifted restlessly as she moved, hunting.

She found his first mistake a hundred feet or so farther on, a tiny bit of broken scrub, and his second, a boot indentation against a gathering of stones, just after. She smiled in spite of herself, her confidence growing, and she hefted the smooth quarterstaff she carried in anticipation. She would have him yet, she promised.

The lake cut into the trees ahead forming a deep cove, and she was forced to swing back to her left through a thick stand of pine. She slowed, moving more cautiously. Her eyes darted. The pines gave way to a mass of thick brush that grew close against a grove of cedar. She skirted the brush, catching sight of a fresh scrape against a tree root. He's getting careless, she thought — or wants me to think him so.

She found the snare at the last moment, just as she was about to put her foot into it. Its lines ran from a carefully concealed noose back into a mass of brush and from there to a stout sapling, bent and tied. Had she not seen it, she would have been yanked from her feet and left dangling.

She found the second snare immediately after, better concealed and designed to catch her avoiding the first. She avoided that one, too, and now became even more cautious.

Even so, she almost missed seeing him in time when he swung down out of the maple not more than fifty yards farther on. Tired of trying to lose her in the woods, he had decided to finish matters in a quicker manner. He dropped silently as she slipped beneath the old shade tree, and it was only her instincts that saved her. She sprang aside as he landed, bringing the quarterstaff about and catching him alongside his great shoulders with an audible thwack. Her attacker shrugged off the blow, coming to his feet with a grunt. He was huge, a man of formidable size who appeared massive in the confines of the tiny forest clearing. He leaped at Wren, and she used the quarterstaff to vault quickly away from him. She slipped on landing, and he was on top of her with a swiftness that was astonishing. She rolled, using the staff to block him, came up underneath with the makeshift dagger and jammed the flat of its blade against his belly.

The sun-browned, bearded face shifted to find her own, and the deepset eyes glanced downward. 'You're dead, Garth,' she told him, smiling. Then her fingers came up to make the signs.

The giant Rover collapsed in mock submission before rolling over and climbing to his feet. Then he smiled, too. They brushed themselves off and stood grinning at each other in the fading light. 'I'm getting better, aren't I?' Wren asked, signing with her hands as she spoke the words.

Garth replied soundlessly, his fingers moving rapidly in the language he had taught her. 'Better, but not yet good enough,' she translated. Her smile broadened as she reached out to clasp his arm. 'Never good enough for you, I suspect. Otherwise, you would be out of a job!'

She picked up the quarterstaff and made a mock feint that caused the other to jump back in alarm. They fenced for a moment, then broke it off and started back toward the lakeshore. There was a small clearing just beyond the cove, not more than a half an hour away, that offered an ideal campsite for the night. Wren had noticed it during the hunt and made for it now.

'I'm tired and I ache and I have never felt better,' the girl said cheerfully as they walked, enjoying the last of the day's sunlight on her back, breathing in the smells of the forest, feeling alive and at peace. She sang a bit, humming some songs of the Rovers and the free life, of the ways that were and the ways that would be. Garth trailed along, a silent shadow at her back.

They found the campsite, built a fire, prepared and ate their dinner, and began trading drinks from a large leather aleskin. The night was warm and comforting, and Wren Ohmsford's thoughts wandered contentedly. They had another five days allotted to them before they were expected back. She enjoyed her outings with Garth; they were exciting and challenging. The big Rover was the best of teachers — one who let his students learn from experience. No one knew more than he did about tracking, concealment, snares, traps, and tricks of all sorts in the fine art of staying alive. He had been her mentor from the first. She had never questioned why he chose her; she had simply felt grateful that he had.

She listened momentarily to the sounds of the forest, trying to visualize out of habit what she heard moving in the dark. It was a strenuous, demanding life she led, but she could no longer imagine leading any other. She had been born a Rover girl and lived with them for all but the very early years of her youth when she had resided in the Southland hamlet of Shady Vale with her cousins, the Ohmsfords. She had been back in the Westland for almost six years now, traveling with Garth and the others, the ones who had claimed her after her parents died, taught her their ways, and showed her their life. All of the Westland belonged to the Rovers, from the Kershalt to the Irrybis, from the Valley of Rhenn to the Blue Divide. Once, it had belonged to the Elves as well. But the Elves were all gone now, disappeared. They had passed back into legend, the Rovers said. They had lost interest in the world of mortal beings and gone back into faerie.

Some disputed it. Some said the Elves were still there, hidden. She didn't know about the truth of that. She only knew that what they had abandoned was a wilderness paradise.

Garth passed her the aleskin and she drank deeply, then handed it back again. She was growing sleepy. Normally, she drank little. But she was feeling especially proud of herself tonight. It wasn't often that she got the best of Garth.

She studied him momentarily, thinking of how much he had come to mean to her. Her time in Shady Vale seemed long ago and far away, although she remembered it well enough. And the Ohmsfords, especially Par and Coll — she still thought about them. They had been her only family once. But it felt as if all that might have happened in another life. Garth was her family now, her father, mother, and brother all rolled into one, the only real family she knew anymore. She was tied to him in ways she had never been tied to anyone else. She loved him fiercely.

Nevertheless, she admitted, she sometimes felt detached from everyone, even him — orphaned and homeless, a stray shunted from one family to the next without belonging to anyone, having no idea at all who she really was. It bothered her that she didn't know more about herself and that no one else seemed to know either. She had asked often enough, but the explanations were always vague. Her father had been an Ohmsford. Her mother had been a Rover. It was unclear how they had died. It was uncertain what had become of any other members of her immediate family. It was unknown who her ancestors had been.

She possessed, in fact, but one item that offered any clue at all as to who she was. It was a small leather bag she wore tied about her neck that contained three perfectly formed stones. Elfstones, one might have thought, until one looked more closely and saw that they were just common rocks painted blue. But they had been found on her as a baby and they were all she had to suggest the heritage that might be hers.

Garth knew something about the matter, she suspected. He had told her that he didn't when she had asked once, but there was something in the way he had made his disavowal that convinced her he was hedging. Garth kept secrets better than most, but she knew him too well to be fooled completely. Sometimes, when she thought about it, she wanted to shake an answer out of him, angry and frustrated at his refusal to be as open with her in this as he was in everything else. But she kept her anger and her frustration to herself. You didn't push Garth. When he was ready to tell her, he would.

She shrugged as she always ended up doing whenever she considered the matter of her family history. What difference did it make? She was who she was, whatever her lineage. She was a Rover girl with a life that most would envy, if they bothered to be honest about it. The whole world belonged to her, because she was tied to no part of it. She could go where she wanted and do what she pleased, and that was more than most could say. Besides, many of her fellow Rovers were of dubious parentage, and you never heard them complain. They reveled in their freedom, in their ability to lay claim to anything and anyone that caught their fancy. Wasn't that good enough for her as well?

She stirred the dirt in front of her with her boot. Of course, none of them were Elven, were they? None of them had the Ohmsford-Shannara blood, with its history of Elven magic. None of them were plagued by the dreams. . . .

Her hazel eyes shifted abruptly as she became aware of Garth looking at her. She signed some innocuous response, thinking as she did so that none of the other Rovers had been as thoroughly trained to survive as she had either and wondering why.

They drank a little more of the ale built the fire up again, and rolled into their blankets. Wren lay awake longer than she wished to, caught up in the unanswered questions and unresolved puzzles that marked her life. When she did sleep, she tossed restlessly beneath her blankets, teased by fragments of dreams that slipped from her like raindrops through her fingers in a summer storm and were forgotten as quickly.

It was dawn when she came awake, and the old man was sitting across from her, poking icly at the ashes of the fire with a long stick. 'It's about time,' he snorted.

She blinked in disbelief, then started sharply out of her blankets. Garth was still sleeping, but awoke with the suddenness of her movement. She reached for the quarterstaff at her side, her thoughts scattering into questions. Where had this old man come from? How had he managed to get so close without waking them?

The old man lifted one sticklike arm reassuringly, saying, 'Don't be getting yourself all upset. Just be grateful I let you sleep.'

Garth was on his feet as well now, crouched, but to Wren's astonishment the old man began speaking to the Rover in his own language, signing, telling him what he had already told Wren, and adding that he meant no harm. Garth hesitated, obviously surprised, then sat back watchfully.

'How did you know to do that?' Wren demanded. She had never seen anyone outside the Rover camp master Garth's language.

'Oh, I know a thing or two about communication,' the old man replied gruffly, a self-satisfied smile appearing. His skin was weather-browned and seamed, his white hair and beard wispy, his lank frame scarecrow thin. A gathering of dusty gray robes hung loosely about him. 'For instance,' he said, 'I know that messages may be sent by writing on paper, by word of mouth, by use of hands ... ' He paused. 'Even by dreams.'

Wren caught her breath sharply. 'Who are you?'

'Well, now,' the old man said, 'that seems to be everyone's favorite question. My name doesn't matter. What matters is that I have been sent to tell you that you can no longer afford to ignore your dreams. Those dreams, Rover girl, come from Allanon.'

He signed as he spoke to Garth, repeating his words with the language of his fingers, as dexterous at the skill as if he had known it all his life. Wren was aware of the big Rover looking at her, but she couldn't take her eyes off the old man. 'How do you know of the dreams?' she asked him softly.

He told her who he was then, that he was Cogline, a former Druid pressed back into service because the real Druids were gone from the Four Lands and there was no other who could go to the members of the Ohmsford family and warn them that the dreams were real. He told her that Allanon's ghost had sent him to convince her of the purpose of the dreams, to persuade her that they spoke the truth, that the Four Lands were in gravest danger, that the magic was almost lost, that only the Ohmsfords could restore it, and that they must come to him on the first night of the new moon to discover what must be done. He finished by saying that he had gone first to Par Ohmsford, then to Walker Boh — recipients of the dreams as well — and now finally he had come to her.

When he was done, she sat thinking for a moment before speaking. 'The dreams have troubled me for some time now,' she confessed. 'I thought them dreams like any other and nothing more. The Ohmsford magic has never been a part of my life . . .'

'And you question whether or not you are an Ohmsford at all,' the old man interrupted. 'You are not certain, are you? If you are not an Ohmsford, then the magic has no part in your life — which might be just as well as far as you're concerned, mightn't it?'

Wren stared at him. 'How do you know all this, Cogline?' She didn't question that he was who he claimed; she accepted it because she believed that it didn't really matter one way or the other. 'How do you know so much about me?' She leaned forward, suddenly anxious. 'Do you know the truth of who I really am?'

The old man shrugged. 'It is not nearly so important to know who you are as who you might be,' he answered enigmatically. 'If you wish to learn something of that, then do as the dreams have asked. Come to the Hadeshorn and speak to Allanon.'

She eased away slowly, glancing momentarily at Garth before looking back. 'You're playing with me,' she told the old man.

'Perhaps.'

'Why?'

'Oh, quite simple, really. If you are intrigued enough by what I say, you might agree to do as I ask and come with me. I chose to chastise and berate the other members of your family. I thought I might try a new approach with you. Time grows short, and I am just an old man. The new moon is only six days distant now. Even on horseback, it will require at least four days to reach the Hadeshorn — five, if I am to make the journey.'

He was signing everything he said, and now Garth made a quick response. The old man laughed. 'Will I choose to make the journey? Yes, by golly, I think I will. I have gone about a shade's business for some weeks now. I believe I am entitled to know the whole of what the culmination of that business might be.' He paused, thoughtful. 'Besides, I am not altogether sure I have been given a choice . . . ' He trailed off.

Wren glanced eastward to where the sun was a pale white ball of fire resting atop the horizon, screened by clouds and mist, its warmth still distant. Gulls swooped across the mirrored waters of the Myrian, fishing. The stillness of the early morning let her thoughts whisper undisturbed within her.

'What did my cousin . . . ?' she began, then caught herself. The word didn't sound right when she spoke it. It distanced her from him in a way she didn't care for. 'What did Par say that he was going to do?' she finished.

'He said he was going to think the matter over,' the old man replied. 'He and his brother. They were together when I found them.'

'And my uncle?'

The other shrugged. 'The same.'

But there was something in his eyes that said otherwise. Wren shook her head. 'You are playing with me again. What did they say?'

The old man's eyes narrowed. 'Rover girl, you try my patience. I haven't the energy to sit about and repeat entire conversations just so you can use that as an excuse for making your decision in this matter. Haven't you a mind of your own? If they go, they will do so for their own reasons and not for any you might provide. Shouldn't you do likewise?'

Wren Ohmsford was a rock. 'What did they say?' she repeated once again, measuring each word carefully before she spoke it.

'What they chose!' the other snapped, his fingers flicking his responses angrily now at Garth, though his eyes never left Wren's. 'Am I a parrot to repeat the phrases of others for your amusement?'

He glared at her a moment, then threw up his hands. 'Very well! Here is the whole of it, then! Young Par, his brother with him, had been chased from Varfleet by the Federation for making use of the magic to tell stories of their family history and the Druids. He thought to go home when I last saw him, to think about the dreams a bit. He will have discovered by now that he cannot do so, that his home is in Federation hands and his parents — your own of sorts, once upon a time — are prisoners!'

Wren started in surprise, but the old man ignored her. 'Walker Boh is another matter. He thinks himself severed from the Ohmsford family. He lives alone and prefers it that way. He wants nothing to do with his family and the world at large and Druids in particular. He thinks that only he knows the proper uses of magic, that the rest of us who possess some small skill are incapable of reason! He forgets who taught him what! He . . . '

'You,' Wren interjected.

'. . . charges about on some self-proclaimed mission of . . .' He stopped short. 'What? What did you say?'

'You,' she repeated, her eyes locking on his. 'You were his teacher once, weren't you?'

There was a moment of silence as the sharp old eyes studied her appraisingly. 'Yes, girl. I was. Are you satisfied now? Is that the revelation you sought? Or do you require something more?'

He had forgotten to sign what he was saying, but Garth seemed to have read his lips in any case. He caught Wren's attention, nodding in approval. Always try to learn something of your adversary that he doesn't want you to know, he had taught her. It gives you an edge.

183

'So he isn't going then, is he?' she pressed. 'Walker, I mean.'

'Ha!' the old man exclaimed in satisfaction. 'Just when I conclude what a smart girl you are, you prove me wrong!' He cocked one eyebrow on his seamed face. 'Walker Boh says he isn't going, and he thinks he isn't going. But he is! The young one, too — Par. That's the way it will be. Things work out the way we least expect them to sometimes. Or maybe that's just the Druid magic at work, twisting those promises and oaths we so recklessly take, steering us where we didn't think we could ever be made to go.' He shook his head in amusement. 'Always was a baffling trick.'

He drew his robes about him and bent forward. 'Now what is it to be with you, little Wren? Brave bird or timid flyaway — which will you be?'

She smiled in spite of herself. 'Why not both, depending on what is needed?' she asked.

He grunted impatiently. 'Because the situation calls for one or the other. Choose.'

Wren let her eyes shift briefly to Garth, then off into the woods, slipping deep into the shadows where the still distant sunlight had not yet penetrated. Her thoughts and questions of the previous night came back to her, darting through her mind with harrying insistence. Well, she could go if she chose, she knew. The Rovers wouldn't stop her, not even Garth — though he would insist on going as well. She could confront the shade of Allanon. She could speak with the shade of a legend, a man many said never existed at all. She could ask the questions of him she had carried about with her for so many years now, perhaps learn some of the answers, possibly come to an understanding about herself that she had lacked before. A rather ambitious task, she thought. An intriguing one.

She felt sunlight slipping across the bridge of her nose, tickling her. It would mean a reunion with Par and Coll and Walker Boh — her other family that maybe wasn't really family at all. She pursed her lips thoughtfully. She might enjoy that.

But it would also mean confronting the reality of her dreams — or at least a shade's version of that reality. And that could mean a change in the course of her life, a life with which she was perfectly content. It could mean disruption of that life, an involvement in matters which she might better avoid.

Her mind raced. She could feel the presence of the little bag with the painted stones pressing against her breast as if to remind her of what might be. She knew the stories of the Ohmsfords and the Druids, too, and she was wary.

Then, unexpectedly, she found herself smiling. Since when had being wary ever stopped her from doing anything? Shades! This was an unlocked door that begged to be opened! How could she live with herself if she passed it up?

The old man interrupted her thoughts. 'Rover girl, I grow weary. These ageing bones require movement to keep from locking up. Let me have your decision. Or do you, like the others in your family, require untold amounts of time to puzzle this matter through?'

Wren glanced over at Garth, cocking one eyebrow. The giant Rover's nod was barely perceptible.

She looked back at Cogline. 'You are so testy, old grandfather!' she chided. 'Where is your patience?'

'Gone with my youth, child,' he said, his voice unexpectedly soft. His hands folded before him. 'Now what's it to be?'

She smiled. 'The Hadeshorn and Allanon,' she answered. 'What did you expect?'

But the old man did not reply.

CHAPTER

14

FIVE DAYS LATER, with the sun exploding streamers of violet and red fire all across the western horizon in the kind of day's end fireworks display that only summer provides, Wren, Garth, and the old man who said he was Cogline reached the base of the Dragon's Teeth and the beginning of the winding, narrow rock trail that led into the Valley of Shale and the Hadeshorn.

Par Ohmsford was the first to see them. He had gone up the trail a few hundred yards to a rock shelf where he could sit and look out over the sweep of Callahorn south and be by himself. He had arrived with Coll, Morgan, Walker, Steff, and Teel one day earlier, and his patience at waiting for the arrival of the first night of the new moon had begun to wear a little thin. He was immersed mostly in his admiration for the majesty of the sunset when he caught sight of the odd trio as they rode their horses out of the westward glare from a screen of poplar trees and started toward him. He came to his feet slowly, refusing to trust his eyes at first. Then, having determined that he was not mistaken, he leaped from his perch and charged back down the trail to alert the others of his little company who were camped immediately below.

Wren got there almost before he did. Her sharp Elven eyes caught sight of him at about the same time he saw her. Acting on impulse and leaving her companions to

follow as best they could, she spurred her horse ahead
recklessly, came charging into camp, vaulted from the
saddle before her mount was fully checked, rushed up to
Par with a wild yell, and hugged him with such enthusiasm that he was almost knocked from his feet. When she
was done with him, she gave the same reception to an
astonished but delighted Coll. Walker got a more reserved
kiss on the cheek and Morgan, whom she barely remembered from her childhood, a handshake and a nod.

While the three Ohmsford siblings — for they seemed
such, despite the fact that Wren wasn't a true sister —
traded hugs and words of greeting, those with them stood
around uncomfortably and sized up one another with
wary glances. Most of the sizing up was reserved for
Garth, who was twice as big as any of the rest of them.
He was dressed in the brightly colored clothing common
to the Rovers, and the garishness of his garb made him
seem larger still. He met the stares of the others without
discomfort, his gaze steady and implacable. Wren remembered him after a moment and began the required series
of introductions. Par followed with Steff and Teel.
Cogline hung back from the others; since everyone
seemed to know who he was, in any case, no formal
introduction was attempted. There were nods and hand-
shakes all around, courtesies observed as expected, but
the wariness in the faces of most did not subside. When
they all moved over to the fire that formed the center of
the little campsite to partake of the dinner that the
Dwarves had been in the process of preparing when
Wren and her companions had appeared, the newly
formed company of nine quickly fragmented into groups.
Steff and Teel turned their attention to the completion of
the meal, mute as they hovered over the pots and cooking
fire, Walker withdrew to a patch of shade under a
scrawny pine, and Cogline disappeared into the rocks
without a word to anyone. He was so quiet about it that
he was gone almost before they realized it. But Cogline
was not really considered a part of the company in any
case, so no one much bothered about it. Par, Coll, Wren,

and Morgan clustered together by the horses, unsaddling them and rubbing them down, and talked about old times, old friends, the places they had been, the things they had seen, and the vicissitudes of life.

'You are much grown, Wren,' Coll marveled. 'Not at all the broomstick little girl I remember when you left us.'

'A rider of horses, wild as the wind! No boundaries for you!' Par laughed, throwing up his hands in a gesture meant to encompass the whole of the land.

Wren grinned back. 'I live a better life than the lot of you, resting on your backsides singing old tales and rousting tired dogs. The Westland's a good country for free-spirited things, you know.' Then her grin faded. 'The old man, Cogline, told me of what's happened in the Vale. Jaralan and Mirianna were my parents for a time, too, and I care for them still. Prisoners, he said. Have you heard anything of them?'

Par shook his head. 'We have been running ever since Varfleet.'

'I am sorry, Par.' There was genuine discomfort in her eyes. 'The Federation does its best to make all of our lives miserable. Even the Westland has its share of soldiers and administrative lackeys, though it's country they mostly ignore. The Rovers know how to avoid them in any case. If need be, you would be welcome to join us.'

Par gave her another quick hug. 'Best that we see how this business of the dreams turns out first,' he whispered.

They ate a dinner of fried meats, fresh-baked hard bread, stewed vegetables, cheese and nuts, and washed it all down with ale and water while they watched the sun disappear beneath the horizon. The food was good, and everyone said so, much to Steff's pleasure, for he had prepared the better part of it. Cogline remained absent, but the others began talking a bit more freely among themselves, all but Teel, who never seemed to want to speak. As far as Par knew, he was the only one besides Steff to whom the Dwarf girl had ever said anything.

When the dinner was complete, Steff and Teel took charge of cleaning the dishes, and the others drifted away in ones and twos as the dusk settled slowly into night. While Coll and Morgan went down to a spring a quarter-mile off to draw fresh water, Par found himself ambling back up the trail that led into the mountains and the Valley of Shale in the company of Wren and the giant Garth.

'Have you been back there yet?' Wren asked as they walked, nodding in the direction of the Hadeshorn.

Par shook his head. 'It's several hours in and no one's much wanted to hurry matters along. Even Walker has refused to go there before the scheduled time.' He glanced skyward where clusters of stars dotted the heavens in intricate patterns and a small, almost invisible crescent moon hung low against the horizon north. 'Tomorrow night,' he said.

Wren didn't reply. They walked on in silence until they reached the shelf of rock that Par had occupied earlier that day. There they stopped, looking back over the country south.

'You've had the dreams, too?' Wren asked him then and went on to describe her own. When he nodded, she said, 'What do you think?'

Par eased himself down on the rock, the other two sitting with him. 'I think that ten generations of Ohmsfords have lived their lives since the time of Brin and Jair, waiting for this to happen. I think that the magic of the Elven house of Shannara, Ohmsford magic now, is something more than we realize. I think Allanon — or his shade, at least — will tell us what that something is.' He paused. 'I think it may turn out to be something wondrous — and something terrible.'

He was aware of her staring at him with those intense hazel eyes, and he shrugged apologetically. 'I don't mean to be overdramatic. That's just the sense I have of things.'

She translated his comments automatically for Garth, who gave no indication of what he thought. 'You and Walker have some use of the magic,' she said quietly. 'I have none. What of that?'

He shook his head. 'I'm not sure. Morgan's magic is

stronger than mine these days and he wasn't called.' He went on to tell her about their confrontation with the Shadowen and the Highlander's discovery of the magic that had lain dormant in the Sword of Leah. 'I find myself wondering why the dreams didn't command him to appear instead of me, for all the use the wishsong has been.'

'But you don't know for certain how strong your magic is, Par,' she said quietly. 'You should remember from the stories that none of the Ohmsfords, from Shea on down, fully understood when they began their quests the uses of the Elven magic. Might it not be the same with you?'

It might, he realized with a shiver. He cocked his head. 'Or you, Wren. What of you?'

'No, no, Par Ohmsford. I am a simple Rover girl with none of the blood that carries the magic from generation to generation in me.' She laughed. 'I'm afraid I must make do with a bag filled with make-believe Elfstones!'

He laughed as well, remembering the little leather bag with the painted rocks that she had guarded so carefully as a child. They traded life stories for a time, telling each other what they had been doing, where they had been, and whom they had encountered on their journeys. They were relaxed, much as if their separation had been but a few weeks rather than years. Wren was responsible for that, Par decided. She had put him immediately at ease. He was struck by the inordinate amount of confidence that she exhibited in herself, such a wild, free girl, obviously content with her Rover life, seemingly unshackled by demands or constraints that might hold her back. She was strong both inwardly and outwardly, and he admired her greatly for it. He found himself wishing that he could display but a fraction of her pluck.

'How do you find Walker?' she asked him after a time.

'Distant,' he said at once. 'Still haunted by demons that I cannot begin to understand. He talks about his mistrust of the Elven magic and the Druids, yet seems to have magic of his own that he uses freely enough. I don't really understand him.'

Wren relayed his comments to Garth, and the giant Rover responded with a brief signing. Wren looked at him sharply, then said to Par, 'Garth says that Walker is frightened.'

Par looked surprised. 'How does he know that?'

'He just does. Because he is deaf, he works harder at using his other senses. He detects other people's feelings more quickly than you or I would — even those that are kept hidden.'

Par nodded. 'Well, he happens to be exactly right in this instance. Walker is frightened. He told me so himself. He says he's frightened of what this business with Allanon might mean. Odd, isn't it? I have trouble imagining anything frightening Walker Boh.'

Wren signed to Garth, but the giant merely shrugged. They sat back in silence for a time, thinking separate thoughts. Then Wren said, 'Did you know that the old man, Cogline, was once Walker's teacher?'

Par looked at her sharply. 'Did he tell you that?'

'I tricked it from him, mostly.'

'Teacher of what, Wren? Of the magic?'

'Of something.' Her dark features turned introspective momentarily, her gaze distant. 'There is much between those two that, like Walker's fear, is kept hidden. I think.'

Par, though he didn't say so, was inclined to agree.

The members of the little company slept undisturbed that night in the shadow of the Dragon's Teeth, but by dawn they were awake again and restless. Tonight was the first night of the new moon, the night they were to meet with the shade of Allanon. Impatiently, they went about their business. They ate their meals without tasting them. They spoke little to one another, moving about uneasily, finding small tasks that would distract them from thinking further on what lay ahead. It was a clear, cloudless day filled with warm summer smells and lazy sunshine, the kind of day that, under other circumstances, might have been enjoyed, but which on this occasion simply seemed endless.

Cogline reappeared about midday, wandering down out of the mountains like some tattered prophet of doom. He looked dusty and unkempt as he came up to them, his hair wild, his eyes shadowed from lack of sleep. He told them that all was in readiness — whatever that meant — and that he would come for them after nightfall. Be ready, he advised. He refused to say anything more, though pressed by the Ohmsfords to do so, and disappeared back the way he had come.

'What do you suppose he is doing up there?' Coll muttered to the others as the ragged figure dwindled into a tiny black speck in the distance and then into nothing at all.

The sun worked its way westward as if dragging chains in its wake, and the members of the little company retreated further into themselves. The enormity of what was about to happen began to emerge in their unspoken thoughts, a specter of such size that it was frightening to contemplate. Even Walker Boh, who might have been assumed to be more at home with the prospect of encountering shades and spirits, withdrew into himself like a badger into its hole and became unapproachable.

Nevertheless, when it was nearing midafternoon, Par happened on his uncle while wandering the cooler stretches of the hills surrounding the springs. They slowed on coming together, then stopped and stood looking at each other awkwardly.

'Do you think he will really come?' Par asked finally.

Walker's pale face was shadowed beneath the protective hood of his cloak, making his face difficult to read. 'He will come,' his uncle said.

Par thought a moment, then said, 'I don't know what to expect.'

Walker shook his head. 'It doesn't matter, Par. Whatever you choose to expect, it won't be enough. This meeting won't be like anything you might envision, I promise you. The Druids have always been very good at surprises.'

'You suspect the worst, don't you?'

'I suspect . . . ' He trailed off without finishing.

'Magic,' said Par.

The other frowned.

'Druid magic — that's what you think we will see tonight, don't you? I hope you are right. I hope that it sweeps and resounds and that it opens all the doors that have been closed to us and lets us see what magic can really do!'

Walker Boh's smile, when it finally overcame his astonishment, was ironic. 'Some doors are better left closed,' he said softly. 'You would do well to remember that.'

He put his hand on his nephew's arm for a moment, then continued silently on his way.

The afternoon crawled toward evening. When the sun at last completed its long journey west and began to slip beneath the horizon, the members of the little company filtered back to the campsite for the evening meal. Morgan was garrulous, an obvious sign of nerves with him, and talked incessantly of magic and swords and all sorts of wild happenings that Par hoped would never be. The others were mostly silent, eating without comment and casting watchful glances northward toward the mountains. Teel wouldn't eat at all, sitting off by herself in a gathering of shadows, the mask that covered her face like a wall that separated her from everyone. Even Steff let her alone.

Darkness descended and the stars began to flicker into view, a scattering here and there at first, and then the sky was filled with them. No moon showed itself; it was the promised time when the sun's pale sister wore black. Daylight's sounds faded and night's remained hushed. The cooking fire crackled and snapped in the silence as conversation lagged. One or two smoked, and the air was filled with the pungent smell. Morgan took out the bright length of the Sword of Leah and began to polish it absently. Wren and Garth fed and curried the horses. Walker moved up the trail a short distance and stood

staring into the mountains. Others sat lost in thought.
Everyone waited.

It was midnight when Cogline returned for them. The old man appeared out of the shadows like a ghost, materializing so suddenly that they all started. No one, not even Walker, had seen him coming.

'It is time,' he announced.

They came to their feet voicelessly and followed him. He took them up the trail from their campsite into the gradually thickening shadows of the Dragon's Teeth. Although the stars shone brightly overhead when they started out, the mountains soon began to close about, leaving the little company shrouded in blackness. Cogline did not slow; he seemed to possess cat's eyes. His charges struggled to keep pace. Par, Coll, and Morgan were closest to the old man, Wren and Garth came next, Steff and Teel behind them, and Walker Boh brought up the rear. The trail steepened quickly after they reached the beginning peaks, and they moved through a narrow defile that opened like a pocket into the mountains. It was silent here, so still that they could hear one another breathe as they labored upward.

The minutes slipped away. Boulders and cliff walls hindered their passage, and the trail wound about like a snake. Loose rock carpeted the whole of the mountains, and the climbers had to scramble over it. Still Cogline pressed on. Par stumbled and scraped his knees, finding the loose rock as sharp as glass. Much of it was a strange, mirrorlike black that reminded him of coal. He scooped up a small piece out of curiosity and stuck it in his pocket.

Then abruptly the mountains split apart before them, and they stepped out onto the rim of the Valley of Shale. It was little more than a broad, shallow depression strewn with crushed stone that glistened with the same mirrored blackness as the rock Par had pocketed. Nothing grew in the valley; it was stripped of life. There was a lake at its center, its greenish black waters moving in sluggish swirls in the windless expanse.

Cogline stopped momentarily and looked back at them. 'The Hadeshorn,' he whispered. 'Home for the spirits of the ages, for the Druids of the past.' His weathered old face had an almost reverent look to it. Then he turned away and started them down into the valley.

Except for the huff of their breathing and the rasp of their boots on the loose rock, the valley, too, was wrapped in silence. Echoes of their movements played in the stillness like children in the slow heat of a midsummer's day. Eyes darted watchfully, seeking ghosts where there were none to find, imagining life in every shadow. It was strangely warm here, the heat of the day captured and held in the airless bowl through the cool of the night. Par felt a trickle of sweat begin to run down his back.

Then they were on the valley floor, closely bunched as they made their way toward the lake. They could see the movement of the waters more clearly now, the way the swirls worked against each other, haphazard, unbidden. They could hear the rippling of tiny waves as they lapped. There was the pungent scent of things ageing and decayed.

They were still several dozen yards from the water's edge when Cogline brought them to a halt, both hands lifting in caution. 'Stand fast, now. Come no closer. The waters of the Hadeshorn are death to mortals, poison to the touch!' He crouched down and put a finger to his lips as if hushing a child.

They did as they were bidden, children indeed before the power they sensed sleeping there. They could feel it, all of them, a palpable thing that hung in the air like wood smoke from a fire. They remained where they were, alert, anxious, filled with a mix of wonder and hesitancy. No one spoke. The star-filled sky stretched away endlessly overhead, canopied from horizon to horizon, and it seemed as if the whole of the heavens was focused on that valley, that lake, and the nine of them who kept watch.

At last Cogline lifted from his crouch and came back to them, beckoning with birdlike movements of his hands to draw them close about him. When they were gathered in a knot that locked them shoulder to shoulder, he spoke.

'Allanon will come just before dawn.' The sharp old eyes regarded them solemnly. 'He wishes me to speak with you first. He is no longer what he was in life. He is just a shade now. His purchase in this world is but the blink of an eye. Each time he crosses over from the spirit world, it requires tremendous effort. He can stay only a little while. What time he is allotted he must use wisely. He will use that time to tell you of the need he has of you. He has left it to me to explain to you why that need exists. I am to tell you of the Shadowen.'

'You've spoken to him?' asked Walker Boh quickly.

Cogline said nothing.

'Why wait until now to tell us about the Shadowen?' Par was suddenly irritated. 'Why now, Cogline, when you could have done so before?'

The old man shook his head, his face both reproving and sympathetic. 'It was not permitted, youngster. Not until all of you had been brought together.'

'Games!' Walker muttered and shook his head in disgust.

The old man ignored him. 'Think what you like, only listen. This is what Allanon would have me tell you of the Shadowen. They are an evil beyond all imagining. They are not the rumors or the tall tales that men would have them be, but creatures as real as you and I. They are born of a circumstance that Allanon in all his wisdom and planning did not foresee. When he passed from the world of mortal men, Allanon believed the age of magic at an end and a new age begun. The Warlock Lord was no more. The Demons of the old world of faerie were again imprisoned within the Forbidding. The Ildatch was destroyed. Paranor was gone into history and the last of the Druids was about to go with it. It seemed the need for magic was past.'

'The need is never past,' Walker said quietly.

Again, the old man ignored him. 'The Shadowen are an aberration. They are a magic that grew out of the use of other magics, a residue of what has gone before. They began as a seeding that lay dormant within the Four Lands, undetected during the time of Allanon, a seeding that came to life only after the Druids and their protective powers were gone. No one could have known they were there, not even Allanon. They were the leavings of magics come and gone, and they were as invisible as dust on a pathway.'

'Wait a minute!' Par interjected. 'What are you saying, Cogline? That the Shadowen are just bits and pieces of some stray magic?'

Cogline took a deep breath, his hands locking before him. 'Valeman, I told you once before that for all the use you have of magic, you still know little about it. Magic is as much a force of nature as the fire at the earth's core, the tidal waves that sweep out of the ocean, the winds that flatten forests or the famine that starves nations. It does not happen and then disappear without effect! Think! What of Wil Ohmsford and his use of the Elfstones when his Elven blood no longer permitted such use? It left as its residue the wishsong that found life in your ancestors! Was that an inconsequential magic? All uses of the magic have effects beyond the immediate. And all are significant.'

'Which magic was it that created the Shadowen?' asked Coll, his blocky face impassive.

The old man shook his wispy head. 'Allanon does not know. There is no way of being certain. It could have happened at any time during the lives of Shea Ohmsford and his descendants. There was always magic in use in those times, much of it evil. The Shadowen could have been born of any part of it.'

He paused. 'The Shadowen were nothing at first. They were the debris of magic spent. Somehow they survived, their presence unknown. It was not until Allanon and Paranor were gone that they emerged into the Four Lands and began to gain strength. There was a vacuum in the order of things by then. A void must be filled in all events, and the Shadowen were quick to fill this one.'

'I don't understand,' Par said quickly. 'What sort of vacuum do you mean?'

'And why didn't Allanon foresee it happening?' added Wren.

The old man held up his fingers and began crooking them downward one by one as he spoke. 'Life has always been cyclical. Power comes and goes; it takes different forms. Once, it was science that gave mankind power. Of late, it has been magic. Allanon foresaw the return of science as a means to progress — especially with the passing of the Druids and Paranor. That was the age that would be. But the development of science failed to materialize quickly enough to fill the vacuum. Partly this was because of the Federation. The Federation kept the old ways intact; it decried the use of any form of power but its own — and its own was primitive and military. It expanded its influence throughout the Four Lands until all were subject to its dictates. The Elves had an effect on matters as well; for reasons we still don't know they disappeared. They were a balancing force, the last people of the faerie world of old. Their presence was necessary, if the transition from magic to science was to be made fault-lessly.'

He shook his head. 'Yet even had the Elves remained in the world of men and the Federation been less a presence, the Shadowen might have come alive. The vacuum was there the moment the Druids passed away. There was no help for it.' He sighed. 'Allanon did not foresee as he should have. He did not anticipate an aberration on the order of the Shadowen. He did what he could to keep the Four Lands safe while he was alive — and he kept himself alive for as long as was possible.'

'Too little of each, it seems,' Walker said pointedly.

Cogline looked at him, and the anger in his voice was palpable. 'Well, Walker Boh. Perhaps one day you will have an opportunity to demonstrate that you can do it better.'

There was a strained moment of silence as the two faced each other in the blackness. Then Cogline looked away. 'You need to understand what the Shadowen are. The Shadowen are parasites. They live off mortal creatures. They are a magic that feeds on living things. They enter them, absorb them, become them. But for some reason the results are not always the same. Young Par, think of the woodswoman that you and Coll encountered at the time of our first meeting. She was a Shadowen of the more obvious sort, a once-mortal creature infected, a ravaged thing that could no more help herself than an animal made mad. But the little girl on Toffer Ridge, do you remember her?'

His fingers brushed Par's cheek lightly. Instantly, the Valeman was filled with the memory of that monster to whom the Spider Gnomes had given him. He could feel her stealing against him, begging him, 'hug me, hug me,' desperate to make him embrace her. He flinched, shaken by the impact of the memory.

Cogline's hand closed firmly about his arm. 'That, too, was a Shadowen, but one that could not be so easily detected. They appear to varying extents as we do, hidden within human form. Some become grotesque in appearance and behavior; those you can readily identify. Others are more difficult to recognize.'

'But why are there some of one kind and some of the other?' Par asked uncertainly.

Cogline's brow furrowed. 'Once again, Allanon does not know. The Shadowen have kept their secret even from him.'

The old man looked away for a long moment, then back again. His face was a mask of despair. 'This is like a plague. The sickness is spread until the number infected multiplies impossibly. Any of the Shadowen can spread the disease. Their magic gives them the means to overcome almost any defense. The more of them there are, the stronger they become. What would you do to stop a plague where the source was unknown, the symptoms undetectable until after they had taken root, and the cure a mystery?'

The members of the little company glanced at one another uneasily in the silence that followed.

Finally, Wren said, 'Do they have a purpose in what they do, Cogline? A purpose beyond simply infecting living things? Do they think as you and I or are they ... mindless?'

Par stared at the girl in undisguised admiration. It was the best question any of them had asked. He should have been the one to ask it.

Cogline was rubbing his hands together slowly. 'They think as you and I, Rover girl, and they most certainly do have a purpose in what they do. But that purpose remains unclear.'

'They would subvert us,' Morgan offered sharply. 'Surely that's purpose enough.'

But Cogline shook his head. 'They would do more still, I think.'

And abruptly Par found himself recalling the dreams that Allanon had sent, the visions of a nightmarish world in which everything was blackened and withered and life was reduced to something barely recognizable. Reddened eyes blinked like bits of fire, and shadow forms flitted through a haze of ash and smoke.

This is what the Shadowen would do, he realized.

But how could they bring such a vision to pass?

He glanced without thinking at Wren and found his question mirrored in her eyes. He recognized what she was thinking instinctively. He saw it reflected in Walker Boh's eyes as well. They had shared the dreams and those dreams bound them, so much so that for an instant their thinking was the same.

Cogline's face lifted slightly, pulling free of the darkness that shaded it. 'Something guides the Shadowen,' he whispered. 'There is power here that transcends anything we have ever known ... '

He let the sentence trail off, ragged and unfinished, as if unable to give voice to any ending. His listeners looked at one another.

'What are we to do?' Wren asked finally.

The old man rose wearily. 'Why, what we came here to do, Rover girl — listen to what Allanon would tell us.'

He moved stiffly away, and no one called after him.

CHAPTER

15

THEY MOVED APART from each other after that, drifting away one by one, finding patches of solitude in which to think their separate thoughts. Eyes wandered restlessly across the valley's glistening carpet of black rock, always returning to the Hadeshorn, carefully searching the sluggishly churning waters for signs of some new movement.

There was none.

Perhaps nothing is going to happen, Par thought. Perhaps it was all a lie after all.

He felt his chest constrict with mixed feelings of disappointment and relief and he forced his thoughts elsewhere. Coll was less than a dozen paces away, but he refused to look at him. He wanted to be alone. There were things that needed thinking through, and Coll would only distract him.

Funny how much effort he had put into distancing himself from his brother since this journey had begun, he thought suddenly. Perhaps it was because he was afraid for him . . .

Once again, this time angrily, he forced his thoughts elsewhere. Cogline. Now there was an enigma of no small size. Who was this old man who seemed to know so much about everything? A failed Druid, he claimed. Allanon's messenger, he said. But those brief descriptions didn't seem nearly complete enough. Par was certain that there was more to him than what he claimed. There was a history of events behind his relationships with Allanon and Walker Boh that was hidden from the rest of them. Allanon would not have gone to a failed Druid for assistance, not even in the most desperate of circumstances. There was a reason for Cogline's involvement with this gathering beyond what any of them knew.

He glanced warily at the old man who stood an uncomfortable number of feet closer than the rest of them to the waters of the Hadeshorn. He knew all about the Shadowen, somehow. He had spoken more than once with Allanon, somehow again. He was the only living human being to have done so since the Druid's death three hundred years ago. Par thought a moment about the stories of Cogline in the time of Brin Ohmsford — a half-crazed old man then, wielding magic against the Mord Wraiths like some sort of broom against dust — that's the picture the tales conjured up. Well, he wasn't like that now. He was controlled. Cranky and eccentric, yes — but mostly controlled. He knew what he was about — enough so that he didn't seem particularly pleased with any of it. He hadn't said that, of course. But Par wasn't blind.

There was a flash of light from somewhere far off in the night skies, a momentary brightness that winked away instantly and was gone. A life ended, a new life begun, his mother used to say. He sighed. He hadn't thought of his parents much since the flight out of Varfleet. He felt a twinge of guilt. He wondered if they were all right. He wondered if he would see them again.

His jaw tightened with determination. Of course he would see them again! Things would work out. Allanon would have answers to give him — about the uses of the magic of the wishsong, the reasons for the dreams, what to do about the Shadowen and the Federation ... all of it.

Allanon would know.

Time slipped away, minutes into hours, the night steadily working its way toward dawn Par moved over to talk with Coll, needing now to be close to his brother. The others shifted, stretched, and moved about uneasily. Eyes grew heavy and senses dulled.

Far east, the first faint twinges of the coming dawn appeared against the dark line of the horizon.

He's not coming, Par thought dismally.

And in answer the waters of the Hadeshorn heaved upward, and the valley shuddered as if something beneath it had come awake. Rock shifted and grated with the movement, and the members of the little company went into a protective crouch. The lake began to boil, the waters to thrash, and spray shot skyward with a sharp hiss. Voices cried out, inhuman and filled with longing. They rose out of the earth, straining against bonds that were invisible to the nine gathered in the valley, but which they could all too readily imagine. Walker's arms flung wide against the sound, scattering bits of silver dust that flared in a protective curtain. The others cupped their ears protectively, but nothing could shut the sound away.

Then the earth began to rumble, thunder that rolled out of its depths and eclipsed even the cries. Cogline's stick-thin arm lifted, pointing rigidly to the lake. The Hadeshorn exploded into a whirlpool, waters churning madly, and from out of the depths rose . . .

'Allanon!' Par cried out excitedly against the fury of sounds.

It was the Druid. They knew him instantly, all of them. They remembered him from the tales of three centuries gone; they recognized him in their heart of hearts, that secret innermost whisper of certainty. He rose into the night air, light flaring about him, released somehow from the waters of the Hadeshorn. He lifted free of the lake to stand upon its surface, a shade from some netherworld, cast in transparent gray, shimmering faintly against the dark. He was cloaked and cowled from head to foot, a tall and powerful image of the man that once was, his long, sharp-featured, bearded face turned toward them, his penetrating eyes sweeping clear their defenses, laying bare their lives for examination and judgment.

Par Ohmsford shivered.

The churning of the waters subsided, the rumbling

ceased, the wails died into a hush that hung suspended across the expanse of the valley. The shade moved toward them, seemingly without haste, as if to discredit Cogline's word that it could stay only briefly in the world of men. Its eyes never left their own. Par had never been so frightened. He wanted to run. He wanted to flee for his life, but he stood rooted to the spot, unable to move.

The shade came to the water's edge and stopped. From somewhere deep within their minds, the members of the little company heard it speak.

— I am Allanon that was —

A murmur of voices filled the air, voices of things no longer living, echoing the shade's words.

— I have called you to me in your dreams — Par, Wren, and Walker. Children of Shannara, you have been summoned to me. The wheel of time comes around again — for rebirthing of the magic, for honoring the trust that was given you, for beginning and ending many things —

The voice, deep and sonorous within them, grew rough with feelings that scraped the bone.

— The Shadowen come. They come with a promise of destruction, sweeping over the Four Lands with the certainty of day after night —

There was a pause as the shade's lean hands wove a vision of his words through the fabric of the night air, a tapestry that hung momentarily in brilliant colors against the misted black. The dreams he had sent them came alive, sketches of nightmarish madness. Then they faded and were gone. The voice whispered soundlessly.

— It shall be so, if you do not heed —

Par felt the words reverberate through his body like a rumble from the earth. He wanted to look at the others, wanted to see what was on their faces but the voice of the shade held him spellbound.

Not so Walker Boh. His uncle's voice was as chilling as the shade's. 'Tell us what you would, Allanon! Be done with it!'

Allanon's flat gaze shifted to the dark figure and settled on him. Walker Boh staggered back a step in spite of himself. The shade pointed.

— Destroy the Shadowen! They subvert the people of the Races, creeping into their bodies, taking their forms as they choose, becoming them, using them, turning them into the misshapen giant and maddened woodswoman you have already encountered — and into things worse still. No one prevents it. No one will, if not you —

'But what are we supposed to do?' Par asked at once, almost without thinking.

The shade had been substantial when it had first appeared, a ghost that had taken on again the fullness of life. But already the lines and shadings were beginning to pale, and he who was once Allanon shimmered with the translucent and ephemeral inconsistency of smoke.

— Shannara child. There are balances to be restored if the Shadowen are to be destroyed — not for a time, not in this age only, but forever. Magic is needed. Magic to put an end to the misuse of life. Magic to restore the fabric of man's existence in the mortal world. That magic is your heritage — yours, Wren's, and Walker's. You must acknowledge it and embrace it —

The Hadeshorn was beginning to roil again, and the members of the little company fell back before its hiss and spray — all but Cogline who stood rock still before the others, his head bowed upon his frail chest.

The shade of Allanon seemed to swell suddenly against the night, rising up before them like a giant. The robes spread wide. The shade's eyes fixed on Par, and the Valeman felt the stab of an invisible finger penetrate his breast.

— Par Ohmsford, bearer of the wishsong's promise, I charge you with recovering the Sword of Shannara. Only through the Sword can truth be revealed and only through truth shall the Shadowen be overcome. Take up the Sword, Par; wield it according to the dictates of your heart — the truth of the Shadowen shall be yours to discover —

The eyes shifted.

— Wren, child of hidden, forgotten lives, yours is a

206

charge of equal importance. There can be no healing of
the Lands or of their people without the Elves of faerie.
Find them and return them to the world of men. Find
them, Rover girl. Only then can the sickness end —

The Hadeshorn erupted with a booming cough.

— And Walker Boh, you of no belief, seek that belief —
and the understanding necessary to sustain it. Search out
the last of the curatives that is needed to give life back to
the Lands. Search out disappeared Paranor and restore
the Druids —

There was astonishment mirrored in the faces of all,
and for an instant it smothered the shouts of disbelief that
struggled to surface. Then everyone was yelling at once,
the words tumbling over one another as each sought to
make himself heard above the tumult. But the cries disappeared instantly as the shade's arms came up in a
sweep that caused the earth to rumble anew.

— Cease —

The waters of the Hadeshorn spit and hissed behind
him as he faced them. It was growing lighter now in the
east; dawn was threatening to break.

The shade's voice was again a whisper.

— You would know more. I wish that it could be so.
But I have told you what I can. I cannot tell you more. I
lack the power in death that I possessed in life. I am
permitted to see only bits and pieces of the world that
was or the future that will be. I cannot find what is
hidden from you for I am sealed away in a world where
substance has small meaning. Each day, the memory of
its slips further from me. I sense what is and what is
possible; that must suffice. Therefore, pay heed to me. I
cannot come with you. I cannot guide you. I cannot
answer the questions you bring with you — not of magic
or family or self-worth. All that you must do for yourselves. My time in the Four Lands is gone, children of
Shannara. As it once was for Bremen, so it is now for me.
I am not chained by shackles of failure as was he, but I
am chained nevertheless. Death limits both time and
being. I am the past. The future of the Four Lands belongs

207

to you and to you alone —

'But you ask impossible things of us!' Wren snapped desperately.

'Worse! You ask things that should never be!' Walker raged. 'Druids come again? Paranor restored?'

The shade's reply came softly.

— I ask for what must be. You have the skills, the heart, the right, and the need to do what I have asked. Believe what I have told you. Do as I have said. Then will the Shadowen be destroyed —

Par felt his throat tighten in desperation. Allanon was beginning to fade.

'Where shall we look?' he cried out frantically. 'Where do we begin our search? Allanon, you have to tell us!'

There was no answer. The shade withdrew further.

'No! You cannot go!' Walker Boh howled suddenly.

The shade began to sink into the waters of the Hadeshorn.

'Druid, I forbid it!' Walker screamed in fury, throwing off sparks of his own magic as he flung his arms out as if to hold the other back.

The whole of the valley seemed to explode in response, the earth shaking until rocks bounced and rattled ferociously, the air filling with a wind that whipped down out of the mountains as if summoned, the Hadeshorn churning in a maelstrom of rage, the dead crying out — and the shade of Allanon bursting into flame. The members of the little company were thrown flat as the forces about them collided, and everything was caught up in a whirlwind of light and sound.

At last it was still and dark again. They lifted their heads cautiously and looked about. The valley was empty of shades and spirits and all that accompanied them. The earth was at rest once more and the Hadeshorn a silent, placid stretch of luminescence that reflected the sun's brilliant image from where it lifted out of the darkness in the east.

Par Ohmsford climbed slowly to his feet. He felt that he might have awakened from a dream.

CHAPTER

16

HEN THEY RECOVERED their composure, the members of the little company discovered that Cogline was missing. At first they thought such a thing impossible, certain that they must be mistaken, and they cast about for him expectantly, searching the lingering nighttime shadows. But the valley offered few places to hide, and the old man was nowhere to be found.

'Perhaps Allanon's shade whisked him away,' Morgan suggested in an attempt to make a joke of it.

Nobody laughed. Nobody even smiled. They were already sufficiently distressed by everything else that had happened that night, and the strange disappearance of the old man only served to unsettle them further. It was one thing for the shades of Druids dead and gone to appear and vanish without warning; it was something else again when it was a flesh-and-blood person. Besides, Cogline had been their last link to the meaning behind the dreams and the reason for their journey here. With the apparent severing of that link, they were all too painfully aware that they were now on their own.

They stood around uncertainly a moment or two longer. Then Walker muttered something about wasting his time. He started back the way he had come, the others of the little company trailing after him. The sun was above the horizon now, golden in a sky that was cloudless and blue, and the warmth of the day was already settling over the barren peaks of the Dragon's Teeth. Par glanced over his shoulder as they reached the valley rim. The Hadeshorn stared back at him, sullen and unresponsive.

The walk back was a silent one. They were all thinking about what the Druid had said, sifting and measuring the revelations and charges, and none of them were ready yet to talk. Certainly Par wasn't. He was so confounded by what he had been told that he was having trouble accepting that he had actually heard it. He trailed the others with Coll, watching their backs as they wound single file through the breaks in the rocks, following the pathway that led down through the cliff pocket to the foothills and their campsite, thinking mostly that Walker had been right after all, that whatever he might have imagined this meeting with the shade of Allanon would be like, he would have imagined wrong. Coll asked him at one point if he were all right and he nodded without replying, wondering inwardly if indeed he would ever be all right again.

Recover the Sword of Shannara, the shade had commanded him. Sticks and stones, how in the world was he supposed to do that?

The seeming impossibility of the task was daunting. He had no idea where to begin. No one, to the best of his knowledge, had even seen the Sword since the occupation of Tyrsis by the Federation — well over a hundred years ago. And it might have disappeared before that. Certainly no one had seen it since. Like most things connected with the time of the Druids and the magic, the Sword was part of a legend that was all but forgotten. There weren't any Druids, there weren't any Elves, and there wasn't any magic — not anymore, not in the world of men. How often had he heard that?

His jaw tightened. Just exactly what was he supposed to do? What were any of them supposed to do? Allanon had given them nothing to work with beyond the bare charging of their respective quests and his assurance that what he asked of them was both possible and necessary.

He felt a hot streak race through him. There had been no mention of his own magic, of the uses of the wishsong that he believed were hidden from him. Nothing had been said about the ways in which it might be employed. He hadn't even been given a chance to ask questions. He didn't know one thing more about the magic than he had before.

Par was angry and disappointed and a dozen other things too confusing to sort out. Recover the Sword of Shannara, indeed! And then what? What was he supposed to do with it? Challenge the Shadowen to some sort of combat? Go charging around the countryside searching them out and destroying them one by one?

His face flushed. Shades! Why should he even *think* about doing such a thing?

He caught himself. Well, that was really the crux of things, wasn't it? Should he consider doing what Allanon had asked — not so much the hunting of the Shadowen with the Sword of Shannara, but the hunting of the Sword of Shannara in the first place?

That was what needed deciding.

He tried pushing the matter from his mind for a moment, losing himself in the cool of the shadows where the cliffs still warded the pathway; but, like a frightened child clinging to its mother, it refused to release its grip. He saw Steff ahead of him saying something to Teel, then to Morgan and shaking his head vehemently as he did so. He saw the stiff set of Walker Boh's back. He saw Wren striding after her uncle as if she might walk right over him. All of them were as angry and frustrated as he was; there was no mistaking the look. They felt cheated by what they had been told — or not told. They had expected something more substantial, something definitive, something that would give them answers to the questions they had brought with them.

Anything besides the impossible charges they had been given!

Yet Allanon had said the charges were not impossible,

that they could be accomplished, and that the three charged had the skills, the heart, and the right to accomplish them.

Par sighed. Should he believe that?

And again he was back to wondering whether or not he should even consider doing what he had been asked.

But he was already considering exactly that, wasn't he? What else was he doing by debating the matter, if not that?

He passed out of the cliff shadows onto the pebble-strewn trail leading downward to the campsite. As he did so, he made a determined effort to put aside his anger and frustration and to think clearly. What did he know that he could rely upon? The dreams had indeed been a summons from Allanon — that much appeared certain now. The Druid had come to them as he had come to Ohmsfords in the past, asking their help against dark magic that threatened the Four Lands. The only difference, of course, was that this time he had been forced to come as a shade. Cogline, a former Druid, had been his messenger in the flesh to assure that the summons was heeded. Cogline had Allanon's trust.

Par took a moment to consider whether or not he really believed that last statement and decided he did.

The Shadowen were real, he went on. They were dangerous, they were evil, they were certainly a threat of some sort to the Races and the Four Lands. They were magic.

He paused again. If the Shadowen were indeed magic, it would probably take magic to defeat them. And if he accepted that, it made much of what Allanon and Cogline had told them more convincing. It made possible the tale of the origin and growth of the Shadowen. It made probable the claim that the balance of things was out of whack. Whether you accepted the premise that the Shadowen were to blame or not, there was clearly much wrong in the Four Lands. Most of the blame for what was bad had been attributed by the Federation to the magic of the Elves and Druids — magic that the old stories claimed was good. But Par thought the truth lay somewhere in between. Magic in and of itself — if you believed in it as Par did — was never bad or good; it was simply power. That was the lesson of the wishsong. It was all in how the magic was used.

Par frowned. That being so, what if the Shadowen were using magic to cause problems among the Races in ways that none of them could see? What if the only way to combat such magic was to turn it against the user, to cause it to revert to the uses for which it was intended? What if Druids and Elves and talismans like the Sword of Shannara were indeed needed to accomplish that end?

There was sense in the idea, he admitted reluctantly.

But was there enough sense?

The campsite appeared ahead, undisturbed since their leave-taking the previous night, streaked by early sunlight and fading shadows. The horses nickered at their approach, still tied to the picket line. Par saw that Cogline's horse was among them. Apparently the old man had not returned here.

He found himself thinking of the way Cogline had come to them before, appearing unexpectedly to each, to Walker, Wren, and himself, saying what he had to say, then departing as abruptly as he had come. It had been that way each time. He had warned each of them what was required, then let them decide what they would do. Perhaps, he thought suddenly, that was what he had done this time, as well — simply left them to decide on their own.

They reached the camp, still without having spoken more than a few brief words to one another, and came to an uneasy halt. There was some suggestion of eating or sleeping first, but everyone quickly decided against it. No one really wanted to eat or sleep; they were neither hungry nor tired. They were ready now to talk about what had happened. They wanted to put the matter to discussion and give voice to the thoughts and emotions that had been building and churning inside them during the walk back.

213

'Very well,' Walker Boh said curtly, after a moment's strained silence. 'Since no one else cares to say it, I will. This whole business is madness. Paranor is gone. The Druids are gone. There haven't been any Elves in the Four Lands in over a hundred years. The Sword of Shannara hasn't been seen for at least that long. We haven't, any of us, the vaguest idea of how to go about recovering any of them — if, indeed, recovery is possible. I suspect it isn't. I think this is just one more instance of the Druids playing games with the Ohmsfords. And I resent it very much!'

He was flushed, his face sharply drawn. Par remembered again how angry he had been back in the valley, almost uncontrolled. This was not the Walker Boh he remembered.

'I am not sure we can dismiss what happened back there as simple game-playing,' Par began, but then Walker was all over him.

'No, of course not, Par — you see all this as a chance to satisfy your misguided curiosity about the uses of magic! I warned you before that magic was not the gift you envisioned, but a curse! Why is it that you persist in seeing it as something else?'

'Suppose the shade spoke the truth?' Coll's voice was quiet and firm, and it turned Walker's attention immediately from Par.

'The truth isn't in those cowled tricksters! When has the truth ever been in them? They tell us bits and pieces, but never the whole! They use us! They have always used us!'

'But not unwisely, not without consideration for what must be done — that's not what the stories tell us.' Coll held his ground. 'I am not necessarily advocating that we do as the shade suggested, Walker. I am only saying that it is unreasonable to dismiss the matter out of hand because of one possibility in a rather broad range.'

'The bits and pieces you speak of — those were always true in and of themselves,' Par added to Coll's surprisingly eloquent defense. 'What you mean is that Allanon never told the whole truth in the beginning. He always

214

held something back.'

Walker looked at them as if they were children, shaking his head. 'A half-truth can be as devastating as a lie,' he said quietly. The anger was fading now, replaced by a tone of resignation. 'You ought to know that much.'

'I know that there is danger in either.'

'Then why persist in this? Let it go!'

'Uncle,' Par said, the reprimand in his voice astonishing even to himself, 'I haven't taken it up yet.'

Walker looked at him for a long time, a tall, pale-skinned figure against the dawn, his face unreadable in its mix of emotions. 'Haven't you?' he replied softly.

Then he turned, gathered up his blankets and gear and rolled them up. 'I will put it to you another way, then. Were everything the shade told us true, it would make no difference. I have decided on my course of action. I will do nothing to restore Paranor and the Druids to the Four Lands. I can think of nothing I wish less. The time of the Druids and Paranor saw more madness than this age could ever hope to witness. Bring back those old men with their magics and their conjuring, their playing with the lives of men as if they were toys?'

He rose and faced them, his pale face as hard as granite. 'I would sooner cut off my hand than see the Druids come again!'

The others glanced at one another in consternation as he turned away to finish putting together his pack.

'Will you simply hide out in your valley?' Par shot back, angry now himself.

Walker didn't look at him. 'If you will.'

'What happens if the shade spoke the truth, Walker? What happens if all it has foreseen comes to pass, and the Shadowen reach extends even into Hearthstone? Then what will you do?'

'What I must.'

'With your own magic?' Par spat. 'With magic taught to you by Cogline?'

His uncle's pale face lifted sharply. 'How did you learn of that?'

Par shook his head stubbornly. 'What difference is there between your magic and that of the Druids, Walker? Isn't it all the same?'

The other's smile was hard and unfriendly. 'Sometimes, Par, you are a fool,' he said and dismissed him.

When he rose a moment later, he was calm. 'I have done my part in this. I came as I was bidden and I listened to what I was supposed to hear. I have no further obligation. The rest of you must decide for yourselves what you will do. As for me, I am finished with this business.'

He strode through them without pausing, moving down to where the horses were tethered. He strapped his pack in place, mounted, and rode out. He never once looked back.

The remaining members of the little company watched in silence. That was a quick decision, Par thought — one that Walker Boh seemed altogether too anxious to make. He wondered why.

When his uncle was gone, he looked at Wren. 'What of you?'

The Rover girl shook her head slowly. 'I haven't Walker's prejudices and predispositions to contend with, but I do have his doubts.' She walked over to a gathering of rocks and seated herself.

Par followed. 'Do you think the shade spoke the truth?'

Wren shrugged. 'I am still trying to decide if the shade was even who it claimed, Par. I sensed it was, felt it in my heart, and yet ...' She trailed off. 'I know nothing of Allanon beyond the stories, and I know the stories but poorly. You know them better than I. What do you think?'

Par did not hesitate. 'It was Allanon.'

'And do you think he spoke the truth?'

Par was conscious of the others moving over to join them, silent, watchful. 'I think there is reason to believe that he did, yes.' He outlined his thoughts as far as he had developed them during the walk back from the

216

valley. He was surprised at how convincing he sounded. He was no longer floundering; he was beginning to gain a measure of conviction in his arguments. 'I haven't thought it through as much as I would like,' he finished. 'But what reason would the shade have for bringing us here and for telling us what it did if not to reveal the truth? Why would it tell us a lie? Walker seems convinced there is a deception at work in this, but I cannot find what form it takes or what purpose it could possibly serve.

'Besides,' he added, 'Walker is frightened of this business — of the Druids, of the magic, of whatever. He keeps something from us. I can sense it. He plays the same game he accuses Allanon of playing.'

Wren nodded. 'But he also understands the Druids.' When Par looked confused, she smiled sadly. 'They do hide things, Par. The hide whatever they do not wish revealed. That is their way. There are things being hidden here as well. What we were told was too incomplete, too circumscribed. However you choose to view it, we are being treated no differently from our ancestors before us.'

There was a long silence. 'Maybe we should go back into the valley tonight and see if the shade won't come to us again,' Morgan suggested in a tone of voice that whispered of doubt.

'Perhaps we should give Cogline a chance to reappear,' Coll added.

Par shook his head. 'I don't think we will be seeing any more of either for now. I expect whatever decisions we make will have to be made without their help.'

'I agree.' Wren stood up again. 'I am supposed to find the Elves and — how did he put it? — return them to the world of men. A very deliberate choice of words, but I don't understand them. I haven't any idea where the Elves are or even where to begin to look for them. I have lived in the Westland for almost ten years now, Garth for many more than that, and between us we have been everywhere there is to go. I can tell you for a fact that there are no Elves to be found there. Where else am I to look?'

She came over to Par and faced him. 'I am going home. There is nothing more for me to do here. I will have to think on this, but even thinking may be of no use. If the dreams come again and tell me something of where to begin this search, then perhaps I will give it a try. But for now . . .'

She shrugged. 'Well. Goodbye, Par.'

She hugged and kissed him, then did the same for Coll and even Morgan this time. She nodded to the Dwarves and began gathering up her things. Garth joined her silently.

'I wish you would stay a bit longer, Wren,' Par tried, quiet desperation welling up like a knot in his stomach at the thought of being left alone to wrestle with this matter.

'Why not come with me instead?' she answered. 'You would probably be better off in the Westland.'

Par looked at Coll, who frowned. Morgan looked away. Par sighed and shook his head reluctantly. 'No, I have to make my own decision first. I have to do that before I can know where I should be.'

She nodded, seeming to understand. She had her things together, and she walked up to him. 'I might think differently if I had the magic for protection like you and Walker. But I don't. I don't have the wishsong or Cogline's teachings to rely on. I have only a bag of painted stones.' She kissed him again. 'If you need me, you can find me in the Tirfing. Be careful, Par.'

She rode out of the camp with Garth trailing. The others watched them go, the tall, curly-haired Rover girl and her giant companion in his bright patchwork clothes. Minutes later, they were specks against the western horizon, their horses almost out of sight.

Par kept looking after them even when they had disappeared. Then he glanced east again after Walker Boh. He felt as if parts of himself were being stolen away.

Coll insisted they have something to eat then, all of them, because it had been better than twelve hours since their last meal and there was no point in trying to think something through on an empty stomach. Par was grateful for the respite, unwilling to confront his own decision-making in the face of the disappointment he felt at the departure of Walker and Wren. He ate the broth that Steff prepared along with some hard bread and fruit, drank several cupfuls of ale, and walked down to the spring to wash. When he returned, he agreed to his brother's suggestion that he lie down for a few minutes and after doing so promptly fell asleep.

It was midday when he woke, his head throbbing, his body aching, his throat hot and dry. He had dreamed snatches of things he would have been just as happy not dreaming at all — of Rimmer Dall and his Federation Seekers hunting him through empty, burned out city buildings; of Dwarves that watched, starving and helpless in the face of an occupation they could do nothing to ease; of Shadowen lying in wait behind every dark corner he passed in his flight; of Allanon's shade calling out in warning with each new hazard, but laughing as well at his plight. His stomach felt unsettled, but he forced the feeling aside. He washed again, drank some more ale, seated himself in the shade of an old poplar tree and waited for the sickness to pass. It did, rather more quickly than he would have expected, and soon he was working on a second bowl of the broth.

Coll joined him as he ate. 'Feeling better? You didn't look well when you first woke up.'

Par finished eating and put the bowl aside. 'I wasn't. But I'm all right now.' He smiled to prove it.

Coll eased down next to him against the roughened tree trunk, settling his solid frame in place, staring out from the comfort of the shade into the midday heat. 'I've been thinking,' he said, the blocky features crinkling thoughtfully. He seemed reluctant to continue. 'I've been thinking about what I would do if you decided to go looking for the Sword.'

Par turned to him at once. 'Coll, I haven't even ...'

'No, Par. Let me finish.' Coll was insistent. 'If there's

one thing I've learned about being your brother, it's to try to get the jump on you when it comes to making decisions. Otherwise, you make them first and once they're made, they might as well be cast in stone!'

He glanced over. 'You may recall that we've had this discussion before? I keep telling you I know you better than you know yourself. Remember that time a few years back when you fell into the Rappahalladran and almost drowned while we were off in the Duln hunting that silver fox? There wasn't supposed to be one like it left in the Southland, but that old trapper said he'd seen one and that was enough for you. The Rappahalladran was cresting, it was late spring, and Dad told us not to try a crossing — made us promise not to try. I knew the minute you made that promise that you would break it if you had to. The very minute you made it!'

Par frowned. 'Well, I wouldn't say . . .'

Coll cut him short. 'The point is, I can usually tell when you've made up your mind about something. And I think Walker was right. I think you've made up your mind about going after the Sword of Shannara. You have, haven't you?'

Par stared at him, surprised.

'Your eyes say you're going after it, Par,' Coll continued calmly, actually smiling. 'Whether it's out there or not, you're going after it. I know you. You're going because you still think you can learn something about your own magic by doing so, because you want to do something fine and noble with it, because you have this little voice inside you whispering that the magic is meant for something. No, no, hold on, now — hear me out.' He held up his hands at Par's attempt to dispute him. 'I don't think there is anything wrong with that. I understand it. But I don't know if you do or whether you can admit to it. And you have to be able to admit to it because otherwise you won't ever be at peace with yourself about why you are going. I know I don't have any magic of my own, but the fact is that in some ways I do understand the problem better than you.'

He paused, somber. 'You always look for the challenges no one else wants. That's part of what's happening here. You see Walker and Wren walk away from this and right away you want to do just the opposite. That's the way you are. You couldn't give it up now if you had to.'

He cocked his head reflectively. 'Believe it or not, I have always admired that in you.'

Then he sighed. 'I know there are other considerations as well. There's the matter of the folks, still under confinement back in the Vale, and us with no home, no real place to go, outlaws of a sort. If we abandon this search, this quest Allanon's shade has given us, where do we go? What possible thing can we do that will change matters more thoroughly than finding the Sword of Shannara? I know there's that. And I know . . .'

Par interrupted. 'You said "we."'

Coll stopped. 'What?'

Par was studying him critically. 'Just then. You said "we." Several times. You said, that if "we" abandon this search and where do "we" go?'

Coll shook his head ruefully. 'So I did. I start talking about you and almost before I know it I'm talking about me as well. But that's exactly the problem, I guess. We're so close that I sometimes think of us as if we were the same — and we're not. We're very different and never more so than in this instance. You have the magic and the chance to learn about it and I don't. You have the quest and I haven't. So what should I do if you go, Par?'

Par waited a moment, then said, 'Well?'

'Well. After all is said and done, after all the arguments for and against have been laid on the table, I keep coming back to a couple of things.' He shifted so he was facing Par. 'First, I'm your brother and I love you. That means I don't abandon you, even when I'm not sure if I agree with what you're doing. I've told you that before. Second, if you go . . .' He paused. 'You are going, aren't you?'

There was a long moment of silence. Par did not reply.

'Very well. If you go, it will be a dangerous journey, and you will need someone to watch your back. And

221

that's what brothers are supposed to do for each other. That's second.'

He cleared his throat. 'Last, I've thought it all out from the point of view of what I would do if I were you, go or not go, measuring what I perceive to be the right and wrong of the matter.' He paused. 'If it were up to me, if I were you, I think I'd go.'

He leaned back against the poplar trunk and waited. Par took a deep breath. 'To be honest, Coll, I think that's just about the last thing I ever expected to hear from you.'

Coll smiled. 'That's probably why I said it. I don't like to be predictable.'

'So you would go, would you? If you were me?' Par studied his brother silently for a moment, letting the possibility play itself out in his mind. 'I don't know if I believe you.'

Coll let the smile broaden. 'Of course you do.'

They were still staring at each other as Morgan wandered up and sat down across from them, faintly puzzled as he saw the same look registered on both faces. Steff and Teel came over as well. All three glanced at one another. 'What's going on?' Morgan asked finally.

Par stared at him momentarily without seeing him. He saw instead the land beyond, the hills dotted with sparse groves, running south out of the barren stretches of the Dragon's Teeth, fading into a heat that made the earth shimmer. Dust blew in small eddies where sudden breezes scooped at the roadway leading down. It was still beneath the tree, and Par was thinking about the past, remembering the times that Coll and he had shared. The memories were an intimacy that comforted him; they were sharp and clear, most of them, and they made him ache in a sweet, welcome way.

'Well?' Morgan persisted.

Par blinked. 'Coll tells me he thinks I ought to do what the shade said. He thinks I ought to try to find the Sword of Shannara.' He paused. 'What do you think, Morgan?'

Morgan didn't hesitate. 'I think I'm going with you. It gets tiresome spending all of my time tweaking the noses of those Federation dunderheads who try to govern Leah. There's better uses for a man like me.' He lunged to his feet. 'Besides, I have a blade that needs testing against things of dark magic!' He reached back in a mock feint for his sword. 'And as all here can bear witness, there's no better way to do so than to keep company with Par Ohmsford!'

Par shook his head despairingly. 'Morgan, you shouldn't joke ...'

'Joke! But that's just the point! All I've been doing for months now is playing jokes! And what good has it done?' Morgan's lean features were hard. 'Here is a chance for me to do something that has real purpose, something far more important than causing Leah's enemies to suffer meaningless irritations and indignities. Come, now! You have to see it as I do, Par. You cannot dispute what I say.' His eyes shifted abruptly. 'Steff, how about you? What do you intend? And Teel?'

Steff laughed, his rough features wrinkling. 'Well now, Teel and I have pretty much the same point of view on the matter. We have already reached our decision. We came with you in the first place because we were hoping to get our hands on something, magic or whatever, that could help our people break free of the Federation. We haven't found that something yet, but we might be getting closer. What the shade said about the Shadowen spreading the dark magic, living inside men and women and children to do so, might explain a good part of the madness that consumes the Lands. It might even have something to do with why the Federation seems so bent on breaking the backs of the Dwarves! You've seen it for yourself — that's surely what the Federation is about. There's dark magic at work there. Dwarves can sense it better than most because the deeper stretches of the Eastland have always provided a hiding place for it. The only difference in this instance is that, instead of hiding, it's out in the open like a crazed animal, threatening us all. So maybe finding the Sword of Shannara as the shade says will be a step toward penning that animal up again!'

'There, now!' Morgan cried triumphantly. 'What better company for you, Par Ohmsford, than that?'

Par shook his head in bewilderment. 'None, Morgan, but . . .'

'Then say you'll do it! Forget Walker and Wren and their excuses! This has meaning! Think of what we might be able to accomplish!' He gave his friend a plaintive look. 'Confound it, Par, how can we lose by trying when by trying we have everything to gain?'

Steff reached over and poked him. 'Don't push so hard, Highlander. Give the Valeman room to breathe!'

Par stared at them each in turn, at the bluff-faced Steff, the enigmatic Teel, the fervently eager Morgan Leah, and finally Coll. He remembered suddenly that his brother had never finished revealing his own decision. He had only said that if he were Par, he would go.

'Coll . . .' he began.

But Coll seemed to read his thoughts. 'If you're going, I'm going.' His brother's features might have been carved from stone. 'From here to wherever this all ends.'

There was a long moment of silence as they faced each other, and the anticipation mirrored in their eyes was a whisper that rustled the leaves of their thoughts as if it were the wind.

Par Ohmsford took a deep breath. 'Then I guess the matter's settled,' he said. 'Now where do we start?'

CHAPTER

17

S USUAL, MORGAN LEAH HAD A PLAN.

'If we expect to have any luck at all locating the Sword, we're going to need help. The five of us are simply too few. After all these years, finding the Sword of Shannara is likely to be like finding the proverbial needle in the haystack — and we don't begin to know enough about the haystack. Steff, you and Teel may be familiar with the Eastland, but Callahorn and the Borderlands are foreign ground. It's the same with the Valemen and myself — we simply don't know enough about the country. And let's not forget that the Federation will be prowling about every place we're likely to go. Dwarves and fugitives from the law aren't welcome in the Southland, the last I heard. We'll have to be on the lookout for Shadowen as well. Truth is, they seem drawn to the magic like wolves to the scent of blood, and we can't assume we've seen the last of them. It will be all we can do to watch our backs, let alone figure out what's happened to the Sword. We can't do it alone. We need someone to help us, someone who has a working knowledge of the Four Lands, someone who can supply us with men and weapons.'

He shifted his gaze from the others to Par and smiled that familiar smile that was filled with secretive amusement. 'We need your friend from the Movement.'

Par groaned. He was none too keen to reassociate with

the outlaws; it seemed an open invitation to trouble. But Steff and Teel and even Coll liked the idea, and after arguing about it for a time he was forced to admit that the Highlander's proposal made sense. The outlaws possessed the resources they lacked and were familiar with the Borderlands and the free territories surrounding them. They would know where to look and what pitfalls to avoid while doing so. Moreover, Par's rescuer seemed a man you could depend upon.

'He told you that if you ever needed help, you could come to him,' Morgan pointed out. 'It seems to me that you could use a little now.'

There was no denying that, so the matter was decided. They spent what remained of the day at the campsite below the foothills leading to the Valley of Shale and the Hadeshorn, sleeping restlessly through the second night of the new moon at the base of the Dragon's Teeth. When morning came, they packed up their gear, mounted their horses and set out. The plan was simple. They would travel to Varfleet, search out Kiltan Forge at Reaver's End in the north city and ask for the Archer — all as Par's mysterious rescuer had instructed. Then they would see what was what.

They rode south through the scrub country that bordered the Rabb Plains until they crossed the east branch of the Mermidon, then turned west. They followed the river through midday and into early afternoon, the sun baking the land out of a cloudless sky, the air dry and filled with dust. No one said much of anything as they traveled, locked away in the silence of their own thoughts. There had been no further talk of Allanon since setting out. There had been no mention of Walker or Wren. Par fingered the ring with the hawk insigne from time to time and wondered anew about the identity of the man who had given it to him.

It was late afternoon when they passed down through the river valley of the Runne Mountains north of Varfleet and approached the outskirts of the city. It sprawled below them across a series of hills, dusty and sweltering against the glare of the westward fading sun. Shacks and hovels ringed the city's perimeter, squalid shelters for men and women who lacked even the barest of means. They called out to the travelers as they passed, pressing up against them for money and food, and Par and Coll handed down what little they had. Morgan glanced back reprovingly, somewhat as a parent might at a naive child, but made no comment.

A little farther on, Par found himself wishing belatedly that he had thought to disguise his Elven features. It had been weeks since he had done so, and he had simply gotten out of the habit. He could take some consolation from the fact that his hair had grown long and covered his ears. But he would have to be careful nevertheless. He glanced over at the Dwarves. They had their travel cloaks pulled close, the hoods wrapping their faces in shadow. They were in more danger than he of discovery. Everyone knew that Dwarves were not permitted to travel in the Southland. Even in Varfleet, it was risky.

When they reached the city proper and the beginnings of streets that bore names and shops with signs, the traffic increased markedly. Soon, it was all but impossible to move ahead. They dismounted and led their horses afoot until they found a stable where they could board them. Morgan made the transaction while the others stood back unobtrusively against the walls of the buildings across the way and watched the people of the city press against one another in a sluggish flow. Beggars came up to them and asked for coins. Par watched a fire-eater display his art to a wondering crowd of boys and men at a fruit mart. The low mutter of voices filled the air with a ragged sound.

'Sometimes you get lucky,' Morgan informed them quietly as he returned. 'We're standing in Reaver's End. This whole section of the city is Reaver's End. Kiltan Forge is just a few streets over.'

He beckoned them on, and they slipped past the steady throng of bodies, working their way into a side street that was less crowded, if more ill-smelling, and soon they were hurrying along a shadowed alley that twisted and turned along a rutted sewage way. Par wrinkled his nose in distaste. This was the city as Coll saw it. He risked a quick glance back at his brother, but his brother was busy watching where he was stepping.

They crossed several more streets before emerging onto one that seemed to satisfy Morgan, who promptly turned right and led them through the crowds to a broad, two-storey barn with a sign that bore the name Kiltan Forge seared on a plaque of wood. The sign and the building were old and splintering, but the furnaces within burned red-hot, spitting and flaming as metals were fed in and removed by tenders. Machines ground, and hammers pounded and shaped. The din rose above the noise of the street and echoed off the walls of the surrounding buildings, to disappear finally into the suffocating embrace of the lingering afternoon heat.

Morgan edged his way along the fringes of the crowd, the others trailing silently after, and finally managed to work his way up to the Forge entrance. A handful of men worked the furnaces under the direction of a large fellow with drooping mustaches and a balding pate colored soot black. The fellow ignored them until they had come all the way inside, then turned and asked, 'Something I can help you with?'

Morgan said, 'We're looking for the Archer.'

The fellow with the mustaches ambled over. 'Who did you say, now?'

'The Archer,' Morgan repeated.

'And who's that supposed to be?' The other man was broad shouldered and caked with sweat.

'I don't know,' Morgan admitted. 'We were just told to ask for him.'

'Who by?'

'Look ...'

'Who by? Don't you know, man?'

It was hot in the shadow of Kiltan Forge, and it was clear that Morgan was going to have trouble with this man if things kept going the way they were. Heads were already starting to turn. Par pushed forward impulsively, anxious to keep from drawing attention to themselves and said, 'By a man who wears a ring that bears the insigne of a hawk.'

The fellow's sharp eyes narrowed, studying the Valeman's face with its Elven features.

'This ring,' Par finished and held it out.

The other flinched as if he had been stung. 'Don't be showing that about, you young fool!' he snapped and shoved it away from him as if it were poison.

'Then tell us where we can find the Archer!' Morgan interjected, his irritation beginning to show through.

There was sudden activity in the street that caused them all to turn hurriedly. A squad of Federation soldiers was approaching, pushing through the crowd, making directly for the Forge. 'Get out of sight!' the fellow with the mustache snapped urgently and stepped away.

The soldiers came into the Forge, glancing about the fire-lit darkness. The man with the mustaches came forward to greet them. Morgan and the Valemen gathered up the Dwarves, but the soldiers were between them and the doorway leading to the street. Morgan edged them all toward the deep shadows.

'Weapons order, Hirehone,' the squad leader announced to the man with the mustaches, thrusting out a paper. 'Need it by week's end. And don't argue the matter.'

Hirehone muttered something unintelligible, but nodded. The squad leader talked to him some more, sounding weary and hot. The soldiers were casting about restlessly. One moved toward the little company. Morgan tried to stand in front of his companions, tried to make the soldier speak with him. The soldier hesitated, a big fellow with a reddish beard. Then he noticed something and pushed past the Highlander. 'You there!' he snapped at Teel. 'What's wrong with you?' One hand reached out, pulling aside the hood. 'Dwarves! Captain, there's...!'

He never finished. Teel killed him with a single thrust of her long knife, jamming the blade through his throat.

He was still trying to talk as he died. The other soldiers reached for their weapons, but Morgan was already among them, his own sword thrusting, forcing them back. He cried out to the others, and the Dwarves and Valemen broke for the doorway. They reached the street, Morgan on their heels, the Federation soldiers a step behind. The crowd screamed and split apart as the battle careened into them. There were a dozen soldiers in pursuit, but two were wounded and the rest were tripping over one another in their haste to reach the Highlander. Morgan cut down the foremost, howling like a madman. Ahead, Steff reached a barred door to a warehouse, brought up the suddenly revealed mace, and hammered the troublesome barrier into splinters with a single blow. They rushed through the darkened interior and out a back door, wheeled left down an alley and came up against a fence. Desperately, they wheeled about and started back.

The pursuing Federation soldiers burst through the warehouse door and came at them.

Par used the wishsong and filled the disappearing gap between them with a swarm of buzzing hornets. The soldiers howled and dove for cover. In the confusion, Steff smashed enough boards of the fence to allow them all to slip through. They ran down a second alley, through a maze of storage sheds, turned right and pushed past a hinged metal gate.

They found themselves in a yard of scrap metal behind the Forge. Ahead, a door to the back of the Forge swung open. 'In here!' someone called.

They ran without questioning, hearing the sound of shouting and blare of horns all about. They shoved through the opening into a small storage room and heard the door slam shut behind them.

Hirehone faced them, hands on hips. 'I hope you turn out to be worth all the trouble you've caused!' he told them.

*

He hid them in a crawlspace beneath the floor of the storage room, leaving them there for what seemed like hours. It was hot and close, there was no light, and the sounds of booted feet tramped overhead twice in the course of their stay, each time leaving them taut and breathless. When Hirehone finally let them out again, it was night, the skies overcast and inky, the lights of the city fragmented pinpricks through the gaps in the boards of the Forge walls. He took them out of the storage room to a small kitchen that was adjacent, sat them down about a spindly table, and fed them.

'Had to wait until the soldiers finished their search, satisfied themselves you weren't coming back or hiding in the metal,' he explained. 'They were angry. I'll tell you — especially about the killing.'

Teel showed nothing of what she was thinking, and no one else spoke. Hirehone shrugged. 'Means nothing to me either.'

They chewed in silence for a time, then Morgan asked, 'What about the Archer? Can we see him now?'

Hirehone grinned. 'Don't think that'll be possible. There isn't any such person.'

Morgan's jaw dropped. 'Then why ...?'

'It's a code,' Hirehone interrupted. 'It's just a way of letting me know what's expected of me. I was testing you. Sometimes the code gets broken. I had to make sure you weren't spying for the Federation.'

'You're an outlaw,' Par said.

'And you're Par Ohmsford,' the other replied. 'Now finish up eating, and I'll take you to the man you came to see.'

They did as they were told, cleaned off their plates in an old sink, and followed Hirehone back into the bowels of Kiltan Forge. The Forge was empty now, save for a single tender on night watch who minded the fire-breathing furnaces that were never allowed to go cold. He paid them no attention. They passed through the cavernous stillness on cat's feet, smelling ash and metal in a sulfurous mix, watching the shadows dance to the fire's cadence.

When they slipped through a side door into the darkness, Morgan whispered to Hirehone, 'We left our horses stabled several streets over.'

'Don't worry about it,' the other whispered back. 'You won't need horses where you're going.'

They passed quietly and unobtrusively down the byways of Varfleet, through its bordering cluster of shacks and hovels and finally out of the city altogether. They traveled north then along the Mermidon, following the river upstream where it wound below the foothills fronting the Dragon's Teeth. They walked for the remainder of the night, crossing the river just above its north-south juncture where it passed through a series of rapids that scattered its flow into smaller streams. The river was down at this time of the year or the crossing would never have been possible without a boat. As it was, the water reached nearly to the chins of the Dwarves at several points, and all of them were forced to walk with their backpacks and weapons hoisted over their heads.

Once across the river, they came up against a heavily forested series of defiles and ravines that stretched on for miles into the rock of the Dragon's Teeth.

'This is the Parma Key,' Hirehone volunteered at one point. 'Pretty tricky country if you don't know your way.'

That was a gross understatement, Par quickly discovered. The Parma Key was a mass of ridges and ravines that rose and fell without warning amid a suffocating blanket of trees and scrub. The new moon gave no light, the stars were masked by the canopy of trees and the shadow of the mountains, and the company found itself in almost complete blackness. After a brief penetration of the woods, Hirehone sat them down to wait for daybreak.

Even in daylight, any passage seemed impossible. It was perpetually shadowed and misted within the mountain forests of the Parma Key, and the ravines and ridges crisscrossed the whole of the land. There was a trail, invisible to anyone who hadn't known it before, a twisting path that Hirehone followed without effort but that left the members of the little company uncertain of the direction in which they were moving. Morning slipped toward midday, and the sun filtered down through the densely packed trees in narrow streamers of brightness that did little to chase the lingering mist and seemed to have strayed somehow from the outer world into the midst of the heavy shadows.

When they stopped for a quick lunch, Par asked their guide if he would tell them how much farther it was to where they were going.

'Not far,' Hirehone answered. 'There.' He pointed to a massive outcropping of rock that rose above the Parma Key where the forest flattened against the wall of the Dragon's Teeth. 'That, Ohmsford, is called the Jut. The Jut is the stronghold of the Movement.'

Par looked, considering. 'Does the Federation know it's there?' he asked.

'They know it's in here somewhere,' Hirehone replied. 'What they don't know is exactly where and, more to the point, how to reach it.'

'And Par's mysterious rescuer, your still-nameless outlaw chief — isn't he worried about having visitors like us carrying back word of how to do just that?' Steff asked skeptically.

Hirehone smiled. 'Dwarf, in order for you to find your way in again, you first have to find your way out. Think you could manage that without me?'

Steff smirked grudgingly, seeing the truth of the matter. A man could wander forever in this maze without finding his way clear.

It was late afternoon when they reached the outcropping they had been pointing toward all day, the shadows of late afternoon falling in thick layers across the wilderness, casting the whole of the forest in twilight. Hirehone had whistled ahead several times during the last hour, each time waiting for an answering whistle before proceeding farther. At the base of the cliffs, a gated lift waited, settled in a clearing, its ropes disappearing skyward into the rocks overhead. The lift was large

233

enough to hold all of them, and they stepped into it, grasping the railing for support as it hoisted them up, slowly, steadily, until at last they were above the trees. They drew even with a narrow ledge and were pulled in by a handful of men working a massive winch. A second lift waited and they climbed aboard. Again they were hoisted up along the face of the rock wall, dangling out precariously over the earth. Par looked down once and quickly regretted it. He caught a glimpse of Steff's face, bloodless beneath its sun-browned exterior. Hirehone seemed unconcerned and whistled idly as they rose.

There was a third lift as well, this one much shorter, and when they finally stepped off they found themselves on a broad, grassy bluff about midway up the cliff that ran back several hundred yards into a series of caves. Fortifications lined the edge of the bluff and ringed the caves, and there were pockets of defense built into the cliff wall overhead where it was riddled with craggy splits. There was a narrow waterfall spilling down off the mountain into a pool, and several gatherings of broad-leaf trees and fir scattered about the bluff. Men scurried everywhere, hauling tools and weapons and crates of stores, crying out instructions, or answering back.

Out of the midst of this organized confusion strode Par's rescuer, his tall form clothed in startling scarlet and black. He was clean-shaven now, his tanned face weather-seamed and sharp-boned in the sunlight, a collection of planes and angles. It was a face that defied age. His brown hair was swept back and slightly receding. He was lean and fit and moved like a cat. He swept toward them with a deep-voiced shout of welcome, one arm extending first to hug Hirehone, then to gather in Par.

'So, lad, you've had change of heart, have you? Welcome, then, and your companions as well. Your brother, a Highlander and a brace of Dwarves, is it? Strange company, now. Have you come to join up?'

He was as guileless as Morgan had ever thought to be, and Par felt himself blush. 'Not exactly. We have a problem.'

'Another problem?' The outlaw chief seemed amused. 'Trouble just follows after you, doesn't it? I'll have my ring back now.'

Par removed the ring from his pocket and handed it over. The other man slipped it back on his finger, admiring it. 'The hawk. Good symbol for a free-born, don't you think?'

'Who are you?' Par asked him bluntly.

'Who am I?' The other laughed merrily. 'Haven't you figured that out yet, my friend? No? Then I'll tell you.' The outlaw chief leaned forward. 'Look at my hand.' He held up the closed fist with the finger pointed at Par's nose. 'A missing hand with a pike. Who am I?'

His eyes were sea green and awash with mischief. There was a moment of calculated silence as the Valeman stared at him in confusion.

'My name, Par Ohmsford, is Padishar Creel,' the outlaw chief said finally. 'But you would know me better as the great, great, great, and then some, grandson of Panamon Creel.'

And finally Par understood.

That evening, over dinner, seated at a table that had been moved purposefully away from those of the other occupants of the Jut, Par and his companions listened in rapt astonishment while Padishar Creel related his story.

'We have a rule up here that everyone's past life is his own business,' he advised them conspiratorially. 'It might make the others feel awkward hearing me talk about mine.'

He cleared his throat. 'I was a landowner,' he began, 'a grower of crops and livestock, the overseer of a dozen small farms and countless acres of forestland reserved for hunting. I inherited the better part of it from my father and he from his father and so on back some years further than I care to consider. But it apparently all began with Panamon Creel. I am told, though I cannot confirm it of course, that after helping Shea Ohmsford recover the

235

Sword of Shannara, he returned north to the Borderlands where he became quite successful at his chosen profession and accumulated a rather considerable fortune. This, upon retiring, he wisely invested in what would eventually become the lands of the Creel family.'

Par almost smiled. Padishar Creel was relating his tale with a straight face, but he knew as well as the Valeman and Morgan that Panamon Creel had been a thief when Shea Ohmsford and he had stumbled on each other.

'Baron Creel, he called himself,' the other went on, oblivious. 'All of the heads of family since have been called the same way. Baron Creel.' He paused, savoring the sound of it. Then he sighed. 'But the Federation seized the lands from my father when I was a boy, stole them without a thought of recompense and in the end dispossessed us. My father died when he tried to get them back. My mother as well. Rather mysteriously.'

He smiled. 'So I joined the Movement.'

'Just like that?' Morgan asked, looking skeptical.

The outlaw chief skewered a piece of beef on his knife. 'My parents went to the governor of the province, a Federation underling who had moved into our home, and my father demanded the return of what was rightfully his, suggesting that if something wasn't done to resolve the matter, the governor would regret it. My father never was given to caution. He was denied his request, and he and my mother were summarily dismissed. On their way back from whence they had come, they disappeared. They were found later hanging from a tree in the forests nearby, gutted and flayed.'

He said it without rancor, matter-of-factly, all with a calm that was frightening. 'I grew up fast after that, you might say,' he finished.

There was a long silence. Padishar Creel shrugged. 'It was a long time ago. I learned how to fight, how to stay alive. I drifted into the Movement, and after seeing how poorly it was managed, formed my own company.' He chewed. 'A few of the other leaders didn't like the idea. They tried to give me over to the Federation. That was their mistake. After I disposed of them, most of the remaining bands came over to join me. Eventually, they all will.'

No one said anything. Padishar Creel glanced up. 'Isn't anyone hungry? There's a good measure of food left. Let's not waste it.'

They finished the meal quickly, the outlaw chief continuing to provide further details of his violent life in the same disinterested tone. Par wondered what sort of man he had gotten himself mixed up with. He had thought before that his rescuer might prove to be the champion the Four Lands had lacked since the time of Allanon, his standard the rallying point for all the oppressed Races. Rumor had it that this man was the charismatic leader for which the freedom Movement had been waiting. But he seemed as much a cutthroat as anything. However dangerous Panamon Creel might have been in his time, Par found himself convinced that Padishar Creel was more dangerous still.

'So, that is my story and the whole of it,' Padishar Creel announced, shoving back his plate. His eyes glittered. 'Any part of it that you'd care to question me about?'

Silence. Then Steff growled suddenly, shockingly, 'How much of it is the truth?'

Everyone froze. But Padishar Creel laughed, genuinely amused. There was a measure of respect in his eyes for the Dwarf that was unmistakable as he said, 'Some of it, my Eastland friend, some of it.' He winked. 'The story improves with every telling.'

He picked up his ale glass and poured a full measure from a pitcher. Par stared at Steff with newfound admiration. No one else would have dared ask that question.

'Come, now,' the outlaw chief interjected, leaning forward. 'Enough of history past. Time to hear what brought you to me. Speak, Par Ohmsford.' His eyes were fixed on Par. 'It has something to do with the magic, hasn't it? There wouldn't be anything else that would bring you here. Tell me.'

Par hesitated. 'Does your offer to help still stand?' he asked instead.

The other looked offended. 'My word is my bond, lad! I said I would help and I will!'

He waited. Par glanced at the others, then said, 'I need to find the Sword of Shannara.'

He told Padishar Creel of his meeting with the ghost of Allanon and the task that had been given him by the Druid. He told of the journey that had brought the five of them gathered to this meeting, of the encounters with Federation soldiers and Seekers and the monsters called Shadowen. He held nothing back, despite his reservations about the man. He decided it was better neither to lie nor to attempt half-truths, better that it was all laid out for him to judge, to accept or dismiss as he chose. After all, they would be no worse off than they were now, whether he decided to help them or not.

When he had finished, the outlaw chief sat back slowly and drained the remainder of the ale from the glass he had been nursing and smiled conspiratorially at Steff. 'It would seem appropriate for me to now ask how much of *this* tale is true!'

Par started to protest, but the other raised his hand quickly to cut him off. 'No, lad, save your breath. I do not question what you've told me. You tell it the way you believe it, that's clear enough. It's only my way.'

'You have the men, the weapons, the supplies and the network of spies to help us find what we seek,' Morgan interjected quietly. 'That's why we're here.'

'You have the spirit for this kind of madness as well, I'd guess,' Steff added with a chuckle.

Padishar Creel rubbed his chin roughly. 'I have more than these, my friends,' he said, smiling like a wolf. 'I have a sense of fate!'

He rose wordlessly and took them from the table to the edge of the bluff, there to stand looking out across the Parma Key, a mass of treetops and ridgelines bathed in the last of the day's sunlight as it faded west across the horizon.

His arm swept the whole of it. 'These are my lands now, the lands of Baron Creel, if you will. But I'll hold them no longer than the ones before them if I do not find a way to unsettle the Federation!' He paused. 'Fate, I told you. That's what I believe in. Fate made me what I am and it will unmake me as easily, if I do not take a hand in its game. The hand I must take, I think, is the one you offer. It is not chance, Par Ohmsford, that you have come to me. It is what was meant to be. I know that to be true, now especially — now, after hearing what you seek. Do you see the way of it? My ancestor and yours, Panamon Creel and Shea Ohmsford, went in search of the Sword of Shannara more than three hundred years ago. Now it is our turn, yours and mine. A Creel and an Ohmsford once again, the start of change in the land, a new beginning. I can feel it!'

He studied them, his sharp face intense. 'Friendship brought you all together; a need for change in your lives brought you to me. Young Par, there are indeed ties that bind us, just as I said when first we met. There is a history that needs repeating. There are adventures to be shared and battles to be won. That is what fate has decreed for you and me!'

Par was a bit confused in the face of all this rhetoric as he asked, 'Then you'll help us?'

'Indeed, I will.' The outlaw chief arched one eyebrow. 'I hold the Parma Key, but the Southland is lost to me — my home, my lands, my heritage. I want them back. Magic is the answer now as it was those many years past, the catalyst for change, the prod that will turn back the Federation beast and send it scurrying for its cave!'

'You've said that several times,' Par interjected. 'Said it several different ways — that the magic can in some way undermine the Federation. But it's the Shadowen that Allanon fears, the Shadowen that the Sword is meant to confront. So why ... ?'

'Ah, ah, lad,' the other interrupted hurriedly. 'You strike to the heart of the matter once again. The answer to your question is this — I perceive threads of cause and effect in everything. Evils such as the Federation and the Shadowen do not stand apart in the scheme of things. They are connected in some way, joined perhaps as Ohmsfords and Creels are joined, and if we can find a way to destroy one, we will find a way to destroy the other!'

The look he gave them was one of such fierce determination that for a long moment no one said anything further. The last of the sunlight was fading away below the horizon, and the gray of twilight cloaked the Parma Key and the lands south and west in a mantle of gauze. The men behind them were stirring from their eating tables and beginning to retire to sleeping areas that lay scattered about the bluff. Even at this high elevation, the summer night was warm and windless. Stars and the beginnings of the first quarter's moon were slipping into view.

'All right,' Par said quietly. 'True or not, what can you do to help us?'

Padishar Creel smoothed back the wrinkles in the scarlet sleeves of his tunic and breathed deeply the smells of the mountain air. 'I can do, lad, what you asked me to do. I can help you find the Sword of Shannara.'

He glanced over with a quick grin and matter-of-factly added, 'You see, I think I know where it is.'

CHAPTER

18

FOR THE NEXT TWO DAYS, Padishar Creel had nothing more to say about the Sword of Shannara. Whenever Par or one of the others of the little company tried to engage him in conversation on the matter, he would simply say that time would tell or that patience was a virtue or offer up some similar platitude that just served to irritate them. He was unfailingly cheerful about it, though, so they kept their feelings to themselves.

Besides, for all the show the outlaw chief made of treating them as his guests, they were prisoners of a sort, nevertheless. They were permitted the run of the Jut, but forbidden to leave it. Not that they necessarily could have left in any event. The winches that raised and lowered the baskets from the heights into the Parma Key were always heavily guarded and no one was allowed near them without reason. Without the lifts to carry them down, there was no way off the bluff from its front. The cliffs were sheer and had been carefully stripped of handholds, and what small ledges and clefts had once existed in the rock had been meticulously chipped away or filled. The cliffs behind were sheer as well for some distance up and warded by the pocket battlements that dotted the high rock.

That left the caves. Par and his friends ventured into the central cavern on the first day, curious to discover what was housed there. They found that the mammoth, cathedrallike central chamber opened off into dozens of smaller chambers where the outlaws stored supplies and weapons of all sorts, made their living quarters when the weather outside grew forbidding, and established training and meeting rooms. There were tunnels leading back into the mountain, but they were cordoned off and watched. When Par asked Hirehone, who had stayed on a few extra days, where the tunnels led, the master of Kiltan Forge smiled sardonically and told him that, like the trails in the Parma Key, the tunnels of the Jut led into oblivion.

The two days passed quickly, despite the frustration of being put off on the subject of the Sword. All five visitors spent their time exploring the outlaw fortress. As long as they stayed away from the lifts and the tunnels they were permitted to go just about anywhere they wished. Not once did Padishar Creel question Par about his companions. He seemed unconcerned about who they were and whether they could be trusted, almost as if it didn't matter. Perhaps it didn't, Par decided after thinking it over. After all, the outlaw lair seemed impregnable.

Par, Coll, and Morgan stayed together most of the time. Steff went with them on occasion, but Teel kept away completely, as aloof and uncommunicative as ever. The Valemen and the Highlander became a familiar sight to the outlaws as they wandered the bluff, the fortifications, and the caverns, studying what man and nature had combined to form, talking with the men who lived and worked there when they could do so without bothering them, fascinated by everything they encountered.

But there was nothing and no one more fascinating than Padishar Creel. The outlaw chief was a paradox. Dressed in flaming scarlet, he was immediately recognizable from anywhere on the bluff. He talked constantly, telling stories, shouting orders, commenting on whatever came to mind. He was unremittingly cheerful, as if smiling was the only expression he had ever bothered to put on. Yet beneath that bright and ingratiating exterior was a core as hard as granite. When he ordered that something be done, it was done. No one ever questioned him. His face could be wreathed in a smile as warm as the summer sun while his voice could take on a frosty edge that chilled to the bone.

He ran the outlaw camp with organization and discipline. This was no ragtag band of misfits at work here. Everything was precise and thorough. The camp was neat and clean and kept that way scrupulously. Stores were separated and cataloged and anything could be found at a moment's notice. There were tasks assigned to everyone, and everyone made certain those tasks were carried out. There were a little more than three hundred men living on the Jut, and not one of them seemed to have the slightest doubt about what he was doing or whom he would answer to, if he were to let down.

On the second day of their stay, two of the outlaws were brought before Padishar Creel on a charge of stealing. The outlaw chief listened to the evidence against them, his face mild, then offered to let them speak in their own defense. One admitted his guilt outright, the other denied it — rather unconvincingly. Padishar Creel had the first flogged and sent back to work and the second thrown over the cliff. No one seemed to give the matter another thought afterward.

Later that same day, Padishar came over to Par when the Valeman was alone and asked if he was disturbed by what had happened. Barely waiting for Par's response, he went on to explain how discipline in a camp such as his was essential, and justice in the event of a breakdown must be swift and sure.

'Appearances often count for more than equities, you see,' he offered rather enigmatically. 'We are a close band here, and we must be able to rely on one another. If a man proves unreliable in camp, he most likely will prove unreliable in the field. And there's more than just his own life at stake there!'

He switched subjects abruptly then, admitting rather apologetically that he hadn't been entirely forthcoming about his background that first night and the truth of the matter was that his parents, rather than being landowners who had been strung up in the woods, had been silk merchants and had died in a Federation prison after they had refused to pay their taxes. He said the other simply made a better story.

When Par encountered Hirehone a short time later, he asked him — Padishar Creel's tale being still fresh in his mind at that point — whether he had known the outlaw chief's parents, and Hirehone said, 'No, the fever took them before I came on board.'

'In prison, you mean?' Par followed up, confused.

'Prison? Hardly. They died while on a caravan south out of Wayford. They were traders in precious metals. Padishar told me so himself.'

Par related both conversations to Coll that night after dinner. They had secluded themselves at the edge of the bluff in a redoubt, where the sounds of the camp were comfortably distant and they could watch the twilight slowly unveil the nighttime sky's increasingly intricate pattern of stars. Coll laughed when Par was finished and shook his head. 'The truth isn't in that fellow when it comes to telling anything about himself. He's more like Panamon Creel than Panamon probably ever thought of being!'

Par grimaced. 'True enough.'

'Dresses the same, talks the same — just as outrageous and quixotic.' Coll sighed. 'So why am I laughing? What are we doing here with this madman?'

Par ignored him. 'What do you suppose he's hiding, Coll?'

'Everything.'

'No, not everything. He's not that sort.' Coll started to protest, but Par put out his hands quickly to calm him. 'Think about it a moment. This whole business of who and what he is has been carefully staged. He spins out these wild tales deliberately, not out of whimsy. Padishar Creel has something else in common with Panamon, if we can believe the stories. He has recreated himself in the minds of everyone around him — drawn a picture of himself that doesn't square from one telling to the next, but is nevertheless bigger than life.' He bent close. 'And you can bet that he's done it for a reason.'

Further speculation about the matter of Padishar Creel's background ended a few minutes later when they were summoned to a meeting. Hirehone collected them with a gruff command to follow and led them across the bluff and into the caves to a meeting chamber where the outlaw chief was waiting. Oil lamps on black chains hung from the chamber ceiling like spiders, their glimmer barely reaching into the shadows that darkened the corners and crevices. Morgan and the Dwarves were there, seated at a table along with several outlaws Par had seen before in the camp. Chandos was a truly ferocious-looking giant with a great black beard, one eye and one ear on the same side of his face missing, and scars everywhere. Ciba Blue was a young, smooth-faced fellow with lank blond hair and an odd cobalt birthmark on his left cheek that resembled a half-moon. Stasas and Drutt were lean, hard, older men with close-cropped dark beards, faces that were seamed and brown, and eyes that shifted watchfully. Hirehone ushered in the Valemen, closed the chamber door, and stood purposefully in front of it.

For just a moment Par felt the hair on the back of his neck prickle in warning.

Then Padishar Creel was greeting them, cheerful and reassuring. 'Ah, young Par and his brother.' He beckoned them onto benches with the others, made quick introductions, and said, 'We are going after the Sword tomorrow at dawn.'

'Where is it?' Par wanted to know at once.

The outlaw chief's smile broadened. 'Where it won't get away from us.'

Par glanced at Coll.

'The less said about where we're going, the better the chance of keeping it a secret.' The big man winked.

'Is there some reason we need to keep it a secret?' Morgan Leah asked quietly.

The outlaw chief shrugged. 'No reason out of the

ordinary. But I am always cautious when I make plans to leave the Jut.' His eyes were hard. 'Humor me, Highlander.'

Morgan held his gaze and said nothing. 'Seven of us will go,' the other continued smoothly. 'Stasas, Drutt, Blue, and myself from the camp, the Valemen and the Highlander from without.' Protests were already starting from the mouths of the others and he moved quickly to squelch them. 'Chandos, you'll be in charge of the Jut in my absence. I want to leave someone behind I can depend upon. Hirehone, your place is back in Varfleet, keeping an eye on things there. Besides, you'd have trouble explaining yourself if you were spotted where we're going.

'As for you, my Eastland friends,' he spoke now to Steff and Teel, 'I would take you if I could. But Dwarves outside the Eastland are bound to draw attention, and we can't be having that. It's risky enough allowing the Valemen to come along with the Seekers still looking for them, but it's their quest.'

'Ours as well now, Padishar,' Steff pointed out darkly. 'We have come a long way to be part of this. We don't relish being left behind. Perhaps a disguise?'

'A disguise would be seen through,' the outlaw chief answered, shaking his head. 'You are a resourceful fellow, Steff — but we can take no chances on this outing.'

'There's a city and people involved, I take it?'

'There is.'

The Dwarf studied him hard. 'I would be most upset if there were games being played here at our expense.'

There was a growl of warning from the outlaws, but Padishar Creel silenced it instantly. 'So would I,' he replied, and his gaze locked on the Dwarf.

Steff held that gaze for a long moment. Then he glanced briefly at Teel and nodded. 'Very well. We'll wait.'

The outlaw chief's eyes swept the table. 'We'll leave at first light and be gone about a week. If we're gone longer than that, chances are we won't be coming back. Are there any questions?'

No one spoke. Padishar Creel gave them a dazzling smile. 'A drink, then? Outside with the others, so they can give us a toast and a wish for success! Up, lads, and strength to us who go to brave the lion in his den!'

He went out into the night, the others following. Morgan and the Valemen trailed, shuffling along thoughtfully.

'The lion in his den, eh?' Morgan muttered half to himself. 'I wonder what he means by that?'

Par and Coll glanced at each other. Neither was certain that they wanted to know.

Par spent a restless night, plagued by dreams and anxieties that fragmented his sleep and left him bleary-eyed with the coming of dawn. He rose with Coll and Morgan to find Padishar Creel and his companions already awake and in the midst of their breakfast. The outlaw chief had shed his scarlet clothing in favor of the less conspicuous green and brown woodsmen's garb worn by his men. The Valemen and the Highlander hurried to dress and eat, shivering a bit from the night's lingering chill. Steff and Teel joined them, wordless shadows hunkered down next to the cooking fire. When the meal was consumed, the seven strapped on their backpacks and walked to the edge of the bluff. The sun was creeping into view above the eastern horizon, its early light a mix of gold and silver against the fading dark. Steff muttered for them to take care and, with Teel in tow, disappeared back into the dark. Morgan was rubbing his hands briskly and breathing the air as if he might never have another chance. They boarded the first lift and began their descent, passing wordlessly to the second and third, the winches creaking eerily in the silence as they were lowered. When they reached the floor of the Parma Key, they struck out into the misty forests, Padishar Creel leading with Blue, the Valemen and the Highlander in the middle, and the remaining two outlaws, Stasas and Drutt, trailing. Within seconds, the rock wall of the Jut had disappeared from view.

They traveled south for the better part of the day, turning west around midafternoon when they encountered the Mermidon. They followed the river until sunset, staying on its north shore, and camped that night just below the south end of the Kennon Pass in the shadow of the Dragon's Teeth. They found a cove sheltered by cypress where a stream fed down out of the rocks and provided them with drinking water. They built a fire, ate their dinner and sat back to watch the stars come out.

After a time, Stasas and Drutt went off to take the first watch, one upstream, one down. Ciba Blue rolled into his blankets and was asleep in moments, his youthful face looking even younger in sleep. Padishar Creel sat with the Valemen and the Highlander, poking at the fire with a stick while he sipped at a flask of ale.

Par had been puzzling over their eventual destination all day, and now he said abruptly to the outlaw chief, 'We're going to Tyrsis, aren't we?'

Padishar glanced over in surprise, then nodded. 'No reason you shouldn't know now.'

'But why look for the Sword of Shannara in Tyrsis? It disappeared from there over a hundred years ago when the Federation annexed Callahorn. Why would it be back there now?'

The other smiled secretively. 'Perhaps because it never left.'

Par and his companions stared at the outlaw chief in astonishment.

'You see, the fact that the Sword of Shannara disappeared doesn't necessarily mean that it went anywhere. Sometimes a thing can disappear and still be in plain sight. It can disappear simply because it doesn't look like what it used to. We see it, but we don't recognize it.'

'What are you saying?' Par asked slowly.

Padishar Creel's smile broadened perceptibly. 'I am saying that the Sword of Shannara may very well be exactly where it was three hundred years ago.'

'Locked away in a vault in the middle of the People's

248

Park in Tyrsis all these years and no one's figured it out?' Morgan Leah was aghast. 'How can that possibly be?'

Padishar sipped speculatively at his flask and said, 'We'll be there by tomorrow. Why don't we wait and see?'

Par Ohmsford was tired from the day's march and last night's lack of sleep. but he was awake a long time, nevertheless, after the others were already snoring. He couldn't stop thinking about what Padishar Creel had said. More than three hundred years ago, after Shea Ohmsford had used it to destroy the Warlock Lord, the Sword of Shannara had been embedded in a block of red marble and entombed in a vault in the People's Park in the Southland city of Tyrsis. There it had remained until the coming of the Federation into Callahorn. It was common knowledge that it had disappeared after that. If it hadn't, why did so many people believe it had? If it was right where it had been three hundred years ago, how come no one recognized it now?

He considered. It was true that much of what had happened during the time of Allanon had lost credibility; many of the tales had taken on the trappings of legend and folklore. By the time the Sword of Shannara disappeared, perhaps no one believed in it anymore. Perhaps no one even understood what it could do. But they at least knew it was *there*! It was a national monument, for goodness sake! So how could they say it was gone if it wasn't? It didn't make sense!

Yet Padishar Creel seemed so positive.

Par fell asleep with the matter still unresolved.

They rose again at sunrise, crossed the Mermidon at a shallows less than a mile upstream and turned south for Tyrsis. The day was hot and still, and the dust of the grasslands filled their nostrils and throats. They kept to the shade when they could, but the country south grew more open as the forests gave way to grasslands. They used their water sparingly and paced themselves as they walked, but the sun climbed steadily in the cloudless summer sky and the travelers soon were sweating freely.

By midday, as they approached the walls of the city, their clothing lay damp against their skin.

Tyrsis was the home city of Callahorn, its oldest city, and the most impregnable fortress in the entire Southland. Situated on a broad plateau, it was warded by towering cliffs to the south, and a pair of monstrous battle walls to the north. The Outer Wall rose nearly a hundred feet above the summit of the plateau, a massive armament that had been breached only once in the city's history when the armies of the Warlock Lord had attacked in the time of Shea Ohmsford. A second wall sat back and within the first, a redoubt for the city's defenders. Once the Border Legion, the Southland's most formidable army, had defended the city. But the Legion was gone now, disbanded when the Federation moved in, and now only Federation soldiers patrolled the walls and byways, occupiers of lands that, until a hundred years ago, had never been occupied. The Federation soldiers were quartered in the Legion barracks within the first wall, and the citizens of the city still lived and worked within the second, housed in the city proper from where it ran back along the plateau to the base of the cliffs south.

Par, Coll, and Morgan had never been to Tyrsis. What they knew of the city, they knew from the stories they heard of the days of their ancestors. As they approached it now, they realized how impossible it was for words alone to describe what they were seeing. The city rose up against the skyline like a great, hulking giant, a construction of stone blocks and mortar that dwarfed anything they had ever encountered. Even in the bright sunlight of midday, it had a black cast to it — as if the sunlight were being absorbed somehow in the rock. The city shimmered slightly, a side effect of the heat, and assumed a mirage-like quality. A massive rampway led up from the plains to the base of the plateau, twisting like a snake through gates and causeways. Traffic was heavy, wagons and animals traveling in both directions in a steady stream, crawling through the heat and the dust.

The company of seven worked their way steadily

closer. As they reached the lower end of the rampway, Padishar Creel turned back to the others and said, 'Careful now, lads. Nothing to call attention to ourselves. Remember that it is as hard to get out of this city as it is to get in.'

They blended into the stream of traffic that climbed toward the plateau's summit. Wheels thudded, traces jingled and creaked, animals brayed, and men whistled and shouted. Federation soldiers manned the checkpoints leading up, but made no effort to interfere with the flow. It was the same at the gates — massive portals that loomed so high overhead that Par was aghast to think that any army had managed to breach them — the soldiers seeming to take no notice of who went in or out. It was an occupied city, Par decided, that was working hard at pretending to be free.

They passed beneath the gates, the shadow of the gatehouse overhead falling over them like a pall. The second wall rose ahead, smaller, but no less imposing. They moved toward it, keeping in the thick of the traffic. The grounds between the walls were clear of everyone but soldiers and their animals and equipment. There were plenty of each, a fair-sized army housed and waiting. Par studied the rows of drilling men out of the corner of one eye, keeping his head lowered in the shadow of his hooded cloak.

Once through the second set of gates, Padishar pulled them from the Tyrsian Way, the main thoroughfare of homes and businesses that wound through the center of the city to the cliff walls and what was once the palace of its rulers, and steered them into a maze of side streets. There were shops and residences here as well, but fewer soldiers and more beggars. The buildings grew dilapidated as they walked and eventually they entered a district of ale houses and brothels. Padishar did not seem to notice. He kept them moving, ignoring the pleas of the beggars and street vendors, working his way deeper into the city.

At last they emerged into a bright, open district

containing markets and small parks. A sprinkling of residences with yards separated the markets, and there were carriages with silks and ribbons on the horses. Vendors sold banners and sweets to laughing children and their mothers. Street shows were being performed on every corner — actors, clowns, magicians, musicians, and animal trainers. Broad, colorful canopies shaded the markets and the park pavilions where families spread their picnic lunches, and the air was filled with shouts, laughter, and applause.

Padishar Creel slowed, casting about for something. He took them through several of the stalls, along tree-shaded blocks where small gatherings were drawn by a multitude of delights, then stopped finally at a cart selling apples. He bought a small sackful for them all to share, took one for himself, and leaned back idly against a lamp pole to eat it. It took Par several moments to realize that he was waiting for something. The Valeman ate his apple with the others and looked about watchfully. Fruits of all sorts were on display in the stalls of a market behind him, there were ices being sold across the way, a juggler, a mime, a girl doing sleight of hand, a pair of dancing monkeys with their trainer, and a scattering of children and adults watching it all. He found his eyes returning to the girl. She had flaming red hair that seemed redder still against the black silk of her clothing and cape. She was drawing coins out of astonished children's ears, then making them disappear again. Once she brought fire out of the air and sent it spinning away. He had never seen that done before. The girl was very good.

He was so intent on watching her, in fact, that he almost missed seeing Padishar Creel hand something to a dark-skinned boy who had come up to him. The boy took what he was given without a word and disppeared. Par looked to see where he had gone, but it was as if the earth had swallowed him up.

They stayed where they were a few minutes longer, and then the outlaw chief said, 'Time to go,' and led them away. Par took a final look at the red-haired girl and saw that she was causing a ring to float in midair before her audience, while a tiny, blond-headed boy leaped and squealed after it.

The Valeman smiled at the child's delight.

On their way back through the gathering of market stalls, Morgan Leah caught sight of Hirehone. The master of Kiltan Forge was at the edge of a crowd applauding a juggler, his large frame wrapped in a great cloak. There was only a momentary glimpse of the bald pate and drooping mustaches, then he was gone. Morgan blinked, deciding almost immediately that he had been mistaken. What would Hirehone be doing in Tyrsis?

By the time they reached the next block, he had dismissed the matter from his mind.

They spent the next several hours in the basement of a storage house annexed to the shop of a weapons-maker, a man clearly in the service of the outlaws, since Padishar Creel knew exactly where in a crevice by the frame to find a key that would open the door and took them inside without hesitating. They found food and drink waiting, along with pallets and blankets for sleeping and water to wash up with. It was cool and dry in the basement, and the heat of the day quickly left them. They rested for a time, eating and talking idly among themselves, waiting for whatever was to come next. Only the outlaw chief seemed to know and, as usual, he wasn't saying. Instead, he went to sleep.

It was several hours before he awoke. He stood up, stretched, took time to wash his face and walked over to Par. 'We're going out,' he said. He turned to the others. 'Everyone else stay put until we get back. We won't be long and we won't be doing anything dangerous.'

Both Coll and Morgan started to protest, then thought better of it. Par followed Padishar up the basement stairs, and the trapdoor closed behind them. Padishar took a moment at the outer door, then beckoned Par after him, and they stepped out into the street.

The street was still crowded, filled with tradesmen and artisans, buyers, and beggars. The outlaw chief took Par south toward the cliffs, striding rapidly as the shadows of late afternoon began to spread across the city. They did not return along any of the avenues that had brought them in, but followed a different series of small, rutted back streets. The faces they passed were masks of studied disinterest, but the eyes were feral. Padishar ignored them, and Par kept himself close to the big man. Bodies pressed up against him, but he carried nothing of value, so he worried less than he might have otherwise.

As they approached the cliffs, they turned onto the Tyrsian Way. Ahead, the Bridge of Sendic lifted over the People's Park, a carefully trimmed stretch of lawn with broad-leaf trees which spread away toward a low wall and a cluster of buildings where the bridge ended. Beyond, a forest grew out of a wide ravine, and beyond that the spires and walls of what had once been the palace of the rulers of Tyrsis rose up against the fading light.

Par studied the park, the bridge, and the palace as they approached. Something about their configuration did not seem quite right. Wasn't the Bridge of Sendic supposed to have ended at the gates of the palace?

Padishar dropped back momentarily. 'So, lad. Hard to believe that the Sword of Shannara could be hidden anywhere so open, eh?'

Par nodded, frowning. 'Where is it?'

'Patience, now. You'll have your answer soon enough.' He put one arm about the Valeman and bent close. 'Whatever happens next, do not act surprised.'

Par nodded. The outlaw chief slowed, moved over to a flower cart and stopped. He studied the flowers, apparently trying to select a batch. He had done so when Par felt an arm go about his waist and turned to find the red-haired girl who practiced sleight of hand pressing up against him.

'Hello, Elf-boy,' she whispered, her cool fingers brushing at his ear as she kissed him on the cheek.

Then two small children were beside them, a girl and a boy, the first reaching up to grasp Padishar's rough hand, the second reaching up to grasp Par's. Padishar smiled, lifted the little girl so that she squealed, kissed her, and gave half of the flowers to her and half to the boy. Whistling, he started the five of them moving into the park. Par had recovered sufficiently to notice that the red-haired girl was carrying a basket covered with a bright cloth. When they were close to the wall that separated the park from the ravine, Padishar chose a maple tree for them to sit under, the red-haired girl spread the cloth, and all of them began unpacking the basket which contained cold chicken, eggs, hard bread and jam, cakes and tea.

Padishar glanced over at Par as they worked. 'Par Ohmsford, meet Damson Rhee, your betrothed for the purposes of this little outing.'

Damson Rhee's green eyes laughed. 'Love is fleeting, Par Ohmsford. Let's make the most of it.' She fed him an egg.

'You are my son,' Padishar added. 'These other two children are your siblings, though their names escape me at the moment. Damson, remind me later. We're just a typical family, out for a late afternoon picnic, should anyone ask.'

No one did. The men ate their meal in silence, listening to the children as they chattered on and acted as if what was happening was perfectly normal. Damson Rhee looked after them, laughing right along with them, her smile warm and infectious. She was pretty to begin with, but when she smiled, Par found her beautiful. When they had finished eating, she did the coin trick with each child, then sent them off to play.

'Let's take a walk,' Padishar suggested, rising.

The three of them strolled through the shade trees, moving without seeming purpose toward the wall that blocked away the ravine. Damson clung lovingly to Par's waist. He found he didn't mind. 'Things have changed somewhat in Tyrsis since the old days,' the outlaw chief said to Par as they walked. 'When the Buckhannah line died out, the monarchy came to an end. Tyrsis, Varfleet, and Kern ruled Callahorn by forming the Council of the Cities. When the Federation made Callahorn a protectorate, the Council was disbanded. The palace had served as an assembly for the Council. Now the Federation uses it — except that no one knows exactly what they use it for.'

They reached the wall and stopped. The wall was built of stone block to a height of about three feet. Spikes were embedded in its top. 'Have a look,' the outlaw chief invited.

Par did. The ravine beyond dropped away sharply into a mass of trees and scrub that had grown so thick it seemed to be choking on itself. Mist curled through the wilderness with an insistence that was unsettling, clinging to even the uppermost reaches of the trees. The ravine stretched away for perhaps a mile to either side and a quarter of that distance to where the palace stood, its door and windows shuttered and dark, its gates barred. The stone of the palace was scarred and dirty, and the whole of it had the look of something that had not seen use for decades. A narrow catwalk ran from the buildings in the foreground to its sagging gates.

He looked back at Padishar. The outlaw chief was facing toward the city. 'This wall forms the dividing line between past and present,' he said quietly. 'The ground we stand upon is called the People's Park. But the true People's Park, the one from the time of our ancestors —' He paused and turned back to the ravine. '— is down there.' He took a moment to let that sink in. 'Look. Below the Federation Gatehouse that wards the catwalk.' Par followed his gaze and caught sight of a scattering of huge stone blocks barely poking up out of the forest. 'That,' the outlaw chief continued somberly, 'is what remains of the real Bridge of Sendic. It was badly cracked, I am told, during the assault on Tyrsis by the Warlock Lord during the time of Panamon Creel. Some years later, it collapsed

256

altogether. This other bridge,' he waved indifferently, 'is merely for show.'

He glanced sideways at Par. 'Now do you see?'

Par did. His mind was working rapidly now, fitting the pieces into place. 'And the Sword of Shannara?' He caught a glimpse of Damson Rhee's startled look out of the corner of his eye.

'Down there somewhere, unless I miss my guess,' Padishar replied smoothly. 'Right where it's always been. You have something to say, Damson?'

The red-haired girl took Par's arm and steered him away from the wall. 'This is what you have come for, Padishar?' She sounded angry.

'Forbear, lovely Damson. Don't let's be judgmental.'

The girl's grip tightened on Par's arm. 'This is dangerous business, Padishar. I have sent men into the Pit before, as you well know, and not one of them has returned.'

Padishar smiled indulgently. 'The Pit — that's what Tyrsians call the ravine these days. Fitting, I suppose.'

'You take too many risks!' the girl pressed.

'Damson is my eyes and ears and strong right arm inside Tyrsis,' the other continued smoothly He smiled at her. 'Tell the Valeman what you know of the Sword, Damson.'

She gave him a dangerous look, then swung her face away. 'The collapse of the Bridge of Sendic occurred at the same time the Federation annexed Callahorn and began occupation of Tyrsis. The forest that now blankets the old People's Park, where the Sword of Shannara was housed, grew up virtually overnight. The new park and bridge came about just as quickly. I asked the old ones of the city some years ago what they remembered, and this is what I learned. The Sword didn't actually disappear from its vault; it was the vault that disappeared into the forest. People forget, especially when they're being told something else. Almost everyone believes there was only one People's Park and one Bridge of Sendic — the ones they see. The Sword of Shannara, if it ever existed, simply disappeared.'

Par was looking at her in disbelief. 'The forest, the bridge, and the park changed overnight?'

She nodded. 'Just so.'

'But ...?'

'Magic, lad,' Padishar Creel whispered in answer to his unfinished question.

They walked on a bit, nearing the brightly colored cloth that contained the remains of their picnic. The children were back, nibbling contentedly at the cakes.

'The Federation doesn't use magic,' Par argued, still confused. 'They have outlawed it.'

'Outlawed its use by others, yes,' the big man acknowledged. 'Perhaps the better to use it themselves? Or to allow someone else to use it? Or some*thing*?' He emphasized the last syllable.

Par looked over sharply. 'Shadowen, you mean?'

Neither Padishar nor Damson said anything. Par's mind spun. The Federation and the Shadowen in league somehow, joined for purposes none of them understood — was that possible?

'I have wondered about the fate of the Sword of Shannara for a long time,' Padishar mused, stopping just out of earshot of the waiting children. 'It is a part of the history of my family as well. It always seemed strange to me that it should have vanished so completely. It was embedded in marble and locked in a vault for two hundred years. How could it simply disappear? What happened to the vault that contained it? Was it all somehow spirited away?' He glanced at Par. 'Damson spent a long time finding out the answer. Only a few remembered the truth of how the disappearance came about. They're all dead now — but they left their story to me.'

His smile was wolfish. 'Now I have an excuse to discover whether that story is true. Is the Sword of Shannara down there in that ravine? You and I shall discover the answer. Resurrection of the magic of the Elven house of Shannara, young Ohmsford — the key, perhaps, to the freedom of the Four Lands. We must know.'

Damson Rhee shook her titian head. 'You are far too eager, Padishar, to throw your life away. And the lives of others like this boy. I will never understand.'

She moved away from them to gather up the children. Par didn't care much for being called a boy by a girl who looked younger still.

'Watch out for that one, Par Ohmsford.' the outlaw chief murmured.

'She doesn't have much faith in our chances,' Par observed.

'Ah, she worries without cause! We have the strength of seven of us to withstand whatever might guard the Pit. And if there's magic as well, we have your wishsong and the Highlander's blade. Enough said.'

He studied the sky. 'It will be dark soon, lad.' He put his arm about the Valeman companionably and moved them forward to join Damson Rhee and the children. 'When it is,' he whispered, 'we'll have a look for ourselves at what's become of the Sword of Shannara.'

CHAPTER

19

A S PADISHAR CREEL'S MAKESHIFT FAMILY reached the edge of the park and prepared to step out onto the Tyrsian Way, Damson Rhee turned to the outlaw chief and said, 'The sentries who patrol the wall make a change at midnight in front of the Federation Gatehouse. I can arrange for a small disturbance that will distract them long enough for you to slip into the Pit — if you are determined on this. Be certain you go in at the west end.'

Then she reached up and plucked a silver coin from behind Par's ear and gave it to him. The coin bore her likeness. 'For luck, Par Ohmsford,' she said. 'You will be needing it if you continue to follow *him*.'

She gave Padishar a hard look, took the children by the hand, and strode off into the crowds without looking back, her red hair shining. The outlaw chief and the Valeman watched her go.

'Who is she, Padishar?' Par asked when she was no longer in view.

Padishar shrugged. 'Whoever she chooses to be. There are as many stories about her origins as there are about my own. Come, now. Time for us to be going as well.'

He took Par back through the city, keeping to the lesser streets and byways. The crowds were still heavy, everyone pushing and shoving, their faces dust-streaked and their tempers short. Twilight had chased the sunlight west, lengthening the shadows into evening, but the heat of midday remained trapped by the city's walls, rising out of the stone of the streets and buildings to hang in the still summer air. It was like being in a furnace. Par glanced skyward. Already the quarter-moon was visible northward, a sprinkling of stars east. He tried to think about what he had learned of the disappearance of the Sword of Shannara, but found himself thinking instead of Damson Rhee.

Padishar had him safely back down in the basement of the storage house behind the weapons shop before dark, where Coll and Morgan waited impatiently to receive them. Cutting short a flurry of questions, the outlaw chief smiled cheerfully and announced that everything was arranged. At midnight the Valemen, the Highlander, Ciba Blue, and he would make a brief foray into the ravine that fronted what had once been the palace of the city's rulers. They would descend using a rope ladder. Stasas and Drutt would remain behind. They would haul the ladder up when their companions were safely down and hide until summoned. Any sentries would be dispatched, the ladder would be lowered again, and they would all disappear back the way they had come.

He was succinct and matter-of-fact. He made no mention of why they were doing all this and none of his own men bothered to ask. They simply let him finish, then turned immediately back to whatever they had been doing before. Coll and Morgan, on the other hand, could barely contain themselves, and Par was forced to take them aside and tell them in detail everything that had happened. The three of them huddled in one corner of the basement, seated on sacks of scrubbing powder. Oil lamps lit the darkness, and the city above them began to go still.

When Par concluded, Morgan shook his head doubtfully.

'It is hard to believe that an entire city has forgotten there was more than one People's Park and Bridge of Sendic,' he declared softly.

'Not hard at all when you remember that they have had more than a hundred years to work on it,' Coll disagreed quickly. 'Think about it, Morgan. How much more than a park and a bridge has been forgotten in that time? The Federation has saddled the Four Lands with three hundred years of revisionist history.'

'Coll's right,' Par said. 'We lost our only true historian when Allanon passed from the Lands. The Druid Histories were the only written compilations the Races had, and we don't know what's become of those. All we have left are the storytellers, with their word-of-mouth recitations, most of them imperfect.'

'Everything about the old world has been called a lie,' Coll said, his dark eyes hard. 'We know it to be the truth, but we are virtually alone in that belief. The Federation has changed everything to suit its own purposes. After a hundred years, it is little wonder that no one in Tyrsis remembers that the People's Park and the Bridge of Sendic are not the same as they once were. The fact of the matter is, who even cares anymore?'

Morgan frowned. 'Perhaps so. But something's still not right about this.' His frown deepened. 'It bothers me that the Sword of Shannara, vault and all, has been down in this ravine all these years and no one's seen it. It bothers me that no one who's gone down to have a look has come back out again.'

'That troubles me, too,' Coll agreed.

Par glanced briefly at the outlaws, who were paying no attention to them. 'None of us thought for a minute that it wouldn't be dangerous trying to recover the Sword,' he whispered, a hint of exasperation in his voice. 'Surely you didn't expect to just walk up and take it? Of course no one's seen it! It wouldn't be missing if they had, would it? And you can bet that the Federation has made certain no one who got down into the Pit got back out again! That's the reason for the guards and the Gatehouse! Besides, the fact that the Federation has gone to so much trouble to hide the old bridge and park suggests to me that the Sword is down there!'

Coll looked at his brother steadily. 'It also suggests that that's where it's meant to stay.'

The conversation broke off and the three of them drifted away to separate corners of the basement. Evening passed quickly into nightfall and the heat of the day finally faded. The little company ate an uneventful dinner amid long stretches of silence. Only Padishar had much of anything to say, ebullient as always, tossing off stories and jokes as if this night were the same as any other, seemingly heedless of the fact that his audience remained unresponsive. Par was too excited to eat or talk and spent the time wondering if Padishar were as unaffected as he appeared. Nothing seemed to alter the mood of the outlaw chief. Padishar Creel was either very brave or very foolish, and it bothered the Valeman that he wasn't sure which it was.

Dinner ended and they sat around talking in hushed voices and staring at the walls. Padishar came over to Par at one point and crouched down beside him. 'Are you anxious to be about our business, lad?' he asked softly.

No one else was close enough to hear. Par nodded.

'Ah, well, it won't be long now.' The outlaw patted his knee. The hard eyes held his own. 'Just remember what we're about. A quick look and out again. If the Sword is there for the taking, fine. If not, no delays.' His smile was wolfish. 'Caution in all things.' He slipped away, leaving Par to stare after him.

The minutes lengthened with the wearing slowness of shadows at midday. Par and Coll sat side by side without speaking. Par could almost hear his brother's thoughts in the silence. The oil lamps flickered and spat. A giant swamp fly buzzed about the ceiling until Ciba Blue killed it. The basement room began to smell close.

Then finally Padishar stood up and said it was time. They came to their feet eagerly, anticipation flickering in their eyes. Weapons were strapped down and cloaks pulled close. They went up the basement stairs through the trapdoor and out into the night.

The city streets were empty and still. Voices drifted out

of ale houses and sleeping rooms, punctuated by raucous laughter and occasional shouts. The lamps were mostly broken or unlit on the back streets that Padishar took them down, and there was only moonlight to guide them through the shadows. They did not move furtively, only cautiously, not wishing to draw attention to themselves. They ducked back into alleyways several times to avoid knots of swaying, singing revellers who were making their way homeward. Drunks and beggars who saw them pass barely glanced up from the doorways and alcoves in which they lay. They saw no Federation soldiers. The Federation left the back streets and the poor of Tyrsis to manage for themselves.

When they reached the People's Park and the Bridge of Sendic, Padishar sent them across the broad expanse of the Tyrsian Way in twos and threes into the shadows of the park, dispatching them in different directions to regroup later, carefully watching the well-lighted Way for any approach of the Federation patrols he knew would be found there. Only one patrol passed, and it saw nothing of the company. A watch was posted before the Gatehouse at the center of the wall which warded the Pit, but the soldiers had lamplight reflecting all about them and could not see outside its glow to the figures lost in the dark beyond. Padishar took the company swiftly through the deserted park west to where the ravine approached its juncture with the cliffs. There, he settled them in to wait.

Par crouched motionlessly in the dark and listened to the sound of his heart pumping in his ears. The silence about him was filled with the hum of insects. Locusts buzzed in raucous cadence in the black. The seven men were concealed in a mass of thicket, invisible to anyone without. But anyone beyond their concealment was invisible to them as well. Par was uneasy with their placement and wondered at its choice. He glanced at Padishar Creel, but the outlaw chief was busy overseeing the untangling of the rope ladder that would lower them into the ravine. . . .

Par hesitated. The Pit. Lower them into the Pit. He

forced himself to say the word.

He took a deep breath, trying to steady himself. He wondered if Damson Rhee was anywhere close.

A patrol of four Federation soldiers materialized out of the dark almost directly in front of them, walking the perimeter of the wall. Though the sound of their boots warned of their coming, it was chilling when they appeared, nevertheless. Par and the others flattened themselves in the scratchy tangle of their concealment. The soldiers paused, spoke quietly among themselves for a moment, then turned back the way they had come, and were gone.

Par exhaled slowly. He risked a quick glance over at the dark bowl of the ravine. It was a soundless, depthless well of ink.

Padishar and the other outlaws were lowering the rope ladder down now, fixing it in place, preparing for the descent. Par came to his feet, eager to relieve muscles that were beginning to cramp, anxious to be done with this whole business. He should have felt confident. He did not. He was growing steadily more uneasy and he couldn't say why. Something was tugging at him frantically, warning him, some sixth sense that he couldn't identify.

He thought he heard something — not ahead in the ravine, but behind in the park. He started to turn, his sharp Elf eyes searching.

Then abruptly there was a flurry of shouts from the direction of the Gatehouse, and cries of alarm pierced the night.

'Now!' Padishar Creel urged, and they bolted their cover for the wall.

The ladder was already knotted in place, tied down to a pair of the wall spikes. Ciba Blue went over first, the cobalt birthmark on his cheek a dark, hollow place in the moonlight. He tested the ladder first with his weight, then disappeared from view.

'Remember, listen for my signal,' Padishar was saying hurriedly to Strasas and Drutt, his voice a rough whisper above the distant shouts.

He was turning to start Par down the ladder after Ciba Blue when a swarm of Federation soldiers appeared out of the dark behind them, armed with spears and crossbows, silent figures that seemed to come from nowhere. Everyone froze. Par felt his stomach lurch with shock. He found himself thinking, 'I should have known, I should have sensed them,' and thinking in the next breath that indeed he had.

'Lay down your weapons,' a voice commanded.

For just an instant, Par was afraid that Padishar Creel would choose to fight rather than surrender. The outlaw chief's eyes darted left and right, his tall form rigid. But the odds were overwhelming. His face relaxed, he gave a barely perceptible smile, and dropped his sword and long knife in front of him wordlessly. The others of the little company did the same, and the Federation soldiers closed about. Weapons were scooped up and arms bound behind backs.

'There's another of them down in the Pit,' a soldier advised the leader of their captors, a smallish man with short-cropped hair and commander's bars on his dark tunic.

The commander glanced over. 'Cut the ropes, let him drop.'

The rope ladder was cut through in a moment. It fell soundlessly into the black. Par waited for a cry, but there was none. Perhaps Ciba Blue had already completed his descent. He glanced at Coll, who just shook his head helplessly.

The Federation commander stepped up to Padishar. 'You should know, Padishar Creel,' he said quietly, his tone measured, 'that you were betrayed by one of your own.'

He waited momentarily for a response, but there was none. Padishar's face was expressionless. Only his eyes revealed the rage that he was somehow managing to contain.

Then the silence was shattered by a terrifying scream

that rose out of the depths of the Pit. It lifted into the night like a stricken bird, hovering against the cliff rock until at last, mercifully, it dropped away.

The scream had been Ciba Blue's, Par thought in horror.

The Federation commander gave the ravine a perfunctory glance and ordered his prisoners led away.

They were taken through the park along the ravine wall toward the Gatehouse, kept in single file and apart from each other by the soldiers guarding them. Par trudged along with the others in stunned silence, the sound of Ciba Blue's scream still echoing in his mind. What had happened to the outlaw down there alone in the Pit? He swallowed against the sick feeling in his stomach and forced himself to think of something else. Betrayed, the Federation commander had said. But by whom? None of them there, obviously — so someone who wasn't. One of Padishar's own . . .

He tripped over a tree root, righted himself and stumbled on. His mind whirled with a scattering of thoughts. They were being taken to the Federation prisons, he concluded. Once there, the grand adventure was over. There would be no more searching for the missing Sword of Shannara. There would be no further consideration of the charge given him by Allanon. No one ever came out of the Federation prisons.

He had to escape.

The thought came instinctively, clearing his mind as nothing else could. He had to escape. If he didn't, they would all be locked away and forgotten. Only Damson Rhee knew where they were, and it had occurred suddenly to Par that Damson Rhee had been in the best position to betray them.

It was an unpleasant possibility. It was also unavoidable.

His breathing slowed. This was the best opportunity to break free that he would get. Once within the prisons, it would be much more difficult to manage. Perhaps Padishar would come up with a plan by then, but Par didn't care to chance it. Uncharitably, perhaps, he was thinking that Padishar was the one who had gotten them into this mess.

He watched the lights of the Gatehouse flicker ahead through the trees of the park. He only had a few minutes more. He thought he could manage it, but he would have to go alone. He would have to leave Coll and Morgan. There wasn't any choice.

Voices sounded from ahead, other soldiers waiting for their return. The line began to string out and some of the guards were straying a bit. Par took a deep breath. He waited until they were passing along a cluster of scrub birch, then used the wishsong. He sang softly, his voice blending into the sounds of the night, a whisper of breeze, a bird's gentle call, a cricket's brief chirp. He let the wishsong's magic reach out and fill the minds of the guards immediately next to him, distracting them, turning their eyes away from him, letting them forget that he was there . . .

And then he simply stepped into the birch and shadows and disappeared.

The line of prisoners passed on without him. No one had noticed that he was gone. If Coll or Morgan or any of the others had seen anything, they were keeping still about it. The Federation soldiers and their prisoners continued moving toward the lights ahead, leaving him alone.

When they were gone, he moved soundlessly off into the night.

He managed to free himself almost immediately of the ropes that held his hands. He found a spike with a jagged edge on the ravine wall a hundred yards from where he had slipped away and, boosting himself up on the wall, sawed through the ropes in only minutes. No alarm had gone up yet from the watch; apparently, he hadn't been missed. Maybe they hadn't bothered to count the original number of their prisoners, he reasoned. After all, it had been dark, and the capture had taken place in a matter of seconds.

At any rate, he was free. So what was he going to do now?

He worked his way back through the park toward the Tyrsian Way, keeping to the shadows, stopping every few seconds to listen for the sounds of the pursuit that never came. He was sweating freely, his turic sticking to his back, his face streaked with dust. He was exhilarated by his escape and devastated by the realization that he didn't know how to take advantage of it. There was no help for him in Tyrsis and no help for him without. He didn't know whom to contact within the city; there was no one he could afford to trust. And he had no idea how to get back into the Parma Key. Steff would help if he knew his companions were in trouble. But how would the Dwarf find out before it was too late to matter?

The lights of the Way came into view through the trees. Par stumbled to the edge of the park, close to its western boundaries, and collapsed in despair against the trunk of an old maple. He had to do something; he couldn't just wander about. He brushed at his face with his sleeve and let his head sink back against the rough bark. He was suddenly sick and it took every ounce of willpower he could muster to prevent himself from retching.

He had to get back to Coll and Morgan. He had to find a way to free them.

Use the wishsong, he thought.

But how?

A Federation patrol came down the Way, boots clumping in the stillness. Par shrank back into the shadows and waited until they were out of sight. Then he moved from his cover along the edge of the park toward a fountain bordering the walk. Once there, he leaned over and hurriedly splashed water on his hands and face. The water ran along his skin like liquid silver.

He paused, letting his head sink against his chest. He was suddenly very tired.

The arm that yanked him around was strong and unyielding, snapping his head back violently. He found himself face to face with Damson Rhee.

'What happened?' she demanded, her voice low.

Frantically, Par reached for his long knife. But his weapons were gone, taken by the Federation. He shoved at the girl, trying to rip free of her grip, but she side-stepped the blow without effort and kicked him so hard in the stomach that he doubled over.

'What are you doing, you idiot?' she whispered angrily.

Without waiting for an answer, she hauled him back into the concealing shadows of the park and threw him to the ground. 'If you try something like that again with me, I will break both your arms!' she snapped.

Par pulled himself up to a sitting position, still looking for a way to escape. But she shoved him back against the ground and crouched close. 'Why don't we try again, my beloved Elf-boy? Where are the others? What has happened to them?'

Par swallowed against his rage. 'The Federation has them! They were waiting for us, Damson! As if you didn't know!'

The anger in her eyes was replaced by surprise. 'What do you mean, "as if I didn't know?"'

'They were waiting for us. We never got past the wall. We were betrayed! The Federation commander told us so! He said it was one of our own — an outlaw, Damson!' Par was shaking.

Damson Rhee's gaze was steady. 'And you have decided that it was me, have you, Par Ohmsford?'

Par forced himself up on his elbows. 'Who better than you? You were the only one who knew what we were about — the only one not taken! No one else knew! If not you, then who could it possibly have been?'

There was a long silence as they stared at each other in the dark. The sound of voices nearby grew slowly distinct. Someone was approaching.

Damson Rhee suddenly bent close. 'I don't know. But it wasn't me! Now lie still until they pass.'

She pushed him into a gathering of bushes, then backed in herself and lay down beside him. Par could feel the warmth of her body. He could smell the sweet scent of her. He closed his eyes and waited. A pair of Federation soldiers worked their way out of the park, paused momentarily, then started back again and were gone.

Damson Rhee put her lips close against Par's ear. 'Do they know you are missing yet?'

Par hesitated. 'I can't be certain,' he whispered back.

She took his chin with her smooth hand and turned his face until it was level with her own. 'I didn't betray you. It may seem as if I must have, but I didn't. If I intended to betray you to the Federation, Par, I would have simply turned you over to that pair of soldiers and been done with it.'

The green eyes glittered faintly with moonlight that had penetrated the branches of their concealment. Par stared at those eyes and found no hint of deception mirrored there. Still, he hesitated.

'You have to decide here and now whether you believe me,' she said quietly.

He shook his head warily. 'It isn't that easy!'

'It has to be! Look at me, Par. I have betrayed no one — not you or Padishar or the others, not now, not ever! Why would I do something like that? I hate the Federation as much as anyone!' She paused, exasperated. 'I told you that this was a dangerous undertaking. I warned you that the Pit was a black hole that swallowed men whole. Padishar was the one who insisted you go!'

'That doesn't make him responsible for what happened.'

'Nor me! What about the distraction I promised? Did it come about as I said it would?'

Par nodded.

'You see! I fulfilled my part of the bargain! Why would I bother if I intended your betrayal?'

271

Par said nothing.

Damson's nostrils flared. 'You will admit to nothing, will you?' She shook back her auburn hair in a flash of color. 'Will you at least tell me what happened?'

Par took a deep breath. Briefly, he related the events that surrounded their capture, including the frightening disappearance of the outlaw Ciba Blue. He kept deliberately vague the circumstances of his own escape. The magic was his business. Its secret belonged to him.

But Damson was not about to be put off. 'So the fact of the matter is, you might as easily be the betrayer as I,' she said. 'How else is it that you managed to escape when the others could not?'

Par flushed, resentful of the accusation, irritated by her persistence. 'Why would I do such a thing to my friends?'

'My own argument exactly,' she replied.

They studied each other wordlessly, each measuring the strength of the other. Damson was right, Par knew. There was as much reason to believe that he had been the betrayer as she. But that didn't change the fact that he knew he wasn't while he didn't know the same of her.

'Decide, Par,' she urged quietly. 'Do you believe me or not?'

Her features were smooth and guileless in the scattering of light, her skin dappled with shadows from the tiny leaves of the bushes. He found himself drawn to her in a way he had not believed possible. There was something special about this girl, something that made him push aside his misgivings and cast out his doubts. The green eyes held him, insinuating and persuasive. He saw only truth in them.

'Okay, I believe you,' he said finally.

'Then tell me how it is that you escaped when the others did not,' she demanded. 'No, don't argue the matter. I must have proof of your own innocence if we are to be of any use to each other or to our friends.'

Par's resolve to keep to himself the secret of the wish-song slipped slowly away. Again, she was right. She was asking only what he would have asked in her place. 'I used magic,' he told her.

She inched closer, as if to judge better the truth of what he was saying. 'Magic? What sort?'

He hesitated yet.

'Sleight of hand? Cloud spells?' she pressed. 'Some sort of vanishing act?'

'Yes,' he replied. She was waiting. 'I have the ability to make myself invisible when I wish.'

There was a long silence. He read the curiosity in her eyes. 'You command real magic, don't you?' she said finally. 'Not the pretend kind that I use, where coins appear and disappear and fire dances on the air. You have the sort that is forbidden. That is why Padishar is so interested in you.' She paused. 'Who are you, Par Ohmsford? Tell me.'

It was still within the park now; the voices of the watch passed from hearing, the night gone deep and silent once more. There might have been no one else in all the world but the two of them. Par weighed the advisability of his reply. He was stepping on stones that floated in quicksand.

'You can see who I am for yourself,' he said finally, hedging. 'I am part Elf and that part of me carries the magic of my forebears. I have their magic to command — or some small part of it, at least.'

She looked at him for a long time then, thinking. At last she seemed to have made up her mind. She crawled from the concealment of the bushes, pulling him out with her. They stood together in the shadows, brushing themselves off, breathing deeply the cool night air. The park was deserted.

She came up to him and stood close. 'I was born in Tyrsis, the child of a forger of weapons and his wife. I had one brother and one sister, both older. When I was eight, the Federation discovered my father was supplying arms to the Movement. Someone — a friend, an acquaintance, I never knew who — betrayed him. Seekers came to our house in the middle of the night, fired it and burned it to the ground. My family was locked inside and burned with it. I escaped only because I was visiting my aunt. Within a year she was dead as well, and I was forced to live in the streets. That is where I grew up. My family was all gone. I had no friends. A street magician took me as his apprentice and taught me my trade. That has been my life.' She paused. 'You deserve to know why it is that I would never betray anyone to the Federation.'

She reached up with her hand and her fingers brushed his cheek for just a moment. Then her hand trailed down to his arm and fastened there.

'Par, we must do whatever it is we are going to do tonight or it will be too late. The Federation knows who they have. Padishar Creel. They will send for Rimmer Dall and his Seekers to question Padishar. Once that happens, rescue will be pointless.' She paused, making certain that he took her meaning. 'We have to help them now.'

Par went cold at the thought of Coll and Morgan in the hands of Rimmer Dall — let alone Padishar. What would the First Seeker do to the leader of the Movement?

'Tonight,' she continued, her voice soft, but insistent. 'While they are not expecting it. They will still have Padishar and the others in the cells at the Gatehouse. They won't have moved them yet. They will be tired, sleepy with the coming of morning. We won't get a better chance.'

He stared at her incredulously. 'You and I?'

'If you agree to come with me.'

'But what can the two of us do?'

She pulled him close. Her red hair shimmered darkly in the moonlight. 'Tell me about your magic. What can you do with it, Par Ohmsford?'

There was no hesitation now. 'Make myself invisible,' he said. 'Make myself appear to be different than I am. Make others think they are seeing things that aren't there.' He was growing excited. 'Just about anything that I want if it's not for too long and not too extended. It's just illusion, you understand.'

She walked away from him, paced into the trees close

by and stopped. She stood there in the shadows, lost in thought. Par waited where he was, feeling the cool night air brush his skin in a sudden breath of wind, listening to the silence that spread across the city like the waters of an ocean across its floor. He could almost swim through that silence, drifting away to better times and places. There was fear in him that he could not suppress — fear at the thought of returning for his friends, fear at the thought of failing in the attempt. But to attempt nothing at all was unthinkable.

Still, what could they do — just this slip of a girl and himself?

As if reading his mind she came back to him then, green eyes intense, seized his arms tightly and whispered, 'I think I know a way, Par.'

He smiled in spite of himself.

'Tell me about it,' he said.

CHAPTER

20

WALKER BOH JOURNEYED DIRECTLY BACK to Hearthstone after taking leave of the company at the Hadeshorn. He rode his horse east across the Rabb, bypassed Storlock and its Healers, climbed the Wolfsktaag through the Pass of Jade, and worked his way upriver along the Chard Rush until he entered Darklin Reach. Three days later he was home again. He talked with no one on the way, keeping entirely to himself as he traveled, pausing only long enough to eat and sleep. He was not fit company for other men and he knew it. He was obsessed with thoughts of his encounter with the shade of Allanon. He was haunted by them.

The Anar was enveloped by a particularly violent midsummer storm within twenty-four hours of his return, and Walker secluded himself truculently in his cottage home while winds lashed its shaved-board walls and rains beat down upon its shingled roof. The forested valley was deluged, wracked by the crack and flash of lightning, shaken by the long, ominous peals of thunder, pelted and washed until it could no longer stand upright. The cadence of the rains obliterated every other sound, and Walker sat amid their constant thrum in brooding silence, wrapped in blankets and a blackness of spirit he would not have thought possible.

He found himself despairing.

It was the inevitability of things that he feared. Walker

Boh, whatever name he chose to bear, was nevertheless an Ohmsford by blood, and he knew that Ohmsfords, despite their misgivings, had always been made to take up the Druid cause. It had been so with Shea and Flick, with Wil, and with Brin and Jair before him. Now it was to be his turn. His and Wren's and Par's. Par embraced the cause willingly, of course. Par was an incurable romantic, a self-appointed champion of the downtrodden and the abused. Par was a fool.

Or a realist, depending on how you viewed the matter. Because, if history proved an accurate indicator, Par was merely accepting without argument what Walker, too, would be forced to embrace — Allanon's will, the cause of a dead man. The shade had come to them like some scolding patriarch out of death's embrace — chiding them for their lack of diligence, scolding them for their misgivings, charging them with missions of madness and self-destruction. Bring back the Druids! Bring back Paranor! Do these things because I say they must be done, because I say they are necessary, because I — a thing of no flesh and dead mind — demand it!

Walker's mood darkened further as the weight of the matter continued to settle steadily over him, a pall mirroring the oppressiveness of the storms without. Change the whole of the face of the world — that was what the shade was asking of them, of Par, Wren, and himself. Take three hundred years of evolution in the Four Lands and dispense with it in an instant's time. What else was the shade asking, if not that? A return of the magic, a return of the wielders of that magic, of its shapers, of all the things ended by this same shade those three hundred years past. Madness! They would be playing with lives in the manner of creators — and they were not entitled!

Through the gray haze of his anger and his fear, he could conjure in his mind the features of the shade. Allanon. The last of the Druids, the keeper of the Histories of the Four Lands, the protector of the Races, the dispenser of magic and secrets. His dark form rose up against the years like a cloud against the sun, blocking

277

away the warmth and the light. Everything that had taken place while he lived bore his touch. And before that, it was Bremen, and before that the Druids of the First Council of the Races. Wars of magic, struggles for survival, the battles between light and dark — or grays perhaps — had all been the result of the Druids.

And now he was being asked to bring all that back.

It could be argued that it was necessary. It had always been argued so. It could be said that the Druids merely worked to preserve and protect, never to shape. But had there ever been one without the other? And necessity was always in the eye of the beholder. Warlock Lords, Demons, and Mord Wraiths past — they had been exchanged for Shadowen. But what were these Shadowen that men should require the aid of Druids and magic? Could not men take it upon themselves to deal with the ills of the world rather than defer to power they scarcely understood? Magic carried grief as well as joy, its dark side as apt to influence and change as its light. Bring it back again, should he, only to give it to men who had repeatedly demonstrated that they were incapable of mastering its truths?

How could he?

Yet without it, the world might become the vision Allanon's shade had shown them — a nightmare of fire and darkness in which only creatures such as the Shadowen belonged. Perhaps it was true after all that magic was the only means of keeping the Races safe against such beings.

Perhaps.

The truth of the matter was that he simply didn't want to be part of what was to happen. He was not a child of the Races of the Four Lands, not in body or in spirit, and never had been. He had no empathy with their men and women. He had no place among them. He had been cursed with magic of his own, and it had stripped him of his humanity and his place among humans and isolated him from every other living thing. Ironic, because he alone had no fear of the Shadowen. Perhaps he could even protect against them, were he asked to do so. But he would not be asked. He was as much feared as they. He was the Dark Uncle, the descendant of Brin Ohmsford, the bearer of her seed and her trust, keeper of some nameless charge from Allanon. . . .

Except, of course, that the charge was nameless no more. The charge was revealed. He was to bring back Paranor and the Druids, out of the void of yesteryear, out of the nothingness.

That was what the shade had demanded of him, and the demand tracked relentlessly through the landscape of his mind, hurdling arguments, circumventing reason, whispering that it was and therefore must be.

So he worried the matter as a dog would its bone, and the days dragged by. The storms passed and the sun returned to bake the plains dry but leave the forestlands weltering in the heat and damp. He went out after a time, walking the valley floor with only Rumor for company, the giant moor cat having wandered down out of the rain forests east with the changing of the weather, luminous eyes as depthless as the despair the Dark Uncle felt. The cat gave him companionship, but offered no solution to his dilemma and no relief from his brooding. They walked and sat together as the days and nights passed, and time hung suspended against a backdrop of events taking place beyond their refuge that neither could know nor see.

Until, on the same night that Par Ohmsford and his companions were betrayed in their attempt to lay hands upon the Sword of Shannara, Cogline returned to the valley of Hearthstone and the illusion of separateness that Walker had worked so hard to maintain was shattered. It was late evening, the sun had gone west, the skies were washed with moonlight and filled with stars, and the summer air was sweet and clean with the smell of new growth. Walker was coming back from a visit to the pinnacle, a refuge he found particularly soothing, the massive stone a source from which it seemed he could draw strength. The cottage door was open and the rooms

279

within lighted as always, but Walker sensed the difference, even before Rumor's purr stilled and his neck ruff bristled.

Cautiously, he moved onto the porch and into the doorway.

Cogline sat at the old wooden dining table, skeletal face bent against the glare of the oil lamps, his gray robes a weathered covering for goods long since past repair. A large, squarish package bound in oilcloth and tied with cord rested close beside him. He was eating cold food, a glass of ale almost untouched at his elbow.

'I have been waiting for you, Walker,' he told the other while he was still in the darkness beyond the entry.

Walker moved into the light. 'You might have saved yourself the trouble.'

'Trouble?' The old man extended a sticklike hand, and Rumor padded forward to muzzle it familiarly. 'It was time I saw my home again.'

'Is this your home?' Walker asked. 'I would have thought you more comfortable amid the relics of the Druid past.' He waited for a response, but there was none. 'If you have come to persuade me to take up the charge given me by the shade, then you should know at once that I will never do so.'

'Oh, my, Walker. Never is such an impossible amount of time. Besides, I have no intention of trying to persuade you to do anything. A sufficient amount of persuading has already been done, I suspect.'

Walker was still standing in the doorway. He felt awkward and exposed and moved over to the table to sit across from Cogline. The old man took a long sip of the ale.

'Perhaps you thought me gone for good after my disappearance at the Hadeshorn,' he said softly. His voice was distant and filled with emotions that the other could not begin to sort out. 'Perhaps you even wished it.'

Walker said nothing.

'I have been out into the world, Walker. I have traveled into the Four Lands, walked among the Races, passed

280

through cities and countrysides; I have felt the pulse of life and found that it ebbs. A farmer speaks to me on the grasslands below the Streleheim, a man worn and broken by the futility of what he has encountered. "Nothing grows," he whispers. "The earth sickens as if stricken by some disease." The disease infects him as well. A merchant of wood carvings and toys journeys from a small village beyond Varfleet, directionless. "I leave," he says, "because there is no need for me. The people cease to have interest in my work. They do nothing but brood and waste away." Bits and pieces of life in the Four Lands, Walker — they wither and fade like a spotting that spreads across the flesh. Pockets here and pockets there — as if the will to go on were missing. Trees and shrubs and growing things fail; animals and men alike sicken and die. All become dust, and a haze of that dust rises up and fills the air and leaves the whole of the ravaged land a still life in miniature of the vision shown us by Allanon.'

The sharp, old eyes squinted up at the other. 'It begins, Walker. It begins.'

Walker Boh shook his head. 'The land and her people have always suffered failings, Cogline. You see the shade's vision because you want to see it.'

'No, not I, Walker.' The old man shook his head firmly. 'I want no part of Druid visions, neither in their being nor in their fulfillment. I am as much a pawn of what has happened as yourself. Believe what you will, I do not wish involvement. I have chosen my life in the same manner that you have chosen yours. You don't accept that, do you?'

Walker smiled unkindly. 'You took up the magic because you wished to. Once-Druid, you had a choice in your life. You dabbled in a mixture of old sciences and magics because they interested you. Not so myself. I was born with a legacy I would have been better born without. The magic was forced upon me without my consent. I use it because I have no choice. It is a millstone that would drag me down. But I do not deceive myself. It has made my life a ruin.' The dark eyes were bitter. 'Do not attempt to compare us, Cogline.'

The other's thin frame shifted. 'Harsh words, Walker Boh. You were eager enough to accept my teaching in the use of that magic once upon a time. You felt comfortable enough with it then to learn its secrets.'

'A matter of survival and nothing more. I was a child trapped in a Druid's monstrous casting. I used you to keep myself alive. You were all I had.' The white skin of his lean face was taut with bitterness. 'Do not look to me for thanks, Cogline. I haven't the grace for it.'

Cogline stood up suddenly, a whiplash movement that belied his fragile appearance. He towered above the dark-robed figure seated across from him, and there was a forbidding look to his weathered face. 'Poor Walker,' he whispered. 'You still deny who you are. You deny your very existence. How long can you keep up this pretense?'

There was a strained silence between them that seemed endless. Rumor, curled on a rug before the fire at the far end of the room, looked up expectantly. An ember from the hearth spat and snapped, filling the air with a shower of sparks.

'Why have you come, old man?' Walker Boh said finally, the words a barely contained thrust of rage. There was a coppery taste in his mouth that he knew came not from anger, but from fear.

'To try to help you,' Cogline said. There was no irony in his voice. 'To give you direction in your brooding.'

'I am content without your interference.'

'Content?' The other shook his head. 'No, Walker. You will never be content until you learn to quit fighting yourself. You work so hard at it. I thought that the lessons you received from me on the uses of the magic might have weaned you away from such childishness — but it appears I was wrong. You face hard lessons, Walker. Maybe you won't survive them.'

He shoved the heavy parcel across the table at the other man. 'Open it.'

Walker hesitated, his eyes locked on the offering. Then he reached out, snapped apart the binding with a flick of his fingers and pulled back the oilcloth.

He found himself looking at a massive, leatherbound book elaborately engraved in gold. He reached out and touched it experimentally, lifted the cover, peered momentarily inside, then flinched away from it as if his fingers had been burned.

'Yes, Walker. It is one of the missing Druid Histories, a single volume only.' The wrinkled old face was intense.

'Where did you get it?' Walker demanded harshly.

Cogline bent close. The air seemed filled with the sound of his breathing. 'Out of lost Paranor.'

Walker Boh came slowly to his feet. 'You lie.'

'Do I? Look into my eyes and tell me what you see.'

Walker flinched away. He was shaking. 'I don't care where you got it or what fantasies you have concocted to make me believe what I know in my heart cannot possibly be so! Take it back to where you got it or let it sink into the bogs! I'll have no part of it!'

Cogline shook his wispy head. 'No, Walker, I'll not take it back. I carried it out of a realm of yesterdays filled with gray haze and death to give it to you. I am not your tormentor — never that! I am the closest thing to a friend you will ever know, even if you cannot yet accept it!' The weathered face softened. 'I said before that I came to help you. It is so. Read the book, Walker. There are truths in there that need learning.'

'I will not!' the other cried furiously.

Cogline stared at the younger man for long minutes, then sighed. 'As you will. But the book remains. Read it or not, the choice is yours. Destroy it even, if you wish.' He drained off the remainder of his ale, set the glass carefully on the table, and looked down at his gnarled hands. 'I am finished here.'

He came around the table and stood before the other. 'Goodbye, Walker. I would stay if it would help. I would give you whatever it is within my power to give you if you would take it. But you are not yet ready Another day, perhaps.'

He turned then and disappeared into the night. He did

not look back as he went. He did not deviate from his course. Walker Boh watched him fade away, a shadow gone back into the darkness that had made him.

The cottage, as if by his going, turned empty and still.

'It will be dangerous, Par,' Damson Rhee whispered. 'If there were a safer way, I should snatch it up in an instant.'

Par Ohmsford said nothing. They were deep within the People's Park once more, crouched in the shadows of a grove of cedar just beyond the broad splash of light cast by the lamps of the Gatehouse. It was midway toward dawn, the deepest, fullest hours of sleep, when everything slowed to a crawl amid dreams and rememberings. The Gatehouse rose up against the moonlit darkness like a gathering of massive blocks stacked one upon the other by a careless child. Barred windows and bolted doors were shallow indentations in a skin made rough and coarse by weather and time. The walls warding the ravine ran off to either side and the crossing bridge stretched away behind, a spider web connecting to the tumbledown ruin of the old palace. A watch had been stationed before the main entry where a pair of matched iron portals stood closed behind a hinged grate of bars. The watch dozed on its feet, barely awake in the enveloping stillness. No sound or movement from the Gatehouse disturbed their rest.

'Can you remember enough of him to conjure up a likeness?' Damson asked, her words a brush of softness against his ear. Par nodded. It was not likely he would ever forget the face of Rimmer Dall.

She was quiet a moment. 'If we are stopped, keep their attention focused on yourself. I will deal with any threats.'

He nodded once more. They waited, motionless within their concealment, listening to the stillness, thinking their separate thoughts. Par was frightened and filled with doubts, but he was mostly determined. Damson and he were the only real chance Coll and the others had. They would succeed in this risky business because they must.

The Gate watch came awake as those patrolling the west wall of the park appeared out of the night. The guards greeted each other casually, spoke for a time and then the watch from the east wall appeared as well. A flask was passed around, pipes were smoked, and then the guards dispersed. The patrols disappeared east and west. The Gate watch resumed their station.

'Not yet,' Damson whispered as Par shifted expectantly.

The minutes dragged by. The solitude that had shrouded the Gatehouse earlier returned anew. The guards yawned and shifted. One leaned wearily on the haft of his poleax.

'Now,' Damson Rhee said. She caught the Valeman by the shoulder and leaned into him. Her lips brushed his cheek. 'Luck to us, Par Ohmsford.'

Then they were up and moving. They crossed into the circle of light boldly, striding out of the shadows as if they were at home in them, coming toward the Gatehouse from the direction of the city. Par was already singing, weaving the wishsong's spell through the night's stillness, filling the minds of the watch with the images he wished them to see.

What they saw were two Seekers cloaked in forbidding black, the taller of the two First Seeker Rimmer Dall.

They snapped to attention immediately, eyes forward, barely looking at the two who approached. Par kept his voice even, the magic weaving a constant spell of disguise in the minds of the willing men.

'Open!' Damson Rhee snapped perfunctorily as they reached the Gatehouse entry.

The guards could not comply quickly enough. They pulled back the hinged grate, released the outer locks and hammered anxiously on the doors to alert the guards within. A tiny door opened and Par shifted the focus of his concentration slightly. Bleary eyes peered out in grouchy curiosity, widened, and the locks released. The doors swung back, and Par and Damson pushed inside.

They stood in a wardroom filled with weapons stacked in wall racks and stunned Federation soldiers. The soldiers had been playing cards and drinking, clearly convinced the night's excitement was over. They were caught off guard by the appearance of the Seekers and it showed. Par filled the room with the faint hum of the wishsong, blanketing it momentarily with his magic. It took everything he had.

Damson understood how tenuous was his hold. 'Everyone out!' she ordered, her voice flinty with anger.

The room emptied instantly. The entire squad dispersed through adjoining doors and disappeared as if formed of smoke. One guard remained, apparently the senior watch officer. He stood uncertainly, stiffly, eyes averted, wishing he were anywhere else but where he was, yet unable to go.

'Take us to the prisoners,' Damson said softly, standing at the man's left shoulder.

The soldier cleared his throat after trying futilely to speak. 'I'll need my commander's permission,' he ventured. Some small sense of responsibility for his assigned duty yet remained to him.

Damson kept her eyes fixed on the man's ear, forcing him thereby to look elsewhere. 'Where is your commander?' she asked.

'Sleeping below,' the man answered. 'I'll wake him.'

'No.' Damson stayed his effort to depart. 'We'll wake him together.'

They went through a heavily bolted door directly across the room and started down a stairwell dimly lit by oil lamps. Par kept the wishsong's music lingering in the frightened guard's ears, teasing him with it, letting him see them as much bigger than life and much more threatening. It was all going as planned, the charade working exactly as Damson and he had hoped. Down the empty stairs they went, circling from landing to landing, the thudding of their boots the only sound in the hollow silence. At the bottom of the well there were two doors.

The one on the left was open and led into a lighted corridor. The guard took them through that door to another, stopped and knocked. When there was no response, he knocked again, sharply.

'What is it, drat you?' a voice snapped.

'Open up at once, Commander!' Damson replied in a voice so cold it made even Par shiver.

There was a fumbling about and the door opened. The Federation commander with the short-cropped hair and the unpleasant eyes stood there, his tunic half buttoned. Shock registered on his face instantly as the wishsong's magic took hold. He saw the Seekers. Worse, he saw Rimmer Dall.

He gave up trying to button his clothing and came quickly into the hall. 'I didn't expect anyone this soon. I'm sorry. Is there a problem?'

'We'll discuss it later, Commander,' Damson said severely. 'For now, take us to the prisoners.'

For just an instant there was a flicker of doubt in the other man's eyes, a shading of worry that perhaps everything was not quite right. Par tightened the hold of the magic on the man's mind, giving him a glimpse of the terror that awaited him should he question the order. That glimpse was enough. The commander hastened back down the corridor to the stairwell, produced a key from a ring at his waist, and opened the second door.

They stepped into a passageway lit by a single lamp hung next to the door. The commander took the lamp in hand and led the way forward. Damson followed. Par motioned the watch officer ahead of him and brought up the rear. His voice was beginning to grow weary from the effort of maintaining the charade. It was more difficult to project to several different points. He should have sent the second man away.

The passageway was constructed of stone block and smelled of mold and decay. Par realized that they were underground, apparently beneath the ravine. Things of considerable size darted from the light, and there were streaks of phosphorescence and dampness in the stone.

287

They had only gone a short distance when they came to the cells. They were low-ceilinged cages, not high enough for a man to stand in, dusty and cobwebbed, the doors constructed of rusted iron bars. The entire company was crammed into the first of these, crouched or sitting on a stone slab floor. Eyes blinked in disbelief, widened as the lie of the magic played hide-and-seek with the truth. Coll knew what was going on. He was already on his feet, pushing to the door, motioning the others up with him. Even Padishar obeyed the gesture, realizing what was about to happen.

'Open the door,' Damson ordered.

Again, the eyes of the Federation commander registered his misgivings.

'Open the door, Commander,' Damson repeated impatiently. 'Now!'

The commander fumbled for a second key within the cluster at his belt, inserted it into the lock and turned. The cell door swung open. Instantly, Padishar Creel had the astonished man's neck in his hands, tightening his grip until the other could scarcely breathe. The watch officer stumbled back, turned, tried unsuccessfully to run over Par, was caught from behind by Morgan, and hammered into unconsciousness.

The prisoners crowded into the narrow passageway, greeting Par and Damson with handclasps and smiles. Padishar paid them no heed. His attention was focused entirely on the hapless Federation commander.

'Who betrayed us?' he said with an impatient hiss.

The commander struggled to free himself, his face turning bright red from the pressure on his throat.

'It was one of us, you said! Who?'

The commander choked. 'Don't ... know. Never saw ...'

Padishar shook him. 'Don't lie to me!'

'Never ... Just a ... message.'

'Who was it?' Padishar insisted, the cords on the back of his hands gone white and hard.

The terrified man kicked out violently, and Padishar

slammed his head sharply against the stone wall. The commander went limp, sagging like a rag doll.

Damson pulled Padishar about. 'Enough of this,' she said evenly, ignoring the fury that still burned in the other's eyes. 'We're wasting time. He clearly doesn't know. Let's get out of here. There's been enough risk-taking for one day.'

The outlaw chief studied her wordlessly for a moment, then let the unconscious man drop. 'I'll find out anyway, I promise you,' he swore.

Par had never seen anyone so angry. But Damson ignored it. She turned and motioned for Par to get moving. The Valeman led the way back up the stairwell, the others trailing behind him in a staggered line. They had devised no plan for getting out again when they had made the decision to come after their friends. They had decided that it would be best simply to take what opportunity offered and make do.

Opportunity gave them everything they needed this night. The wardroom was empty when they reached it, and they moved swiftly to pass through. Only Morgan paused, rummaging through the weapons rack until he had located the confiscated Sword of Leah. Smiling grimly, he strapped it across his back and went after the others.

Their luck held. The guards outside were overpowered before they knew what was happening. All about, the night was silent, the park empty, the patrols still completing their rounds, the city asleep. The members of the little band melted into the shadows and vanished.

As they hurried away, Damson swung Par around and gave him a brilliant smile and a kiss full on the mouth. The kiss was hungry and filled with promise.

Later, when there was time to reflect, Par Ohmsford savored that moment. Yet it was not Damson's kiss that he remembered most from the events of that night. It was the fact that the magic of the wishsong had proven useful at last.

CHAPTER

21

THE DRUID HISTORY became for Walker Boh a challenge that he was determined to win.

For three days after Cogline's departure, Walker ignored the book. He left it on the dining table, still settled amid its oilcloth wrappings and broken binding cord, its burnished leather cover collecting motes of dust and gleaming faintly in sunshine and lamplight. He disdained it, going about his business as if it weren't there, pretending it was a part of his surroundings which he could not remove, testing himself against its temptation. He had thought at first to rid himself of it immediately, then decided against it. That would be too easy and too quickly second-guessed later on. If he could withstand its lure for a time, if he could live in its presence without giving in to his understandable desire to uncover its secrets, then he could dispose of it with a clean conscience. Cogline expected him either to open it or dispose of it at once. He would do neither. The old man would get no satisfaction in his efforts to manipulate Walker Boh.

The only one who paid any attention to the parcel was Rumor, who sniffed at it from time to time but otherwise ignored it. The three days passed and the book sat unopened.

But then something odd happened. On the fourth day of this odd contest, Walker began to question his reasoning. Did it really make any better sense to dispose of the book after a week or even a month than it did to dispose of it immediately? Would it matter either way? What did it demonstrate other than a sort of perverse hardheadedness on his part? What sort of game was he playing and for whose benefit was he playing it?

Walker mulled the matter over as the daylight hours waned and darkness closed about, then sat staring at the book from across the room while the fire in the hearth burned slowly to ash and the midnight hour neared.

'I am not being strong,' he whispered to himself. 'I am being frightened.'

He considered the possibility in the silence of his thoughts. Finally he stood up, crossed the room to the dining table and stopped. For a moment, he hesitated. Then he reached down and picked up the Druid History. He hefted it experimentally.

Better to know the Demon that pursues you than to continue to imagine him.

He crossed back to his reading chair and seated himself once more, the book settled on his lap. Rumor lifted his massive head from where he slept in front of the fire, and his luminous eyes fixed on Walker. Walker stared back. The cat blinked and went back to sleep.

Walker Boh opened the book.

He read it slowly, working his way through its thick parchment pages with deliberate pacing, letting his eyes linger on the gold edges and ornate calligraphy, determined that now that the book was opened nothing should be missed. The silence after midnight deepened, broken only by an occasional throaty sound from the sleeping moor cat and the snapping of embers in the fire. Only once he thought to wonder how Cogline had really come by the book — surely not out of Paranor! — and then the matter was forgotten as the recorded history caught him up and swept him away as surely as if he were a leaf upon a windswept ocean.

The time chronicled was that of Bremen when he was among the last of the Druids, when the Warlock Lord and his minions had destroyed nearly all of the members of the Council. There were stories of the dark magic that had changed the rebel Druids into the horrors they had become. There were accounts of its varied uses, conjurings, and incantations that Bremen had uncovered but had been smart enough to fear. All of the frightening secrets of what the magic could do were touched upon, interspersed with the cautions that so many who tried to master the power would ignore. It was a time of upheaval and frightening change in the Four Lands, and Bremen alone had understood what was at stake.

Walker paged ahead, growing anxious now. Cogline had meant him to read something particular within this history. Whatever it was, he had not yet come upon it.

The Skull Bearers had seized Paranor for themselves, the chronicles related. Paranor, they had thought, would now be their home. But the Warlock Lord had felt threatened there, wary of latent magic within the stones of the Keep, within the depths of the earth where the furnaces beneath the castle fortress burned. So he had called the Skull Bearers to him and gone north. . . .

Walker frowned. He had forgotten that part. For a time Paranor had been abandoned completely when it could have belonged to the rebels. After all, the Second War of the Races had dragged on for years.

He paged ahead once more, skimming the words, searching without knowing exactly what it was he was searching for. He had forgotten his resolve of earlier, his promise to himself that he was not going to be caught up in Cogline's snare. His curiosity and intellect were too demanding to be stayed by caution. There were secrets here that no man had set eyes upon for hundreds of years, knowledge that only the Druids had enjoyed, dispensing it to the Races as they perceived necessary and never otherwise. Such power! How long had it been hidden from everyone but Allanon, and before him Bremen, and before him Galaphile and the first Druids, and before them . . .?

He stopped reading, aware suddenly that the flow of

the narrative had changed. The script had turned smaller, more precise. There were odd markings amid the words, runes that symbolized gestures.

Walker Boh went cold to his bones. The silence that enveloped the room became enormous, an unending, suffocating ocean.

Shades! he whispered in the darkest corner of his mind. *It is the invocation for the magic that sealed away Paranor!*

His breathing sounded harsh in his own ears as he forced his eyes away from the book. His pale face was taut. This was what Cogline had meant him to find — why, he didn't know — but this was it. Now that he had found it, he wondered if he might not be better off closing the book at once.

But that was the fear whispering in his ear again, he knew.

He lowered his eyes once more and began to read. The spell was there, the invocation of magic that Allanon had used three hundred years ago to close away Paranor from the world of men. He found to his surprise that he understood it. His training with Cogline was more complete than he would have imagined. He finished the narrative of the spell and turned the page.

There was a single paragraph. It read:

Once removed, Paranor shall remain lost to the world of men for the whole of time, sealed away and invisible within its casting. One magic alone has the power to return it — that singular Elfstone which is colored Black and was conceived by the faerie people of the old world in the manner and form of all Elfstones, combining nevertheless in one stone alone the necessary properties of heart, mind, and body. Whosoever shall have cause and right shall wield it to its proper end.

That was all it said. Walker read on, found that the subject matter abruptly changed and skipped back. He read the paragraph again, slowly, searching for anything he might have missed. There was no question in his mind that this was what Cogline had meant him to find. A Black Elfstone. A magic that could retrieve lost Paranor. The means to the end of the charge that the shade of Allanon had given him.

Bring back Paranor and restore the Druids. He could hear again the words of the charge in his mind.

Of course, there were no longer any Druids. But maybe Allanon intended that Cogline should take up the cause, once Paranor was restored. It seemed logical despite the old man's protestations that his time was past — but Walker was astute enough to recognize that where Druids and their magics were concerned logic often traveled a tortuous path.

He was two-thirds of the way through the history. He spent another hour finishing it, found nothing further that he believed was intended for him, and turned back again to the paragraph on the Black Elfstone. Dawn was creeping out of the east, a faint silver light in the dark horizon. Walker rubbed his eyes and tried to think. Why was there so little digression on the purpose and properties of this magic? What did it look like and what could it do? It was a single stone instead of three — why? How was it that no one had ever heard of it before?

The questions buzzed around inside his head like trapped flies, annoying and at the same time intriguing him. He read the paragraph several times more — read it, in fact, until he could recite it from memory — and closed the book. Rumor stretched and yawned on the floor in front of him, lifted his head and blinked.

Talk to me, cat, Walker thought. *There are always secrets that only a cat knows. Maybe this is one of them.*

But Rumor only got up and went outside, disappearing into the fading shadows.

Walker fell asleep then and did not come awake again until midday. He rose, bathed and dressed anew, ate a slow meal with the closed book in front of him and went out for a long walk. He passed south through the valley to a favorite glade where a stream rippled noisily over a meandering rock bed and emptied into a pool that contained tiny fish colored brilliant red and blue. He lingered there for a time, thinking, then returned again to the cottage. He sat on the porch and watched the sun creep westward in a haze of purple and scarlet.

'I should never have opened the book,' he chided himself softly, for its mystery had proven irresistible after all. 'I should have bound it back up and dropped it into the deepest hole I could find.'

But it was too late for that. He had read it and knowledge acquired could not be readily forgotten. A sense of futility mingled with anger. He had thought it impossible that Paranor could be restored. Now he knew that there was a magic that could do exactly that. Once again, there was that sense of the inevitability of things prophesied by the Druids.

Still, his life was his own, wasn't it? He needn't accept the charge of Allanon's shade, whatever its viability.

But his curiosity was relentless. He found himself thinking of the Black Elfstone, even when he tried not to. The Black Elfstone was out there, somewhere, a forgotten magic. Where? Where was it?

That and all the other questions pressed in about him as the evening passed. He ate his dinner, walked again for a time, read from the few precious books of his own library, wrote a bit in his journal, and mostly thought of that single, beguiling paragraph on the magic that would bring back Paranor.

He thought about it as he prepared for bed.

He was still thinking about it as midnight approached.

Teasingly, insinuatingly, it wormed about restlessly inside his mind, suggesting this possibility and that, opening doors just a crack into unlighted rooms, hinting at understandings and insights that would bring him the knowledge he could not help but crave.

And with it, perhaps, peace of mind.

His sleep was troubled and restless. The mystery of the Black Elfstone was an irritation that would not be dispelled.

By morning, he had decided that he must do something about it.

Par Ohmsford came awake that morning with a decision of his own to make. It had been five days since Damson and he had rescued Coll, Morgan, Padishar Creel, and the other two outlaws from the cells of the Federation Gatehouse, and the bunch of them had been on the run ever since. They had not attempted to leave the city, certain that the gates would be closely watched and the risk of discovery too great. They had not returned to the basement of the weapon-maker's shop either, feeling that it might have been compromised by their mysterious betrayer. Instead, they had skipped from one shelter to the next, never remaining more than one night, posting guards throughout their brief stay at each, jumping at every sound they heard and every shadow they saw.

Well, enough was enough. Par had decided that he was through running.

He rose from the makeshift bed he occupied in the attic of the grain house and glanced over at Coll next to him, who was still asleep. The others were already up and presumably downstairs in the main warehouse, which was closed until the beginning of the work week. Gingerly he crossed to the tiny, shuttered window that let in what small amount of light the room enjoyed and peered out. The street below was empty except for a stray dog sniffing at a refuse bin and a beggar sleeping in the door of the tin factory across the way. Clouds hung low and gray across the skies, threatening rain before the close of the day.

When he crossed back to pull on his boots, he found Coll awake and looking at him. His brother's coarse hair was ruffled and his eyes were clouded with sleep and disgruntlement.

'Ho-hum, another day,' Coll muttered and then yawned hugely. 'What fascinating storage room will we be visiting today, do you suppose?'

'None, as far as I'm concerned.' Par dropped down beside him.

Coll's eyebrows arched. 'That so? Have you told Padishar?'

'I'm on my way.'

'I suppose you have an alternative in mind — to hiding out, that is.' Coll pushed himself up on one elbow. 'Because I don't think Padishar Creel is going to give you the time of day if you don't. He hasn't been in the best of moods since he found out he might not be as well-loved among his men as he thought he was.'

Par doubted that Padishar Creel ever had allowed himself to become deluded enough to believe that he was well-loved by his men, but Coll was certainly right enough about the outlaw chief's present temperament. His betrayal at the hands of one of his own men had left him taciturn and bitter. He had retreated somewhere deep inside himself these several days past, still clearly in command as he led them through the network of Federation patrols and checkpoints that had been thrown out across the city, still able to find them refuge when it seemed there could be none, but at the same time had become uncharacteristically withdrawn from everyone about him. Damson Rhee had come with them, whether by choice or not Par still wasn't sure, but even she could not penetrate the defenses the outlaw chief had thrown up around himself. Except for exercising his authority as leader, Padishar had removed himself from them as surely as if he were no longer physically present.

Par shook his head. 'Well, we have to do something besides simply hop about from place to place for the rest of our lives.' He was feeling rather sullen about matters himself. 'If there's a need for a plan, Padishar should come up with one. Nothing's being accomplished the way things stand now.'

Coll sat up and began dressing. 'You probably don't want to hear this, Par, but it may be time to rethink this whole business of allying ourselves with the Movement.

We might be better off on our own again.'

Par said nothing. They finished dressing and went downstairs to find the others. There was cold bread, jam, and fruit for breakfast, and they ate it hungrily. Par could not understand how he could be so famished after doing so little. He listened as he ate to Stasas and Drutt compare notes on hunting in the forests of their respective homes somewhere below Varfleet. Morgan was keeping watch by the doors leading into the warehouse and Coll went to join him. Damson Rhee sat on an empty packing crate nearby, carving something. He had seen little of her during the past several days; she was often out with Padishar, scouting the city while the rest of them hid.

Padishar was nowhere to be seen.

After eating, Par went back upstairs to gather his things together, anticipating that, whatever the result of his confrontation with Padishar, it would likely involve a move.

Damson followed him up. 'You grow restless,' she observed when they were alone. She seated herself on the edge of his pallet, shaking back her reddish mane. 'An outlaw's life is not quite what you had in mind, is it?'

He smiled faintly. 'Sitting about in warehouses and basements isn't quite what I had in mind. What is Padishar waiting around for?'

She shrugged. 'What we all wait around for from time to time — that little voice buried somewhere deep inside that tells us what to do next. It might be intuition or it might be common sense or then again it might be the advent of circumstances beyond our control.' She gave him a wicked smile. 'Is it speaking now to you?'

'Something certainly is.' He sat down next to her. 'Why are you still here, Damson? Does Padishar keep you?'

She laughed. 'Hardly. I come and go as I please. He knows I was not the one who betrayed him. Or you, I think.'

'Then why stay?'

She considered him thoughtfully for a moment. 'Maybe I stay because you interest me,' she said at last. She paused as if she wanted to say more, but thought of better of it. She smiled. 'I have never met anyone who uses real magic. Just the pretend kind, like me.'

She reached up and deftly plucked a coin from behind his ear. It was carved from cherry wood. She handed it to him. It bore her likeness on one side and his on the other. He looked up at her in surprise. 'That's very good.'

'Thank you.' He thought she colored slightly. 'You may keep it with the other for good luck.'

He tucked the coin into his pocket. They sat silent for a time, exchanging uncertain glances. 'There isn't much difference, you know, between your kind of magic and mine,' he said finally. 'They both rely on illusion.'

She shook her head. 'No, Par. You are wrong. One is an acquired skill, the other innate. Mine is learned and, once learned, has become all it can. Yours is constantly growing, and its lessons are limitless. Don't you see? My magic is a trade, a way to make a living. Your magic is much more; it is a gift around which you must build your life.'

She smiled, but there was a hint of sadness in it. She stood up. 'I have work to do. Finish your packing.' She moved past him and disappeared down the ladder.

The morning hours crawled past and still Padishar did not return. Par busied himself doing nothing, growing anxious for something — anything — to happen. Coll and Morgan drifted over from time to time, and he spoke to them of his intention to confront the outlaw chief. Neither seemed very optimistic about his chances.

The skies grew more threatening, the wind picking up until it made a rather mournful howl about the loose-fitting jambs and shutters of the old building they were housed in, but still it didn't rain. Card games were played to pass the time and topics of conversation exhausted

It was nearing midafternoon when Padishar returned. He slipped in through the front doors without a word, crossed the room to Par and motioned him to follow. He took the Valeman into a small office situated at the back on the main floor and shut the door behind them.

When they were alone, he seemed at a loss for words.

'I have been thinking rather carefully about what we should do,' he said finally. 'Or, if you prefer, what we should not do. Any mistake we make now could be our last.'

He pulled Par over to a bench that had been shoved back against the wall and sat them both down. 'There's the problem of this traitor,' he said quietly. His eyes were bright and hard with something Par couldn't read. 'I was certain at first that it must be one of us. But it isn't me or Damson. Damson is above suspicion. It isn't you. It might be your brother; but it isn't him either, is it?'

He made it a statement of fact rather than a question. Par shook his head in agreement.

'Or the Highlander.'

Par shook his head a second time.

'That leaves Ciba Blue, Stasas, and Drutt. Blue is likely dead; that means that if he's the one, he was stupid enough to let himself get killed in the bargain. Doesn't sound like Blue. And the other two have been with me almost from the first. It is inconceivable that either of them would betray me — whatever the price offered or the reason supplied. Their hatred of the Federation is nearly a match for my own.'

The muscles in his jaw tightened. 'So perhaps it isn't any of us after all. But who else could have discovered our plan? Do you see what I mean? Your friend the Highlander mentioned this morning something he had almost forgotten. When we first came into the city and went down to the market stalls, he thought he saw Hirehone. He thought then he was mistaken; now he wonders. Forgetting momentarily the fact that Hirehone held my life in his hands any number of times before this and did not betray me, how would he have gone about doing so now? No one, outside of Damson and those I brought with me, knew the where, when, how or why of what we were about. Yet those Federation soldiers were waiting for us. They knew.'

Par had forgotten momentarily his plan to tell Padishar he was fed up with matters. 'Then who was it?' he asked eagerly. 'Who could it have been?'

Padishar's smile was forced. 'The question plagues me like flies a sweating horse. I don't know yet. You may rest assured that sooner or later I will. For the moment, it doesn't matter. We have bigger fish to fry.'

He leaned forward. 'I spent the morning with a man I know, a man who has access to what happens within the higher circles of Federation authority in Tyrsis. He is a man I am certain of, one I can trust. Even Damson doesn't know of him. He told me some interesting things. It seems that you and Damson came to my rescue just in time. Rimmer Dall arrived early the next morning to see personally to my questioning and ultimate disposal.' The outlaw chief's voice emitted a sigh of satisfaction. 'He was very disappointed to find I had left early.'

Padishar shifted his weight and brought his head close to Par's. 'I know you are impatient for something to happen, Par. I can read the signs of it in you as if you were a notice posted on the wall by my bed. But haste results in an early demise in this line of work, so caution is always necessary.' He smiled again. 'But you and I, lad — we're a force to be reckoned with in this business of the Federation and their games-playing. Fate brought you to me, and she has something definite in mind for the two of us, something that will shake the Federation and their Coalition Council and their Seekers and all the rest right to the foundation of their being!'

One hand clenched before Par's face, and the Valeman flinched back in spite of himself. 'So much effort has been put into hiding all traces of the old People's Park — the Bridge of Sendic destroyed and rebuilt, the old park walled away, guards running all about like ants at a picnic dinner! Why? Because there's something down there that they don't want anyone to know about! I can feel it, lad! I am as convinced of it now as I was when we went in five nights ago!'

'The Sword of Shannara?' Par whispered.

Padishar's smile was genuine this time. 'I'd stake ten years of my life on it! But there's still only one way to find out, isn't there?'

He brought his hands up to grip Par's shoulders. The weathered, sharp-boned face was a mask of cunning and ruthless determination. The man who had led them for the past five days had disappeared; this was the old Padishar Creel speaking.

'The man I spoke to, the one who has ears in the Federation chambers, tells me that Rimmer Dall believes we've fled. He thinks us back within the Parma Key. Whatever we came here for we've given up on, he's decided. He lingers in the city only because he has not decided what needs doing next. I suggest we give him some direction, young Par.'

Par's eyes widened. 'What ...'

'What he least expects, of course!' Padishar anticipated his question and pounced on it. 'The last thing he and his black-cloaked wolves will look for — that's what!' His eyes narrowed. 'We'll go back down into the Pit!'

Par quit breathing.

'We'll go back down before they have a chance to figure out where we are or what we intend, back down into that most carefully guarded hidey-hole, and if the Sword of Shannara is there, why we'll snatch it away from under their very noses!'

He brought an astonished Par to his feet with a jerk. 'And we'll do it tonight!'

CHAPTER

22

I T WAS NEARING TWILIGHT by the time Walker Boh reached his destination. He had been journeying northward from Hearthstone since midmorning, traveling at a comfortable pace, not hurrying, allowing himself adequate time to think through what he was about to do. The skies had been clear and filled with sunshine when he had set out, but as the day lengthened toward evening clouds began to drift in from the west and the air turned misty and gray. The land through which he traveled was rugged, a series of twisting ridges and drops that broke apart the symmetry of the forests and left the trees leaning and bent like spikes driven randomly into the earth. Deadwood and outcroppings of rock blocked the trail repeatedly and mist hung shroudlike in the trees, trapped there, it seemed, unmoving.

Walker stopped. He stared downward between two massive, jagged ridgelines into a narrow valley which cradled a tiny lake. The lake was barely visible, screened away by pine trees and a thick gathering of mist that clung tenaciously above its surface, swirling sluggishly, listlessly, haphazardly in the nearly windless expanse.

The lake was the home of the Grimpond.

Walker did not pause long, starting down into the valley almost immediately. The mist closed quickly about him as he went, filling his mouth with its metallic taste, clouding his vision of what lay ahead. He ignored the sensations that attacked him — the pressing closeness, the imagined whispers, the discomfiting deadness — and kept his concentration focused on putting one foot in front of the other. The air grew quickly cool, a damp layer of gauze against his skin that smelled of things decayed. The pines rose up about him, their numbers increasing until there was nowhere they did not stand watch. Silence cloaked the valley and there was only the soft scrape of his boots against the stone.

He could feel the eyes of the Grimpond watching.

It had been a long time.

Cogline had warned him early about the Grimpond. The Grimpond was the shade that lived in the lake below, a shade older than the world of the Four Lands itself. It claimed to predate the Great Wars. It boasted that it had been alive in the age of faerie. As with all shades, it had the ability to divine secrets hidden from the living. There was magic at its command. But it was a bitter and spiteful creature, trapped in this world for all eternity for reasons no one knew. It could not die and it hated the substance-less, empty existence it was forced to endure. It vented itself on the humans who came to speak with it, teasing them with riddles of the truths they sought to uncover, taunting them with their mortality, showing them more of what they would keep hidden than what they would reveal.

Brin Ohmsford had come to the Grimpond three hundred years earlier to find a way into the Maelmord so that she might confront the Ildatch. The shade toyed with her until she used the wishsong to ensnare it by trickery, forcing it to reveal what she wished to discover. The shade had never forgotten that; it was the only time a human had bested it. Walker had heard the story any number of times while growing up. It was only after he came north to Hearthstone to live, forsaking the Ohmsford name and legacy, that he discovered that the Grimpond was waiting for him. Brin Ohmsford might be dead and gone, but the Grimpond was alive forever and it had determined that someone must be made to pay for its humiliation. If not the one directly responsible, why then another of that one's bloodline would do nicely.

Cogline advised him to stay clear. The Grimpond would see him destroyed if it was given the opportunity. His parents had been given the same advice and had heeded it. But Walker Boh had reached a point in his life where he was through making excuses for who and what he was. He had come to the Wilderun to escape his legacy; he did not intend to spend the rest of his life wondering if there was something out there that could undo him. Best to deal with the shade at once. He went looking for the Grimpond. Because the shade never appeared to more than one person at a time, Cogline was forced to remain behind. When the confrontation came, it was memorable. It lasted for almost six hours. During that time, the Grimpond assailed Walker Boh with every imaginable trick and ploy at its disposal, divulging real and imagined secrets of his present and his future, showering him with rhetoric designed to drive him into madness, revealing to him visions of himself and those he loved that were venomous and destructive. Walker Boh withstood it all. When the shade exhausted itself, it cursed Walker as he would not have believed possible and disappeared back into the mist.

Walker returned to Hearthstone, feeling that the matter of the past was settled. He let the Grimpond alone and the Grimpond — though it could be argued that he had no choice since he was bound to the waters of the lake — did the same to him.

Until today, Walker Boh had not been back.

He sighed. It would be more difficult this time, since this time he wanted something from the shade. He could pretend otherwise. He could keep to himself the truth of why he had come — to learn from the Grimpond the whereabouts of the mysterious Black Elfstone. He could talk about this and that, or assume some role that would confuse the creature, since it loved games and the playing of them. But it was unlikely to make any difference.

Somehow the Grimpond always divined the reason you were there.

Walker Boh felt the mist brush against him with the softness of tiny fingers, clinging insistently. This was not going to be pleasant.

He continued ahead as daylight failed and darkness closed about. Shadows, where they could find purchase in the graying haze, lengthened in shimmering parody of their makers. Walker wrapped his cloak closer to his body, thinking through the words he would say to the Grimpond, the arguments he would put forth, the games he would play if forced to do so. He recounted in his mind the events of his life that the shade was likely to play upon — most of them drawn from his youth when he was discomfited by his differences and beset by his insecurities.

'Dark Uncle' they had called him even then — the playmates of Par and Coll, their parents, and even people of the village of Shady Vale that didn't know him. Dark for the color of his life and being, this pale, withdrawn young man who could sometimes read minds, who could divine things that would happen and even cause them to be so, who could understand so much of what was hidden from others. Par and Coll's strange uncle, without parents of his own, without a family that was really his, without a history that he cared to share. Even the Ohmsford name didn't seem to fit him. He was always the 'Dark Uncle', somehow older than everyone else, not in years but in knowledge. It wasn't knowledge that he had learned; it was knowledge he had been born with. His father had tried to explain. It was the legacy of the wishsong's magic that caused it. It manifested itself this way. But it wouldn't last; it never did. It was just a stage he must pass through because of who he was. But Par and Coll did not have to pass through it, Walker would argue in reply. No, only you and I, only the children of Brin Ohmsford, because we hold the trust, his father would whisper. We are the chosen of Allanon....

He swept the memories from his mind angrily, the

bitterness welling up anew. The 'chosen of Allanon' had his father said? The 'cursed of Allanon' was more like it.

The trees gave way before him abruptly, startling him with the suddenness of their disappearance. He stood at the edge of the lake, its rocky shores wending into the mist on either side, its waters lapping gently, endlessly in the silence. Walker Boh straightened. His mind tightened and closed down upon itself as if made of iron, his concentration focused, his thoughts cleared.

A solitary statue, he waited.

There was movement in the fog, but it emanated from more than one place. Walker tried to fix on it, but it was gone as quickly as it had come. From somewhere far away, above the haze that hung across the lake, beyond the rock walls of the ridgelines enfolding the narrow valley, a voice whispered in some empty heaven.

Dark Uncle.

Walker heard the words, tauntingly close and at the same time nowhere he would ever be, not from inside his head or from any other place discernible, but there nevertheless. He did not respond to them. He continued to wait.

Then the scattered movements that had disturbed the mist moments earlier focused themselves on a single point, coming together in a colorless outline that stood upon the water and began to advance. It took surer form as it came, growing in size, becoming larger than the human shape it purported to represent, rising up as if it might crush anything that stood in its way. Walker did not move. The ethereal shape became a shadow, and the shadow became a person. . . .

Walker Boh watched expressionlessly as the Grimpond stood before him, suspended in the mist, its face lifting out of shadow to reveal who it had chosen to become.

'Have you come to accept my charge, Walker Boh?' it asked.

Walker was startled in spite of his resolve. The dark, brooding countenance of Allanon stared down at him.

The warehouse was hushed, its cavernous enclosure blanketed by stillness from floor to ceiling as six pairs of eyes fastened intently on Padishar Creel.

He had just announced that they were going back down into the Pit.

'We'll be doing it differently this time,' he told them, his raw-boned face fierce with determination, as if that alone might persuade them to his cause. 'No sneaking about through the park with rope ladders this go-around. There's an entry into the Pit from the lower levels of the Gatehouse. That's how we'll do it. We'll go right into the Gatehouse, down into the Pit and back out again — and no one the wiser.'

Par risked a quick glance at the others. Coll, Morgan, Damson, the outlaws Stasas and Drutt — there was a mix of disbelief and awe etched on their faces. What the outlaw chief was proposing was outrageous; that he might succeed, even more so. No one tried to interrupt. They wanted to hear how he was going to do it.

'The Gatehouse watch changes shift twice each day — once at sunrise, once at sunset. Two shifts, six men each. A relief comes in for each shift once a week, but on different days. Today is one of those days. A relief for the day shift comes in just after sunset. I know; I made it a point to find out.'

His features creased with the familiar wolfish smile. 'Today a special detail will arrive a couple of hours before the shift change because there's to be an inspection of the Gatehouse quarters this evening at the change, and the Commander of the Gatehouse wants everything spotless. The day watch will be happy enough to let the detail past to do its work, figuring it's no skin off their noses.' He paused. 'That detail, of course, will be us.'

He leaned forward, his eyes intense. 'Once inside, we'll dispatch the night watch. If we're quiet enough about it, the day watch won't even know what's happening. They'll continue with their rounds, doing part of our job for us — keeping everyone outside. We'll bolt the door from within as a precaution in any case. Then we'll go down through the Gatehouse stairs to the lower levels and out into the Pit. It should still be light enough to find what we're looking for fairly quickly. Once we have it, we'll go back up the stairs and out the same way we came in.'

For a moment, no one said anything. Then Drutt said, his voice gravelly, 'We'll be recognized, Padishar. Bound to be some of the same soldiers there as when we was taken.'

Padishar shook his head. 'There was a shift change three days ago. That was the shift that was on duty when we were seized.'

'What about that commander?'

'Gone until the beginning of the work week. Just a duty officer.'

'We'd need Federation uniforms.'

'We have them. I brought them in yesterday.'

Drutt and Stasas exchanged glances. 'Been thinking about this for a time, have you?' the latter asked.

The outlaw chief laughed softly. 'Since the moment we walked out of those cells.'

Morgan, who had been seated on a bench next to Par, stood up. 'If anything goes wrong and they discover what we're about, they'll be all over the Gatehouse. We'll be trapped, Padishar.'

The big man shook his head. 'No, we won't. We'll carry in grappling hooks and ropes with our cleaning equipment. If we can't go back the way we came, we'll climb out of the Pit using those. The Federation will be concentrating on getting at us through the Gatehouse entry. It won't even occur to them that we don't intend to come back that way.'

The questions died away. There was a long silence as the six sifted through their doubts and fears and waited for something inside to reassure them that the plan would work. Par found himself thinking that there were an awful lot of things that could go wrong.

'Well, what's it to be?' Padishar's patience gave out. 'Time's something we don't have to spare. We all know that there's risks involved, but that's the nature of the business. I want a decision. Do we try it or not? Who says we do? Who's with me?'

Par listened to the silence lengthen. Coll and Morgan were statues on the bench to either side of him. Stasas and Drutt, who it seemed might speak first, now had their eyes fixed firmly on the floor. Damson was looking at Padishar, who in turn was looking at her. Par realized all at once that no one was going to say anything, that they were all waiting on him.

He surprised himself. He didn't even have to think about it. He simply said, 'I'll go.'

'Have you lost your mind?' Coll whispered urgently in his ear. Stasas and Drutt had Padishar's momentary attention, declaring that they, too, would go. 'Par, this was our chance to get out!'

Par leaned close to him. 'He's doing this for me, don't you see? I'm the one who wants to find the Sword! I can't let Padishar take all the risks! I have to go!'

Coll shook his head helplessly. Morgan, with a wink at Par over Coll's shoulder, cast his vote in favour of going as well. Coll just raised his hand wordlessly and nodded.

That left Damson. Padishar had his sharp gaze fixed on her, waiting. It suddenly occurred to Par that Padishar needn't have asked who wanted to go with him; he simply could have ordered it. Padishar had told him earlier that he didn't believe it was any of them — but he might have it in his mind to make sure.

'I will wait for you in the park,' Damson Rhee said, and everyone stared at her. She did not seem to notice. 'I would have to disguise myself as a man in order to go in with you. That is one more risk you would be taking — and to what end? There is nothing I can offer by being with you. If there is trouble, I will be of better use to you on the outside.'

Padishar's smile was immediately disarming. 'Your

thinking is correct as usual, Damson. You will wait in the park.'

It seemed to Par that he was a little too quick to agree.

Geysers exploded and died from the flat, gray surface of the lake, and the spray felt like bits of ice where it landed on Walker Boh's skin.

'Tell me why you come here, Dark Uncle?' Allanon's shade whispered.

Walker felt the chill burn away as his determination caught fire. 'I need tell you nothing,' he replied. 'You are not Allanon. You are only the Grimpond.'

Allanon's visage shimmered and faded in the half-light, replaced by Walker's own. The Grimpond emitted a hollow laugh. 'I am you, Walker Boh. Nothing more and nothing less. Do you recognize yourself?

His face went through a flurry of transformations — Walker as a child, as a boy, as a youth, as a man. The images came and went so quickly that Walker could barely register them. It was somehow terrifying to watch the phases of his life pass by so quickly. He forced himself to remain calm.

'Will you speak with me, Grimpond?' he asked.

'Will you speak with yourself?' came the reply.

Walker took a deep breath. 'I will. But for what purpose should I do so? There is nothing to talk about with myself. I already know all that I have to say.'

'Ah, as do I, Walker. As do I.'

The Grimpond shrank until it was the same size as Walker. It kept his face, taunting him with it, letting it reveal flashes of age that would one day claim it, giving it a beaten cast as if to demonstrate the futility of his life.

'I know why you have come to me,' the Grimpond said suddenly. 'I know the private-most thoughts of your mind, the little secrets you would keep even from yourself. There need be no games between us, Walker Boh. You are surely my equal in the playing of them, and I have no wish to do battle with you again. You have come to ask where you must go to find the Black Elfstone. Fair enough. I will tell you.'

Immediately, Walker mistrusted the shade. The Grimpond never volunteered anything without twisting it. He nodded in response, but said nothing.

'How sad you seem, Walker,' soothed the shade. 'No jubilation at my submission, no elation that you will have what you want? Is it so difficult then to admit that you have dispensed with pride and self-resolution, that you have forsaken your lofty principles, that you have been won over after all to the Druid cause?'

Walker stiffened in spite of himself. 'You misread matters, Grimpond. Nothing has been decided.'

'Oh, yes, Dark Uncle! Everything has been decided! Make no mistake. Your life weaves out before my eyes as a thread straight and undeviating, the years a finite number, their course determined. You are caught in the snare of the Druid's words. His legacy to Brin Ohmsford becomes your own, whether you would have it so or not. You have been shaped!'

'Tell me, then, of the Black Elfstone,' Walker tried.

'All in good time. Patience, now.'

The words died away into the stillness, the Grimpond shifting within its covering of mist. Daylight had faded into darkness, the gray turned black, the moon and stars shut away by the valley's thick haze. Yet there was light where Walker stood, a phosphorescence given off by the waters beneath the air on which the Grimpond floated, a dull and shallow glow that played wickedly through the night.

'So much effort given over to escaping the Druids,' the Grimpond said softly. 'What foolishness.' Walker's face dissipated and was replaced by his father's. His father spoke. 'Remember, Walker, that we are the bearers of Allanon's trust. He gave it to Brin Ohmsford as he lay dying, to be passed from one generation to the next, to be handed down until it was needed, sometime far, far in the distant future . . .'

His father's visage leered at him. 'Perhaps now?'

Images flared to life above him, born on the air as if tapestries threaded on a frame, woven in the fabric of the mist. One after another they appeared, brilliant with color, filled with the texture and depth of real life.

Walker took a step back, startled. He saw himself in the images, anger and defiance in his face, his feet positioned on clouds above the cringing forms of Par and Wren and the others of the little company who had gathered at the Hadeshorn to meet with the shade of Allanon. Thunder rolled out of a darkness that welled away into the skies overhead, and lightning flared in jagged streaks. Walker's voice was a hiss amid the rumble and the flash, the words his own, spoken as if out of his memory. *I would sooner cut off my hand than see the Druids come again!* And then he lifted his arm to reveal that his hand, indeed, was gone.

The vision faded, then sharpened anew. He saw himself again, this time on a high, empty ridgeline that looked out across forever. The whole world spread away below him, the nations and their Races, the creatures of land and water, the lives of everyone and everything that were. Wind whipped at his black robes and whistled ferociously in his ears. There was a girl with him. She was woman and child both, a magical being, a creature of impossible beauty. She stunned him with the intensity of her gaze, depthless black eyes from which he could not turn away. Her long, silver hair flowed from her head in a shimmering mass. She reached for him, needing his balance to keep her footing on the treacherous rock — and he thrust her violently away. She fell, tumbling into the abyss below, soundless as she shrank from sight, silver hair fading into a ribbon of brightness and then into nothing at all.

Again, the vision faded, then returned. He saw himself a third time, now in a castle fortress that was empty of life and gray with disuse. Death stalked him relentlessly, creeping through walls and along corridors, cold fingers probing for signs of his life. He felt the need to run from it, knew that he must if he were to survive — and yet he couldn't. He stood immobile, letting Death approach him, reach for him, close about him. As his life ended, the cold filled him, and he saw that a dark, robed shape stood behind him, holding him fast, preventing him from fleeing. The shape bore the face of Allanon.

The visions disappeared, the colors faded, and the gray mist returned, shifting sluggishly in the lake's phosphorescent glow. The Grimpond brought its robed arms downward slowly, and the lake hissed and spit with dissatisfaction. Walker Boh flinched from the spray that cascaded down upon him.

'What say you, Dark Uncle?' the Grimpond whispered. It bore Walker's pale face once more.

'That you play games still,' Walker said quietly. 'That you show lies and half-truths designed to taunt me. That you have shown me nothing of the Black Elfstone.'

'Have I not?' The Grimpond shimmered darkly. 'Is it all a game, do you think? Lies and half-truths only?' The laugh was mirthless. 'You must think what you will, Walker Boh. But I see a future that is hidden from you, and it would be foolish to believe I would show you none of it. Remember, Walker. I am you, the telling of who and what you are — just as I am for all who come to speak with me.'

Walker shook his head. 'No, Grimpond, you can never be me. You can never be anyone but who you are — a shade without identity, without being, exiled to this patch of water for all eternity. Nothing you do, no game you play, can ever change that.'

The Grimpond sent spray hissing skyward, anger in its voice. 'Then go from me, Dark Uncle! Take with you what you came for and go!' The visage of Walker disappeared and was replaced by a death's head. 'You think my fate has nothing to do with you? Beware! There is more of me in you than you would care to know!'

Robes flared wide, throwing shards of dull light into the mist. 'Hear me, Walker! Hear me! You wish to know of the Black Elfstone? Then, listen! Darkness hides it, a black that light can never penetrate, where eyes turn a man to stone and voices turn him mad! Beyond, where only the dead lie, is a pocket carved with runes, the signs of time's passing. Within that pocket lies the Stone!'

The death's head disappeared into nothingness, and only the robes remained, hanging empty against the mist. 'I have given you what you wish, Dark Uncle,' the shade whispered, its voice filled with loathing. 'I have done so because the gift will destroy you. Die, and you will end your cursed line, the last of it! How I long to see that happen! Go, now! Leave me! I bid you swift journey to your doom!'

The Grimpond faded into the mist and was gone. The light it had brought with it dissipated as well. Darkness cloaked the whole of the lake and the shore surrounding it, and Walker was left momentarily sightless. He stood where he was, waiting for his vision to clear, feeling the chill touch of the mist as it brushed against his skin. The Grimpond's laughter echoed in the silence of his mind.

Dark Uncle came the harsh whisper.

He cast himself in stone against it. He sheathed himself in iron.

When his vision returned, and he could make out the vague shape of the trees behind him, he turned from the lake with his cloak wrapped close about him and walked away.

CHAPTER

23

FTERNOON SLID TOWARDS EVENING. A slow, easy rain fell on the city of Tyrsis, washing its dusty streets, leaving them slick and glistening in the fading light. Storm clouds brushed low against the trees of the People's Park, trailing downward in ragged streamers of mist to curl about the roughened trunks. The park was empty, silent save for the steady patter of the rain.

Then footsteps broke the silence, a heavy thudding of boots, and a Federation squad of six materialized out of the gray, cloaked and hooded, equipment packs rattling. A pair of blackbirds perched on a peeling birch glanced over alertly. A dog rummaging amid the garbage slunk quickly away. From a still-dry doorway, a homeless child huddled against the chill and peered out, caution mirrored in its eyes. No other notice was taken. The streets were deserted, the city hunkered down and unseeing in the damp, unpleasant gloom.

Padishar Creel took his little band across the circle of the Tyrsian Way and into the park. Wrapped against the weather, they were indistinguishable one from the other, one from anyone else. They had come all the way from their warehouse lair without challenge. They had barely seen another living thing. Everything was going exactly as planned.

Par Ohmsford watched the faint, dark outline of the

Gatehouse appear through the haze of the trees and felt his mind fold in upon itself. He hunched his shoulders against the chill of the rain and the heat of the sweat that ran beneath his clothing. He was trapped within himself and yet at the same time able to watch from without as if disembodied. The way forward was far darker than the day's light made it seem. He had stumbled into a tunnel, its walls round and twisting and so smooth he could not find a grip. He was falling, his momentum carrying him relentlessly toward the terror he sensed waiting ahead.

He was in danger of losing control of himself, he knew. He had been afraid before, yes — when Coll and he had fled Varfleet, when the woodswoman appeared to confront them below the Runne, when Cogline told them what they must do, when they crossed the Rainbow Lake in night and fog with Morgan, when they fought the giant in the forests of the Anar, when they ran from the Gnawl in the Wolfsktaag, and when the Spider Gnomes and the girl-child who was a Shadowen had seized him. He had been afraid when Allanon had come. But his fear then and since was nothing compared to what it was now. He was terrified.

He swallowed against the dryness he felt building in his throat and tried to tell himself he was all right. The feeling had come over him quite suddenly, as if it were a creature that had lain in wait along the rain-soaked streets of the city, its tentacles lashing out to snare him. Now he was caught up in a grip that bound him like iron and there was no way to break free. It was pointless to say anything to the others of what he was experiencing. After all, what could he say that would have any meaning — that he was frightened, even terrified? And what, did he suppose, were they?

A gust of wind shook the water-laden trees and showered him with droplets. He licked the water from his lips, the moisture cool and welcome. Coll was a bulky shape immediately ahead, Morgan another one behind. Shadows danced and played about him, nipping at his fading courage. This was a mistake, he heard himself whispering from somewhere deep inside. His skin prickled with the certainty of it.

He had a sense of his own mortality that had been missing before, locked away in some forgotten storeroom of his mind, kept there, he supposed, because it was so frightening to look upon. It seemed to him in retrospect as if he had treated everything that had gone before as some sort of game. That was ridiculous, he knew; yet some part of it was true. He had gone charging about the countryside, a self-declared hero in the mold of those in the stories he sang about, determined to confront the reality of his dreams, decided that he would know the truth of who and what he was. He had thought himself in control of his destiny; he realized now that he was not.

Visions of what had been swept through his mind in swift disarray, chasing one another with vicious purpose. He had caromed from one mishap to the next, he saw — always wrongly believing that his meddling was somehow useful. In truth, what had he accomplished? He was an outlaw running for his life. His parents were prisoners in their own home. Walker believed him a fool. Wren had abandoned him. Coll and Morgan had stayed with him only because they felt he needed looking after. Padishar Creel believed him something he could never be. Worst of all, as a direct result of his misguided decision to accept the charge of a man three hundred years dead, five men were about to offer up their lives.

'Watch yourself,' he had cautioned Coll in a vain attempt at humor as they departed their warehouse concealment. 'Wouldn't want you tripping over those feet, duck's weather or no.'

Coll had sniffed. 'Just keep your ears pricked. Shouldn't be hard for someone like you.'

Teasing, playing at being brave. Fooling no one.

Allanon! He breathed the Druid's name like a prayer in the silence of his mind. *Why don't you help me?*

But a shade, he knew, could help no one. Help could come only from the living.

There was no more time to think, to agonize over

decisions past making, or to lament those already made. The trees broke apart, and the Gatehouse was before them. A pair of Federation guards standing watch stiffened as the patrol approached. Padishar never hesitated. He went directly to them, informed them of the patrol's purpose, joked about the weather, and had the doors open within moments. In a knot of lowered heads and tightened cloaks, the little band hastened inside.

The men of the night watch were gathered about a wooden table playing cards, six of them, heads barely lifting at the arrival of the newcomers. The watch commander was nowhere to be seen.

Padishar glanced over his shoulder, nodded faintly to Morgan, Stasas and Drutt, and motioned them to spread out about the table. As they did so, one of the players glanced up suspiciously.

'Who're you?' he demanded.

'Clean-up detail,' Padishar answered. He moved around behind the speaker and bent over to read his cards. 'That's a losing hand, friend.'

'Back off, you're dripping on me,' the other complained.

Padishar hit him on the temple with his fist, and the man dropped like a stone. A second followed almost as fast. The guards surged to their feet, shouting, but the outlaws and Morgan felled them all in seconds. Par and Coll began pulling ropes and strips of cloth from their packs.

'Drag them into the sleeping quarters, tie and gag them,' Padishar whispered. 'Make sure they can't escape.'

There was a quick knock at the door. Padishar waited until the guards were dispatched, then cracked the peep window. Everything was fine, he assured the guards without, who thought they might have heard something. The card game was breaking up; everyone thought it would be best to start getting things in order.

He closed the window with a reassuring smile.

After the men of the night watch were secured in the sleeping quarters, Padishar closed the door and bolted it.

He hesitated, then ordered the locks to the entry doors thrown as well. No point in taking any chances, he declared. They couldn't afford to leave any of their company behind to make certain they were not disturbed.

With oil lamps to guide them, they descended through the gloom of the stairwell to the lower levels of the Gatehouse, the sound of the rain lost behind the heavy stone. The dampness penetrated, though, so chill that Par found himself shivering. He followed after the others in a daze, prepared to do whatever was necessary, his mind focused on putting one foot in front of the other until they were out of there. There was no reason to be frightened, he kept telling himself. It would all be over quick enough.

At the lower level, they found the watch commander sleeping — a new man, different from the one that had been waiting for them when they had tried to slip over the ravine wall. This one fared no better. They subdued him without effort, bound and gagged him, and locked him in his room.

'Leave the lamps,' Padishar ordered.

They bypassed the watch commander's chambers and went down to the end of the hall. A single, ironbound door stood closed before them, twice as high as their tallest, the angular Drutt. A massive handle, emblazoned with the wolf's head insigne of the Seekers, jutted out. Padishar reached down with both hands and twisted. The latch gave, the door slid open. Mist and darkness filled the gap, and the stench of decay and mold slithered in.

'Stay close, now,' Padishar whispered over his shoulder, his eyes dangerous, and stepped out into the gloom.

Coll turned long enough to reach back and squeeze Par's shoulder, then followed.

They stood in a forest of jumbled tree trunks, matted brush, vines, brambles, and impenetrable mist. The thick, sodden canopy of the treetops overhead all but shut out the little daylight that remained. Mud oozed and sucked in tiny bogs all about them. Things flew in ragged jumps through the gloom — birds or something less pleasant, they couldn't tell which. Smells assailed them — the decay and the mold, but something more as well, something even less tolerable. Sounds rose out of the murk, distant, indistinguishable, threatening. The Pit was a well of endless gloom.

Every nerve ending on Par Ohmsford's body screamed at him to get out of there.

Padishar motioned them ahead. Drutt followed, then Coll, Par, Morgan, and Stasas, a line of rain-soaked forms. They picked their way forward slowly, following the edge of the ravine, moving in the direction of the rubble from the old Bridge of Sendic. Par and Coll carried the grappling hooks and ropes, the others drawn weapons. Par glanced over his shoulder momentarily and saw the light from the open door leading back into the Gatehouse disappear into the mist. He saw the Sword of Leah glint dully in Morgan's hand, the rain trickling off its polished metal.

The earth they walked upon was soft and yielding, but it held them as they pushed steadily into the gloom. The Pit had the feel of a giant maw, open and waiting, smelling of things already eaten, its breath the mist that closed them away. Things wriggled and crawled through the pools of stagnant water, oozed down decaying logs, and flashed through bits of scrub like quicksilver. The silence was deafening; even the earlier sounds had disappeared at their approach. There was only the rain, slow and steady, seeping downward through the murk.

They walked for what seemed to Par a very long time. The minutes stretched away in an endless parade until there was no longer either beginning or end to them. How far could it be to the fallen bridge, he wondered? Surely they should be there by now. He felt trapped within the Pit, the wall of the ravine on his left, the trees and mist to his right, gloom and rain overhead and all about. The black cloaks of his companions gave them the look of mourners at a funeral, buriers of the dead.

Then Padishar Creel stopped, listening. Par had heard it, too — a sort of hissing sound from somewhere deep within the murk, like steam escaping from a fissure. The others craned their necks and peered unsuccessfully about. The hissing stopped, the silence filling again with the sound of their breathing and the rain.

Padishar's broadsword glimmered as he motioned them ahead once more. He took them more quickly now, as if sensing that all was not right, that speed might have to take precedence over caution. Scores of massive, glistening trunks came and went, silent sentinels in the gloom. The light was fading rapidly, turned from gray to cobalt.

Par sensed suddenly that something was watching them. The hair on the back of his neck stiffened with the feel of its gaze, and he glanced about hurriedly. Nothing moved in the mist; nothing showed.

'What is it?' Morgan whispered in his ear, but he could only shake his head.

Then the stone blocks of the shattered Bridge of Sendic came into view, bulky and misshapen in the gloom as they jutted like massive teeth from the tangled forest. Padishar hurried forward, the others following. They moved away from the ravine wall and deeper into the trees. The Pit seemed to swallow them in its mist and dark. Bridge sections lay scattered amid the stone rubble beneath the covering of the forest, moss-grown and worn, spectral in the failing light.

Par took a deep breath. The Sword of Shannara had been embedded blade downward in a block of red marble and placed in a vault beneath the protective span of the Bridge of Sendic, the old legends told.

It had to be here, somewhere close.

He hesitated. The Sword was embedded in red marble; could he free it? Could he even enter the vault?

His eyes searched the mist. What if it was buried beneath the rubble of the bridge? How would they reach it then?

So many unanswered questions, he thought, feeling suddenly desperate. Why hadn't he asked them before? Why hadn't he considered the possibilities?

The cliffs loomed faintly through the murky haze. He could see the west corner of the crumbling palace of the Kings of Callahorn, a dark shadow through a break in the trees. He felt his throat tighten. They were almost to the far wall of the ravine. They were almost out of places to look.

I won't leave without the Sword, he swore wordlessly. *No matter what it takes, I won't!* The fire of his conviction burned through him as if to seal the covenant.

Then the hissing sounded again, much closer now. It seemed to be coming from more than one direction. Padishar slowed and stopped, turning guardedly. With Drutt and Stasas on either side, he stepped out a few paces to act as a screen for the Valemen and the Highlander, then began inching cautiously along the fringe of the broken stone.

The hissing grew louder, more distinct. It was no longer hissing. It was breathing.

Par's eyes searched the darkness frantically. Something was coming for them, the same something that had devoured Ciba Blue and all those before him who had gone down into the Pit and not come out again. His certainty of it was terrifying. Yet it wasn't for their stalker that he searched. It was for the vault that held the Sword of Shannara. He was desperate now to find it. He could see it suddenly in his mind, as clear as if it were a picture drawn and mounted for his private viewing. He groped for it uncertainly, within his mind, then without in the mist and the dark.

Something strange began to happen to him.

He felt a tightening within that seemed grounded in the magic of the wishsong. It was a pulling, a tugging that wrenched against shackles he could neither see nor understand. He felt a pressure building within himself that he had never experienced before.

Coll saw his face and went pale. 'Par?' he whispered anxiously and shook him.

Red pinpricks of light appeared in the mist all about them, burning like tiny fires in the damp. They shifted and winked and drew closer. Faces materialized, no longer human, the flesh decaying and half-eaten, the features twisted and fouled. Bodies shambled out of the night, some massive, some gnarled, all misshapen beyond belief. It was as if they had been stretched and wrenched about to see what could be made of them. Most walked bent over; some crawled on all fours.

They closed about the little company in seconds. They were things out of some loathsome nightmare, the fragments and shards of sleep's horror come into the world of waking. Dark, substanceless wraiths flitted in and out of their bodies, through mouths and eyes, from the pores of skin and the bristles of hair.

Shadowen!

The pressure inside Par Ohmsford grew unbearable. He felt something drop away in the pit of his stomach. He was seeing the vision in his dreams come alive, the dark world of animallike humans and Shadowen masters. It was Allanon's promise come to pass.

The pressure broke free. He screamed, freezing his companions with the sharpness of his cry. The sound took form and became words. He sang, the wishsong ripping through the air as if a flame, the magic lighting up the darkness. The Shadowen jerked away, their faces horrible in the unexpected glare, the lesions and cuts on their bodies vivid streaks of scarlet. Par stiffened, flooded with a power he had never known the wishsong to possess. He was aware of a vision within his mind — a vision of the Sword of Shannara.

The light from the magic, only an illusion at first, was suddenly real. It brightened, lancing the darkness in a way that Par found strangely familiar, flaring with intensity as it probed the gloom. It twisted and turned like a captured thing trying to escape, winding past the stone wreckage of the fallen Bridge of Sendic, leaping across the carcasses of fallen trees, burning through the ragged brush to where a singular stone chamber sat alone amid a tangle of vines and grasses not a hundred yards from where he stood.

He felt a surge of elation race through him.

There!

The word hissed in the white silence of his mind, cocooned away from the magic and the chaos. He saw weathered black stone, the light of his magic burning into its pocked surface, scouring its cracks and crevices, picking out the scrolled words carved into its facing:

Herein lies the heart and soul of the nations.
Their right to be free men,
Their desire to live in peace,
Their courage . . .

His strength gave out suddenly before he could complete his reading, and the magic flared sharply and died into blackness, gone as quickly as it had come. He staggered backward with a cry, and Coll caught him in his arms. Par couldn't hear himself. He couldn't hear anything but the strange ringing that was the wishsong's residue, the leavings of a magic he now realized he had not yet begun to understand.

And in his mind the vision lingered, a shimmering image at the forefront of his thoughts — all that remained of what moments earlier the magic had uncovered in the mist and dark.

The weathered stone vault. The familiar words in scroll.

The Sword of Shannara.

Then the ringing stopped, the vision disappeared, and he was back in the Pit, drowning in weakness. The Shadowen were closing, shambling forward from all directions to trap them against the stone of the bridge. Padishar stepped forward, tall and forbidding, to confront the nearest, a huge bearish thing with talons for hands. It reached for him and he cut at it with the broadsword — once, twice, a third time — the strokes so rapid Par could barely register them. The creature sagged back, limbs drooping — but it did not fall. It barely seemed aware of what had been done to it, its eyes fixed, its features

325

twisting with some inner torment.

Par watched the Shadowen through glazed eyes. Its limbs reconnected in the manner of the giant they had fought in the Anar.

'Padishar, the Sword ...' he started to say, but the outlaw chief was already shouting, directing them back the way they had come, retreating along the wall of stone. 'No!' Par shrieked in dismay. He could not put into words the certainty he felt. They had to reach the Sword. He lurched up, trying to break free of Coll, but his brother held him fast, dragging him along with the others.

The Shadowen attacked in a shambling rush. Stasas went down, dragged beyond the reach of his companions. His throat was ripped out and then something dark entered his body while he was still alive, gasping. It jerked him upright, brought him about to face them, and he became another attacker. The company retreated, swords slashing. Ciba Blue appeared — or what was left of him. Impossibly strong, he blocked Drutt's sword, caught hold of his arms, and wrapped himself about his former comrade like a leech. The outlaw shrieked in pain as first one arm and then the other was ripped from his body. His head went last. He was left behind then, Ciba Blue's remains still fastened to him, feeding.

Padishar was alone then, besieged on all sides. He would have been dead if he were not so quick and so strong. He feinted and slashed, dodging the fingers that grappled for him, twisting to stay free. Hopelessly outnumbered, he began to give ground quickly.

It was Morgan Leah who saved him. Abandoning his role as defender of Par and Coll, the Highlander rushed to the aid of the outlaw chief. His red hair flying, he charged into the midst of the Shadowen. The Sword of Leah arced downward, catching fire as it struck. Magic surged through the blade and into the dark things, burning them to ash. Two fell, three, then more. Padishar fought relentlessly beside him, and together they began cutting a path through the gathering of eyes, calling wildly for Par and Coll to follow. The Valemen stumbled after them, avoiding the grasp of Shadowen who had slipped behind. Par abandoned all hope of reaching the Sword. Two of their number were already dead; the rest of them would be killed as well if they didn't get out of there at once.

Back toward the wall of the ravine they staggered, warding off the Shadowen as they went, the magic of the Sword of Leah keeping the creatures at bay. They seemed to be everywhere, as if the Pit were a nest in which they bred. Like the woodswoman and the giant, they seemed impervious to any damage done to them by conventional weapons. Only Morgan could hurt them; it was magic that they could not withstand.

The retreat was agonizingly slow. Morgan grew weary, and as his own strength drained away so did the power of the Sword of Leah. They ran when they could, but more and more frequently the Shadowen blocked their way. Par attempted in vain to invoke the magic of the wish-song; it simply would not come. He tried not to think of what that meant, still struggling to make sense of what had occurred, to understand how the magic had broken free. Even in flight, his mind wrestled with the memory. How could he have lost control like that? How could the magic have provided him with that strange light, a thing that was real and not illusion? Had he simply willed it to be? What was it that had happened to him?

Somehow they reached the wall of the ravine and sagged wearily against it. Shouts sounded from the park above and torches flared. Their battle with the Shadowen had alerted the Federation watch. In moments, the Gatehouse would be under siege.

'The grappling hooks!' Padishar gasped.

Par had lost his, but Coll's was still slung across his shoulder. The Valeman stepped back, uncoiled the rope and heaved the heavy iron skyward. It flew out of sight and caught. Coll tested it with his weight and it held.

Padishar braced Par against the wall, and their eyes met. Behind him, the forests of the Pit were momentarily empty. 'Climb,' he ordered roughly. His breath came in short gasps. He pulled Coll to him as well. 'Both of you.

Climb until you are safely out, then flee into the park. Damson will find you and take you back to the Jut.'

'Damson,' Par repeated dumbly.

'Forget your suspicions and mine as well,' the outlaw whispered harshly. There was a glint of something sad in his hard eyes. 'Trust her, lad — she is the better part of me!'

The Shadowen materialized once more out of the murk, their breathing a slow hiss in the night air. Morgan had already pushed out from the wall to face them. 'Get out of here, Par,' he called back over his shoulder.

'Climb!' Padishar Creel snapped. 'Now!'

'But you . . .' Par began.

'Shades!' the other exploded. 'I remain with the High-lander to see that you escape! Don't waste the gesture!' He caught Par roughly by the shoulders. 'Whatever happens to any of the rest of us, you must live! The Shannara magic is what will win this fight one day, and you are the one who must wield it! Now go!'

Coll took charge then, half-pushing and half-lifting Par onto the rope. It was knotted, and the Valeman found an easy grip. He began to climb, tears of frustration filling his eyes. Coll followed him up, urging him on, his blocky face taut beneath its sheen of sweat.

Par paused only once to glance downward. Shadowen ringed Padishar Creel and Morgan Leah as they stood protectively before the ravine wall.

Too many Shadowen.

The Valeman looked away again. Biting back against his rage, he continued to climb into the mist and black.

Morgan Leah did not turn around as the scraping of boots on the ravine wall faded away; his eyes remained fixed on the encircling Shadowen. He was aware of Padishar standing at his left shoulder. The Shadowen were no longer advancing on them; they were hanging back guardedly at the edge of the mist's thick curtain, keeping their distance. They had learned what Morgan's weapon could do, and they had grown cautious.

Mindless things, the Highlander thought bitterly. *I could have come to a better end than this, you'd think!*

He feinted at the nearest of them, and they backed away.

Morgan's weariness dragged at him like chains. It was the work of the magic, he knew. Its power had gone all through him, a sort of inner fire drawn from the sword, an exhilarating rush at first, then after a time simply a wearing down. And there was something more. There was an insidious binding of the magic to his body that made him crave it in a way he could not explain, as if to give it up now, even to rest, would somehow take away from who and what he was.

He was suddenly afraid that he might not be able to relinquish it until he was too weak to do otherwise.

Or too dead.

He could no longer hear Par and Coll climbing. The Pit was again encased in silence save for the hissing of the Shadowen.

Padishar leaned close to him. 'Move, Highlander!' he rasped softly.

They began to ease their way down the ravine wall, slowly at first, and then, when the Shadowen did not come at them right away, more quickly. Soon they were running, stumbling really, for they no longer had the strength to do anything more. Mist swirled about them, gray tendrils against the night. The trees shimmered in the haze of falling rain and seemed to move. Morgan felt himself ease into a world of unfeeling half-sleep that stole away time and place.

Twice more the Shadowen attacked as they fled, brief forays each time, and twice they were driven back by the magic of the Sword of Leah. Grotesque bodies launched themselves like slow rolling boulders down a mountainside and were turned to ash. Fire burned in the night, quick and certain, and Morgan felt a bit of himself fall away with each burst.

He began to wonder if in some strange way he was killing himself.

Above, where the park lay hidden behind the wall of the ravine, the shouts continued to grow, reaching out to them like a false lifeline of hope. There were no friends to be found there, Morgan knew. He stumbled, and it required an incredible amount of effort to right himself.

And then, at last, the Gatehouse came into view, a shadowy, massive tower lifting out of the trees and mist.

Morgan was dimly aware that something was wrong.

'Get through the door!' Padishar Creel cried frantically, shoving at him so hard he almost fell.

Together they sprinted for the door — or where the door should have been, for it was unexplainably missing. No light seeped through the opening they had left; the stone wall was black and faceless. Morgan felt a surge of fear and disbelief well up in the pit of his stomach.

Someone — or something — had sealed off their escape!

With Padishar a step behind, he came up against the Gatehouse wall, against the massive portal that had admitted them into the Pit, now closed and barred against their re-entry. They heaved against it in desperation, but it was fastened securely. Morgan's fingers searched its edges, probing, finding to his horror small markings all about, markings they had somehow overlooked before, runes of magic that glowed faintly in the graying mist and prevented their escape more certainly than any lock and key ever could.

Behind him, he could hear the Shadowen massing. He wheeled away, rushed the night things in a frenzy and caused them to scatter. Padishar was hammering at the invisible lock, not yet aware that it was magic and not iron that kept them out.

Morgan turned back, his lean face a mask of fury. 'Stand away, Padishar!' he shouted.

He went at the door as if it were one of the Shadowen, the Sword of Leah raised, its blade a brilliant silver streak against the dark. Down came the weapon like a hammer — once, twice, then again and again. The runes carved into the door's iron surface glowed a deep, wicked green.

Sparks flew with each blow, shards of flame that screamed in protest. Morgan howled as if gone mad, and the power of the sword's magic drew the last of his strength from him in a rush.

Then everything exploded into white fire, and Morgan was consumed by darkness.

Par lifted himself out of the Pit's murky blackness to the edge of the ravine wall and pulled himself up. Cuts and scrapes burned his arms and legs. Sweat stung his eyes, and his breath came in short gasps. For a moment, his vision blurred, the night about him an impenetrable mask dotted with weaving bits of light.

Torches, he realized, clustered about the entry to the Gatehouse. There were shouts as well and a hammering of heavy wood. The watch and whoever else had been summoned were trying to break down the bolted door.

Coll came over the wall behind him, grunting with the effort as he dropped wearily to the cool, sodden earth. Rain matted his dark hair where the hood of his cloak had fallen away, and his eyes glittered with something Par couldn't read.

'Can you walk?' his brother whispered anxiously.

Par nodded without knowing if he could or not. They came to their feet slowly, their muscles aching, their breathing labored. They stumbled from the wall into the shadow of the trees and paused in the blackness, waiting to discover if they had been seen, listening to the commotion that surrounded the Gatehouse.

Coll bent his head close. 'We have to get out of here, Par.' Par's eyes lifted accusingly. 'I know! But we can't help them anymore. Not now, at least. We have to save ourselves.' He shook his head helplessly. 'Please!'

Par clasped him momentarily and nodded into his shoulder, and they stumbled ahead. They made their way slowly, keeping to the blackest shadows, staying clear of the paths leading in toward the Gatehouse. The rain had stopped without their realizing it, and the great trees shed their surface water in sudden showers as the wind gusted in intermittent bursts. Par's mind spun with the memory of what had happened to them, whispering anew the warning it had given him earlier, teasing him with self-satisfied, purposeless glee. Why hadn't he listened? it whispered. Why had he been so stubborn?

The lights of the Tyrsian Way burned through the darkness ahead, and moments later they stumbled to the edge of the street. There were people clustered there, dim shapes in the night, faceless shadows that stood mute witness to the chaos beyond. Most were farther down near the park's entry and saw nothing of the two ragged figures who emerged. Those who did see quickly looked away when they recognized the Federation uniforms.

'Where do we go now?' Par whispered, leaning against Coll for support. He was barely able to stand.

Coll shook his head wordlessly and pulled his brother toward the street, away from the lights. They had barely reached its cobblestones when a lithe figure materialized out of the shadows some fifty feet away and moved to intercept them. *Damson*, Par thought. He whispered her name to Coll, and they slowed expectantly as she hurried up.

'Keep moving,' she said quietly, boosting Par's free arm about her shoulders to help Coll support him. 'Where are the others?'

Par's eyes lifted to meet hers. He shook his head slowly and saw the stricken look that crossed her face.

Behind them, deep within the park, there was a brilliant explosion of fire that rocketed skyward into the night. Gasps of dismay rose out of those gathered on the streets.

The silence that followed was deafening.

'Don't look back,' Damson whispered, tight-lipped.

The Valemen didn't need to.

Morgan Leah lay sprawled upon the scorched earth of the Pit, steam rising from his clothing, the acrid stench of smoke in his mouth and nostrils. Somehow he was still alive, he sensed — barely. Something was terribly wrong with him. He felt broken, as if everything had been smashed to bits within his skin, leaving him an empty, scoured shell. There was pain, but it wasn't physical. It was worse somehow. a sort of emotional agony that wracked not only his body but his mind as well.

'Highlander!'

Padishar's rough voice cut through the layers of hurt and brought his eyes open. Flames licked the ground inches away.

'Get up — quickly!' Padishar was pulling at him, hauling him forcibly to his feet, and he heard himself scream. A muddled sea of trees and stone blocks swam in the mist and darkness, slowly steadied and at last took shape.

Then he saw. He was still gripping the hilt of the Sword of Leah, but its blade was shattered. No more than a foot remained, a jagged, blackened shard.

Morgan began to shake. He could not stop himself. 'What have I done?' he whispered.

'You saved our lives, my friend!' Padishar snapped, dragging him forward. 'That's what you did!' Light poured through a massive hole in the wall of the Gatehouse. The door that had been sealed against their return had disappeared. Padishar's voice was labored. 'Your weapon did that. Your magic. Shattered that door into smoke! Gives us the chance we need, if we're quick enough. Hurry, now! Lean on me. Another minute or two . . .'

Padishar shoved him through the opening. He was dimly aware of the corridor they stumbled down, the stairs they climbed. The pain continued to rip through his body, leaving him incoherent when he tried to speak. He could not take his eyes from the broken sword. His sword — his magic — himself. He could not differentiate between them.

Shouts and a heavy thudding broke into his thoughts, causing him to flinch. 'Easy, now,' Padishar cautioned, the outlaw's voice a buzzing in his ears that seemed to come from very far away.

They reached the ward room with its weapons and debris. There was a frantic pounding on the entry doors. Their iron shielding was buckled and staved.

'Lie here,' Padishar ordered, leaning him back against the wall to one side. 'Say nothing when they enter, just keep still. With luck, they'll think us victims of what's happened here and nothing more. Here, give me that.' He reached down and pried the broken Sword of Leah from Morgan's nerveless fingers. 'Back in its case with this, lad. We'll see to its fixing later.'

He shoved the weapon into its shoulder scabbard, patted Morgan's cheek, and moved to open the entry doors.

Black-garbed Federation soldiers poured into the room, shouting and yelling and filling the chamber with a din that was suffocating. A disguised Padishar Creel shouted and yelled back, directing them down the stairwell, into the sleeping quarters, over this way and out that. There was mass confusion. Morgan watched it all without really understanding or even caring. The sense of indifference he felt was outweighed only by his sense of loss. It was is if his life no longer had a purpose, as if any reason for it had evaporated as suddenly and thoroughly as the blade of the Sword of Leah.

No more magic, he thought over and over. I have lost it. I have lost everything.

Then Padishar was back, hauling him to his feet again, steering him through the chaos of the Gatehouse to the entry doors and from there into the park. Bodies surged past, but no one challenged them. 'It's a fine madness we've let loose with this night's work,' Padishar muttered darkly. 'I just hope it doesn't come back to haunt us.'

He took Morgan swiftly from the circle of the Gatehouse lights into the concealing shadows beyond.

Moments later, they were lost from sight.

CHAPTER

24

I T WAS JUST AFTER DAWN when Par Ohmsford came awake the first time. He lay motionless on his pallet of woven mats, collecting his scattered thoughts in the silence of his mind. It took him awhile to remember where he was. He was in a storage shed behind a gardening shop somewhere in the center of Tyrsis. Damson had brought them there last night to hide after . . .

The memory returned to him in an unpleasant rush, images that swept through his mind with horrific clarity.

He forced his eyes open and the images disappeared. A faint wash of gray, hazy light seeped through cracks in the shuttered windows of the shed, lending vague definition to the scores of gardening tools stacked upright like soldiers at watch. The smell of dirt and sod filled the air, rich and pungent. It was silent beyond the walls of their concealment, the city still sleeping.

He lifted his head cautiously and glanced about. Coll was asleep beside him, his breathing deep and even. Damson was nowhere to be seen.

He lay back again for a time, listening to the silence, letting himself come fully awake. Then he rose, gingerly easing himself from beneath his blankets and onto his feet. He was stiff and cramped, and there was an aching in his joints that caused him to wince. But his strength was back; he could move about again unaided.

Coll stirred fitfully, turning over once before settling down again. Par watched his brother momentarily, studying the shadowed line of his blunt features, then stepped over to the nearest window. He was still wearing his clothing; only his boots had been removed. The chill of early morning seeped up from the plank flooring into his stockinged feet, but he ignored it. He put his eye to a crack in the shutters and looked out. It had stopped raining, but the skies were clouded and the world had a damp, empty look. Nothing moved within the range of his vision. A jumbled collection of walls, roofs, streets and shadowed niches stared back at him from out of the mist.

The door behind him opened, and Damson stepped noiselessly into the shed. Her clothing was beaded with moisture and her red hair hung limp.

'Here, what are you doing?' she whispered, her forehead creasing with annoyance. She crossed the room quickly and took hold of him as if he were about to topple over. 'You're not to be out of bed yet! You're far too weak! Back you go at once!'

She steered him to his pallet and forced him to lie down again. He made a brief attempt to resist and discovered that he had less strength than he first believed.

'Damson, listen ...' he began, but she quickly put a hand over his mouth.

'No, you listen, Elf-boy.' She paused, staring down at him as she might at a curious discovery. 'What is the matter with you, Par Ohmsford? Haven't you an ounce of common sense to call your own? You barely escaped with your life last night and already you are looking to risk it again. Haven't you the least regard for yourself?'

She took a deep breath, and he found himself thinking suddenly of how warm her hand felt against his face. She seemed to read his thoughts and lifted it away. Her fingers trailed across his cheek.

He caught her hand in his and held it. 'I'm sorry. I couldn't sleep anymore. I was drifting in and out of nightmares about last night.' Her hand felt small and light in his own. 'I can't stop thinking about Morgan and Padishar . . .'

He trailed off, not wanting to say more. It was too frightening, even now. Next to him, Coll's eyes blinked open and fixed on him. 'What's going on?' he asked sleepily.

Damson's fingers tightened on Par's. 'Your brother cannot seem to sleep for worrying about everyone but himself.'

Par stared up at her wordlessly for a moment, then said, 'Is there any news, Damson?'

She smiled faintly. 'I will make a bargain with you. If you promise me that you will try to go back to sleep for a time — or at least not leave this bed — I promise you that I will try to learn the answer to your question. Fair enough?'

The Valeman nodded. He found himself pondering anew Padishar's final admonition to him: *Trust her. She is the better part of me!*

Damson glanced over at Coll. 'I depend on you to make certain that he keeps his word.' Her hand slipped from Par's and she stood up. 'I will bring back something to eat as well. Stay quiet, now. No one will disturb you here.'

She paused momentarily, as if reluctant even then to leave, then turned and disappeared out the door.

Silence filled the shadowed room. The brothers looked at each other without speaking for a moment, and then Coll said quietly, 'She's in love with you.'

Par flushed, then quickly shook his head. 'No. She's just being protective, nothing more.'

Coll lay back, sighed and closed his eyes. 'Oh, is that it?' He let his breathing slow. Par thought he was sleeping again when he suddenly said, 'What happened to you last night, Par?'

Par hesitated. 'You mean the wishsong?'

Coll's eyes slipped open. 'Of course I mean the wishsong.' He glanced over sharply. 'I know how the magic works better than anyone other than yourself, and I've never seen it do that. That wasn't an illusion you created; that was the real thing! I didn't think you could do that.'

'I didn't either.'

'Well?'

Par shook his head. What had happened indeed? He closed his eyes momentarily and then opened them again. 'I have a theory,' he admitted finally. 'I came up with it between sleep and bad dreams, you might say. Remember how the magic of the wishsong came about in the first place? Wil Ohmsford used the Elfstones in his battle with the Reaper. He had to in order to save the Elf-girl Amberle. Shades, we've told that story often enough, haven't we? It was dangerous for him to do so because he hadn't enough true Elf blood to allow it. It changed him in a way he couldn't determine at first. It wasn't until after his children were born, until after Brin and Jair, that he discovered what had been done. Some part of the Elf magic of the Stones had gone into him. That part was passed to Brin and Jair in the form of the wishsong.'

He raised himself up on one elbow; Coll did likewise. The light was sufficient now to let them see each other's faces clearly. 'Cogline told us that first night that we didn't understand the magic. He said that it works in different ways — something like that — but that until we understood it, we could only use it in one. Then, later, at the Hadeshorn, he told us how the magic changes, leaving wakes in its passing like the water of a lake disturbed. He made specific reference to Wil Ohmsford's legacy of magic, the magic that became the wishsong.'

He paused. The room was very still. When he spoke again, his voice sounded strange in his ears. 'Now suppose for a moment that he was right, that the magic is changing all the time, evolving in some way. After all, that's what happened when the magic of the Elfstones passed from Wil Ohmsford to his children. So what if it has changed again, this time in me?'

Coll stared. 'What do you mean?' he asked finally. 'How do you think it could change?'

'Suppose that the magic has worked its way back to what it was in the beginning. The blue Elfstones that Allanon gave to Shea Ohmsford when they went in search of the Sword of Shannara all those years ago had the power to seek out that which was hidden from the holder.'

'Par!' Coll breathed his name softly, the astonishment apparent in his voice.

'No, wait. Let me finish. Last night, the magic released itself in a way it has never done before. I could barely control it. You're right, Coll; there was no illusion in what it did. But it did respond in a recognizable way. It sought out what was hidden from me, and I think it did so because subconsciously I willed it.' His voice was fierce. 'Coll. Suppose that the power that once was inherent in the magic of the Elfstones is now inherent in the magic within me!'

There was a long silence between them. They were close now, their faces not two feet apart, their eyes locked. Coll's rough features were knotted in concentration, the enormity of what Par was suggesting weighing down on him like a massive stone block. Doubt mirrored in his eyes, then acceptance, and suddenly fear.

His face went taut. His rough voice was very soft. 'The Elfstones possessed another property as well. They could defend the holder against danger. They could be a weapon of tremendous power.'

Par waited, saying nothing, already knowing what was coming.

'Do you think that the magic of the wishsong can now do the same for you?'

Par's response was barely audible. 'Yes, Coll. I think maybe it can.'

By midday, the haze of early morning had burned away and the clouds had moved on. Sunshine shone down on Tyrsis, blanketing the city in heat. Puddles and streams evaporated as the temperature rose, the stone and clay of the streets dried, and the air grew humid and sticky.

Traffic at the gates of the Outer Wall was heavy and slow moving. The Federation guards on duty, double the usual number as a result of the previous night's disturbance, were already sweating and irritable when the bearded gravedigger approached from out of the back streets beyond the inner wall. Travelers and merchants alike moved aside at his approach. He was ragged and stooped, and he smelled to the watch as if he had been living in a sewer. He was wheeling a heavy cart in front of him, the wood rotted and splintered. There was a body in the cart, wrapped in sheets and bound with leather ties.

The guards glanced at one another as the gravedigger trudged up to them, his charge wheeled negligently before him, rolling and bouncing.

'Hot one for work, isn't it, sirs?' the gravedigger wheezed, and the guards flinched in spite of themselves from the stench of him.

'Papers,' said one perfunctorily.

'Sure, sure.' One ragged hand passed over a document that looked as if it had been used to wipe up mud. The gravedigger gestured at the body. 'Got to get this one in the ground quick, don't you know. Won't last long on a day such as this.'

One of the guards stepped close enough to prod the corpse with the point of his sword. 'Easy now,' the gravedigger advised. 'Even the dead deserve some respect.'

The soldier looked at him suspiciously, then shoved the sword deep into the body and pulled it out again. The gravedigger cackled. 'You might want to be cleaning your sword there, sir — seeing as how this one died of the spotted fever.'

The soldier stepped back quickly, pale now. The others retreated as well. The one holding the gravedigger's papers handed them hastily back and motioned him on.

The gravedigger shrugged, picked up the handles of the cart and wheeled his body down the long ramp toward the plain below, whistling tunelessly as he went.

What a collection of fools, Padishar Creel thought disdainfully to himself.

When he reached the first screening of trees north, the city of Tyrsis a distant grayish outline against the swelter, Padishar eased the handles of the cart down, shoved the body he had been hauling aside, took out an iron bar and began prying loose the boards of the cart's false bottom. Gingerly, he helped Morgan extricate himself from his place of hiding. Morgan's face was pale and drawn, as much from the heat and discomfort of his concealment as from the lingering effects of last night's battle.

'Take a little of this.' The outlaw chief offered him an aleskin, trying unsuccessfully not to look askance. Morgan accepted the offering wordlessly. He knew what the other was thinking — that the Highlander hadn't been right since their escape from the Pit.

Abandoning the cart and its body, they walked a mile further on to a river where they could wash. They bathed, dressed in clean clothes that Padishar had hidden with Morgan in the cart's false bottom, and sat down to have something to eat.

The meal was a silent one until Padishar, unable to stand it any longer, growled, 'We can see about fixing the blade, Highlander. It may be the magic isn't lost after all.'

Morgan just shook his head. 'This isn't something anyone can fix,' he said tonelessly.

'No? Tell me why. Tell me how the sword works, then. You explain it to me.' Padishar wasn't about to let the matter alone.

Morgan did as the other asked, not because he particularly wanted to, but because it was the easiest way to get Padishar to stop talking about it. He told the story of how the Sword of Leah was made magic, how Allanon dipped its blade in the waters of the Hadeshorn so that Rone Leah would have a weapon with which to protect Brin Ohmsford. 'The magic was in the blade, Padishar,' he finished. He was having trouble being patient by now. 'Once broken, it cannot be repaired. The magic is lost.'

Padishar frowned doubtfully, then shrugged. 'Well, it was lost for a good cause, Highlander. After all, it saved our lives. A good trade any day of the week.'

Morgan looked up at him, his eyes haunted. 'You don't understand. There was some sort of bond between us, the sword and me. When the sword broke, it was as if it was happening to me! It doesn't make sense, I know — but it's there anyway. When the magic was lost, some part of me was lost as well.'

'But that's just your sense of it now, lad. Who's to say that won't change?' Padishar gave him an encouraging smile. 'Give yourself a little time. Let the wound heal, as they say.'

Morgan put down his food, disinterested in eating, and hunched his knees close against his chest. He remained quiet, ignoring the fact that the outlaw chief was waiting for a response, contemplating instead the nagging recognition that nothing had gone right since their decision to go down into the Pit after the missing Sword of Shannara.

Padishar's brow furrowed irritably. 'We have to go,' he announced abruptly and stood up. When Morgan didn't move right away, he said, 'Now, listen to me, Highlander. We're alive and that's the way we're going to stay, sword or no sword, and I'll not allow you to continue acting like some half-dead puppy ...'

Morgan came to his feet with a bound. 'Enough, Padishar! I don't need you worrying about me!' His voice sounded harsher than he had meant it to, but he could not disguise the anger he was feeling. That anger quickly found a focus. 'Why don't you try worrying about the Valemen? Do you have any idea at all what's happened to them? Why have we left them behind like this?'

'Ah.' The other spoke the word softly. 'So that's what's really eating at you, is it? Well, Highlander, the Valemen are likely better off than we are. We were seen getting out of that Gatehouse, remember? The Federation isn't so stupid that it will overlook the report of what happened and the fact that two so-called guards are somehow missing. They'll have our description. If we hadn't gotten out of the city right away, we likely wouldn't have gotten out at all!'

He jabbed his finger at the Highlander. 'Now the Valemen, on the other hand — no one saw them. No one will recognize their faces. Besides, Damson will have them in hand by now. She knows to bring them to the Jut. She'll get them out of Tyrsis easily enough when she has the chance.'

Morgan shook his head stubbornly. 'Maybe. Maybe not. You were confident as well about our chances of retrieving the Sword of Shannara and look what happened.'

Padishar flushed angrily. 'The risks involved in that were hardly a secret to any of us!'

'Tell that to Stasas and Drutt and Ciba Blue!'

The big man snatched hold of Morgan's tunic and yanked him forward violently. His eyes were hard with anger. 'Those were my friends that died back there, Highlander — not yours. Don't be throwing it up in my face! What I did, I did for all of us. We need the Sword of Shannara! Sooner or later we're going to have to go back for it — Shadowen or not! You know that as well as I! As for the Valemen, I don't like leaving them any better than you do! But we had precious little choice in the matter!'

Morgan tried unsuccessfully to jerk free. 'You might have gone looking for them, at least!'

'Where? Where would I look? Do you think they would be hidden in any place we could find? Damson's no fool! She has them tucked away in the deepest hole in Tyrsis! Shades, Highlander! Don't you realize what's happening back there? We uncovered a secret last night that the Federation has gone to great pains to conceal! I'm not sure either of us understands what it all means yet, but it's enough that the Federation thinks we might! They'll want us dead for that!'

His voice was a snarl. 'I caught a glimpse of what's to

come when I passed you through the gates. The Federation authorities no longer concern themselves merely with doubling guards and increasing watch patrols. They have mobilized the entire garrison! Unless I am badly mistaken, young Morgan Leah, they have decided to eliminate us once and for all — you and me and any other members of the Movement they can run to earth. We are a real threat to them now, because, for the first time, we begin to understand what they are about — and that's something they will not abide!'

His grip tightened, fingers of stone. 'They'll come hunting us, and we had best not be anywhere we can be found!'

He released the Highlander with a shove. He took a deep breath and straightened. 'In any case, I don't choose to argue the matter with you. I am leader here. You fought well back there in the Pit, and perhaps it cost you something. But that doesn't give you the right to question my orders. I understand the business of staying alive better than you, and you had best remember it.'

Morgan was white with rage, but he kept himself in check. He knew there was nothing to be gained by arguing the matter further; the big man was not about to change his mind. He knew as well, deep down inside where he could admit it to himself, that what Padishar was saying about staying around in an effort to find Par and Coll was the truth.

He stepped away from Padishar and smoothed his rumpled clothing carefully. 'I just want to be certain that we are agreed that the Valemen will not be forgotten.'

Padishar Creel's smile was quick and hard. 'Not for a moment. Not by me, at least. You are free to do as you choose in the matter.'

He wheeled away, moving off into the trees. After a moment's hesitation, Morgan swallowed his anger and pride and followed.

Par came awake for the second time that day toward

midafternoon. Coll was shaking him and the smell of hot soup filled the close confines of their shelter. He blinked and sat up slowly. Damson stood at a pruning bench, spooning broth into bowls, the steam rising thickly as she worked. She glanced over at the Valeman and smiled. Her flaming hair shimmered brightly in the shards of sunlight that filtered through the cracks in the shuttered windows, and Par experienced an almost irresistible need to reach out and stroke it.

Damson served the Valemen the soup together with fresh fruit, bread, and milk, and Par thought it was the most wonderful meal he had ever tasted. He ate everything he was given, Coll with him, both ravenous beyond what they would have thought possible. Par was surprised that he had been able to go back to sleep, but he was unquestionably the better for it, his body rested now and shed of most of its aches and pains There was little talk during the meal, and that left him free to think. His mind had begun working almost immediately on waking, skipping quickly from the memory of last night's horrors to the prospect of what lay ahead — to sift through the information he had gathered, to consider carefully what he suspected, to make plans for what he now believed must be.

The process made him shudder inwardly with excitement and foreboding. Already, he discovered, he was beginning to relish the prospect of attempting the unthinkable.

When the Valemen had finished eating, they washed in a basin of fresh water. Then Damson sat them down again and told them what had become of Padishar and Morgan.

'They escaped,' she began without preamble. Her green eyes reflected amusement and awe. 'I don't know how they managed it, but they did. It took me awhile to verify that they had indeed gotten free, but I wanted to make certain of what I was being told '

Par grinned at his brother in relief. Coll stifled his own grin and instead simply shrugged. 'Knowing those two, they probably talked their way out,' he responded gruffly.

'Where are they now?' Par asked. He felt as if years had been added back onto his life. Padishar and Morgan had escaped — it was the best news he could have been given.

'That I don't know,' Damson replied, shrugging. 'They seem to have disappeared. Either they have gone to ground in the city or — more likely — they have left it altogether and are on their way back to the Jut. The latter seems the better guess because the entire Federation garrison is mobilizing and there's only one reason they would do that. They mean to go after Padishar and his men in the Parma Key. Apparently, whatever he — and you — did last night made them very angry. There are all sorts of rumors afloat. Some say dozens of Federation soldiers were killed at the Gatehouse by monsters. Some say the monsters are loose in the city. Whatever the case, Padishar will have read the signs as easily as I. He'll have slipped out by now and gone north.'

'You're certain the Federation hasn't found him instead?' Par was still anxious.

Damson shook her head. 'I would have heard.' She was propped against the leg of the pruning bench as they sat on the pallets that had served as their beds the night before. She let her head tilt back against the roughened wood so that the soft curve of her face caught the light. 'It is your turn now. Tell me what happened, Par. What did you find in the Pit?'

With help from Coll, Par related what had befallen them, deciding as he did that he would do as Padishar had urged, that he would trust Damson in the same way that he had trusted the outlaw chief. Thus he told her not only of their encounter with the Shadowen, but of the strange behavior of the wishsong, of the unexpected way its magic had performed, even of his suspicions of the influence of the Elfstones.

When he had finished, the three of them sat staring wordlessly at one another for a moment, of different minds as they reflected on what the foray into the Pit had uncovered and what it all meant.

Coll spoke first. 'It seems to me that we have more questions to answer now than we did when we went in.'

'But we know some things, too, Coll,' Par argued. He bent forward, eager to speak. 'We know that there is some sort of connection between the Federation and the Shadowen. The Federation has to know what it has down there; it can't be ignorant of the truth. Maybe it even helped create those monsters. For all we know they might be Federation prisoners thrown into the Pit like Ciba Blue and changed into what we found. And why are they still down there if the Federation isn't keeping them so? Wouldn't they have escaped long ago if they could?'

'As I said, there are more questions than answers,' Coll declared. He shifted his heavy frame to a more comfortable position.

Damson shook her head. 'Something seems wrong here. Why would the Federation have any dealings with the Shadowen? The Shadowen represent everything the Federation is against — magic, the old ways, the subversion of the Southland and its people. How would the Federation even go about making such an arrangement? It has no defense against the Shadowen magic. How would it protect itself?'

'Maybe it doesn't have to,' Coll said suddenly. They looked at him. 'Maybe the Federation has given the Shadowen someone else to feed on besides itself, someone the Federation has no use for in any case. Perhaps that's what became of the Elves.' He paused. 'Perhaps that's what's happening now to the Dwarves.'

They were silent as they considered the possibility. Par hadn't thought about the Dwarves for a time, the horrors of Culhaven and its people shoved to the back of his mind these past few weeks. He remembered what he had seen there — the poverty, the misery, the oppression. The Dwarves were being exterminated for reasons that had never been clear. Could Coll be right? Could the Federation be feeding the Dwarves to the Shadowen as part of some unspeakable bargain between them?

347

His face tightened in dismay. 'But what would the Federation get in return?'

'Power,' Damson Rhee said immediately. Her face was still and white.

'Power over the Races, over the Four Lands,' Coll agreed, nodding. 'It makes sense, Par.'

Par shook his head slowly. 'But what happens when there is no one left but the Federation? Surely someone must have thought of that. What keeps the Shadowen from feeding on them as well?'

No one answered. 'We're still missing something,' Par said softly. 'Something important.'

He rose, walked to the other side of the room, stood looking into space for a long moment, shook his head finally, turned, and came back. His lean face was stubborn with determination as he reseated himself.

'Let's get back to the matter of the Shadowen in the Pit,' he declared quietly, 'since that, at least, is a mystery that we might be able to solve.' He folded his legs in front of him and eased forward. He looked at each of them in turn, then said, 'I think that the reason they are down there is to keep anyone from getting to the Sword of Shannara.'

'Par!' Coll tried to object, but his brother cut him off with a quick shake of his head.

'Think about it a moment, Coll. Padishar was right. Why would the Federation go to all the trouble of remaking the People's Park and the Bridge of Sendic? Why would they hide what remains of the old park and bridge in that ravine? Why, if not to conceal the Sword? And we've seen the vault, Coll! We've seen it!'

'The vault, yes — but not the Sword,' Damson pointed out quietly, her green eyes intense as they met those of the Valemen.

'But if the Sword isn't down in the Pit as well, why are the Shadowen there?' Par asked at once. 'Surely not to protect an empty vault! No, the Sword is still in its vault, just as it has been for three hundred years. That's why Allanon sent me after it — he knew it was there, waiting to be found.'

'He could have saved us a lot of time and trouble by telling us as much,' said Coll pointedly.

Par shook his head. 'No, Coll. That isn't the way he would do it. Think about the history of the Sword. Bremen gave it to Jerle Shannara some thousand years ago to destroy the Warlock Lord and the Elf King couldn't master it because he wasn't prepared to accept what it demanded of him. When Allanon chose Shea Ohmsford to finish the job five hundred years later, he decided that the Valeman must first prove himself. If he was not strong enough to wield it, if he did not want it badly enough, if he were not willing to give enough of himself to the task that finding it entailed, then the power of the Sword would prove too much for him as well. And he knew if that happened, the Warlock Lord would escape again.'

'And he believes it will be the same now with you,' Damson finished. She was looking at Par as if she were seeing him for the first time. 'If you are not strong enough, if you are not willing to give enough, the Sword of Shannara will be useless to you. The Shadowen will prevail.'

Par's answering nod was barely discernible.

'But why would the Shadowen — or the Federation, for that matter — leave the Sword in the Pit all these years?' Coll demanded, irritated that they were even talking about the matter after what had happened to them last night. 'Why not simply remove it — or better yet, why not destroy it?'

Par's face was intense. 'I don't think either the Federation or the Shadowen can destroy it — not a talisman of such power. I doubt that the Shadowen can even touch it. The Warlock Lord couldn't. What I can't figure out is why the Federation hasn't taken it out and hidden it.'

He clasped his hands tightly before him. 'In any case, it doesn't matter. The fact remains the Sword is still there, still in its vault.' He paused, eyes level. 'Waiting for us.'

Coll gaped at him, realizing for the first time what he was suggesting. For a moment, he couldn't speak at all.

349

'You can't be serious, Par,' he managed finally, the disbelief in his voice undisguised. 'After what happened last
night? After seeing . . .' He forced himself to stop, then
snapped, 'You wouldn't last two minutes.'

'Yes, I would,' Par replied. His eyes were bright with
determination. 'I know I would. Allanon told me as
much.'

Coll was aghast. 'Allanon! What are you talking
about?'

'He said we had the skills needed to accomplish what
was asked — Walker, Wren, and myself. Remember? In
my case, I think he was talking about the wishsong. I
think he meant that the magic of the wishsong would
protect me.'

'Well, it's done a rather poor job of it up to now!' Coll
snapped, lashing out furiously.

'I didn't understand what it could do then. I think I do
now.'

'You think? You think? Shades, Par!'

Par remained calm. 'What else are we to do? Run back
to the Jut? Run home? Spend the rest of our days sneaking about?' Par's hands were shaking. 'Coll, I haven't any
choice. I have to try.'

Coll's strong face closed in upon itself in dismay, his
mouth tightening against whatever outburst threatened to
break free. He wheeled on Damson, but the girl had her
eyes locked on Par and would not look away.

The Valeman turned back, gritting his teeth. 'So you
would go back down into the Pit on the strength of an
unproven and untested belief. You would risk your life on
the chance that the wishsong — a magic that has failed to
protect you three times already against the Shadowen —
will somehow protect you now. And all because of what
you perceive as your newfound insight into a dead man's
words!' He drew his breath in slowly. 'I cannot believe
you would do anything so . . . stupid! If I could think of
anything worse to call it, I would!'

'Coll . . .'

'No, don't say another word to me! I have gone with

350

you everywhere, followed after you, supported you, done everything I could to keep you safe — and now you plan to throw yourself away! Just waste your life! Do you understand what you are doing, Par? You are sacrificing yourself! You still think you have some special ability to decide what's right! You are obsessed! You can't ever let go, even when common sense tells you you should!'

Coll clenched his fists before him. His face was rigid and furrowed, and it was all he could do to keep his voice level. Par had never seen him so angry. 'Anyone else would back away, think it through, and decide to go for help. But you're not planning on any of that, are you? I can see it in your eyes. You haven't the time or the patience. You've made up your mind. Forget Padishar or Morgan or anyone else but yourself. You mean to have that Sword! You'd even give up your life to have it, wouldn't you?'

'I am not so blind . . .'

'Damson, you talk to him!' Coll interrupted, desperate now. 'I know you care for him; tell him what a fool he is!'

But Damson Rhee shook her head. 'No. I won't do that.' Coll stared at her, stunned. 'I haven't the right,' she finished softly.

Coll went silent then, his rough features sagging in defeat. No one spoke immediately, letting the momentary stillness settle across the room. Daylight had shifted with the sun's movement west, gone now to the far side of the little storage shed, the shadows beginning to lengthen slightly in its wake. A scattering of voices sounded from somewhere in the streets beyond and faded away. Par felt an aching deep within himself at the look he saw on his brother's face, at the sense of betrayal he knew Coll was feeling. But there was no help for it. There was but one thing Par could say that would change matters, and he was not about to say it.

'I have a plan,' he tried instead. He waited until Coll's eyes lifted. 'I know what you think, but I don't propose to take any more chances than I have to.' Coll gave him an incredulous look, but kept still. 'The vault sits close to the base of the cliffs, just beneath the walls of the old palace. If I could get into the ravine from the other side, I would have only a short distance to cover. Once I had the Sword in my hands, I would be safe from the Shadowen.'

There were several huge assumptions involved in that last statement, but neither Coll nor Damson chose to raise them. Par felt the sweat bead on his forehead. The difficulty of what he was about to suggest was terrifying.

He swallowed. 'That catwalk from the Gatehouse to the old palace would give me a way across.'

Coll threw up his hands. 'You plan to go back into the Gatehouse yet a third time?' he exclaimed, exasperated beyond reason.

'All I need is a ruse, a way to distract . . .'

'Have you lost your mind completely? Another ruse won't do the trick! They'll be looking for you this go-around! They'll spy you out within two seconds of the time you . . .'

'Coll!' Par's own temper slipped.

'He is right,' Damson Rhee said quietly.

Par wheeled on her, then caught himself. He jerked back toward his brother. Coll dared him to speak, red-faced, but silent. Par shook his head. 'Then I'll have to come up with another way.'

Coll looked suddenly weary. 'The truth of the matter is, there isn't any other way.'

'There might be one.' It was Damson who spoke, her low voice compelling. 'When the armies of the Warlock Lord besieged Tyrsis in the time of Balinor Buckhannah, the city was betrayed twice over from within — once by the front gates, the second time by passageways that ran beneath the city and the cliffs backing the old palace to the cellars beneath. Those passageways might still exist, giving us access to the ravine from the palace side.'

Coll looked away wordlessly, disgust registering on his blocky features. Clearly, he had hoped for better than this from Damson.

Par hesitated, then said carefully, 'That all happened more than four hundred years ago. I had forgotten about

352

those passageways completely — even telling the stories as often as I do.' He hesitated again. 'Do you know anything about them — where they are, how to get into them, whether they can be traversed anymore?'

Damson shook her head slowly, ignoring the deliberate lift of Coll's eyebrows. She said, 'But I know someone who might. If he will talk to us.' Then she met Coll's gaze and held it. There was a sudden softness in her face that surprised Par. 'We all have a right to make our own choices,' she said quietly.

Coll's eyes seemed haunted. Par studied his brother momentarily, debating whether to say anything to him, then turned abruptly to Damson. 'Will you take me to this person — tonight?'

She stood up then, and both Valemen rose with her. She looked small between them, almost delicate; but Par knew the perception was a false one. She seemed to deliberate before saying, 'That depends. You must first promise me something. When you go back into the Pit, however you manage it, you will take Coll and me with you.'

There was a stunned silence. It was hard to tell which of the Valemen was more astonished. Damson gave them a moment to recover, then said to Par, 'I'm not giving you any choice in the matter, I'm afraid. I cannot. You would feel compelled to do the right thing and leave us both behind to keep us safe — which would be exactly the wrong thing. You need us with you.'

Then she turned to Coll. 'And we need to be there, Coll. Don't you see? This won't end, any of it, not Federation oppression nor Shadowen evil nor the sickness that infects all the Lands, until someone makes it end. Par may have a chance to do that. But we cannot let him try it alone. We have to do whatever we can to help because this is our fight, too. We cannot just sit back and wait for someone else to come along and help us. No one will. If I've learned anything in this life, it's that.'

She waited, looking from one to the other. Coll looked confused, as if he thought there ought to be an obvious alternative to his choices but couldn't for the life of him recognize what it was. He glanced briefly at Par and away again. Par had gone blank, his gaze focused on the floor, his face devoid of expression.

'It is bad enough that I must go,' he said finally.

'Worse than bad,' Coll muttered.

Par ignored him, looking instead at Damson. 'What if it turns out that only I can go in?'

Damson came up to him, took his hands in her own and squeezed them. 'That won't happen. You know it won't.' She leaned up and kissed him softly. 'Are we agreed?'

Par took a deep breath, and a frightening sense of inevitability welled up inside. Coll and Damson Rhee — he was risking both their lives by going after the Sword. He was being stubborn beyond reason, intractable to the point of foolhardiness; he was letting himself be caught up in his own self-perceived needs and ambitions. There was every reason to believe that his insistence would kill them all.

Then give it up, he whispered fiercely to himself. *Just walk away.*

But even as he thought it, he knew he wouldn't.

'Agreed,' he said.

There was a brief silence. Coll looked up and shrugged. 'Agreed,' he echoed quietly.

Damson reached up to touch Par's face, then stepped over to Coll and hugged him. Par was more than a little surprised when his brother hugged her back.

CHAPTER

25

IT WAS DUSK ON THE FOLLOWING DAY when Padishar Creel and Morgan Leah finally reached the Jut. Both were exhausted.

They had traveled hard since leaving Tyrsis, stopping only for meals. They had slept less than six hours the previous night. Nevertheless, they would have arrived even sooner and in better condition if not for Padishar's insistence on doing everything possible to disguise their trail. Once they entered the Parma Key, he backtracked continuously, taking them down ravines, through riverbeds and over rocky outcroppings, all the while watching the land behind him like a hawk.

Morgan had thought the outlaw chief overcautious and, after growing impatient enough, had told him so. 'Shades, Padishar, we're wasting time! What do you think is back there anyway?'

'Nothing we can see, lad,' had been the other's enigmatic reply.

It was a sultry evening, the air heavy and still, and the skies hazy where the red ball of the sun settled into the horizon. As they rose in the basket lift toward the summit of the Jut, they could see night's shadows begin to fill the few wells of daylight that still remained in the forests below, turning them to pools of ink. Insects buzzed annoyingly about them, drawn by their body sweat. The swelter of the day lay across the land in a suffocating blanket. Padishar still had his gaze turned south toward Tyrsis, as if he might spy whatever it was he suspected had followed them. Morgan looked with him, but as before saw nothing. The big man shook his head. 'I can't see it,' he whispered. 'But I can feel it coming.'

He didn't explain what he meant by that and the Highlander didn't ask. Morgan was tired and hungry, and he knew that nothing either Padishar or he did was likely to change the plans of whatever might be out there. Their journey was completed, they had done everything humanly possible to disguise their passing, and there wasn't anything to be gained by worrying now. Morgan felt his stomach rumble and thought of the dinner that would be waiting. Lunch that day had been a sparse affair — a few roots, stale bread, hard cheese, and some water.

'I realize that outlaws are supposed to be able to subsist on next to nothing, but surely you could have done better than this!' he had complained. 'This is pathetic!'

'Oh, surely, lad!' the outlaw chief had replied. 'And next time you be the gravedigger and I'll be the body!'

Their differences had been put aside by then — not forgotten perhaps, but at least placed in proper perspective. Padishar had dismissed their confrontation five minutes after it ended, and Morgan had concluded by the end of the day that things were back to normal. He bore a grudging respect for the man — for his brash and decisive manner, because it reminded the Highlander of his own, for the confidence he so readily displayed in himself, and for the way he drew other men to him. Padishar Creel wore the trappings of leadership as if they were his birthright, and somehow that seemed fitting. There was undeniable strength in Padishar Creel; it made you want to follow him. But Padishar understood that a leader must give something back to his followers. Acutely aware of Morgan's role in bringing the Valemen north, he had made a point of acknowledging the legitimacy of the Highlander's concern for their safety. Several times after their argument he had gone out of his way to reassure

Morgan that Par and Coll Ohmsford would never be abandoned, that he would make certain that they were safe. He was a complex, charismatic fellow, and Morgan liked him despite a nagging suspicion that Padishar Creel would never in the world be able to deliver everything he promised.

Outlaws clasped Padishar's hand in greeting at each station of their ascent. If they believe so strongly in him, Morgan asked himself, shouldn't I?

But he knew that belief was as ephemeral as magic. He thought momentarily of the broken sword he carried. Belief and magic forged as one, layered into iron, then shattered. He took a deep breath. The pain of his loss was still there, deep and insidious despite his resolve to put it behind him, to do as Padishar had suggested and to give himself time to heal. There was nothing he could do to change what had happened, he had told himself; he must get on with his life. He had lived for years without the use of the sword's magic — without even knowing it existed. He was no worse off now than he had been then. He was the same man.

And yet the pain lingered. It was an emptiness that scraped the bones of his body from within, leaving him fragmented and in search of the parts that would make him whole again. He could argue that he was unchanged, but what he had experienced through wielding of the magic had left its stamp upon him as surely as if he had been branded by a hot iron. The memories remained, the images of his battles, the impressions made by the power he had been able to call upon, the strength he had enjoyed. It was lost to him now. Like the loss of a parent or a sibling or a child, it could never be completely forgotten.

He looked out across the Parma Key and felt himself shrinking away to nothing.

When they reached the Jut, Chandos was waiting. Padishar's one-eyed second-in-command looked larger and blacker than Morgan remembered, his bearded, disfigured face furrowed and lined, wrapped in a great cloak that seemed to lend his massive body added size. He seized Padishar's hand and gripped it hard. 'Good hunting?'

'Dangerous would be a better word for it,' the big man replied shortly.

Chandos glanced at Morgan. 'The others?'

'They've fought their last, save for the Valemen. Where's Hirehone? Somewhere about or gone back to Varfleet?'

Morgan glanced quickly at him. So Padishar was still looking to discover who had betrayed them, he thought. There had been no mention of the master of Kiltan Forge since Morgan had reported seeing him in Tyrsis.

'Hirehone?' Chandos looked puzzled. 'He left after you did, same day. Went back to Varfleet like you told him, I expect. He's not here.' He paused. 'You have visitors, though.'

Padishar yawned. 'Visitors?'

'Trolls, Padishar.'

The outlaw chief came awake at once. 'You don't say? Trolls? Well, well. And how do they come to be here?'

They started across the bluff toward the fires, Padishar and Chandos shoulder to shoulder, Morgan trailing. 'They won't say,' Chandos said. 'Came out of the woods three days back, easy as you please, as if finding us here wasn't any trouble at all for them. Came in without a guide, found us like we were camped in the middle of a field with our pennants flying.' He grunted. 'Twenty of them, big fellows, down out of the north country, the Charnals. Kelktic Rock, they call themselves. Just hung about until I went down to talk to them, then asked to speak with you. When I said you were gone, they said they'd wait.'

'No, is that so? Determined, are they?'

'Like falling rock looking to reach level ground. I brought them up when they agreed to give over their arms. Didn't seem right leaving them sitting down in the Parma Key when they'd come all that way to find you — and done such a good job of it in the bargain.' He smirked within his beard. 'Besides, I figured three hundred of us ought to be able to stop a handful of Trolls.'

Padishar laughed softly. 'Doesn't hurt to be cautious, old friend. Takes more than a shove to bring down a Troll. Where are they?'

'Over there, the fire on the left.'

Morgan and Padishar peered through the gloom. A cluster of faceless shadows were already on their feet, watching their approach. They looked huge. Unconsciously, Morgan reached back to finger the handle of his sword, remembering belatedly that a handle was just about all he had.

'The leader's name is Axhind,' Chandos finished, his voice deliberately low now. 'He's the Maturen.'

Padishar strode up to the Trolls, his weariness shed somewhere back, his tall form commanding. One of the Trolls stepped forward to meet him.

Morgan Leah had never seen a Troll. He had heard stories about them, of course; everyone told stories about the Trolls. Once, long before Morgan was born, Trolls had come down out of the Northland, their traditional home, to trade with the members of the other Races. For a time, some of them had even lived among the men of Callahorn. But all that ended with the coming of the Federation and its crusade for Southland domination. Trolls were no longer welcome below the Streleheim, and the few who had come south quickly went north again. Reclusive by nature, it took very little to send them back to their mountain strongholds. Now, they never came out — or at least no one Morgan knew had ever heard of them coming out. To find a band this far south was very unusual.

Morgan tried not to stare at the visitors, but it was hard. The Trolls were heavily muscled, almost grotesque, their bodies tall and wide, their skin nut-brown and rough like bark. Their faces were flat and nearly featureless. Morgan couldn't find any ears at all. They wore leather and heavy armor, and great cloaks lay scattered about their fire like discarded shadows.

'I'm Baron Creel, Leader of the Movement.' Padishar's voice boomed out.

The Troll facing him rumbled something incomprehensible. Morgan caught only the name Axhind. The two gripped hands briefly, then Axhind beckoned Padishar to sit with him at their fire. The Trolls stepped aside as the outlaw chief and his companions moved into the light to seat themselves. Morgan glanced about uneasily as the massive creatures closed about. He had never felt so unprotected. Chandos seemed unconcerned, positioning himself behind Padishar and a few feet back. Morgan eased down next to him.

The talk began in earnest then, but the Highlander didn't understand any of it. It was all done in the guttural language of the Trolls, a language of which Morgan knew nothing. Padishar seemed comfortable with it, however, pausing only infrequently to consider what he was saying. There was a great deal of what sounded like grunting, some heavy slurs, and much of what was said was emphasized by sharp gestures.

'How does Padishar speak their language?' Morgan whispered early on to Chandos.

The other never even glanced at him. 'We see a bit more of life in Callahorn than you Highlanders,' he said.

Morgan's hunger was threatening to consume him, but he forced it from his mind, holding himself erect against encroaching weariness, keeping himself deliberately still. The talk went on. Padishar seemed pleased with its direction.

'They want to join us,' Chandos whispered after a time, apparently deciding that Morgan should be rewarded for his patience. He listened some more. 'Not just these few — an entire twenty-one tribes!' He grew excited. 'Five thousand men! They want to make an alliance!'

Morgan grew excited himself. 'With us? Why?'

Chandos didn't answer right away, motioning for Morgan to wait. Then he said, 'The Movement has approached them before, asked them to help. But they always believed it too divided, too undependable. They've changed their minds of late.' He glanced over briefly. 'They say Padishar has pulled the separate factions together sufficiently to reconsider. They're looking for a way to slow the Federation advance on their homelands.' His rough voice was filled with satisfaction. 'Shades, what a stroke of good fortune this might turn out to be!'

Axhind was passing out cups now and filling them with something from a great jar. Morgan took the cup he was offered and glanced down. The liquid it contained was as black as pitch. He waited until both the Troll leader and Padishar saluted, then drank. It was all he could do to keep from retching. Whatever he had been given tasted like bile.

Chandos caught the look on his face. 'Troll milk,' he said and smiled.

They drained the offering, even Morgan who found it curbed his appetite in a way he would not have thought possible. Then they rose. Axhind and Padishar shook hands once more, and the Southlanders moved away.

'Did you hear?' Padishar asked quietly as they disappeared into the shadows. Stars were beginning to wink into view overhead, and the last of the daylight had faded away. 'Did you hear it all, the whole of it?'

'Every last word,' Chandos replied, and Morgan nodded wordlessly.

'Five thousand men! Shades! We could challenge the best that the Federation had to offer if we had a force like that!' Padishar was ecstatic. 'There might be two thousand and some that the Movement could call upon, and more than that from the Dwarves! Shades!'

He slammed his fist into his open palm, then reached over and clapped both Chandos and Morgan heartily on the back. 'It's about time something went our way, wouldn't you agree, lads?'

Morgan had dinner after that, sitting alone at a table near the cooking fire, his appetite restored by the smells that emanated from the stew kettles. Padishar and Chandos had gone off to confer on what had been happening during the former's absence, and Morgan saw no need to be part of that. He looked about for Steff and Teel, but there was no sign of either, and it wasn't until he had almost finished eating that Steff appeared out of the darkness and slumped down beside him.

'How did it go?' the Dwarf asked perfunctorily, forgoing any greeting, his gnarled hands clutched about a tankard of ale he had carried over. He looked surprisingly worn.

Briefly, Morgan related the events of the past week. When he had finished, Steff rubbed at his cinnamon beard and said, 'You're lucky to be alive — any of you.' His scarred face was haggard-looking; the mix of half-light and shadows seemed to etch more deeply its lines. 'There's been some strange happenings taking place while you were away.'

Morgan pushed back his plate and looked over, waiting.

The Dwarf cleared his throat, glancing about before he spoke. 'Teel took sick the same day you left. They found her collapsed by the bluff about noon. She was breathing, but I couldn't bring her awake. I took her inside and wrapped her in blankets and sat with her for most of a week. I couldn't do anything for her. She just lay there, barely alive.' He took a deep breath. 'I thought she'd been poisoned.'

His mouth twisted. 'Could of been, it seemed to me. Lots in the Movement have no use for the Dwarves. But then she woke finally, retching and so weak she could barely move. I fed her broth to give her back her strength, and she came around finally. She doesn't know what happened to her. She said the last thing she remembered was wondering something about Hirehone ...'

Morgan's sharp intake of breath stopped him. 'That mean something to you, Morgan?'

Morgan nodded faintly. 'It might. I thought I saw Hirehone in Tyrsis after we arrived there. He shouldn't have been, and I decided then I must have been mistaken. I'm not so certain now. Someone gave us over to the

Federation. It could have been Hirehone.'

Steff shook his head. 'Doesn't sound right. Why Hirehone, of all people? He could have turned us in that first time in Varfleet. Why wait until now?' The stocky form shifted. 'Besides, Padishar trusts him completely.'

'Maybe,' Morgan muttered, sipping at his ale. 'But Padishar was quick enough to ask about him when we got back here.'

Steff considered that a moment, then dismissed the matter. 'There's more. They found a handful of guards at the cliff edge two days back, night watch, the ones on the lifts, all dead, their throats torn out. No sign of who did it.' He looked away momentarily, then back again. Shadows darkened his eyes. 'The baskets were all up, Morgan.'

They stared at each other. Morgan frowned. 'So it was someone already here who did it?'

'Don't know. Seems like. But what was the reason for it, then? And if it was someone from the outside, how did they get up and then back down again with the baskets in place?'

Morgan looked off into the shadows and thought about it, but no answers would come. Steff rose. 'I thought you should know. Padishar will hear on his own, I expect.' He drained his tankard. 'I've got to get back to Teel; I don't like leaving her alone after what's happened. She's still awfully weak.' He rubbed his forehead and grimaced. 'I don't feel so well myself.'

'Off you go, then,' Morgan said, rising with him. 'I'll come see you both in the morning. Right now, though, I'm in desperate need of about two days' sleep.' He paused. 'You know about the Trolls?'

'Know about them?' Steff gave him a wry smile. 'I've spoken with them already. Axhind and I go back a ways.'

'Well, well. Another mystery. Tell me about it tomorrow, will you?'

Steff began moving away. 'Tomorrow it is.' He was almost out of sight when he said, 'Better watch your back, Highlander.'

Morgan Leah had already decided as much.

He slept well that night and woke rested. The midmorning sun had crested the tree line and begun to heat up the day. There was activity in the outlaw camp, more so than usual, and Morgan was immediately anxious to find out what was happening. He thought momentarily that the Valemen might have returned, but then discarded the possibility, deciding that he would have been awakened if they had. He pulled on his clothing and boots, rolled up his blankets, washed, ate, and went down to the bluff edge. He caught sight of Padishar immediately, dressed once more in his crimson garb, shouting orders and directing men this way and that.

The outlaw chief glanced over as the Highlander approached and grunted. 'I trust the noise didn't wake you.' He turned to yell instructions to a gathering of men by the lifts before continuing in a normal tone of voice, 'I would hate to think you were disturbed.'

Morgan muttered something under his breath, but stopped when he caught a glimpse of the other's mocking grin. 'Ah, ah. Just teasing you a bit, Highlander,' the other soothed. 'Let's not begin the day on the wrong foot — there's too much that needs doing. I've sent scouts to sweep the Parma Key to reassure myself that my neck hairs misled me about what's out there, and I've sent south for Hirehone. We will see what we will see. Meanwhile, the Trolls await, Axhind and his brood. Close kin, the bunch of them, I'm told. Yesterday was merely an overture. Today we talk about the how and the wherefore of it all. You want to come along?'

Morgan did. Buckling on the scabbard that held the remains of the Sword of Leah, which he was carrying now mostly out of habit, he followed Padishar along the bluff face and then back toward the campsite where the Trolls were already gathering. As they walked, he asked if there was any news of Par and Coll. There wasn't. He looked about expectantly for Steff and Teel, but there was no sign of either. He promised himself that he would seek them out later.

When they reached the Trolls, Axhind embraced the outlaw chief, then greeted the Highlander with a solemn nod and a handclasp like iron, and beckoned them both to take seats. Moments later, Chandos appeared with several companions, men Morgan didn't know, and the meeting got underway.

It lasted the remainder of the morning and the better part of the afternoon. Once again, Morgan was unable to follow what was being said, and this time Chandos was too preoccupied with his own participation to worry about him. Morgan listened attentively nevertheless, studying the gestures and movements of the bearish Trolls, trying to read something of what they were thinking behind their expressionless faces. He was mostly unsuccessful. They looked like great tree stumps brought to life and given the rudiments of human form to allow them to move about. Few did much of anything besides watch. The ones who spoke did so sparingly, even Axhind. There was an economy of effort behind everything they did. Morgan wondered briefly what they were like in a fight and decided that he probably already knew.

The sun moved across the sky, changing the light from dim to bright and back again, erasing and then lengthening shadows, filling the day with heat and then letting it linger in a suffocating swelter that left everyone shifting uncomfortably in a futile search for relief. There was a short break for lunch, an exchange of ales and wines, and even a brief allusion to the Highlander that had something to do with the extent of the support that the Movement enjoyed. Morgan stayed wisely silent during that exchange. He knew he had been brought there for support, not to contradict.

The afternoon was waning when the runner appeared, winded and frightened-looking. Padishar caught sight of him, frowned in annoyance at the interruption, and excused himself. He listened intently to what the runner had to say, hesitated, then glanced at the Highlander and beckoned. Morgan came to his feet in a hurry. He did not care for what he saw in Padishar Creel's face.

Padishar dismissed the runner when Morgan reached them. 'They found Hirehone,' he said softly, evenly. 'Out along the west edge of the Parma Key, close to the path we followed on our return. He's dead.' His eyes shifted uncomfortably. 'The patrol that found him said he looked as if he had been turned inside out.'

Morgan felt his throat tighten at the image. 'What's going on, Padishar?' he asked quietly.

'Be sure you let me know when you figure it out, Highlander. Meantime, there's worse news still. My neck hairs never lie. There's a Federation army not two miles off — the garrison at Tyrsis or I'm not my mother's favorite son.' The hard face creased with lines of irony. 'They're coming right for us, lad. Not a whit of deviation in their approach. Somehow they've discovered where we are — and I guess we both know how that might have happened, don't we?'

Morgan was stunned. 'Who?' He barely breathed the word.

Padishar shrugged and laughed softly. 'Does it really matter now?' He glanced over his shoulder. 'Time to finish up here. I don't relish telling Axhind and his clan what's happened, but it wouldn't do to play games. If I were them, I'd disappear out of here faster than a hare gone to ground.'

The Trolls were of a different mind, however. When the meeting broke up, Axhind and his companions showed no inclination to leave. Instead, they requested their weapons back — an impressive collection of axes, pikes, and broadswords — and on receiving them sat down and began in a leisurely fashion to sharpen the blades. It seemed as if they were looking for a fight.

Morgan went off to find the Dwarves. They were camped in a small, secluded grove of fir at the far end of the cliff base where an outcropping of rock formed a natural shelter from the weather. Steff greeted him without much enthusiasm. Teel was sitting up, her

366

strange, masked face revealing nothing of her thoughts, though her eyes glittered watchfully. She looked stronger, her dusky hair brushed out, her hands steady as they accepted Morgan's own. He spoke with her briefly, but she said almost nothing in return. Morgan gave them the news of Hirehone and the approaching Federation army. Steff nodded soberly; Teel didn't even do that. He left them feeling vaguely dissatisfied with the entire visit.

The Federation army arrived with the coming of nightfall, spread out in the forestlands directly below the cliffs of the Jut, and began clearing the land for its use, working with the industrious determination of ants. They streamed out of the trees, several thousand strong, their pennants flying, their weapons gleaming. Standards were raised before each company — banners of solid black with one red and one white stripe where there were regular Federation soldiers and a grinning white wolf's head where there were Seekers. Tents went up, weapons racks were assembled, supplies were positioned to the rear, and fires sparked to life. Almost immediately teams of men began building siege weapons, and the sounds of saws felling trees and axes hewing limbs filled the air.

The outlaws watched from the heights, their own fortifications already in place. Morgan watched with them. They seemed relaxed and easy. There were only three hundred of them, but the Jut was a natural fortification that could resist an army five times the size of this one. The lifts had already been drawn to the bluff, and now there was no way up or down except by scaling the walls. That would require climbing by hand, ladder, or grappling hook. Even a handful of men could put a stop to that.

It was fully dark by the time Morgan was able to speak again with Padishar. They stood by the lifts, now under heavy guard, and looked out over the broad scattering of watch fires below. The men of the Federation continued to work, the sound of their building rising out of the darkened forests into the still night air.

'I don't mind telling you that all this effort bothers me,'

the outlaw chief muttered, his brow furrowing.

Morgan frowned with him. 'Even with siege equipment, how can they possibly hope to reach us?'

Padishar shook his head. 'They can't. That's what bothers me.'

They watched a bit longer, then Padishar steered Morgan to a secluded part of the bluff, keeping him close as he whispered. 'I needn't remind you that we've been betrayed twice now. Whoever's responsible is still out there — probably still among us. If the Jut's to be taken, that's my guess as to how it's to be done.'

He turned to Morgan, his strong, weathered face close. 'I'll do my part to see that the Jut's kept secure. But you keep your eyes open as well, Highlander. You might see things differently from me, being fresh here. Maybe you'll see something I'd otherwise miss. Watch us all, and it's a big favor I'll owe you if you turn up something.'

Morgan nodded wordlessly. It gave him a purpose for being there, something he was beginning to suspect he lacked. He was consumed by the feeling of emptiness he had experienced on shattering his sword. He was distressed that he had been forced to leave Par and Coll Ohmsford behind. This charge, if nothing else, would give him something to concentrate on. He was grateful to Padishar for that.

When they finished, he went to the armorer and asked to be given a broadsword. He picked one that suited him, withdrew his own broken sword and replaced it with the new one. Then he hunted about for a discarded scabbard until he found one the Sword of Leah would fit, cut the scabbard to the sword's shortened length, bound the severed end, and strapped the makeshift sheath carefully to his belt.

He felt better about himself for the first time in days.

He slept well that night, too — even though the Federation continued to assemble its siege weapons until dawn. When the sun appeared, the building ceased. He woke then, the sudden stillness disconcerting, pulled on his clothes, strapped on his weapons, and hurried down to the bluff edge. The outlaws were settling into place, arms at the ready. Padishar was there, with Steff, Teel, and the contingent of Trolls. All watched silently what was taking place below.

The Federation army was forming up, squads into companies. They were well drilled, and there was no confusion as they marched into place. They encircled the base of the Jut, stretching from one end of the cliffs to the other, their lines just out of range of long bow and sling. Scaling ladders and ropes with grappling hooks were piled next to them. Siege towers stood ready, though the towers were crude and scarcely a third of the height of the cliffs leading up. Commanders barked orders crisply, and the gaps between companies slowly began to fill.

Morgan touched Steff briefly on the shoulder. The Dwarf glanced about uncertainly, nodded without saying anything and looked away again.

Morgan frowned. Steff wasn't carrying any weapons.

Trumpets sounded, and the Federation lines straightened. Everything went still once more. Sunlight glinted off armor and weapons as the skies in the east brightened. Dew glistened off leaves and grasses, the birdsongs lifted cheerfully, the sound of water running came from somewhere distant, and it seemed to Morgan Leah that it might have been any of a thousand mornings he had greeted when he still roamed and hunted the hills of his homeland.

Then from back in the trees, behind the long lines of soldiers, something moved. There was a jerking of limbs and trunks and a rasping of scraped bark. The Federation ranks suddenly split in two, opening a hole that was better than a hundred feet across. The outlaws and their allies stiffened expectantly, frowns creasing their faces as the forest continued to shake with the approach of whatever was hidden there.

Shades, Morgan whispered to himself.

The thing emerged from out of the fading shadows. It

was huge, a creature of impossible size, an apparition composed of the worst bits and pieces of things scavengers might have left. It was formed of hair and sinew and bone, but at the same time of metal plates and bars. There were jagged ends and shiny surfaces, iron grafted onto flesh, flesh grown into iron. It had the look of a monstrous, misshapen crustacean or worm, but was neither. It shambled forward, its glittering eyes rolling upward to find the edge of the bluff. Pinchers clicked like knives and claws scraped heedlessly the roughened stone.

For an instant, Morgan thought it was a machine. Then, a heartbeat later, he realized it was alive.

'Demon's blood!' Steff cried in recognition, his gruff voice angry and frightened. 'They've brought a Creeper!'

Hunching its way slowly through the ranks of the Federation army, the Creeper came for them.

CHAPTER

26

ORGAN LEAH REMEMBERED THE STORIES THEN. It seemed as if there had always been stories of the Creepers, tales that had been handed down from grandfather to father, from father to son, from generation to generation. They were told in the Highlands and in most parts of the Southland he had visited. Men whispered of the Creepers over glasses of ale around late night fires and sent shivers of excitement and horror down the spines of boys like Morgan, who listened at the circle's edge. No one put much stock in the stories, though; after all, they were told in the same breath as those wild imaginings of Skull Bearers and Mord Wraiths and other monsters out of a time that was all but forgotten. Yet no one was quite ready to dismiss them out-of-hand, either. Because whatever the men of the Southland might believe, there were Dwarves in the Eastland who swore by them.

Steff was one of those Dwarves. He had repeated the stories to Morgan — long after Morgan had already heard them — not as legend but as truth. They had happened, he insisted. They were real.

It was the Federation, he told Morgan, who made the Creepers. A hundred years ago, when the war against the Dwarves had bogged down deep in the wilderness of the Anar, when the armies of the Southland were thwarted by the jungle and the mountains and by the tangle of brush and the walls of rock that prevented them from engaging and trapping their elusive quarry, the Federation had called the Creepers to life. The Dwarves had taken the offensive away from the Federation by then, a sizeable resistance force that was determined to avoid capture and to harass the invaders until they were driven from their homeland. From their fortress lairs within the maze of canyons and defiles of the Ravenshorn and the cavelike hollows of the surrounding forests, the Dwarves counterattacked the heavier and more cumbersome Federation armies almost at will and slipped away with the ease of night's shadows. The months dragged on as the Federation effort stalled, and it was then that the Creepers appeared.

No one knew for certain where they came from. There were some who claimed they were simply machines constructed by the Federation builders, juggernauts without capacity to think, whose only function was to bring down the Dwarf fortifications and the Dwarves with them. There were others who said that no machine could have done what the Creepers did, that such things possessed cunning and instinct. A few whispered that they were formed of magic. Whatever their origin, the Creepers materialized within the wilderness of the central Anar and began to hunt. They were unstoppable. They tracked the Dwarves relentlessly and, when they caught up to them, destroyed them all. The war ended in a little more than a month, the Dwarf armies annihilated, the backbone of the resistance shattered.

After that, the Creepers vanished as mysteriously as they had appeared, as if the earth might have swallowed them whole. Only the stories remained, growing more lurid and at the same time less accurate with each telling, losing the force of truth as time passed, until only the Dwarves themselves remained certain of what had happened.

Morgan Leah stared downward for a moment longer as the stories of his childhood came to life, then wrenched his eyes away from the drop, away from the nightmare below, and looked frantically at Steff. The Dwarf was staring back at him, half-turned as if to bolt from the fortifications, his scarred face stricken.

'A Creeper, Morgan. A Creeper — after all these years. Do you know what that means?'

Morgan didn't have time to speculate. Padishar Creel was suddenly beside them, having heard the Dwarf speak. His hands gripped Steff's shoulders and he pulled the other about to face him. 'Tell me now, quickly! What do you know of this thing?'

'It's a Creeper,' Steff repeated, his voice stiff and unnatural, as if naming it said everything.

'Yes, yes, fine and well!' Padishar snapped impatiently. 'I don't care what it is I want to know how to stop it!'

Steff shook his head slowly, as if trying to clear it, as if dazed and unable to think. 'You can't stop it. There isn't any way to stop it. No one has ever found a way.'

There were mutterings from the men closest to them as they heard the Dwarf's words, and a sense of restless misgiving began to ripple through the lines of defenders. Morgan was stunned; he had never heard Steff sound so defeated. He glanced quickly at Teel. She had moved Steff away from Padishar protectively, her eyes bits of hard, glistening rock within her mask.

Padishar ignored them, turning instead to face his own men. 'Stand where you are!' he roared angrily at those who had begun to whisper and move back. The whispers and the movement stopped immediately. 'I'll skin the first rabbit who does otherwise!'

He gave Steff a withering glance. 'No way, is there? Not for you, perhaps — though I would have thought it otherwise and you a better man, Steff.' His voice was low, controlled. 'No way? There's always a way!'

There was a scraping sound from below, and they all pushed back to the breastworks. The Creeper had reached the base of the cliff wall and was beginning to work its way up, finding its grip in cracks and crevices where human hands and feet could not hope to find purchase. Sunlight glinted off patches of armor-plating and bits of iron rod, and the muscles of its wormlike body rippled. The marching drums of the Federation had begun to sound, pounding a steady cadence to mark the monster's approach.

Padishar leaped recklessly atop the defenses. 'Chandos! A dozen archers to me — now!'

The archers appeared immediately and as rapidly as they could manage sent a rain of arrows into the Creeper. It never slowed. The arrows bounced off its armor or buried themselves in its thick hide without effect. Even its eyes, those hideous black orbs that shifted and turned lazily with the movement of its body, seemed impervious.

Padishar withdrew the archers. A cheer went up from the ranks of the Federation army and a chanting began, matching the throb of the drums. The outlaw chief called for spearmen, but even the heavy wooden shafts and iron heads could not slow the monster's approach. They broke off or shattered on the rocks, and the Creeper came on.

Massive boulders were brought forward and sent rolling over the cliff edge. Several crashed into the Creeper. They grazed it or struck it full on, and the result was the same. It kept coming. The mutterings resumed, born of fear and frustration. Padishar shouted angrily to quiet them, but the task was growing harder. He called for brush to be brought forward, had it fired and sent tumbling into the Creeper — to no effect. Furious, he had a cask of cooking oil brought up, broken open and spilled down the cliff wall, then ignited. It burned ferociously against the barren rock, engulfing the approaching Creeper in a haze of black smoke and flames. Cries rose from the ranks of the Federation and the drums went still. Heat lifted into the morning air in waves so suffocating that the defenders were forced back. Morgan retreated with the rest, Steff and Teel next to him. Steff's face was drawn and pale, and he seemed strangely disoriented. Morgan helped him step away, unable to fathom what had happened to his friend.

'Are you sick?' he asked, whispering to the other as he eased him to a sitting position. 'Steff, what's wrong?'

374

But the other didn't appear to have an answer. He simply shook his head. Then with an effort he said, 'Fire won't stop it. It's been tried, Morgan. It doesn't work.'

He was right. When the flames and the heat died away enough to permit the defenders to return to the walls, the Creeper was still there, working its way steadily upward, almost halfway up by now, as scorched and blackened as the rock to which it clung but otherwise unchanged. The drumming and the chanting from the Federation soldiers below resumed, an eager, confident swell of sound that engulfed the whole of the Jut.

The outlaws were dismayed. Arguments began to spring up, and it was clear that by now no one believed that the Creeper could be stopped. What would they do when it reached them? Seemingly invulnerable to spears and arrows, could it be stopped by swords? The frantic outlaws could make a pretty good guess.

Only Axhind and his Rock Trolls seemed unperturbed by what was happening. They stood at the far end of the outlaw defenses, protecting a shelf that slanted down from the main bluff to the cliff wall, weapons held ready, a small island of calm amid the tumult. They were not talking. They did not appear nervous. They were watching Padishar Creel, apparently waiting to see what he would do next.

Padishar was quick to show them. He had noticed something that everyone else had missed, and it gave him a glimmer of hope for the besieged outlaws.

'Chandos!' he called out, shoving and pushing his men back into place as he walked down the breastworks. His burly, black-bearded lieutenant appeared. 'Bring up whatever oil we've got — cooking, cleaning, anything! Don't waste time asking questions, just do it!'

Chandos closed his mouth and hurried off. Padishar wheeled and came back down the line toward Morgan and the Dwarves. 'Ready one of the lifts!' he called past them. Then unexpectedly he stopped. 'Steff. How are these things on slick surfaces, these Creepers? How do they grip?'

Steff looked at him blankly, as if the question were too perplexing for him to consider. 'I don't know.'

'But they have to grip to climb, don't they?' the other demanded. 'What happens if they can't?'

He wheeled away without waiting for an answer. The morning had grown hot, and he was sweating heavily now. He stripped off his tunic, throwing it aside irritably. Snatching a set of cross belts from another outlaw, he buckled them on, picked up a short-handled axe, shoved it through one of the belt loops, and moved ahead to the lifts. Morgan followed, beginning to see now what the outlaw planned to do. Chandos hurried up from the caves, followed by a knot of men carrying casks of varying sizes and weights.

'Load them,' Padishar ordered, motioning. When the loading was begun, he put his hands on his lieutenant's broad shoulders. 'I'm going over in the lift, down where the beast climbs, and dump the oil on it.'

'Padishar!' Chandos was horrified.

'No, listen now. The Creeper can't get up here if it can't climb, and it can't climb if it can't grip. The oil will make everything so slick the slug won't be able to move. It might even fall.' He grinned fiercely. 'Wouldn't that put a nice finish to things?'

Chandos shook his woolly head, a frantic look in his eyes. The Trolls had drifted over and were listening. 'You think the Federation will let you get that far? Their bowmen will cut you to pieces!'

'Not if you keep them back, they won't.' The grin vanished. 'Besides, old friend — what other choice do we have?'

He sprang into the lift, crouching within the shelter of its railing to present the smallest target possible. 'Just don't let me drop,' he shouted and gripped the axe tightly.

The lift went over the side, Chandos letting it down quickly, bringing the boom close above where the Creeper worked its way upward, now high on the wall, a large black smudge that oozed across the rock. A howl went up from the Federation army as they saw what was happening, and lines of bowmen surged forward. The outlaws were waiting. Shooting unobstructed from their defenses far above, they broke the assault in moments. Immediately more lines rushed forward, and arrows began to shatter against the cliff face all about the dropping lift. The outlaws returned the Federation fire. Again, the assault broke apart and fell back.

But by now catapults had been brought forward, and massive rocks began to hurtle into the cliff face, smashing all about the fragile lift as Federation marksmen sought to find the range. One barrage of loose rock hammered into the lift and sent it careering into the wall. Wood splintered and cracked. From directly below, the Creeper looked up.

Morgan Leah stood at the edge of the bluff and watched in horror, Steff and Teel beside him. The lift with Padishar Creel twisted and spun as if caught in a fierce wind.

'Hold him!' Chandos screamed to the men on the ropes, turning back in dismay. 'Hold him steady!'

But they were losing him. The rope slipped and the effort to retrieve it dragged its handlers toward the cliff edge where they frantically struggled to brace themselves. Federation arrows raked the bluff, and two of the handlers dropped. No one took their place, uncertain what to do in the chaos of the attack. Chandos looked back over his shoulder, eyes wide. The rope slipped further.

They can't hold it, Morgan realized in horror.

He darted forward, shouting frantically. But Axhind was quicker. With a speed that belied his size, the Maturen of the Kelltic Rock bounded through the onlookers and seized the rope in his massive hands. The other holders fell back in confusion. Alone, the giant Troll held the lift and Padishar Creel. Then another Troll appeared and then two more. Bracing themselves, they hauled back on the rope as Chandos shouted instructions from the edge.

Morgan peered out over the bluff again. The Parma Key stretched away in a sea of deep green that disappeared into a midmorning sky that was cloudless and blue, filled with sweet smells and a sense of timelessness. The Jut was an island of chaos in its midst. At the base of the cliffs, Federation soldiers lay dying in heaps. The orderly lines were ragged now, their neat formations scattered in the rush to attack. Catapults launched their missiles and arrows flew from everywhere. The lift still dangled from its rope, a tiny bit of bait that was seemingly only inches above the black monstrosity that hunched its way steadily closer.

Then suddenly, almost unexpectedly, Padishar Creel lifted into view, short-handled axe splintering the first of the oil casks and spilling its contents down the cliff side and over the Creeper. The head and upper body of the creature were coated in the glistening liquid, and the Creeper stopped moving. The contents of a second cask followed the first, and then the contents of a third. The Creeper and the cliff wall were saturated. Arrows from Federation bows pinged all about Padishar as he stood exposed. Then he was struck, once, twice, and he went down.

'Haul him up!' Chandos screamed.

The Trolls jerked on the line in response, the watching outlaws howling in fury and shooting down into the ranks of the Federation archers.

But then somehow Padishar was back on his feet, and the last two remaining casks were splintered and their contents dumped down the rock wall onto the Creeper. The beast hung there, no longer moving, letting the oil run down into it, under it, over it, streams of glistening oil and grease spreading down the cliff face in the harsh glare of the morning sun.

A catapult struck the lift squarely then and shattered it to pieces. The outlaws on the bluff cried out as the lift fell apart. But Padishar did not fall; he caught hold of the rope and dangled there, arrows and stones flying all about him, a perfect target. There was blood on his chest and arms, and the muscles of his body were corded with the effort it required for him to hang on.

Swiftly the rope came up, Padishar Creel was hauled to the edge of the bluff, and his men reached out to pull him to safety. For a moment the battle was forgotten. Chandos shouted in vain for everyone to get back, but the outlaws ignored him as they crowded around their fallen leader. Then Padishar was on his feet, blood streaming down his body from his wounds, arrows protruding from deep within his right shoulder and through the fleshy part of his left side, his face pale and drawn with pain. Reaching down, he snapped the arrow in his side in two and with a grimace pulled the shaft clear.

'Get back to the wall!' he roared. 'Now!'

The outlaws scattered. Padishar pushed past Chandos and staggered to the breastworks, peering down at the Creeper.

The Creeper was still hanging there, still not moving, as if glued to the rock. The Federation archers and catapults were continuing their barrage on the outlaw defenses, but the effort had become a halfhearted one as they, too, waited to see what would happen.

'Fall, drat you!' Padishar cried furiously.

The Creeper stirred, shifting slightly, edging right, trying to maneuver away from the glistening sheet of oil. Claws rasped as it hunched and squirmed to keep its hold. But the oil had done its job. The creature's grip began to loosen, slowly at first, then more rapidly as one after another of its appendages slipped free. A howl of dismay went up from the Federation ranks a cheer from the outlaws. The Creeper was sliding down more quickly now, skidding on a track of oil that followed after it relentlessly, coating its tubular body. Its grip gave way altogether and down it went, tumbling, rolling, falling with a crunch of metal and bone. When it struck the earth at last, dust rose in a massive cloud, and the whole of the cliff face shook with the impact.

The Creeper lay motionless at the base of the cliffs, its oiled bulk shuddering.

'That's more like it!' Padishar Creel sighed and slid down the breastworks into a sitting position, his eyes closing wearily.

'You've finished him sure enough!' Chandos exclaimed, dropping into a crouch beside him. His smile was ferocious. Morgan, standing close at hand, found himself grinning as well.

But Padishar simply shook his head. 'This doesn't finish anything. That was today's horror. Tomorrow will surely bring another. And what do we do for oil then, with the last of it spilled out today?' The dark eyes opened. 'Cut this other arrow out of me so I can get some sleep.'

The Federation did not attack again that day. It withdrew its army to the edge of the forest, there to tend to the dead and wounded. Only the catapults were left in place, sending their loads skyward periodically, though most fell short and the assault proved more annoying than effective.

The Creeper, unfortunately, was not dead. After a time, it seemed to recover, and it rolled over sluggishly and crawled off into the shelter of the Parma Key. It was impossible to guess how badly it had been damaged, but no one was ready to predict that they had seen the last of it.

Padishar Creel was treated for his wounds, bound up and put to bed. He was weak from loss of blood and in no small amount of pain, but his injuries would not leave him disabled. Even as Chandos was seeing to his care, Padishar was giving instructions for continuing the defense of the Jut. A special weapon was to be built. Morgan heard Chandos speak of it as he gathered a select group of men and sent them off into the largest of the caves to construct it. Work began almost immediately, but when Morgan asked what it was that was being assembled, Chandos was unwilling to talk about it.

'You'll see it when it's completed, Highlander,' he

responded gruffly. 'Leave it at that.'

Morgan did, but only because he hadn't any other choice. At something of a loss as to what to do with himself, he drifted over to where Steff had been taken by Teel and found his friend wrapped in blankets and feverish. Teel watched suspiciously as the Highlander felt Steff's forehead, a watchdog that no longer trusted anyone. Morgan could hardly blame her. He spoke quietly with Steff for a few moments, but the Dwarf was barely conscious. It seemed better to let him sleep. The Highlander stood up, glanced a final time at the unresponsive Teel, and walked away.

He spent the remainder of the day passing back and forth between the fortifications and the caves, checking on the Federation army and the secret weapon and on Padishar Creel and Steff. He didn't accomplish much, and the hours of the late morning and then the afternoon passed slowly. Morgan found himself wondering once again what good he was doing anyone, trapped at the Jut with these outlaws, resistance fighters or no, far from Par and Coll and what really mattered. How would he ever find the Valemen again, now that they had been separated? Certainly they would not attempt to come into the Parma Key, not while a Federation army had them under siege. Damson Rhee would never permit it.

Or would she? It suddenly occurred to Morgan that she might, if she thought there was a safe way to do so. That made him think. What if there was more than one way into the Jut? Didn't there have to be, he asked himself? Even with the defenses as strong as they were, Padishar Creel would never take the chance that they might somehow be breached, leaving the outlaws trapped against the rocks. He would have an escape route, another way out. Or in.

He decided to find out. It was almost dusk, however, before he got his chance. Padishar was awake again by then, and Morgan found him sitting on the edge of his bed, heavily bandaged, streaks of blood showing vividly against his weathered skin, studying a set of crudely sketched drawings with Chandos. Another man would still be sleeping, trying to regain his strength; Padishar looked ready to fight. The men glanced up as he approached, and Padishar tucked the drawings out of sight. Morgan hesitated.

'Highlander,' the other greeted. 'Come sit with me.'

Surprised, Morgan came over, taking a seat on a packing crate filled with metal fittings. Chandos nodded, got up without a word and walked out.

'And how is our friend the Dwarf?' Padishar asked, rather too casually. 'Better, now?'

Morgan studied the other man. 'No. Something is very wrong with him, but I don't know what it is.' He paused. 'You don't trust anyone, do you? Not even me.'

'Especially not you.' Padishar waited a moment, grinned disarmingly, and then made the smile disappear in the quickness of an eye's blink. 'I can't afford to trust anyone anymore. Too much has happened to suggest that I shouldn't.' He shifted his weight and grimaced with the pain it caused. 'So tell me. What brings you to visit? Have you seen something you think I should know about?'

The truth was that with the excitement of the events of that morning, Morgan had forgotten about the charge that Padishar had given him to try to find out who it was that had betrayed them. He didn't say so, however; he simply shook his head.

'I have a question,' he said. 'About Par and Coll Ohmsford. Do you think that Damson Rhee might still try to bring them here? Is there another way into the Jut that she might use?'

The look that Padishar Creel gave him was at once indecipherable and filled with meaning. There was a long silence, and Morgan felt himself grow suddenly cold as he realized how it must look for him to be asking such a question.

He took a deep breath. 'I'm not asking where it is, only if . . .'

'I understand what you're asking and why,' the other said, cutting short his protestation. The hard face furrowed about the eyes and mouth. Padishar said nothing for a moment, studying the Highlander intently. 'As a matter-of-fact, there is another way,' he said finally. 'You must have figured that out on your own, though. You understand enough of tactics to know that there must always be more than one way in or out of a refuge.'

Morgan nodded wordlessly.

'Well, then, Highlander, I can only add that Damson would not put the Valemen at risk by trying to bring them here while the Jut was under siege. She would keep them safe in Tyrsis or elsewhere, whatever the situation might require.'

He paused, eyes hard with hidden thoughts. Then he said, 'No one but Damson, Chandos and I know the other way — now that Hirehone is dead. Better that we keep it so until the identity of our traitor is discovered, don't you think? I wouldn't want the Federation walking in through the back door while we were busy holding shut the front.'

Morgan hadn't considered the possibility of such a thing happening until now. It was a chilling thought. 'Is the back way secure?' he asked hesitantly.

Padishar pursed his lips. 'Very. Now take yourself off to dinner, Highlander. And remember to keep your eyes open.'

He turned back to his drawings. Morgan hesitated a moment, thinking to say something more, then turned abruptly and left.

That night, as daylight faded into evening and stars began to appear, Morgan sat alone at the far end of the bluff where a grove of aspen trees sheltered a small grassy clearing, looked out across the valley of the Parma Key to where the moon, half-full again, lifted slowly out of the horizon into the darkening skies, and marshalled his powers of reason. The camp was quiet now except for the muffled sounds of work being done back in the caves on Padishar's secret weapon. The catapults and bows were stilled, the men of both the Federation army and the

Movement sleeping or lost in their own private contemplations. Padishar was meeting with the Trolls and Chandos, a meeting to which Morgan had not been invited. Steff was resting, his fever seemingly no worse, but his strength sapped and his general health no better. There was nothing to be done, nothing to occupy the time but to sleep or think, and Morgan Leah had chosen the latter.

For as long as he could remember, he had been clever. It was a gift, admittedly, one that could be traced to his ancestors, to men such as Menion and Rone Leah — real princes in those days, heroes — but an ability, too, that Morgan had worked long and hard to perfect. The Federation had supplied him with both a purpose and a direction for his skill. He had spent almost the whole of his youth concentrating on finding ways to outwit the Federation officials who occupied and governed his homeland, to irritate them at every opportunity so that they might never feel secure, to make them experience a futility and a frustration that would one day drive them from Leah forever. He was very good at it; perhaps he was the best there was. He knew all the tricks, had conceived most of them himself. He could outthink and outsmart almost anyone, if he were given time and opportunity to do so.

He smiled ruefully. At least, that was what he had always told himself. Now it was time to prove that it was so. It was time to figure out how the Federation had known so often what they were about, how it was that they had been betrayed — the outlaws, the Valemen, the little company from Culhaven, everyone connected with this misadventure — and most important of all, who was responsible.

It was something he could reason out.

He let his lean frame drape itself against the grassy base of a twisted, old trunk, drew his knees partway up to his chest, and considered what he knew.

The list of betrayals was a long one. Someone had informed the Federation when Padishar had taken them into Tyrsis to recover the Sword of Sharnara. Someone had found out what they were going to do and gotten word to the Federation watch commander ahead of their arrival. One of your own, the watch commander had told Padishar. Then someone had revealed the location of the Jut to the army that now besieged it — again, someone who knew where it could be found and how to find it.

He frowned. The betrayals had actually begun before that, though. If you accepted the premise — and he was now prepared to — that someone had sent the Gnawl to track them in the Wolfsktaag and had gotten word to the Shadowen on Toffer Ridge where the Spider Gnomes could snatch Par, why then the betrayals went all the way back to Culhaven.

So had someone been tracking them all the way from Culhaven?

He discarded the possibility immediately. No one could have managed such a feat.

But there was more to the puzzle. There was the sighting of Hirehone in Tyrsis and his subsequent murder in the Parma Key. And there was the killing of the lift watch with the lifts still drawn up. What did those events have to do with anything?

He let all the pieces sift through his mind for a few minutes, waiting to see if he would discover something he had missed. Night birds called out from below in the darkness of the Parma Key, and the wind blew gently across his face, warm and fragrant. When nothing further occurred, he took each piece in turn and tried to fit it to the puzzle, working to see if a recognizable picture would emerge. The minutes paraded past him silently. The pieces refused to fit.

He was missing something.

He rubbed his hands together briskly. He would try it another way. He would eliminate what didn't work and see what was left. He took a steadying breath and relaxed.

No one could have followed them — not for all that

time. So it must be someone among them. One of them. But if that someone were responsible for the Gnawl and the Shadowen as well as everything that had happened since their arrival at the outlaw camp, then didn't it have to be one of the members of the original company? Par, Coll, Steff, Teel, or himself? He went back to Teel momentarily, for he knew less of her than of any of them. He could not bring himself to believe it was either of the Valemen or Steff. But why was Teel any better as a candidate? Hadn't she suffered at least as much as Steff?

Besides, what did Hirehone have to do with any of this? Why were the men of the lift watch killed?

He caught himself. They were killed so that someone could either get in or get out of the outlaw camp undetected. It made sense. But the lifts were drawn up. They had to have been killed after bringing someone into the camp — killed perhaps to hide that someone's identity.

He wrestled with the possibilities. It all kept coming back to Hirehone. Hirehone was the key. What if it had been Hirehone he had seen in Tyrsis? What if Hirehone had indeed betrayed them to the Federation? But Hirehone had never returned to the Jut after leaving. So how could he have killed the watch? And why would he be killed after doing so in any case? And by whom? Could there be more than one traitor involved — Hirehone and someone else?

Something clicked into place.

Morgan Leah jerked forward in recognition. Who was the enemy here — the real enemy? Not the Federation. The real enemy was the Shadowen. Wasn't that what Allanon's shade had told them? Wasn't that what they had been warned against? And the Shadowen could take the form and body and speech of anyone. Some of them could, at least — the most dangerous. Cogline had said so.

Morgan felt his pulse quicken and his face flush with excitement. They weren't dealing with a human being in this matter. They were dealing with a Shadowen! The pieces of the puzzle suddenly began to fit together. A Shadowen could have hidden among them and they would not have known. A Shadowen could have summoned a Gnawl, sent word to Toffer Ridge to another of its kind, have gotten to Tyrsis ahead of Padishar's company, have spied out its purpose, and slipped away again before its return. A Shadowen could get close enough. And it could disguise itself as Hirehone. No, not disguise — it could *be* Hirehone! And it could have killed him when he had served his purpose, and killed the lift watch because they would have reported seeing it, no matter whose face it had worn. It had revealed the location of the Jut to the Federation army — even mapped a path for them to follow!

Who? All that remained was to determine . . .

Morgan sagged back slowly against the trunk of the aspen behind him, the puzzle suddenly complete. He knew who. Steff or Teel. It had to be one or the other. They were the only ones, besides himself, who had been with the company from the very beginning, from Culhaven to the Jut, to Tyrsis and back. Teel had been unconscious practically the entire time Padishar's band was in Tyrsis. That would have given either of the Dwarves, or more specifically the Shadowen within, the opportunity to slip away and then back again. They were alone much of the time in any case — just the two of them.

He stiffened against the weight of his suspicions as they bore down on him. For an instant, he thought he was crazy, that he should discard his reasoning entirely and start over again. But he couldn't do that. He knew he was right.

The wind brushed at him, and he pulled his cloak closer in spite of the evening's warmth. He sat without moving in the protective shadow of his haven and examined carefully the conclusions he had reached, the reasonings he had devised, the speculations that had slowly assumed the trappings of truth. It was silent now in the outlaw camp, and he could imagine himself to be

the only human being living in all the vast, dark expanse
of the Parma Key.

Shades.

Steff or Teel.

His instincts told him it was Teel.

CHAPTER

27

IT WAS THREE DAYS AFTER they had made their decision to go back down into the Pit to recover the Sword of Shannara that Damson at last took the Valemen from their garden shed hideaway into the streets of Tyrsis. By then Par was beside himself with impatience. He had wanted to go immediately; time was everything, he had argued. But Damson had flatly refused. It was too dangerous, she insisted. Too many Federation patrols were still combing the city. They had to wait. Par had been left with no choice but to do so.

Even now, when she finally judged the margin of risk small enough to permit them to venture forth, it was on a night when reasonable men would think twice about doing so, a night that was bone-cold, the city wrapped in a blanket of mist and rain that prevented even friends of long standing from recognizing each other from a distance of more than a few feet and sent the few citizens who had worked past their normal quitting time scurrying down the glistening, empty streets for the warmth and comfort of their homes.

Damson had provided the little company with foul weather cloaks, hooded and caped, and they wore them now pulled close as they made their way through the damp and the silence. Their boots thudded softly on the stone roadway as they walked, echoing in the silence, filling up the night with a strange, rushed cacophony. Water dripped from eaves and trickled down mortared grooves, and the mist settled on their skin with a chill, possessive adherence that was faintly distasteful. They followed the back streets as always, avoiding the Tyrsian Way and the other main thoroughfares where Federation patrols still kept watch, steering into the narrow avenues that burrowed like tunnels through the colorless, semi-abandoned blocks of the city's poor and homeless.

They were on their way to find the Mole.

'That is how he is known,' Damson told them just before they went out. 'All of the street people call him that because that is what he chooses to call himself. If he ever had a real name, I doubt that he remembers it. His past is a closely kept secret. He lives in the sewers and catacombs beneath Tyrsis, a recluse. He almost never comes out into the light. His whole world is the underbelly of the city, and no one knows more about it than he does.'

'And if there are still passageways that run beneath the palace of the Kings of Tyrsis, the Mole will know about them?' Par pressed.

'He will know.'

'Can we trust him?'

'The problem is not whether we can trust him, but whether he will decide to trust us. As I said, he is very reclusive. He may not even choose to talk with us.'

And Par said simply, 'He must.'

Coll said nothing. He had said little the entire day, barely a word since they had decided to go back into the Pit. He had swallowed the news of what they were going to do as if he had ingested a medicine that would either cure or kill him and he was waiting to see which it would be. He seemed to have decided that it was pointless to debate the matter further or to argue what he perceived as the folly of their course of action, so he had taken a fatalistic stance, bowing to the inevitability of Par's determination and the fortune or misfortune that would befall them because of it, and he had gone into a shell as hard and impenetrable as iron.

He trailed now as they made their way through the murk of the Tyrsian evening, tracking Par as closely as his own shadow, intruding with his silent presence in a way that distressed rather than comforted. Par didn't like feeling that way about his brother, but there was no help for it. Coll had determined his own role. He would neither accept what Par was doing nor cut himself free of it. He would simply stick it out, for better or worse, until a resolution was reached.

Damson steered them to the top of a narrow flight of stone steps that cut through a low wall connecting two vacant, unlighted buildings and wound its way downward into the dark. Par could hear water running, a low gurgle that splashed and chugged through some obstruction. They made a cautious descent of the slick stone, finding a loose, rusted railing that offered an uncertain handhold. When they reached the end of the stairs, they found themselves on a narrow walkway that ran parallel to a sewer trench. It was down the trench that the water ran, spilling from a debris-choked passageway that opened from underneath the streets above.

Damson took the Valemen into the tunnel.

It was black inside and filled with harsh, pungent smells. The rain disappeared behind them. Damson paused, fumbled about in the dark for a moment, then produced a torch coated with pitch on one end, which she managed to light with the aid of a piece of flint. The firelight brightened the gloom enough to permit them to see their way a few steps at a time, and so they proceeded. Unseen things scurried away in the darkness ahead, soundless but for the scratching of tiny claws. Water dripped from the ceiling, ran down the walls, and churned steadily through the trench. The air was chill and empty of life.

They reached a second set of stairs descending further into the earth and took them. They passed through several levels this time, and the sound of the water faded. The scratchings remained, however, and the chill clung to them with irritating persistence. The Valemen pulled their cloaks tighter. The stairs ended and a new passageway began, this one narrower than the other. They were forced to crouch in order to proceed, and the dampness gave way to dust. They moved ahead steadily, and the minutes slipped past. They were deep beneath the city by now, well within the core of rock and earth that formed the plateau on which Tyrsis rested. The Valemen had lost all sense of direction.

When they reached the bottom of a dry well with an iron ladder that led up, Damon paused. 'It is not far now,' she said quietly. 'Just another several hundred yards when we reach the top of this ladder. We should find him then — or he us. He brought me here once long ago when I showed him a bit of kindness.' She hesitated. 'He is very gentle, but peculiar as well. Be careful how you treat him.'

She took them up the ladder to a landing that opened into a series of passageways. It was warmer there, less dusty, the air stale but not malodorous. 'These tunnels were bolt holes once for the city's defenders; at some points they lead all the way down to the plains.' Her red hair shimmered as she brushed it back from her face. 'Stay close to me.'

They entered one of the corridors and started down. The pitch coating on the torch head sizzled and steamed. The tunnel twisted about, crisscrossed other tunnels, wound through rooms shored up with timbers and fastening bolts, and left the Valemen more confused than ever as to where they were. But Damson never hesitated, certain of her way, either reading signs that were hidden from them or calling to memory a map that she kept within her head.

At last they entered a room that was the first of several, all interconnected, large chambers with wooden beams, stone block floors, walls from which hangings and tapestries dangled, and a storehouse of bizarre treasures. Piled floor to ceiling, wall to wall, there were trunks of old clothing, piles of furniture crammed and laden with clasps, fittings, writings gone almost to dust, feathers, cheap jewelry, and toy animals of all sorts, shapes, and sizes. The animals were all carefully arranged, some seated in groups, some lined up on shelves and on divans, some placed at watch atop bureaus and at doorways. There were a few rusted weapons scattered about and an armful of baskets woven from cane and rush.

There were lights as well — oil lamps fastened to the beams overhead and the walls beneath, filling the rooms with a vague brightness, the residual smoke venting through airholes that disappeared at the corners of the room into the rock above.

The Valemen looked about expectantly. There was no one there.

Damson did not seem surprised. She led them into a room, dominated by a trestle table and eight highback chairs of carved oak, and motioned for them to sit. There were animals occupying all the chairs, and the Valemen looked inquiringly at the girl.

'Choose your place, pick up the animal that's seated there, and hold it,' she advised and proceeded to show them what she meant. She selected a chair with a worn, stuffed velvet rabbit resting on it, lifted the tattered creature, and placed it comfortably on her lap as she sat down.

Coll did the same, his face empty as he fixed his gaze on a spot on the far wall, as if convinced that what was happening was no stranger than what he had expected. Par hesitated, then sat down as well, his companion something that might have been either a cat or a dog — it was impossible to tell which. He felt vaguely ridiculous.

They sat there then and waited, not speaking, barely looking at each other. Damson began stroking the worn fur backing on her rabbit. Coll was a statue. Par's patience began to slip as the minutes passed and nothing happened.

Then one after another, the lights went out. Par started to his feet, but Damson said quickly, 'Sit still.'

All of the lights but one disappeared. The one that

remained was at the opening of the first room they had entered. Its glow was distant and barely reached to where they sat. Par waited for his eyes to adjust to the near darkness; when they did, he found himself staring at a roundish, bearded face that had popped up across from him two seats down from Damson. Blank, dilated ferret eyes peered at him, shifted to find Coll, blinked, and stared some more.

'Good evening to you, Mole,' Damson Rhee said.

The Mole lifted his head a shade; his neck and shoulders came into view, and his hands and arms lifted onto the table. He was covered with hair, a dark, furry coat. It grew on every patch of skin showing, save for where his nose and cheeks and a swatch of forehead glimmered like ivory in the faint light. His rounded head swiveled slowly, and his child's fingers locked together in a pose of contentment.

'Good evening to you, lovely Damson,' he said.

He spoke in a child's voice, but it sounded queer somehow, as if he were speaking out of a barrel or through a screen of water. His eyes moved from Par to Coll, from Coll to Par.

'I heard you coming and put on the lights for you,' he said. 'But I don't much like the lights, so now that you are here, I have put them out again. Is that all right?'

Damson nodded. 'Perfectly.'

'Whom have you brought with you on your visit?'

'Valemen.'

'Valemen?'

'Brothers, from a village south of here, a long way away. Par Ohmsford. Coll Ohmsford.'

She pointed to each and the eyes shifted. 'Welcome to my home. Shall we have tea?'

He disappeared without waiting for an answer, moving so quietly that, try as he might, even in the almost utter silence, Par could not hear him. He could smell the tea as it was brought, yet failed to see it materialize until the cups were placed before him. There were two of them, one regular size and one quite tiny.

They were old, and the paint that decorated them was faded and worn.

Par watched doubtfully while Damson offered a sip from the smaller cup to the toy rabbit she held. 'Are all the children fine?' she asked conversationally.

'Quite well,' the Mole replied, seated again now where he had first appeared. He was holding a large bear, to whom he offered his own cup. Coll and Par followed the ritual without speaking. 'Chalt, you know, has been bad again, sneaking his tea and cookies when he wishes, disrupting things rather thoroughly. When I go up to hear the news through the street grates and wall passages, he seems to believe he has license to reorganize things to his own satisfaction. Very annoying.' He gave the bear a cross look. 'Lida had a very bad fever, but is recovered now. And Westra cut her paw.'

Par glanced at Coll, and this time his brother glanced back.

'Anyone new to the family?' Damson asked.

'Everlind,' the Mole said. He stared at her for a moment, then pointed to the rabbit she was holding. 'She came to live with us just two nights ago. She likes it much better here than on the streets.'

Par hardly knew what to think. The Mole apparently collected junk discarded by the people of the city above and brought it down into his lair like a pack rat. To him, the animals were real — or at least that was the game he played. Par wondered uneasily if he knew the difference.

The Mole was looking at him. 'The city whispers of something that has upset the Federation — disruptions, intruders, a threat to its rule. The street patrols are increased and the gate watches challenge everyone. There is a tightening of the chains.' He paused, then turned to Damson. He said, almost eagerly, 'It is better to be here, lovely Damson — here, underground.'

Damson put down her cup. 'The disruption is part of the reason we have come, Mole.'

The Mole didn't seem to hear. 'Yes, better to be underground, safe within the earth, beneath the streets and the towers, where the Federation never comes.'

Damson shook her head firmly. 'We are not here for sanctuary.'

The Mole blinked, disappointment registering in his eyes. He set his own cup aside and the animal he held with it, and he cocked his rounded head. 'I found Everlind at the back of the home of a man who provides counting services for the Federation tax collectors. He is quick with numbers and tallies far more accurately than others of his skill. Once, he was an advisor to the people of the city, but the people couldn't pay him as well as the Federation, so he took his services there. All day long, he works in the building where the taxes are held, then goes home to his family, his wife and his daughter, to whom Everlind once belonged. Last week, the man bought his daughter a new toy kitten, silky white fur and green button eyes. He bought it with money the Federation gave him from what they had collected. So his daughter discarded Everlind. She found the new kitten far prettier to look upon.'

He looked at them. 'Neither the father nor the daughter understand what they have given up. Each sees only what is on the surface and nothing of what lies beneath. That is the danger of living above ground.'

'It is,' Damson agreed softly. 'But that is something we must change, those of us who wish to continue to live there.'

The Mole rubbed his hands again, looking down at them as he did so, lost in some contemplation of his own. The room was a still life in which the Mole and his visitors sat among the discards and rejects of other lives and listened to what might have been the whisper of their own.

The Mole looked up again, his eyes fixing on Damson. 'Beautiful Damson, what is it that you wish?'

Damson's willowy form straightened, and she brushed back the stray locks of her fiery hair. 'There were once tunnels beneath the palace of the Kings of Tyrsis. If they are still there, we need to go into them.'

The Mole stiffened. 'Beneath the palace?'

'Beneath the palace and into the Pit.'

There was a long silence as the Mole stared at her unblinking. Almost unconsciously, his hands went out to retrieve the animal he had been holding. He patted it gently. 'There are things out of darkest night and mind in the pit,' he said softly.

'Shadowen,' Damson said.

'Shadowen? Yes, that name suits them. Shadowen.'

'Have you seen them, Mole?'

'I have seen everything that lives in the city. I am the earth's own eyes.'

'Are there tunnels that lead into the Pit? Can you take us through them?'

The Mole's face lost all expression, then pulled away from the table's edge and dropped back into shadow. For an instant, Par thought he was gone. But he was merely hiding, returned to the comfort of the dark to consider what he was being asked. The toy animal went with him, and the girl and the Valemen were left alone as surely as if the little fellow had truly disappeared. They waited patiently, not speaking.

'Tell them how we met,' the Mole spoke suddenly from his concealment. 'Tell them how it was.'

Damson turned obediently to the Valemen. 'I was walking in one of the parks at night, just as the dusk was ending, the stars brightening in the sky. It was summer, the air warm and filled with the smell of flowers and new grass. I rested on a bench for a moment, and Mole appeared beside me. He had seen me perform my magic on the streets, hidden somewhere beneath them as he watched, and he asked me if I would do a trick especially for him. I did several He asked me to come back the next night, and I did. I came back each night for a week, and then he took me underground and showed me his home and his family. We became friends.'

'Good friends, lovely Damson. The best of friends.' The Mole's face slipped back into view, easing from the shadows. The eyes were solemn. 'I cannot refuse anything you ask of me. But I wish you would not ask this.'

'It is important, Mole.'

'You are more important,' the Mole replied shyly. 'I am afraid for you.'

She reached over slowly and touched the back of his hand. 'It will be all right.'

The Mole waited until she took her hand away, then quickly tucked his own under the table. He spoke reluctantly. 'There are tunnels all through the rock beneath the palace of the Kings of Tyrsis. They connect with cellars and dungeons that lie forgotten. Some, one or two perhaps, open into the Pit.'

Damson nodded. 'We need you to take us there.'

The Mole shivered. 'Dark things — Shadowen — will be there. What if they find us? What will we do?'

Damson's eyes locked on Par. 'This Valeman has use of magic as well, Mole. But it is not magic like mine that plays tricks and entertains, it is real magic. He is not afraid of the Shadowen. He will protect us.'

Par felt his stomach tighten at the words — words that made promises he knew deep down inside he might not be able to keep.

The Mole was studying him once more. His dark eyes blinked. 'Very well. Tomorrow I will go into the tunnels and make certain they can still be traversed. Come back when it is night again, and if the way is open I will take you.'

'Thank you, Mole,' Damson said.

'Finish your tea,' the Mole said quietly, not looking at her.

They sat in silence in the company of the toy animals and did so.

It was still raining when they left the maze of underground tunnels and sewer channels and slipped back through the empty streets of the city. Damson led the way, surefooted in the mist and damp, a cat that didn't mind the wet. She returned the Valemen to the storage shed behind the gardening shop and left them there to get some sleep. She said she would return for them after midday. There were things that she needed to do first

But Par and Coll didn't sleep. They kept watch instead, sitting at the windows and looking out into a curtain of fog that was filled with the movement of things that weren't there and thick with the reflected light of the coming day. It was almost morning by then, and the sky was brightening in the east. It was cold in the shed, and the brothers huddled in blankets and tried to put aside their discomfort and the disquieting thought of what lay ahead.

For a long time neither of them spoke. Finally Par, his impatience used up, said to his brother, 'What are you thinking about?'

Coll took a moment to consider, then simply shook his head.

'Are you thinking about the Mole?'

Coll sighed. 'Some.' He hunched himself within his blanket. 'I should be worried about placing my life in the hands of a fellow who lives underground with the relics of other people's lives for possessions and toy animals for companions, but I'm not. I don't really know why that is. I guess it is because he doesn't seem any stranger than anyone else connected with what's happened since we left Varfleet. Certainly, he doesn't seem any crazier.'

Par didn't respond to that. There wasn't anything he could say that hadn't already been said. He knew his brother's feelings. He pulled his own blanket tight and let his eyes close against the movement of the fog. He wished the waiting was over and that it was time to get started. He hated the waiting.

'Why don't you go to sleep?' he heard Coll say.

'I can't,' he replied. His eyes slipped open again. 'Why don't you?'

Coll shrugged. The movement seemed an effort. Coll was lost within himself, struggling to maintain direction while mired in a steadily tightening morass of circumstances and events from which he knew he should extricate himself but could not.

'Coll, why don't you let me do this alone?' Par said suddenly, impulsively. His brother looked over. 'I know we've already had this discussion; don't bother reminding me. But why don't you? There isn't any reason for you to go. I know what you think about what I'm doing. Maybe you're right. So stay here and wait for me.'

'No.'

'But why not? I can look out for myself.'

Coll stared. 'As a matter-of-fact, you can't,' he said quietly. His rough features crinkled with disbelief. 'I think that might be the most ridiculous thing I've ever heard you say.'

Par flushed angrily. 'Just because . . .'

'There hasn't been a single moment during this entire expedition or trek or whatever you want to call it that you haven't needed help from someone.' The dark eyes narrowed. 'Don't misunderstand me. I'm not saying you were the only one. We've all needed help, needed each other — even Padishar Creel. That's the way life works.' One strong hand lifted and a finger jabbed Par roughly. 'The thing is, everyone but you realizes and accepts it. But you keep trying to do everything on your own, trying to be the one who knows best, who has all the answers, recognizes all the options and has some special insight the rest of us lack that allows you to decide what's best. You blind yourself to the truth. Do you know what, Par? The Mole, with his family of toy animals and his underground hideout — you're just like him. You're exactly the same. You create your own reality — it doesn't matter what the truth is or what anyone else thinks.'

He slipped his hand back into his blanket and pulled the covering tight again. 'That's why I'm going. Because you need me to go. You need me to tell you the difference between the toy animals and the real ones.'

He turned away again, directing his gaze back out the rain-streaked window to where the night's fading shadows continued to play games in the mist.

Par's mouth tightened. His brother's face was infuriatingly calm. 'I know the difference, Coll!' he snapped

Coll shook his head. 'No you don't. It's all the same to you. You decide whatever you want to decide and that's the end of the matter. That's the way it was with Allanon's ghost. That's the way it was with the charge he gave you to find the Sword of Shannara. That's the way it is now. Toy animals or real ones, the fact of what they are doesn't matter. What matters is how you perceive it.'

'That's not true!' Par was incensed.

'Isn't it? Then tell me this. What happens tomorrow if you're mistaken? About anything. What if the Sword of Shannara isn't there? What if the Shadowen are waiting for us? What if the wishsong doesn't work the way you think it will? Tell me, Par. What if you're just plain wrong?'

Par gripped the edges of his blanket until his knuckles were white.

'What happens if the toy animals turn out to be real ones? What do you plan to do then?' He waited a moment, then said, 'That's why I'm going, too.'

'If if turns out that I'm wrong, what difference will it make if you do go?' Par shouted furiously.

Coll didn't respond right away. Then slowly he looked over once again. He gave Par a small, ironic smile. 'Don't you know?'

He turned away again. Par bit his lip in frustration. The rain picked up momentarily, the drops beating on the shed's wooden roof with fresh determination. Par felt suddenly small and frightened, knowing that his brother was right, that he was being foolish and impulsive, that his insistence in going back into the Pit was risking all their lives, but knowing too that it didn't make any difference; he must go. Coll was right about that as well; the decision had been made and he would not change it. He remained rigid and upright next to his brother, refusing to give way to his fears, but within he curled tight and tried to hide from the faces they showed him.

Then Coll said quietly, 'I love you, Par. And I suppose

when you get right down to it, that's why I'm going most of all.'

Par let the words hang in the silence that followed, unwilling to disturb them. He felt himself uncurl and straighten, and a flush of warmth spread through him. When he tried to speak, he could not. He let his breath out in a long, slow, inaudible sigh.

'I need you with me, Coll,' he managed finally. 'I really do.'

Coll nodded. Neither of them said anything after that.

CHAPTER

28

WALKER BOH RETURNED TO HEARTHSTONE following his confrontation with the Grimpond and for the better part of a week did nothing more than consider what he had been told. The weather was pleasant, the days warm and sunny, the air filled with fragrant smells from the woodland trees and flowers and streams. He felt sheltered by the valley; he was content to remain in seclusion there. Rumor provided all the company he required. The big moor cat trailed after him on the long walks he took to while away his days, padding silently down the solitary trails, along the moss-covered stream banks, through the ancient massive trees, a soundless and reassuring presence. At night, the two sat upon the cottage porch, the cat dozing, the man staring skyward at the canopy of moon and stars.

He was always thinking. He could not stop thinking. The memory of the Grimpond's words haunted him even at Hearthstone, at his home, where nothing should have been able to threaten him. The words played unpleasant games within his mind, forcing him to confront them, to try to reason through how much of what they whispered was truth and how much a lie. He had known it would be like this before he had gone to see the Grimpond — that the words would be vague and distressing and that they would speak riddles and half-truths and leave him with a tangled knot of threads leading to the answers he sought, a knot that only a clairvoyant could manage to sort out. He had known and still he was not prepared for how taxing it would be.

He was able to determine the location of the Black Elfstone almost immediately. There was only one place where eyes could turn a man to stone and voices drive him mad, one place where the dead lay in utter blackness — the Hall of Kings, deep in the Dragon's Teeth. It was said that the Hall of Kings had been fashioned even before the time of the Druids, a vast and impenetrable cavern labyrinth in which the dead monarchs of the Four Lands were interred, a massive crypt in which the living were not permitted, protected by darkness, by statues called Sphinxes that were half-man, half-beast and could turn the living to stone, and by formless beings called Banshees who occupied a section of the caverns called the Corridor of Winds and whose wail could drive men mad instantly.

And the Tomb itself, where the pocket carved with runes hid the Black Elfstone, was watched over by the serpent Valg.

At least it was, if the serpent was still alive. There had been a terrible battle fought between the serpent and the company under Allanon's leadership, who had gone in search of the Sword of Shannara in the time of Shea Ohmsford. The company had encountered the serpent unexpectedly and been forced to battle its way clear. But no one had ever determined if the serpent had survived that battle. As far as Walker knew, no one had ever gone back to see.

Allanon might have returned once upon a time, of course. But Allanon had never said.

The difficulty in any event was not in determining the mystery of the Elfstone's whereabouts, but in deciding whether or not to go after it. The Hall of Kings was a dangerous place, even for someone like Walker who had less to fear than ordinary men. Magic, even the magic of a Druid, might not be protection enough — and Walker's magic was far less than Allanon's had ever been. Walker was concerned as well with what the Grimpond hadn't told him. There was certain to be more to this than what had been revealed; the Grimpond never gave out everything it knew. It was holding something back, and that was probably something that could kill Walker.

There was also the matter of the visions. There had been three of them, each more disturbing than the one before. In the first, Walker had stood on clouds above the others in the little company who had come to the Hadeshorn and the shade of Allanon, one hand missing, mocked by his own claim that he would lose that hand before he would allow the Druids to come again. In the second, he had pushed to her death a woman with silver hair, a magical creature of extraordinary beauty. In the third, Allanon had held him fast while death reached to claim him.

There was some measure of truth in each of these visions, Walker knew — enough truth so that he must pay heed to them and not simply dismiss them as the Grimpond's tauntings. The visions meant something; the Grimpond had left it to him to figure out what.

So Walker Boh debated. But the days passed and still the answers he needed would not come. All that was certain was the location of the Black Elfstone — and its claim upon the Dark Uncle grew stronger, a lure that drew him like a moth to flame, though the moth understood the promise of death that waited and flew to it nevertheless.

And fly to it Walker did as well in the end. Despite his resolve to wait until he had puzzled out the Grimpond's riddles, his hunger to reclaim the missing Elfstone finally overcame him. He had thought the conversation through until he was sick of repeating it in his mind. He became convinced that he had learned all from it that he was going to learn. There was no other course of action left to him but to go in search of the Black Elfstone and to discover by doing what he could discover in no other way. It would be dangerous; but he had survived dangerous situations before. He resolved not to be afraid, only to be careful.

He left the valley at the close of the week, departing with the sunrise, traveling afoot, wearing a long forest cloak for protection against the weather and carrying only a rucksack full of provisions. Most of what he would need he would find on the way. He walked west into Darklin Reach and did not look back until Hearthstone was lost from view. Rumor remained behind. It was difficult to leave the big cat; Walker would have felt better having him along. Few things living would challenge a full-grown moor cat. But it would be dangerous for Rumor as well outside the protective confines of the Eastland, where he could not conceal himself as easily and where his natural protection would be stripped from him. Besides, this was Walker's quest and his alone.

The irony of his choosing to make the quest at all did not escape him. He was the one who had vowed never to have anything to do with the Druids and their machinations. He had gone grudgingly with Par on his journey to the Hadeshorn. He had left the meeting with the shade of Allanon convinced that the Druid was playing games with the Ohmsfords, using them to serve his own hidden purposes. He had practically thrown Cogline from his own home, insisting that the other's efforts to teach the secrets of the magic had retarded his growth rather than enhanced it. He had threatened to take the Druid History that the old man had brought him and throw it into the deepest bog.

But then he had read about the Black Elfstone, and somehow everything had changed. He still wasn't sure why. His curiosity was partly to blame, his insatiable need to know. Was there such a thing as the Black Elfstone? Could it bring back disappeared Paranor as the history promised? Questions to be answered — he could never resist the lure of their secrets. Such secrets had to be solved, their mysteries revealed. There was knowledge waiting to be discovered. It was the purpose to which he had dedicated his life.

He wanted to believe that his sense of fairness and compassion made him go as well. Despite what he believed about the Druids, there might be something in Paranor itself — if, indeed, the Druid's Keep could be brought back — that would help the Four Lands against the Shadowen. He was uneasy with the possibility that in not going he was condemning the Races to a future like that which the Druid shade had described.

He promised himself as he departed that he would do no more than he must and certainly no more than he believed reasonable. He would remain, first and always, his own master rather than the plaything that Allanon's shade would have him be.

The days were still and sultry, the summer's heat building as he traversed the forest wilderness. Clouds were massed in the west, somewhere below the Dragon's Teeth. There would be storms waiting in the mountains.

He passed along the Chard Rush, then climbed into the Wolfsktaag and out again. It took him three days of easy travel to reach Storlock. There he reprovisioned with the help of the Stors and on the morning of the fourth day set out to cross the Rabb Plains. The storms had reached him by then, and rain began to fall in a slow, steady drizzle that turned the landscape gray. Patrols of Federation soldiers on horseback and caravans of traders appeared and faded like wraiths without seeing him. Thunder rumbled in the distance, muted and sluggish in the oppressive heat, a growl of dissatisfaction echoing across the emptiness.

Walker camped that night on the Rabb Plains, taking shelter in a cottonwood grove. There was no dry wood for a fire and Walker was already drenched through, so he slept wrapped in his cloak, shivering with the damp and cold.

Morning brought a lessening of the rains, the clouds thinning and letting the sun's brightness shine through in a screen of gray light. Walker roused himself stoically, ate a cold meal of fruit and cheese, and struck out once more. The Dragon's Teeth rose up before him, sullen and dark. He reached the pass that led upward into the Valley of Shale and the Hadeshorn and, beyond, the Hall of Kings.

That was as far as he went that day. He made camp beneath an outcropping of rock where the earth was still dry. He found wood, built a fire, dried his clothes, and warmed himself. He would be ready now when tomorrow came and it was time to enter the caverns. He ate a hot meal and watched the darkness descend in a black pall of clouds, mist, and night across the empty reaches about him. He thought for a time about his boyhood and wondered what he might have done to make it different. It began to rain again, and the world beyond his small fire disappeared.

He slept well. There were no dreams, no nervous awakenings. When he woke, he felt rested and prepared to face whatever fate awaited him. He was confident, though not carelessly so. The rain had stopped again. He listened for a time to the sounds of the morning waking around him, searching for hidden warnings. There were none.

He wrapped himself in his forest cloak, shouldered his rucksack, and started up.

The morning slipped away as he climbed. He was more cautious now, his eyes searching across the barren rock, defiles, and crevices for movement that meant danger, his ears sorting through the small noises and scrapes for those that truly menaced. He moved quietly, deliberately, studying the landscape ahead before proceeding into it, choosing his path with care. The mountains about him were vast, empty, and still — sleeping giants rooted so utterly by time to the earth beneath that even if they somehow managed to wake they would find they could no longer move.

He passed into the Valley of Shale. Black rock glistened damply within its bowl, and the waters of the Hadeshorn stirred like a thick, greenish soup. He circled it warily and left it behind.

Beyond, the slope steepened and the climb grew more difficult. The wind began to pick up, blowing the mist away until the air was sharp and clear and there was only the gray ceiling of the clouds between Walker and the earth. The temperature dropped, slowly at first, then rapidly until it was below freezing. Ice began to appear on the rock, and snow flurries swirled past his face in small gusts. He wrapped his cloak about him more tightly and pressed on.

His progress slowed then, and for a very long time it seemed to Walker as if he were not moving at all. The pathway was uneven and littered with loose stone, twisting and inding its way through the larger rocks. The wind blew into him remorselessly, biting at his face and hands, buffeting him so that it threatened to knock him backward. The mountainside remained unchanging, and it was impossible to tell at any given point how far he had come. He quit trying to hear or see anything beyond what lay immediately in front of him and limited his concentration to putting one foot in front of the other, drawing into himself as far as he could to block away the cold.

He found himself thinking of the Black Elfstone, of how it would look and feel, of what form its magic might take. He played with the vision in the silence of his mind, shutting out the world he traveled through and the discomfort he was feeling. He held the image before him like a beacon and used it to brighten the way.

It was noon when he entered a canyon, a broad split between the massive peaks with their canopy of clouds that opened into a valley and beyond the valley into a narrow, twisting passageway that disappeared into the rock. Walker traversed the canyon floor to the defile and started in. The wind died away to a whisper, an echo that breathed softly in the suddenly enfolding stillness. Mist trapped by the peaks collected in pools. Walker felt the chill lose its bite. He came out of himself again, newly alert, tense as he searched the dark rifts and corners of the corridor he followed.

Then the walls fell away and his journey was finished.

The entrance to the Hall of Kings stood before him, carved into the wall of the mountain, a towering black maw, bracketed by huge stone sentries fashioned in the shape of armor-clad warriors, the blades of their swords jammed downward into the earth. The sentries faced out from the cavern mouth, faces scarred by wind and time, eyes fastened on Walker as if they might somehow really see.

Walker slowed, then stopped. The way forward was wrapped in darkness and silence. The wind, its echo still ringing in his ears, had faded away completely. The mist was gone. Even the cold had mutated into a sort of numbing, empty chill.

What Walker felt at that moment was unmistakable. The feeling wrapped about him like a second skin, permeated his body, and reached down into his bones. It was the feeling of death.

He listened to the silence. He searched the blackness. He waited. He let his mind reach out into the void. He could discover nothing.

The minutes faded away.

Finally Walker Boh straightened purposefully, hitched up the rucksack, and started forward once again.

It was midafternoon in the Westland where the Tirfing stretched from the sun-baked banks of the Mermidon south along the broad, empty stretches of the Shroudslip. The summer had been a dry one, and the grasses were withered from the heat, even where there had been a measure of shade to protect them. Where there had been no shade at all, the land was burned bare.

Wren Ohmsford sat with her back against the trunk of a spreading oak, close to where the horses nosed into a muddy pool of water, and watched the sun's fire turn red against the western sky, edging toward the horizon and the day's close. The glare blinded her to anything approaching from that direction, and she shaded her eyes watchfully. It was one thing to be caught napping by Garth; it was something else again to let her guard down against whoever it was that was tracking them.

She pursed her lips thoughtfully. It had been more than two days now since they had first discovered they were being followed — sensed it, really, since their shadow had remained carefully hidden from them. He or she or it — they still didn't know. Garth had backtracked that morning to find out, stripping off his brightly colored clothing and donning mud-streaked plains garb, shading his face, hands, and hair, disappearing into the heat like a wraith.

Whoever was tracking them was in for an unpleasant surprise.

Still, it was nearing day's end and the giant Rover hadn't returned. Their shadow might be more clever than they imagined.

'What does it want?' she mused to herself.

She had asked Garth the same question that morning, and he had drawn his finger slowly across his throat. She tried to argue against it, but she lacked the necessary conviction. It could be an assassin following them as easily as anyone else.

Her gaze wandered to the expanse of the plains east. It was disturbing enough to be tracked like this. It was even more disturbing to realize that it probably had something to do with her inquiries about the Elves.

She sighed fitfully, vaguely irritated with the way things were working out. She had come back from her meeting with the shade of Allanon in an unsettled state, dissatisfied with what she had heard, uncertain as to what she should do. Common sense told her that what the shade had asked of her was impossible. But something inside, that sixth sense she relied upon so heavily, whispered that maybe it wasn't, that Druids had always known more than humans, that their warnings and chargings to the people of the Races had always had merit. Par believed. He was probably already in search of the missing Sword of Shannara. And while Walker had departed from them in a rage, vowing never to have anything to do with the Druids, his anger had been momentary. He was too rational, too controlled to dismiss the matter so easily. Like her, he would be having second thoughts.

She shook her head ruefully. She had believed her own decision irrevocable for a time. She had persuaded herself that common sense must necessarily govern her course of action, and she had returned with Garth to her people, putting the business of Allanon and the missing Elves behind her. But the doubts had persisted, a nagging sense of something being not quite right about her determination to drop the matter. So, almost reluctantly, she had begun to ask questions about the Elves. It was easy enough to do; the Rovers were a migrating people and traveled the Westland from end to end during the course of a year's time, trading for what they needed, bartering with what they had. Villages and communities came and went, and there were always new people to talk to. What harm could it do then to inquire about the Elves?

Sometimes she had asked her questions directly, sometimes almost jokingly. But the answers she had received were all the same. The Elves were gone, had been since before anyone could remember, since before the time of their grandfathers and grandmothers. No one had ever seen an Elf. Most weren't sure there had ever really been any to see.

Wren had begun to feel foolish even asking, had begun to consider giving up asking at all. She broke away from her people to hunt with Garth, anxious to be alone to think, hoping to gain some insight into the dilemma through solitary consideration of it.

And then their shadow had appeared, stalking them. Now she was wondering if there wasn't something to be found out after all.

She saw movement out of the corner of her eye, a vague blur in the swelter of the plains, and she came cautiously to her feet. She stood without moving in the shadow of the oak as the shape took form and became Garth. The giant Rover trotted up to her, sweat coating his heavily muscled frame. He seemed barely winded, a tireless machine that even the intense midsummer heat could not affect. He signed briefly, shaking his head. Whoever was out there had eluded him.

Wren held his gaze a moment, then reached down to hand him the waterskin. As he drank, she draped her lanky frame against the roughened bark of the oak and stared out into the empty plains. One hand came up in an unconscious movement to touch the small leather bag about her neck. She rolled the contents thoughtfully between her fingers. Make-believe Elfstones. Her good luck charm. What sort of luck were they providing her now?

She brushed aside her uneasiness, her sun-browned face a mask of determination. It didn't matter. Enough was enough. She didn't like being followed, and she was going to put an end to it. They would change the direction of their travel, disguise their trail, backtrack once or twice, ride all night if need be, and lose their shadow once and for all.

She took her hand away from the bag and her eyes were fierce.

Sometimes you had to make your own luck.

Walker Boh entered the Hall of Kings on cat's feet, passing noiselessly between the massive stone sentinels, stepping through the cavern mouth into the blackness beyond. He paused there, letting his eyes adjust. There was light, a faint greenish phosphorescence given off by the rock. He would not need to light a torch to find the way.

A picture of the caverns flashed momentarily in his mind, a reconstruction of what he expected to find. Cogline had drawn it for him on paper once, long ago. The old man had never been into the caverns himself, but others of the Druids had, Allanon among them, and Cogline had studied the maps that they had devised and revealed their secrets to his pupil. Walker felt confident that he could find the way.

He started ahead.

The passageway was broad and level, its walls and floor free from sharp projections and crevices. The near-dark was wrapped in silence, deep and hushed, and there was only the faint echo of his boots as he walked. The air was bone-chilling, a cold that had settled into the mountain rock over the centuries and could not be dislodged. It seeped into Walker despite his clothing and made him shiver. A prickling of unpleasant feelings crept through him — loneliness, insignificance, futility. The caverns dwarfed him; they reduced him to nothing, a tiny creature whose very presence in such an ancient, forbidden place was an affront. He fought back against the feelings, recognizing what they would do to him, and after a brief struggle they faded back into the cold and the silence.

He reached the cave of the Sphinxes shortly after. He paused again, this time to steady his mind, to take himself deep down inside where the stone spirits couldn't reach him. When he was there, wrapped in whispers of caution and warning, blanketed in words of power, he went forward. He kept his eyes fixed on the dusty floor, watching the stone pass away, looking only at the next few feet he must cover.

In his mind, he saw the Sphinxes looming over him, massive stone monoliths fashioned by the same hands that had made the sentinels. The Sphinxes were said to have human faces carved on the bodies of beasts — creatures of another age that no living man had ever seen. They were old, so incredibly ancient that their lives could be measured by hundreds of generations of mortal men. So many dead monarchs had passed beneath their gaze, carried from life to endless rest within their mountain tombs. So many, and none had returned.

Look at us, they whispered! *See how wondrous we are!*

He could sense their eyes on him, hear the whisper of their voices in his mind, feel them tearing and ripping at the layers of protection he had fashioned for himself, begging him to look up. He moved more quickly now, fighting to banish the whispers, resisting the urge to obey them. The stone monsters seemed to howl at him, harsh and insistent.

Walker Boh! Look at us! You must!

414

He struggled forward, his mind swarming with their voices, his resolve crumbling. Sweat beaded on his face despite the cold, and his muscles knotted until they hurt. He gritted his teeth against his weakness, chiding himself for it, thinking suddenly of Allanon in a bitter, desperate reminder that the Druid had come this way before him with seven men under his protection and had not given in.

In the end, neither did he. Just as he thought he would, that he must, he reached the far end of the cavern and stepped into the passageway beyond. The whispers faded and were gone. The Sphinxes were left behind. He looked up again, carefully resisted the urge to glance back, then moved ahead once more.

The passageway narrowed and began to wind downward. Walker slowed, uncertain as to what might lurk around the darkened corners. The greenish light could be found only in small patches here, and the corridor was thick with shadows. He dropped into a crouch, certain that something waited to attack him, feeling its presence grow nearer with every step he took. He considered momentarily using his magic to light the passageway so that he might better see what hid from him, but he quickly discarded the idea. If he invoked the magic, he would alert whatever might be there that he possessed special powers. Better to keep the magic secret, he thought. It was a weapon that would serve him best if its use was unexpected.

Yet nothing appeared. He shrugged his uneasiness aside and pressed on until the passageway straightened and began to widen out again.

Then the sound began.

He knew it was coming, that it would strike all at once, and still he was not prepared when it came. It lashed out at him, wrapping about with the strength of iron chains, dragging him ahead. It was the scream of wind through a canyon, the howl and rip of storms across a plain, the pounding of seas against shoreline cliffs. And beneath, just under the skin of it, was the horrifying shriek of souls

415

in unimaginable pain, scraping their bones against the rock of the cavern walls.

Frantically, Walker Boh brought his defenses to bear. He was in the Corridor of Winds, and the Banshees were upon him. He blocked everything away in an instant, closing off the terrifying sound with a strength of will that rocked him, focusing his thoughts on a single picture within his mind — an image of himself. He constructed the image with lines and shadings, coloring in the gaps, giving himself life and strength and determination. He began to walk forward. He muffled the sounds of the Banshees until they were no more than a strange buzzing that whipped and tore about him, trying to break through. He watched the Corridor of Winds pass away about him, a bleak and empty cavern in which everything was invisible but the sound of the Banshees wailing, a whirl of color that flashed like maddened lightning through the black.

Nothing Walker did would lessen it. The shrieks and howls hammered into him, buffeting his body as if they were living things. He could feel his strength ebbing as it had before the onslaught of the Sphinxes, his defenses giving way. The fury of the attack was frightening. He fought back against it, a hint of desperation creeping through him as he watched the image he had drawn of himself begin to shimmer and disappear. He was losing control. In another minute, maybe two, his protection would crumble completely.

And then, once again, he broke clear just when it seemed he must give way. He stumbled from the Corridor of Winds into a small cave that lay beyond. The screams of the Banshees vanished. Walker collapsed against the closest wall, sliding down the smooth rock into a sitting position, his entire body shaking. He breathed in and out slowly, steadily, coming back to himself in bits and pieces. Time slowed, and for a moment he allowed his eyes to close.

When he opened them again, he was looking at a pair of massive stone doors fastened to the rock by iron hinges. Runes were carved into the doors, the ancient markings as red as fire.

He had reached the Assembly, the Tomb where the Kings of the Four Lands were interred.

He climbed to his feet, hitched up the rucksack, and walked to the doors. He studied the markings a moment, then placed one hand carefully upon them and shoved. The door swung open and Walker Boh stepped through.

He stood in a giant, circular cavern streaked by greenish light and shadow. Sealed vaults lined the walls, the dead within closed away by mortar and stone. Statues stood guarding their entombed rulers, solemn and ageless. Before each was piled the wealth of the master in casks and trunks — jewels, furs, weapons, treasures of all sorts. They were so covered with dust that they were barely recognizable. The walls of the chamber loomed upward until they disappeared, the ceiling an impenetrable canopy of black.

The chamber appeared empty of life.

At its far end, a second pair of doors stood closed. It was beyond that the serpent Valg had lived. The Pyre of the Dead was there, an altar on which the deceased rulers of the Four Lands lay in state for a requisite number of days before their interment. A set of stone stairs led down from the altar to a pool of water in which Valg hid. Supposedly, the serpent kept watch over the dead. Walker wouldn't have been surprised to learn that he just fed on them.

He listened for long moments for the sound of anything moving, anything breathing. He heard nothing. He studied the Tomb. The Black Elfstone was hidden here — not in the cavern beyond. If he were quick and if he were careful, he might avoid having to discover whether or not the serpent Valg was still alive.

He began moving slowly, noiselessly past the crypts of the dead, their statues and their wealth. He ignored the treasures; he knew from Cogline that they were coated with a poison instantly fatal to anyone who touched them. He picked his way forward, skirting each bastion of death, studying the rock walls and the rune markings that decorated them. He circled the chamber and found himself back where he had started.

Nothing.

His brow furrowed in thought. Where was the pocket that contained the Black Elfstone?

He studied the cavern a second time, letting his eyes drift through the haze of greenish light, skipping from one pocket of shadows to the next. He must have missed something. What was it?

He closed his eyes momentarily and let his thoughts reach out, searching the blackness. He could feel something, a very small presence that seemed to whisper his name. His eyes snapped open again. His lean, ghostlike face went taut. The presence was not in the wall; it was in the floor!

He began moving again, this time directly across the chamber, letting himself be guided by what he sensed waiting there. It was the Black Elfstone, he concluded. An Elfstone would have life of its own, a presence that could summon if called upon. He strode away from the statues and their treasures, away from the vaults, no longer even seeing them, his eyes fastening on a point almost at the center of the cavern.

When he reached that point, he found a rectangular slab of rock resting evenly on the floor. Runes were carved in its surface, markings so faded that he could not make them out. He hesitated, uneasy that the writing was so obscured. But if the runes were Elven script, they might be thousands of years old; he could not expect to be able to read them now.

He knelt down, a solitary figure in the center of the cavern, isolated even from the dead. He brushed at the stone markings and tried a moment longer to decipher them. Then, his patience exhausted, he gave up. Using both hands, he pushed at the stone. It gave easily, moving aside without a sound.

He felt a momentary rush of excitement.

The hole beneath was dark, so cloaked in shadow that

he could make nothing out. Yet there was something . . .

Casting aside momentarily the caution that had served him so well, Walker Boh reached down into the opening.

Instantly, something wrapped about his hand, seizing him. There was a moment of excruciating pain and then numbness. He tried to jerk free, but he could not move. Panic flooded through him. He still could not see what was down there.

Desperate now, he used the magic, his free hand summoning light and sending it swiftly down into the hole.

What he saw caused him to go cold. There was no Elfstone. Instead, a snake was fastened to his hand, coiled tightly about it. But this was no ordinary snake. This was something far more deadly, and he recognized it instantly. It was an Asphinx, a creature out of the old legends, conceived at the same time as its massive counterparts in the caves without, the Sphinxes. But the Asphinx was a creature of flesh and blood until it struck. Only then did it turn to stone.

And whatever it struck turned to stone as well.

Walker's teeth clenched against what he saw happening. His hand was already turning gray, the Asphinx still wrapped firmly about it, dead now and hardened, cemented against the floor of the compartment in a tight spiral from which it could not be broken loose.

Walker Boh pulled violently against the creature's grasp. But there was no escape. He was embedded in stone, fastened to the Asphinx and the cavern floor as surely as if by chains.

Fear ripped through him, tearing at him as a knife edge might his flesh. He was poisoned. Just as his hand was turning to stone, so would the rest of him. Slowly. Inexorably.

Until he was a statue.

CHAPTER

29

DAWN AT THE JUT brought a change in the weather as the leading edge of the storm that was passing through Tyrsis drifted north into the Parma Key. It was still dark when the first cloud banks began to blanket the skies, blotting out the moon and stars and turning the whole of the night an impenetrable black. Then the wind died, its whisper fading away almost before anyone still awake in the outlaw camp noticed it was gone, and the air became still and sullen. A few drops fell, splashing on the upturned faces of the watch, spattering onto the dry, dusty rock of the bluff in widening stains. Everything grew hushed as the drops came quicker. Steam rose off the floor of the forestland below, lifting above the treetops to mix with the clouds until there was nothing left to see, even with the sharpest eyes. When dawn finally broke, it came as a line of brightness along the eastern horizon so faint that it went almost unnoticed. By then, the rain was falling steadily, a heavy drizzle that sent everyone scurrying for shelter, including the watch.

Which was why no one saw the Creeper.

It must have come out of the forest under cover of darkness and begun working its way up the cliffside when the clouds took away the only light that would have revealed its presence. There were sounds of scraping as it climbed, the rasp of its claws and armor-plating as it dragged itself upward, but the sounds were lost in the rumble of distant thunder, the splatter of the rain, and the movement of men and animals in the camps. Besides, the outlaws on watch were tired and irritable and convinced that nothing was going to happen before dawn.

The Creeper was almost on top of them before they realized their mistake and began to scream.

The cries brought Morgan Leah awake with a start. He had fallen asleep in the grove of asper at the far end of the bluff, still mulling over what to do about his suspicions as to the identity of the traitor. He was curled in a ball under the canopy of the largest tree, his hunting cloak wrapped about him for warmth. His muscles were so sore and cramped that at first he could not bring himself to stand. But the cries grew quickly more frantic, filled with terror. Ignoring his own discomfort, he forced himself to his feet, pulled free the broadsword he had strapped to his back, and stumbled out into the rain.

The bluff was in pandemonium. Men were charging back and forth everywhere, weapons drawn, dark shadows in a world of grayness and damp. A few torches appeared, bright beacons against the black, but their flames were extinguished almost immediately by the downpour. Morgan hurried ahead, following the tide, searching the gloom for the source of the madness.

And then he saw it. The Creeper was atop the bluff, rearing out of the chasm, looming over the outlaw fortifications and the men who threatened it, its claws digging into the rock to hold it fast. A dead man dangled from one of its massive pinchers, cut nearly in half — one of the watch who had realized what was happening too late.

The outlaws surged forward recklessly, seizing poles and spears, jamming them into the Creeper's massive body, trying desperately to force the monster back over the edge. But the Creeper was huge; it towered above them like a wall. Morgan slowed in dismay. They might as well have been trying to turn a river from its course. Nothing that large could be dislodged by human strength alone.

The Creeper lunged forward, throwing itself into its attackers. Poles and spears snapped and splintered as it hurtled down. The men caught beneath died instantly, and several more were quickly snatched up by the pinchers. An entire section of the Jut's fortifications collapsed under the creature's weight. The outlaws fell back as it hunched its way into them, smashing weapons, stores, and campsites, catching up anything that moved. Blows from swords and knives rained down on its body, but the Creeper seemed unaffected. It advanced relentlessly, stalking the men who retreated from it, destroying everything in its path.

'Free-born!' the cry rang out suddenly. 'To me!'

Padishar Creel materialized from out of nowhere, a bright scarlet figure in the rain and mist, rallying his men. They cried out in answer and rushed to stand beside him. He formed them quickly into squads; half counterattacked the Creeper with massive posts to fend off the pinchers while the balance hacked at the monster's sides and back. The Creeper writhed and twisted, but came on.

'Free-born, free-born!' the cries sounded from everywhere, lifting into the dawn, filling the grayness with their fury.

Then Axhind and his Rock Trolls appeared, their massive bodies armored head to foot, wielding their huge battleaxes. They attacked the Creeper head-on, striking for the pinchers. Three died almost instantly, torn apart so fast that they disappeared in a blur of limbs and blood. But the others cut and hacked with such determination that they shattered the left pincher, leaving it broken and useless. Moments later, they cut it off entirely.

The Creeper slowed. A trail of bodies littered the ground behind it. Morgan still stood between the monster and the caves, undecided as to what he should do and unable to understand why. It was as if he had become mired in quicksand. He saw the beast lift itself clear of the earth. Its head and pinchers came up, and it hung suspended like a snake about to strike, braced on the back half of its body, prepared to throw itself on its attackers and smash them. The Trolls and the outlaws fell back in a rush, shouting to one another in warning.

Morgan looked for Padishar, but the outlaw chief had disappeared. The Highlander could not find him anywhere. For an instant, he thought Padishar must have fallen. Rain trickled down his face into his eyes, and he blinked it away impatiently. His hand tightened on the handle of his broadsword, but still he hung back.

The Creeper was inching forward, casting right and left to protect against flanking attacks. A twitch of its tail sent several men flying. Spears and arrows flew into it and bounced away. Steadily it came on, forcing the defenders ever closer to the caves. Soon, there would be nowhere left for them to go.

Morgan Leah was shaking. *Do something!* his mind screamed.

In that same instant Padishar reappeared at the mouth of the largest of the Jut's caves, calling out to his men to fall back. Something huge lumbered into view behind him, creaking and rumbling as it came. Morgan squinted through the gloom and mist. Lines of men appeared, hauling on ropes, and the thing behind Padishar began to take shape. Morgan could see it now as it cleared the cavern entrance and crawled into the light.

It was a great, wooden crossbow.

Padishar had its handlers wheel it into position facing the Creeper. Atop its base, Chandos used a heavy winch to crank back the bowstring. A massive, sharpened bolt was fitted in place.

The Creeper hesitated, as if to measure the potential danger of this new weapon. Then, lowering itself slightly, it advanced, pinchers clicking in anticipation.

Padishar ordered the first bolt fired when the creature was still fifty feet away. The shot flew wide. The Creeper picked up speed as Chandos hurriedly rewound the bowstring. The crossbow fired again, but the bolt glanced off a section of armor-plating and caromed away. The Creeper was knocked sideways, slowed momentarily by the force of the blow, and then it straightened itself and came on.

Morgan saw at once that there would be no time for a third shot. The Creeper was too close. Yet Chandos stayed atop the crossbow, desperately cranking back the bowstring a third time. The Creeper was only yards away. Outlaws and Trolls harassed it from all sides, axes and swords hammering against it, but it refused to be deterred. It recognized the crossbow as the only thing it really had to fear and moved swiftly to destroy it.

Chandos shoved the third bolt into place and reached for the trigger.

He was too late. The Creeper lunged and came down atop the crossbow, smashing into its works. Wood splintered, and the wheels supporting the weapon gave way. Chandos was thrown into the night. Men scattered everywhere, crying out. The Creeper shifted atop the wreckage, then lifted free. It drew itself up deliberately, sensing its victory, knowing it needed only one further lunge to finish the job.

But Padishar Creel was quicker. While the other outlaws fled, Chandos lay unconscious in the darkness, and Morgan struggled with his indecision, Padishar attacked. Little more than a scarlet blur in the mist and half-light of the rain-soaked dawn, the outlaw chief seized one of the crossbow bolts that had been spilled from its rack, darted beneath the Creeper and braced the bolt upright against the earth. The Creeper never saw him, so intent was it on destroying the crossbow. The monster hammered down, smashing through the already crippled weapon onto the iron-tipped bolt. The force of its lunge sent the bolt through iron and flesh, in one side of its body and out the other.

Padishar barely managed to roll clear as the Creeper struck the earth.

Back the monster reared, shuddering with pain and surprise, transfixed on the bolt. It lost its balance and toppled over, writhing madly in an effort to dislodge the killing shaft. It crashed to the ground, belly up, coiling into a ball. 'Free-born!' Padishar Creel cried out, and the outlaws and Trolls were upon it. Bits and pieces of the creature flew apart as swords and axes hacked. The second pincher was sheared off. Padishar shouted encouragement to his men, attacked with them, swinging his broadsword with every ounce of strength he possessed.

The battle was ferocious. Though badly injured, the Creeper was still dangerous. Men were pinned beneath it and crushed, sent flying as it thrashed, and ripped by its claws. All efforts to put an end to it were stymied until finally another of the scattered crossbow bolts was brought forward and rammed through the monster's eye and into its brain. The Creeper convulsed one last time and went still.

Morgan Leah watched it all as if from a great distance, too far removed from what was happening to be of any use. He was still shaking when it ended. He was bathed in sweat. He had not lifted a finger to help.

There was a change in the outlaw camp after that, a shift in attitude that reflected the growing belief that the Jut was no longer invulnerable. It was apparent almost immediately. Padishar slipped into the blackest of moods, railing at everyone, furious at the Federation for using a Creeper, at the dead monster for the damage it had inflicted, at the watch for not being more alert, and at himself especially for not being better prepared. His men went about their tasks grudgingly, a dispirited bunch that slogged through the rain and murk and mumbled darkly to themselves. If the Federation had sent one Creeper, they said, what was to prevent it from sending another? If another was sent, what would they do to stop this one? And what would they do if the Federation sent something worse?

Eighteen men died in the attack and twice that number were injured, some of whom would be dead before the day was out. Padishar had the casualties buried at the far end of the bluff and the injured moved into the largest cave, which was converted into a temporary hospital. There were medicines and some few men with experience in treating battle wounds to administer them, but the outlaws did not have the services of a genuine Healer. The cries of the injured and dying lingered in the early morning stillness.

The Creeper was dragged to the edge of the bluff and thrown over. It was a difficult, exhausting task, but Padishar would not tolerate the creature's presence on the bluff a second longer than was necessary. Ropes and pulleys were used, one end of the lines fastened to the monster's dead bulk, the other end passed through the hands of dozens of men who pulled and strained as the Creeper was hauled inch by inch through the wreckage of the camp. It took the outlaws all morning. Morgan worked with them, not speaking to anyone, trying hard to remain inconspicuous, still struggling to understand what had happened to him.

He figured it out finally. He was still immersed in the effort to drag the Creeper to the bluff edge, his body aching and weary, but his mind grown unexpectedly sharp. It was the Sword of Leah that was responsible, he realized — or more accurately, the magic it contained, or had once contained. It was the loss of the magic that had crippled him and had caused him to be so indecisive, so frightened. When he had discovered the magic of the Sword, he had thought himself invincible. The feeling of power was like nothing he had ever experienced or would have believed possible. With that sort of power at his command, he could do anything. He could still remember what it had felt like to stand virtually alone against the Shadowen in the Pit. Wondrous. Exhilarating.

But draining, as well. Each time he invoked the power, it seemed to take something away from him.

When he had broken the Sword of Leah and lost all use of the magic, he had begun to understand just how much it was that had been taken from him. He sensed the change in himself almost immediately. Padishar had insisted he was mistaken, had told him he would forget his loss, that he would heal, and that time would see him back to the way he had been. He knew now that it wasn't so. He would never heal — not completely. Having once used the magic, he was changed irrevocably. He couldn't give it up; he wasn't the same man without it. Though he had possessed it only briefly, the effect of having had it for even that long was permanent. He hungered to have it back again. He needed to have it back. He was lost without it; he was confused and afraid. That was the reason he had failed to act during the battle with the Creeper. It was not that he lacked a sense of what he should do or how he should do it. It was that he no longer could invoke the magic to aid him.

Admitting this cost him something he couldn't begin to define. He continued to work, a machine without feelings, numbed by the thought that loss of the magic could paralyze him so. He hid himself in his thoughts, in the rain and the gray, hoping that no one — especially Padishar Creel — had noticed his failure, agonizing over what he would do if it happened again.

After a time, he found himself thinking about Par. He had never considered before what it must be like for the Valeman to have to continually struggle with his own magic. Forced to confront what the magic of the Sword of Leah meant to him, Morgan thought he understood how difficult it must be for Par. How had his friend learned to live with the uncertainty of the wishsong's power? What did he feel when it failed him, as it had so many times on their journey to find Allanon? How had he managed to accept his weakness? It gave Morgan a measure of renewed strength to know that the Valeman had some-how found a way.

By midday, the Creeper was gone and the damage it had caused to the camp was mostly repaired. The rain ceased finally as the storms drifted east, scraping along the rim of the Dragon's Teeth. The clouds broke apart, and sunlight appeared through the breaks in long, narrow streamers that played across the dark green spread of the

Parma Key. The mist burned off, and all that remained was a sheen of dampness that blanketed everything with a lustrous silver coating.

The Federation immediately hauled forward their catapults and siege towers and renewed their assault on the Jut. The catapults flung their stones and the siege towers were lined with archers who kept a steady fire on the outlaw camp. No effort was made to scale the heights; the attack was limited to a constant barrage against the bluff and its occupants, a barrage that lasted through the afternoon and went on into the night, a steady, constant, ceaseless harassment. There was nothing that the outlaws could do to stop it; their attackers were too far away and too well-protected. There was nowhere outside of the caves where it was safe to walk. It seemed clear that the loss of the Creeper hadn't discouraged the Federation. The siege would not be lifted. It would go on until the defenders were sufficiently weakened to be overcome by a frontal assault. If it were to take days or weeks or months, the end would be the same. The Federation army was content to wait.

On the heights, the defenders dodged and darted through the rain of missiles, yelled defiantly down at their attackers, and went about their work as best they could. But in the privacy of their shelters they grumbled and muttered their suspicions with renewed conviction. No matter what they had once believed, the Jut could not be held.

Morgan Leah was faced with worries of his own. The Highlander had deliberately gone off by himself and was secluded once more within the shelter of the aspen grove at the far end of the bluff, away from the major defensive positions of the camp where most of the Federation attack was being concentrated. Having managed to put aside for the moment the matter of his inability to accept losing the magic of the Sword of Leah, he was now forced to confront the equally troubling dilemma of his suspicions as to the identity of the traitor.

It was difficult to know what to do. Surely he should

428

tell someone. He *had* to tell someone. But who?

Padishar Creel? If he told Padishar, the outlaw chief might or might not believe him, but in either case he was unlikely to leave the matter to chance. Padishar didn't care a fig for either Steff or Teel at this point; he would simply do away with them — both of them. After all, there was no way of knowing which one it was — or even if it was either. And Padishar was in no mood to wait around for the answer.

Morgan shook his head. He couldn't tell Padishar.

Steff? If he chose to do that, he was deciding, in effect, that Teel was the traitor. That was what he wanted to believe, but was that the truth of the matter? Even if it was, he knew what Steff's reaction would be. His friend was in love with Teel. Teel had saved his life. He would hardly be willing to accept what Morgan was telling him without some sort of proof to back it up. And Morgan didn't have any proof — at least, nothing you could hold in your hand and point to. Speculation was all he had, well-reasoned or not.

He eliminated Steff.

Someone else? There wasn't anyone else. He would have told Par or Coll if they were there, or Wren, or even Walker Boh. But the members of the Ohmsford family were scattered to the four winds, and he was alone. There was no one he could trust.

He sat within the trees and listened to the distant shouts and cries of the defenders, to the sound of catapults and bows, the creaking of iron and wood, the hum of missiles sent flying, and the ping and crash and thud of their impact. He was isolated, an island within the heart of a battle that had somehow caught him up, lost in a sea of indecision and doubt. He had to do something — but the direction he should take refused to reveal itself. He had wanted so badly to be a part of the fight against the Federation, to come north to join the outlaws, to undertake the search for the Sword of Shannara, to see the Shadowen destroyed. Such aspirations he had harbored when he had set out — such bold plans! He was to be shed of his claustrophobic existence in the Highlands, his meaningless tweaking of the noses of the bureaucrats the Federation had sent to govern, finished at least with conducting meaningless experiments in aggravation against men who could change nothing, even if they wished to do so. He was to do something grand, something wonderful ...

Something that would make a difference.

Well, now he had his chance. He could make the difference no one else could. And there he sat, paralyzed.

Afternoon drifted into evening, the siege continued unabated, and Morgan's dilemma remained unresolved. He left the grove once to check on Steff and Teel — or more accurately, perhaps, to spy on them, to see if they might give anything away. But the Dwarves seemed no different from before. Steff was still weak and able to converse for only a few minutes before dropping off to sleep; Teel was taciturn, guarded. He studied them both as surreptitiously as he could, working at seeing something that would give him a clue as to whether his suspicions had any basis in fact — any possibility of truth at all — and he left as empty-handed as he had come.

It was almost dark when Padishar Creel found him. He was lost in thought, still trying to puzzle through what course of action he should take, and he didn't hear the big man approach. It wasn't until Padishar spoke that he realized anyone was there.

'Keeping to yourself quite a bit, aren't you?'

Morgan jumped. 'What? Oh, Padishar. Sorry.'

The big man sat down across from him. His face was tired and streaked with dust and sweat. If he noticed Morgan's uneasiness, he didn't let on. He stretched his legs and leaned back, supporting himself on his elbows, wincing from the pain of his wounds. 'This has been a foul day, Highlander,' he said. It came out in a long sigh of aggravation. 'Twenty-two men dead now, another two likely to be gone by morning, and here we cower like foxes brought to bay.'

Morgan nodded without responding. He was trying

desperately to decide what he should say.

'Truth is, I don't much care for the way this is turning out.' The hard face was impossible to read. 'The Federation will lay siege to this place until we've all forgotten why it was that we came here in the first place, and that doesn't do much to advance my plans or the hopes of the free-born. Bottled up like we are, we're not much use to anyone. There's other havens, and there'll be other times to square matters with those cowards who would send things conceived of dark magic to do their work rather than face us themselves.' He paused. 'So I've decided that it's time to think about getting out.'

Morgan sat forward now. 'Escape?'

'Out that back door we talked about. I thought you should know. I'll be needing your help.'

Morgan stared. 'My help?'

Padishar straightened slowly to a sitting position. 'I want someone to carry a message to Tyrsis — to Damson and the Valemen. They need to know what's happened. I'd go myself, but I have to stay to see the men safely out. So I thought you might be interested.'

Morgan agreed at once. 'I am. I'll do it.'

The other's hand lifted in warning. 'Not so fast. We won't be leaving the hut right away, probably not for another three days or so. The injured shouldn't be moved just yet. But I'll want you to leave sooner. Tomorrow, in fact. Damson's a smart girl with a good head on her shoulders, but she's wilful. I've been thinking matters over a bit since you asked me whether she might attempt to bring the Valemen here. I could be wrong; she might try to do just that. You have to make certain she doesn't.'

'I will.'

'Out the back door, then — as I've said. And you go alone.'

Morgan's brow furrowed.

'Alone, lad. Your friends stay with me. First, you can't be wandering about Callahorn with a pair of Dwarves in tow — even if they were up to it, which at least the one isn't. The Federation would have you in irons in two

431

minutes. And second, we can't be taking any chances after all the treachery that's been done. No one is to know your plans.'

The Highlander considered a moment. Padishar was right. There was no point in taking needless risks. He would be better off going by himself and telling no one what he was about — especially Steff and Teel. He almost gave voice to what he was thinking, then thought better of it. Instead, he simply nodded.

'Good. The matter is settled. Except for one thing.' Padishar climbed back to his feet. 'Come with me.'

He took Morgan through the camp and into the largest of the caves that opened on the cliffs backing the bluff, led him past the bay in which the wounded were being cared for and into the chambers beyond. The tunnels began there, a dozen or more, opening off each other, disappearing back into the darkness. Padishar had picked up a torch on their way in; now he touched it to one that burned from an iron bracket hammered into the cave wall, glanced about for a moment to reassure himself that no one was paying any special attention, then beckoned Morgan ahead. Ignoring the tunnels, he guided the Highlander through the piles of stores to the very deepest part of the caves, several hundred feet back into the cliff rock to a wall where crates were stacked twenty feet high. It was quiet there, the noise left behind. Again he glanced back, scanning the darkness.

Then, handing his torch to Morgan, he reached up with both hands, fitted his fingers into the seams of the crates and pulled. An entire section swung free, a false front on hidden hinges that opened into a tunnel beyond.

'Did you see how I did that, lad?' he asked softly. Morgan nodded.

Padishar took back his torch and poked it inside. Morgan leaned forward. The walls of the secret tunnel twisted and wound downward into the rock until they were lost from view.

'It goes all the way through the mountain,' Padishar said. 'Follow it to its end and you come out above the

432

Parma Key just south of the Dragon's Teeth, east of the Kennon Pass.' He looked at Morgan pointedly. 'If you were to attempt to find your way through the other passageways — the ones I keep a guard on for show — we might never see you again. Understand?'

He shoved the secret door closed again and stepped back. 'I'm showing you all this now because, when you're ready to go, I won't be with you. I'll be out there, keeping a close watch on your backside.' He gave Morgan a small, hard smile. 'Be certain you get clear quickly.'

They went back through the storage chambers and out through the main cavern to the bluff. It was dark now, the last of the daylight faded into dusk. The outlaw chief stopped, stretched and took a deep breath of evening air.

'Listen to me, lad,' he said quietly. 'There's one thing more. You have to stop brooding about what happened to that sword you carry. You can't haul that burden around with you and expect to stay clearheaded; it's much too heavy a load, even for a determined fellow like you. Lay it down. Leave it behind you. You've got enough heart in you to manage without it.'

He knows about this morning, Morgan realized at once. He knows and he's telling me that it's all right.

Padishar sighed. 'Every bone in my body aches, but none of them aches nearly so bad as my heart. I hate what's happened here. I hate what's been done to us.' He looked squarely at Morgan. 'That's what I mean about useless baggage. You think about it.'

He turned and strode off into the dark. Morgan almost called him back. He even took a step after him, thinking that now he would tell him his suspicions about the traitor. It would have been easy to do so. It would have freed him of the frustration he felt at having to keep the matter to himself. It would have absolved him of the responsibility of being the only one who knew.

He wrestled with his indecision as he had wrestled with it all that day.

But once again he lost.

He slept after that, wrapping himself in his cloak and curling up on the ground within the shadow of the aspen. The earth had dried after the morning rain; the night was warm, and the air was filled with the smells of the forest. His sleep was dreamless and complete. Worries and indecisions slipped away like water shed from his skin. Banished were the wraiths of his lost magic and of the traitor, driven from his mind by the weariness that wrapped protectively about him and gave him peace. He drifted, suspended in the passing of time.

And then he came awake.

A hand clutched his shoulder, tightening. It happened so abruptly, so shockingly, that for a moment he thought he was being attacked. He thrashed himself clear of his cloak and bounded to his feet, wheeling about frantically in the dark.

He found himself face to face with Steff.

The Dwarf was crouched before him, wrapped in his blankets, his hair stiff and spiky, his scarred face pale and drawn and sweating despite the night's comfortable feel. His dark eyes burned with fever, and there was something frightened and desperate in their look.

'Teel's gone,' he whispered harshly.

Morgan took a deep, steadying breath. 'Gone where?' he managed, one hand still fastened tightly about the handle of the dagger at his waist.

Steff shook his head, his breathing ragged in the night's silence. 'I don't know. She left about an hour ago. I saw her. She thought I was sleeping, but ...' He trailed off. 'Something's wrong, Morgan. Something.' He could barely speak. 'Where is she? Where's Teel?'

And instantly, Morgan Leah knew.

CHAPTER

30

I T WAS ON THAT SAME NIGHT that Par Ohmsford went after the Sword of Shannara for the final time.

Darkness had descended on the city of Tyrsis, a cloak of impenetrable black. The rain and mist had turned into fog so thick that the roofs and walls of buildings, the carts and stalls of the markets, even the stones of the streets disappeared into it as if they had melted away. Neither moon nor stars could be seen, and the lights of the city flickered like candles that might be snuffed out at any instant.

Damson Rhee led the Valemen from the garden shed into the haze, cloaked and hooded once more. The fog was suffocating; it was damp and heavy and it clung to clothing and skin alike in a fine sheen. The day had ended early, shoved into nightfall by the appearance of the fog as it rose out of the grasslands below the bluff and built upon itself like a tidal wave until it simply rolled over Tyrsis' walls and buried her. The chill of the previous night had been replaced by an equally unpleasant warmth that smelled of must and rot. All day the people of the city muttered in ill-disguised concern over the strangeness of the weather; when the last of the day's thin, gray light began to fade, they barricaded themselves in their homes as if they were under siege.

Damson and the Valemen found themselves virtually

435

alone in the silent, shrouded streets. When travelers passed by, once or twice only, their presence was but momentary, as if ghosts that had ventured forth from the netherworld only to be swallowed back up again. There were sounds, but they were distant and unrecognizable, muffled by the haze so completely that they lacked both a source and a direction. Footsteps, the soft thudding of boots, rose into the silence from out of nowhere and disappeared the same way. Things moved about them, shapes and forms without definition that floated rather than walked and that came and went with the blink of an eye.

It was a night for imagining things that weren't there.

Par did his best to avoid that, but he was only partially successful. He harboured within him ghosts of his own making, and they seemed to find their identity in the shadows that played in the mist. There, left of the pinprick of light that was a streetlamp, rose the promise Par had made to keep Coll and Damson safe this night when they went down into the Pit — a small, frightened wisp of nothing. There, just behind it, was his belief that he possessed in the magic of the wishsong sufficient power to keep that promise, that he could somehow use the wishsong as the Elfstones had once been used — not as a maker of images and deceptions, but as a weapon of strength and power. His belief chased after his promise, smaller and frailer yet. Across the way, crawling along the barely visible wall of a shop front, hunching itself across the stone blocks as if mired in quicksand, was the guilt he felt at heeding no one but himself as he sought to vindicate both promise and belief — a guilt that threatened to rise up and choke him.

And hanging over all of them like a giant bird of prey — over promise, belief, and guilt, at home within the faceless night, blind and reckless and cast in stone — was his determination to heed the charge of the shade of Allanon and retrieve from the Pit and its Shadowen the missing Sword of Shannara.

It was down there in its vault, he reasurred himself in

the privacy of his thoughts. The Sword of Shannara. It was waiting for him.

But the ghosts would not be banished, and the whisper of their doubts swarmed about his paper-thin self-assurance like scavengers, insistent in their purpose, taunting him for his pride and his foolish certainty, teasing him with vivid images of the fate that awaited them all if he was wrong. He walled himself away from the ghosts, just as he had walled himself away all along. But he could not ignore their presence. He could not pretend they weren't there. He fled down inside himself as the three companions worked their way slowly, blindly through the empty city streets, the fog, and the damp and found refuge in the hard core of his resolve. He was risking everything on being right. But what if he wasn't? Who, besides Coll and Damson, would suffer for his mistake?

He thought for a time about those from whom he had become separated on his odyssey — those who had faded away into the events that had brought him to this night. His parents were Federation prisoners, under house arrest at their home in the village of Shady Vale — kind, gentle folk who had never hurt anyone and knew nothing of what this business was about. What, he wondered, would happen to them if he failed? What of Morgan Leah, the sturdy Dwarf Steff, and the enigmatic Teel? He supposed that even now they were hatching plans against the Federation, hidden away at the Jut, deep within the protective confines of the Parma Key. Would his failure exact a price from them as well? And what of the others who had come to the Hadeshorn? Walker Boh had returned to Hearthstone. Wren had gone back into the Westland. Cogline had disappeared.

And Allanon. What of the Druid shade? What of Allanon, who might never even have existed?

But this wasn't a mistake and he wasn't wrong. He knew it. He was certain of it.

Damson slowed. They had reached the narrow stone steps that wound downward to the sewers. She glanced back at Par and Coll momentarily, her green eyes hard. Then, beckoning them after, she began her descent. The Valemen followed. Par's ghosts went with him, closing tightly about, their breath as real as his own as it brushed against his face. Damson led the way; Coll brought up the rear. No one spoke. Par was not certain he could speak if he tried. His mouth and throat felt as if they were lined with cotton.

He was afraid.

Once again, Damson produced a torch to light the way, a flare of brightness in the dark, and they moved noiselessly ahead. Par glanced at Damson and Coll in turn. Their faces were pale and taut. Each met his gaze briefly and looked away.

It took them less than an hour to reach the Mole. He was waiting for them when they climbed out of the dry well, hunched down in the shadows, a bristling cluster of hair from which two glittering eyes peeked out.

'Mole?' Damson called softly to him.

For a moment, there was no response. The Mole was crouched within a cleft in the rock wall of the chamber, almost invisible in the dark. If it hadn't been for the torch Damson bore, they would have missed him completely. He stared out at them without speaking, as if measuring the truth of who they appeared to be. Finally, he shuffled forward a foot or two and stopped.

'Good evening, lovely Damson,' he whispered. He glanced briefly at the Valemen but said nothing to them.

'Good evening, Mole,' Damson replied. She cocked her head. 'Why were you hiding?'

The Mole blinked like an owl. 'I was thinking.'

Damson hesitated, her brow furrowing. She stuck the torch into a crack in the rock wall behind her where the light would not disturb her strange friend. Then she crouched down in front of him. The Valemen remained standing.

'What have you discovered, Mole?' Damson asked quietly.

The Mole shifted. He was wearing some sort of leather

438

pants and tunic, but they were almost completely enveloped in the fur of his body. His feet were covered with hair as well. He wore no shoes.

'There is a way into the palace of the Kings of Tyrsis and from there into the Pit,' the Mole said. He hunched lower. 'There are also Shadowen.'

Damson nodded. 'Can we get past them?'

The Mole rubbed his nose with his hand. Then he studied her expectantly for a very long time, as if discovering something in her face that before this had somehow escaped his notice. 'Perhaps,' he said finally. 'Shall we try?'

Damson smiled briefly and nodded again. The Mole stood up. He was tiny, a ball of hair with arms and legs that looked as if they might have been stuck on as an afterthought. What was he, Par wondered? A Dwarf? A Gnome? What?

'This way,' the Mole said, and beckoned them after him into a darkened passageway. 'Bring the torch if you wish. We may use it for a while.' He glanced pointedly at the Valemen. 'But there must be no talking.'

So it began. He took them down into the bowels of the city, its deepest sewers, the catacombs that tunneled its basements and sublevels, passageways that no one had used for hundreds of years. Dust lay upon the rock and earthen floors in thick layers that showed no signs of having ever been disturbed. It was warmer here; the damp and fog did not penetrate. The corridors burrowed into the cliffs, rising and falling through rooms and chambers that had once been used as bolt holes for the defenders of the city, to store foodstuffs and weapons, and on occasion to hide the entire population — men, women, and children — of Tyrsis. There were doors now and then, all rusted and falling off their hinges, bolts broken and shattered, wooden timbers rotting. Rats stirred from time to time in the darkness, but fled at the approach of the humans and the light.

Time slipped away. Par lost all track of how long they navigated the underground channels, working their way steadily forward behind the squat form of the Mole. He let them rest now and again, though he himself did not appear to need to. The Valemen and the girl carried water and some small food to keep their strength up, but the Mole carried nothing. He didn't even appear to have a weapon. When they stopped, those few brief times, they sat about in a circle in the near dark, four solitary humans buried under hundreds of feet of rock, three sipping water and nibbling food, the fourth watching like a cat, all of them silent participants in some strange ritual.

They walked until Par's legs began to ache. Dozens of corridors lay behind them, and the Valeman had no idea where they were or what direction they were going. The torch they had started out with had burned away and been replaced twice. Their clothing and boots were coated with dust, their faces streaked with it. Par's throat was so parched he could barely swallow.

Then the Mole stopped. They were in a dry well through which a scattering of tunnels ran. Against the far wall, a heavy iron ladder had been bolted into the rock. It rose into the dark and disappeared.

The Mole turned, pointed up and held one scruffy finger to his mouth. No one needed to be told what that meant.

They climbed the ladder in silence, one foot after the other, listening to the rungs creak and groan beneath their weight. The torchlight cast their shadows on the walls of the well in strange, barely recognizable shapes. The corridors beneath faded into the black.

At the top of the ladder there was a hatchway. The Mole braced himself on the ladder and lifted. The hatchway rose an inch or two, and the Mole peeked out. Satisfied, he pushed the hatchway open, and it fell over with a hollow thud. The Mole scrambled out, Damson and the Valemen on his heels.

They stood in a huge empty cellar, a stone-block dungeon with enormous casks banded by strips of iron, shackles and chains scattered about, cell doors fashioned of iron bars, and countless corridors that disappeared at every turn into black holes. A single broad stairway at the far end of the cellar lifted into shadow. The silence was immense, as if become so much a part of the stone that it echoed with a voice of its own. Darkness hung over everything, chased only marginally by the smoking light of the single torch the company bore.

The Mole edged close against Damson and whispered something. Damson nodded. She turned to the Valeman, pointed to where the stairs rose into the black and mouthed the word 'Shadowen.'

The Mole took them quickly through the cellar to a tiny door set into the wall on their right, unlatching it soundlessly, ushering them through, then closing it tightly behind them. They were in a short corridor that ended at another door. The Mole took them through this door as well and into the room beyond.

The room was empty with nothing in it but some pieces of wood that might have come from packing crates, some loose pieces of metal shielding, and a rat that scurried hastily into a crack in the wall's stone blocks.

The Mole tugged at Damson's sleeve and she bent down to listen. When he had finished, she faced the Valemen.

'We have come under the city, through the cliffs at the west end of the People's Park and into the palace. We are in its lower levels, down where the prisons used to be. It was here that the armies of the Warlock Lord attempted a breakthrough in the time of Balinor Buckhannah, the last King of Tyrsis.'

The Mole said something else. Damson frowned. 'The Mole says that there may be Shadowen in the chambers above us — not Shadowen from the Pit, but others. He says he can sense them, even if he cannot see them.'

'What does that mean?' Par asked at once.

'It means that sensing them is as close as he cares to get.' Damson's face tilted away from the torchlight as she scanned the ceiling of the room. 'It means that if he gets close enough to see them, they can undoubtedly see him as well.'

Par followed her gaze uneasily. They had been talking in whispers, but was it safe to do even that? 'Can they hear us?' he asked, lowering his voice further, pressing his mouth close to her ear.

She shook her head. 'Not here, apparently. But we won't be able to talk much after this.' She looked over at Coll. He was motionless in the dark. 'Are you all right?' Coll nodded, white-faced nevertheless, and she looked back at Par. 'We are some distance from the Pit still. We have to use the catacombs under the palace to reach the cliff hatch that will let us in. Mole knows the way. But we have to be very careful. There were no Shadowen in the tunnels yesterday when he explored, but that may have changed.'

Par glanced at the Mole. He was squatting down against one wall, barely visible at the edge of the torch-light, eyes gleaming as he watched them. One hand stroked the fur of his arm steadily.

The Valeman felt a twinge of uneasiness. He shifted his feet until he had placed Damson between the Mole and himself. Then he said, so that he believed only she could hear, 'Are you sure we can trust him?'

Damson's pale face did not change expression, but her eyes seems to look somewhere far, far away. 'As sure as I can be.' She paused. 'Do you think we have a choice?'

Par shook his head slowly.

Damson's smile was faint and ironic. 'Then I guess there is no point worrying about it, is there?'

She was right, of course. There was no help for his suspicions unless he agreed to turn back, and Par Ohmsford had already decided that he would never do that. He wished that he could test the magic of the wishsong, that he had thought to do so earlier — just to see if it could do what he thought it could. That would provide some reassurance. Yet he knew, even as he completed the thought, that there was no way to test the magic, at least not in the way that he needed to — that it would not reveal itself. He could make images, yes. But he could not summon the wishsong's real power, not until there was something to use it against. And maybe not even then.

But the power was there, he insisted once again, a desperate reassurance against the whisperings of his ghosts. It had to be.

'We won't be needing this anymore,' Damson said, gesturing with the torch. She handed it to Par, then fished through her pockets and produced a pair of strange white stones streaked with silver. She kept one and handed him the other. 'Put out the torch.' she instructed him. 'Then place your hands tightly about the stone to warm it. When you feel its heat, open them.'

Par doused the torch in the dust, smothering the flame. The room went completely black. He put the strange stone between his hands and held it there. After a few seconds, he could feel it grow warm. When he took one hand away, the stone gave off a meager silver light. As his eyes adjusted, he saw that the light was strong enough to reveal the faces of his companions and an area beyond of several feet.

'If the light begins to dim, warm the stone again with your hands.'

She closed her hand over his, tight about the stone, held it there, then lifted it away. The silver light radiated even more brightly. Par smiled in spite of himself, the amazement in his eyes undisguised. 'That's a nice trick, Damson,' he breathed.

'A bit of my own magic, Valeman,' she said softly, and her eyes fixed on him. 'Street magic from a street girl. Not so wonderful as the real thing, but reliable. No smoke, no smell, easily tucked away. Better than torchlight, if we want to stay hidden.'

'Better,' he agreed.

The Mole took them from the room then, guiding them into the black without the benefit of any light at all, apparently needing none. Damson followed, carrying one stone, Par came after carrying the other, and Coll once again brought up the rear. They went out through a second door into a passageway that twisted about and ran

443

past other doors and rooms. They moved soundlessly, their boots scraping softly on the stone, their breathing a shallow hiss, their voices stilled.

Par found himself wondering again about the Mole. Could the Mole be trusted? Was the little fellow what he claimed to be or something else? The Shadowen could appear as anyone. What if the Mole was a Shadowen? So many questions once again, and no answers to be found. There was no one he could trust, he thought bleakly — no one but Coll. And Damson. He trusted Damson.

Didn't he?

He beat back the sudden cloud of doubt that threatened to envelop him. He could not afford to be asking such questions now. It was too late to make any difference, if the answers were the wrong ones. He was risking everything on his judgment of Damson, and he must believe that his judgment was correct.

Thinking again of the Shadowen enigma, the mystery of who and what they were and how they could be so many things, he was led to wonder suddenly if there were Shadowen in the outlaw camp, if the enemy they were so desperately seeking to remain hidden from was in fact already among them. The traitor that Padishar Creel sought could be a Shadowen, one that only looked human, that only seemed to be one of them. How were they to know? Was magic the only test that would reveal them? Was that to be the purpose of the Sword of Shannara, to reveal the true identity of the enemy they sought? It was what he had wondered from the moment Allanon had sent him in search of the Sword. But how impossible it seemed that the talisman could be meant for such endless, exhausting work. It would take forever to test it against everyone who might be a Shadowen.

He heard in his mind the whisper of Allanon's voice.

Only through the Sword can truth be revealed and only through truth shall the Shadowen be overcome.

Truth. The Sword of Shannara was a talisman that revealed truth, destroyed lies, and laid bare what was real against the pretense of what only seemed so. That was the use to which Shea Ohmsford had put it when the little Valeman had defeated the Warlock Lord. It must be the use for which the talisman was meant this time as well.

They climbed a long, spiral staircase to a landing. A door in the wall before them stood closed and bolted. The wall behind and the ceiling above were lost in shadow. The drop below seemed endless. They crowded together on the landing while the Mole worked the bolts, first one, then another, then a third. One by one, the metal grating softly, they slid free. The Mole twisted the handle slowly. Par could hear the sound of his own breathing, of his pulse, and of his heartbeat, all working in response to the fear that coursed through him. He could feel Shadowen watching, hidden in the dark. He could sense their presence. It was irrational, imagined — but there nevertheless.

Then the Mole had the door open, and they slipped quickly through.

They found themselves in a tiny, windowless room with a stairwell in the exact center that spiralled down into utter pitch and a door to the left that opened into a empty corridor. Light filtered through slits in the walls of the corridor, faint and wispy. At the corridor's far end, maybe a hundred feet away, a second door stood closed.

The Mole motioned them into the corridor and shut the first door behind them. Par edged over to one of the slits in the wall and peered out. They were somewhere in the palace, above ground again. Cliffs rose up before him, their slopes a tangle of pine trees. Above the trees, clouds hung thick across the skyline, their underbellies flat and hard and sullen.

Par drew back. Darkness was beginning to give way to daylight. It was almost morning. They had been walking all night.

'Lovely Damson,' the Mole was saying softly as Par rejoined them. 'There is a catwalk ahead that crosses the palace court. Using it will save us considerable time. If you and your friends will keep watch, I will make certain the shadow things are nowhere about.'

Damson nodded. 'Where do you want us?'

Where he wanted them was at each end of the corridor, listening for the sound of anything that might approach. It was agreed that Coll would remain where he was. Par and Damson went on with the Mole to the corridor's far end. There, after a reassuring nod, the Mole slipped past them through the door and was gone.

The Valeman and the girl sat across from each other, close against the door. Par glanced back down the dimly lighted corridor to make certain that Coll was in sight. His brother's rough face lifted briefly, and Par gave a cursory wave. Coll waved back.

They sat in silence then, waiting. The minutes passed and the Mole did not return.

Par grew uneasy. He edged closer to Damson. 'Do you think he is all right?' he asked in a whisper.

She nodded without speaking.

Par sat back again, took a deep breath, and let it out slowly. 'I hate waiting like this.'

She made no response. Her head tilted back against the wall and her eyes closed. She remained like that for a long time. Par thought she might be sleeping. He looked down the corridor again at Coll, found him exactly as he had left him, and turned back to Damson. Her eyes were open, and she was looking at him.

'Would you like me to tell you something about myself that no one else knows?' she asked quietly.

He studied her face wordlessly — her fine, even features, so intense now, her emerald eyes and pale skin shadowed under the sweep of her red hair. He found her beautiful and enigmatic, and he wanted to know everything about her.

'Yes,' he replied.

She moved over until their shoulders were touching. She glanced at him briefly, then looked away. He waited.

'When you tell someone a secret about yourself, it is like giving a part of yourself away,' she said. 'It is a gift, but it is worth much more than something you buy. I don't tell many people things about myself. I think it is because I have never had much besides myself, and I don't want to give what little I have away.'

She looked down and her hair spilled forward, veiling her face so that he couldn't see it clearly. 'But I want to give something to you. I feel close to you. I have from the very beginning, from that first day in the park. Maybe it is because we have the magic in common — we share that. Maybe that is what makes me feel we're alike. Your magic is different from mine, but that doesn't matter. What matters is that using the magic is how we live. It is what we are. Magic gives us our identity.'

She paused, and he thought she might be waiting for a response, so he nodded. He could not tell if she saw the nod or not.

She sighed. 'Well, I like you, Elf-boy. You are stubborn and determined, and sometimes you don't take notice of anything or anyone around you — only of yourself. But I am like that, too. Maybe that is how we keep ourselves from becoming exactly like everyone else. Maybe it is how we survive.'

She paused, then faced him. 'I was thinking that if I were to die, I would want to leave something of myself with you, something that only you would have. Something special.'

Par started to protest, but she put her fingers quickly against his mouth. 'Just let me finish. I am not saying that I think I will die, but it is surely possible. So perhaps telling you this secret will protect me against it, like a talisman, and keep me safe from harm. Do you see?'

His mouth tightened and she took her fingers away. 'Do you remember when I first told you about myself, that night you escaped from the Federation watch after the others were captured? I was trying to convince you that I was not your betrayer. We told ourselves some things about each other. You told me about the magic, about how it worked. Do you remember?'

He nodded. 'You told me that you were orphaned

when you were eight, that the Federation was responsible.'

She drew her knees up like a child. 'I told you that my
family died in a fire set by Federation Seekers after it was
discovered that my father was supplying weapons to the
Movement. I told you a street magician took me in shortly
after and that is how I learned my trade.'

She took a deep breath and shook her head slowly.
'What I told you was not entirely true. My father didn't
die in the fire. He escaped. With me. It was my father
who raised me, not an aunt, not a street magician. I grew
up with street magicians and that is how I learned my
trade, but it was my father who looked after me. It is my
father who looks after me still.'

Her voice shook. 'My father is Padishar Creel.'

Par stared in wonderment. 'Padishar is your father?'

Her eyes never left him. 'No one knows but you. It is
safer that way. If the Federation found out who I was,
they would use me to get to him. Par, what you needed to
know that night when I told you about my childhood was
that I could never betray anyone after the way my family
was betrayed to the Federation. That much was true. That
is why my father, Padishar Creel, is so furious that there
might be a traitor among his own men. He can never
forget what happened to my mother, brother, and sister.
The possibility of losing anyone close to him again
because of someone's treachery terrifies him.'

She paused, studying him intently. 'I promised never
to tell anyone who I really was, but I am breaking that
promise for you. I want you to know. It is something I can
give you that will belong only to you.'

She smiled then, and some of the tension drained out
of him. 'Damson,' he said, and he found himself smiling
back at her. 'Nothing had better happen to you. If it does,
it will be my fault for talking you into bringing me down
here. How will I face Padishar, then?' His voice was a soft
whisper of laughter. 'I wouldn't be able to go within a
hundred miles of him!'

She started laughing as well, shaking soundlessly at

the thought, and she shoved him as if they were children at play. Then she reached over and hugged herself against him. He let her hold him without responding for a moment, his eyes straying to where Coll sat, a vague shadow at the other end of the hall. But his brother wasn't looking. There had been friends and traitors mixed up in this enterprise from the beginning, and it had been all but impossible to tell which was which. Except for Coll. And now Damson.

He put his arms around her and hugged her back.

Moments later, the Mole returned. He came upon them so quietly that they didn't even know he was there until the door began to open against them. Par released Damson and jumped to his feet, the blade of his long knife flashing free. The Mole peeked through the door and then ducked hurriedly out of sight again. Damson grabbed Par's arm. 'Mole!' she whispered. 'It's all right!'

The Mole's roundish face eased back into view. Upon seeing that the weapon had been put away, he came all the way through. Coll was already hastening down the corridor. When he joined them, the Mole said, calm again, 'The catwalk is clear and will stay that way if we hurry. But be very quiet, now.'

They slipped from the corridor and found themselves on a balcony that encircled a vast, empty rotunda. They moved quickly along it, passing scores of closed, latched doors and shadowed alcoves. Halfway around, the Mole led them into a hall and down its length to a set of iron-barred doors that opened out over the main courtyard of the palace. A catwalk ran across the drop to a massive wall. The courtyard had once been a maze of gardens and winding pathways; now there were only crumbling flagstones and bare earth. Beyond the wall lay the dark smudge of the Pit.

The Mole beckoned anxiously. They stepped onto the catwalk, feeling it sway slightly beneath their combined weight, hearing it creak in protest. The wind blew in quick gusts, and the sound it made as it rushed over the bare stone walls and across the empty courtyard was a low, sad moan. Weeds whipped and shuddered below them and debris scattered about the court, careening from wall to wall. There was no sign of life, no movement in the shadows and murk, no Shadowen in sight.

They crossed the catwalk quickly, once they were upon it, ignoring the creak and groan of its iron stays. They kept their feet moving, their hands on the railing, and their eyes focused carefully ahead, watching the palace wall draw closer. When the crossing was completed they stepped hurriedly onto the battlement, each reaching back to help the next person, grateful to be done.

The Mole took them into a stairwell where they found a fresh set of steps winding downward into blackness. Using the light of the stones Damson had supplied, they descended silently. They were close now; the stone of the wall was all that separated them from the Pit. Par's excitement sent the blood pumping through him, a pounding in his ears, and his nerve endings tightened.

Just a few more minutes . . .

At the bottom of the stairwell, there was a passageway that ended at a weathered, ironbound wooden door. The Mole walked to the door and stopped. When he turned back to face them, Par knew at once what lay beyond.

'Thank you, Mole,' he said softly.

'Yes, thank you,' Damson echoed.

The Mole blinked shyly. Then he said, 'You can look through here.'

He reached up and carefully pulled back a tiny shutter that revealed a slit in the wood. Par stepped forward and peered out.

The floor of the Pit stretched away before him, a vast, fog-bound wilderness of trees and rock, a bottomland that was strewn with decaying logs and tangled brush, a darkness in which shadows moved and shapes formed and faded again like wraiths. The wreckage of the Bridge of Sendic lay just to the right and disappeared into the gray haze.

Par squinted into the murk a moment longer. There was no sign of the vault that held the Sword of Shannara.

But he had seen it, right there, just beyond the wall of the palace. The magic of the wishsong had revealed it. It was out there. He could feel its presence like a living thing.

He let Damson take a lock, then Coll. When Coll stepped back, the three of them stood facing one another.

Par slipped out of his cloak. 'Wait for me here. Keep watch for the Shadowen.'

'Keep watch for them yourself,' Coll said bluntly, shrugging off his own cloak. 'I'm going with you.'

'I'm going, too,' said Damson.

But Coll blocked her way instantly. 'No, you're not. Only one of us can go besides Par. Look about you, Damson. Look at where we are. We're in a box, a trap. There is no way out of the Pit except through this door and no way out of the palace except back up the stairs and across the catwalk. The Mole can watch the catwalk, but he can't watch this door at the same time. You have to do that.'

Damson started to object, but Coll cut her short. 'Don't argue, Damson. You know I'm right. I've listened to you when I should; this time you listen to me.'

'It doesn't matter who listens to whom. I don't want either of you going,' insisted Par sharply.

Coll ignored him, shifting his short sword in his belt until it was in front of him. 'You don't have any choice.'

'Why shouldn't I be the one to go?' Damson demanded angrily.

'Because he's my brother!' Coll's voice cracked like a whip, and his rough features were hard. But when he spoke next, his voice was strangely soft. 'It has to be me; it's why I came in the first place. It's why I'm here at all.'

Damson went still, frozen and voiceless. Her gaze shifted. 'All right,' she agreed, but her mouth was tight and angry as she said it. She turned away. 'Mole, watch the catwalk.'

The little fellow was glancing at each of them in turn, a mix of uncertainty and bewilderment in his bright eyes.

451

'Yes, lovely Damson,' he murmured and disappeared up the stairs.

Par started to say something more, but Coll took him by the shoulders and pushed him back up against the weathered door. Their eyes met and locked.

'Let's not waste any more time arguing about this, huh?' Coll said. 'Let's just get it over with. You and me.'

Par tried to twist free, but Coll's big hands were like iron clamps. He sagged back, frustrated. Coll released him. 'Par,' he said, and the words were almost a plea. 'I spoke the truth. I have to go.'

They faced each other in silence. Par found himself thinking of what they had come through to reach this point, of the hardships they had endured. He wanted to tell Coll that it all meant something, that he loved him, that he was frightened for him now. He wanted to remind his brother about his duck feet, to warn him that duck feet were too big to sneak around in. He thought he might scream.

But, instead, he said simply, 'I know.'

Then he moved to the heavy, weathered door, released its fastenings and pulled on its worn handle. The door swung open, and the half-light and fog, the rancid smells and cloying chill, the hiss of swamp sounds, and the high, distant call of a solitary bird rushed in.

Par looked back at Damson Rhee. She nodded. That she would wait? That she understood? He didn't know.

With Coll beside him, he stepped out into the Pit.

CHAPTER

31

WHERE WAS TEEL?

Morgan Leah knelt hurriedly beside Steff, touched his face, and felt the chill of his friend's skin through his fingers. Impulsively, he put his hands on Steff's shoulders and gripped him, but Steff did not seem to feel it. Morgan took his hands away and rocked back on his heels. His eyes scanned the darkness about him, and he shivered with something more than the cold. The question repeated itself in his mind, racing from corner to corner as if trying to hide, a dark whisper.

Where was Teel?

The possibilities paraded before him. Gone to get Steff a drink of water, something hot to eat, another blanket perhaps? Gone to look around, spooked from her sleep by one of those instincts or sixth-senses that kept you alive when you were constantly being hunted? Close by, about to return?

The possibilities shattered into broken pieces and disappeared. No. He knew the answer. She had gone into the secret tunnel. She had gone there to lead the soldiers of the Federation into the Jut from the rear. She was about to betray them one final time.

No one but Damson, Chandos, and I know the other way — now that Hirehone is dead.

That was what Padishar Creel had told him, speaking

453

of the hidden way out, the tunnel — something Morgan had all but forgotten until now. He shivered at the clarity of the memory. If his reasoning was correct and the traitor was a Shadowen who had taken Hirehone's identity to follow them to Tyrsis, then that meant the Shadowen had possession of Hirehone's memories and knew of the tunnel as well.

And if the Shadowen was now Teel . . .

Morgan felt the hairs on the back of his neck prickle. It would take the Federation months to take the Jut by siege. But what if the siege was nothing more than a decoy? What if the Creeper itself had been, even in failing, just a decoy? What if the Federation's intent from the beginning was to take the Jut from within, by betrayal once again, through the tunnel that was to be the outlaws' escape?

I have to do something!

Morgan Leah felt leaden. He must leave Steff and get to Padishar Creel at once. If his suspicions about Teel were correct, she had to be found and stopped.

If.

The horror of what he was thinking knotted in his throat — that Teel could be the very worst of the enemies that had hunted them all since Culhaven, that she could have deceived them so completely, especially Steff, who believed that he owed her his life, and who was in love with her. The knot tightened. He knew that the horror he felt didn't come from the possibility of the betrayal — it came from the certainty of it.

Steff saw something of that horror mirrored in his eyes and grappled angrily with him. 'Where is she, Morgan? You know! I can see it!'

Morgan did not try to break away. Instead, he faced his friend and said, 'I think I know. But you have to wait here, Steff. You have to let me go after her.'

'No.' Steff shook his head adamantly, his scarred face knotting. 'I'm going with you.'

'You can't. You're too sick . . .'

'I'm going, Morgan! Now where is she?'

The Dwarf was shaking with fever, but Morgan knew that he was not going to be able to free himself unless he did so by force. 'All right,' he agreed, taking a slow breath. 'This way.'

He put his arm under his friend to support him and started into the dark. He could not leave Steff behind, even knowing how difficult it would make things having his friend along. He would simply do what he must in spite of him. He stumbled suddenly and sought his way back to his feet, hauling Steff up with him, not having seen the coil of rope that lay on the ground in his path. He forced himself to slow, realizing as he did so that he hadn't even taken time yet to think through what he was going to do. His mind began to sort out the specifics of what he had surmised. Teel was the traitor. He must accept that. Steff could not, but he must. Teel was the one . . .

He stopped himself.

No. Not Teel. Don't call that thing Teel. Teel is dead. Or close enough to being dead that there is no distinction to be made. So, not Teel. The Shadowen that hid in Teel.

His breathing grew rapid as he hastened through the night, Steff clinging to him. The Shadowen must have left her body and taken Hirehone's in order to follow Padishar's little company to Tyrsis and betray it to the Federation. Then it had abandoned Hirehone's body, returned to the camp, killed the watch because it could not ascend the Jut unseen, and reinhabited Teel. Steff had never realized what was happening. He had believed Teel poisoned. The Shadowen had let him think as much. It had even managed to cast suspicion on Hirehone with that tale of following him to the bluff before falling into unconsciousness. He wondered how long Teel had been a Shadowen. A long time, he decided. He pictured her in his mind, nothing more than a shell, a hollow skin, and his teeth ground at the image. He remembered Par's description of what it had been like when the Shadowen on Toffer Ridge, the one who had taken the body of the little girl, had tried to come into him. He remembered the horror and revulsion the Valeman had expressed. That was what it must have been like for Teel.

There was no further time to consider the matter. They were approaching the main cave. The entrance was ablaze with torchlight. Padishar Creel stood there. The outlaw chief was awake, just as Morgan had hoped he would be, brilliant in his scarlet clothing, talking with the men who cared for the sick and injured, his broadsword and long knives strapped in place.

'What are you doing?' Steff cried angrily. 'This is between you and me, Morgan! Not him!'

But Morgan ignored his protestations, dragging him into the light. Padishar Creel turned as the two men staggered up to him and caught hold of them by the shoulders.

'Whoa, now, lads — slow down! What's the reason for charging about in the dark like this?' The other man's grip tightened as Steff tried to break free, and the rough voice lowered. 'Careful, now. Your eyes say something's frightened you. Let's keep it to ourselves. What's happened?'

Steff was rigid with anger, and his eyes were hard. Morgan hesitated. The others in Padishar's company were looking at them curiously, and they were close enough to hear what he might say. He smiled disarmingly. 'I think I've found the person you've been looking for,' he said to the big man.

Padishar's face went taut momentarily, then quickly relaxed. 'Ah, that's all, is it?' He spoke as much to his men as to them, his voice almost joking. 'Well, well, come on outside a minute and tell me about it.' He put his arm about their shoulders as if all was well, waved to those listening and steered the Highlander and the Dwarf outside.

There he backed them into the shadows. 'What is it you've found?' he demanded.

Morgan glanced at Steff, then shook his head. He was sweating now beneath his clothes, and his face was flushed. 'Padishar,' he said. 'Teel's missing. Steff doesn't know what's happened to her. I think she might have gone down into the tunnel.'

He waited, his gaze locked on the big man, silently pleading with him not to demand more, not to make him explain. He still wasn't certain, not absolutely, and Steff would never believe him in any case.

Padishar understood. 'Let's have a look. You and I, Highlander.'

Steff seized him by the arm. 'I'm coming too.' His face was bathed in sweat, and his eyes were glazed, but there was no mistaking his determination in the matter.

'You haven't the strength for it, lad.'

'That's my concern!'

Padishar's face turned sharply into the light. It was crisscrossed with welts and cuts from last night's battle, tiny lines that seemed to reflect the deeper scars the Dwarf bore. 'And none of mine,' he said quietly. 'So long as you understand.'

They went into the sick bay, where Padishar took one of the other outlaws aside and spoke softly to him. Morgan could just make out what was being said.

'Rouse Chandos,' Padishar ordered. 'Tell him I want the camp mobilized. Check the watch, be certain it's awake and alive. Make ready to move everyone out. Then he's to come after me into the hidden tunnel, the bolt hole. With help. Tell him I said that we're all done with secrecy, so it doesn't matter now who knows what he's about. Now get to it!'

The man scurried off, and Padishar beckoned wordlessly to Morgan and Steff. He led them through the main cavern into the deep recesses where the stores were kept. He lit three torches, kept one for himself and gave one each to the Highlander and the Dwarf. Then he took them into the very back of the farthest chamber where the cases were stacked against the rock wall, handed his torch to Morgan, grabbed the cases in both hands and pulled. The false front opened into the tunnel beyond. They slipped through the opening, and Padishar pulled the packing crates back into place.

'Stay close,' he warned.

They hurried into the dark, the torches smoking above them, casting their weak yellow light against the shadows. The tunnel was wide, but it twisted and turned. Rock outcroppings made the passage hazardous; there were stalactites and stalagmites both, wicked stone icicles. Water dripped from the ceiling and pooled in the rock, the only sound in the silence other than their footsteps. It was cold in the caves, and the chill quickly worked its way through Morgan's clothes. He shivered as he trailed after Padishar. Steff trailed them both, walking haltingly on his own, his breathing ragged and quick.

Morgan wondered suddenly what they were going to do when they found Teel.

He made a mental check of his weapons. He had the newly acquired broadsword strapped across his back, a dagger in his belt, and another in his boot. At his waist, he wore the shortened scabbard and the remains of the Sword of Leah.

Not much help against a Shadowen, he thought worriedly. And how much use would Steff be, even after he discovered the truth? What would he do?

If only I still had the magic . . .

He forced the thought away from him, knowing what it would lead to, determined that he would not allow his indecision to bind him again.

The seconds ticked by, and the echo of their passing reverberated in the sound of the men's hurried footsteps. The walls of the tunnel narrowed down sharply, then broadened out again, a constant change of size and shape. They passed through a series of underground caverns where the torchlight could not even begin to penetrate the shadows that cloaked the hollow, vaulted roofs. A little farther on, a series of crevices opened before them, several almost twenty feet across. Bridges had been built to span them, wooden slats connected by heavy ropes, the ropes anchored in the rock by iron pins. The bridges swayed and shook as they crossed, but held firm.

All the while they walked, they kept watch for Teel. But there was no sign of her.

Steff was beginning to have trouble keeping up. He was enormously strong and fit when well, but whatever sickness had attacked him — if indeed it was a sickness and he had not been poisoned as Morgan was beginning to surmise — had left him badly worn. He fell repeatedly and had to drag himself up again each time. Padishar never slowed. The big man had meant what he said — Steff was on his own. The Dwarf had gotten this far on sheer determination, and Morgan did not see how he could maintain the pace the outlaw chief was setting much longer. The Highlander glanced back at his friend, but Steff didn't seem to see him, his haunted eyes searching the shadows, sweeping the curtain of black beyond the light.

They were more than a mile into the mountain when a glimmer of light appeared ahead, a pinprick that quickly became a glow. Padishar did not slow or bother to disguise his coming. The tunnel broadened, and the opening ahead brightened with the flicker of torches. Morgan felt his heartbeat quicken.

They entered a massive underground cavern ablaze with light. Torches were jammed into cracks in the walls and floors, filling the air with smoke and the smell of charred wood and burning pitch. At the center of the cavern a huge crevice split the chamber floor end to end, a twisted maw that widened and narrowed as it worked its way from wall to wall. Another bridge had been built to span the crevice at its narrowest juncture, this one a massive iron structure. Machinery had been installed on the near side of the crevice to raise and lower it. The bridge was down at the moment, linking the halves of the cavern floor. Beyond, the flat rock stretched away to where the tunnel disappeared once more into darkness.

Teel stood next to the bridge machinery, hammering.

Padishar Creel came to a stop, and Morgan and Steff quickly came up beside him. Teel hadn't heard or seen them yet, their footfalls muffled by the sounds she was making as she hammered, their torchlight enveloped by the cavern's own brightness.

Padishar laid down his torch. 'She's jammed the machinery. The bridge can't be raised again.' His eyes found Steff's. 'If we let her, she will bring the Federation right to us.'

Steff stared wildly. 'No!' he gasped in disbelief.

Padishar ignored him. He unsheathed his broadsword and started forward.

Steff lunged after him, tripping, falling, then crying out frantically, 'Teel!'

Teel whirled about. She held an iron bar in her hands, the smooth surface bright with nicks from where she had been smashing the bridge works. Morgan could see the damage clearly now, winches split apart, pulleys forced loose, gears stripped. Teel's hair glittered in the light, flashing with traces of gold. She faced them, her mask revealing nothing of what she was thinking, an expressionless piece of leather strapped about her head, the eyeholes dark and shadowed.

Padishar closed both big hands about the broadsword, lifting its blade into the light. 'End of the line for you, girl,' he snapped.

The echo filled the cavern, and Steff came to his feet, lurching ahead. 'Padishar, wait!' he howled.

Morgan jumped to intercept him, caught hold of his arm and jerked him about. 'No, Steff, that isn't Teel! Not anymore!' Steff's eyes were bright with anger and fear. Morgan lowered his voice, speaking quickly, calmly. 'Listen to me. That's a Shadowen, Steff. How long since you've seen the face beneath that mask? Have you looked at it? It isn't Teel under there anymore. Teel's been gone a long time.'

The anger and fear turned to horror. 'Morgan, no! I would know! I could tell if it wasn't her!'

'Steff, listen . . .'

'Morgan, he's going to kill her! Let me go!'

Steff jerked free and Morgan grabbed him again. 'Steff, look at what she's done! She's betrayed us!'

'No!' the Dwarf screamed and struck him.

Morgan went down in a heap, the force of the blow

460

leaving him stunned. His first reaction was surprise; he hadn't thought it possible that Steff could still possess such strength. He pushed himself to his knees, watching as the Dwarf raced after Padishar, screaming something the Highlander couldn't understand.

Steff caught up with the big man when they were just a few steps from Teel. The Dwarf threw himself on Padishar from behind, seizing his sword arm, forcing it down. Padishar shouted in fury, tried to break free and failed. Steff was all over him, wrapped about him like a second skin.

In the confusion, Teel struck. She was on them like a cat, the iron bar lifted. The blows hammered down, quick and unchallenged, and in a matter of seconds both Padishar and Steff lay bleeding on the cavern floor.

Morgan staggered to his feet alone to face her.

She came for him unhurriedly, and as she did so there was a moment in which all of his memories of her came together at once. He saw her as the small, waiflike girl that he had met at Culhaven in the darkened kitchen of Granny Elise and Auntie Jilt, her honey-colored hair just visible beneath the folds of her hooded cloak, her face concealed by the strange leather mask. He saw her listening at the edges of the campfire's light to the conversation shared by the members of the little company who had journeyed through the Wolfsktaag. He saw her crowded close to Steff at the base of the Dragon's Teeth before they went to meet with the shade of Allanon, suspicious, withdrawn, fiercely protective.

He forced the images away, seeing her only as she was now, striking down Padishar and Steff, too swift and strong to be what she pretended. Even so, it was hard to believe that she was a Shadowen, harder still to accept that they had all been fooled so completely.

He pulled free the broadsword and waited. He would have to be quick. Maybe he would have to be more than quick. He remembered the creatures in the Pit. Iron alone hadn't been enough to kill them.

Teel went into a crouch as she reached him, her eyes

dark pools within the mask, the look that was reflected there hard and certain. Morgan gave a quick feint, then cut viciously at the girl's legs. She sidestepped the blow easily. He cut again — once, twice. She parried, and the shock of the sword blade striking the iron bar washed through him. Back and forth they lunged, each waiting for the other to provide an opening.

Then a series of blows brought the flat of the broadsword against the iron bar and the blade shattered. Morgan ripped at the bar with what was left, the handle catching it and twisting it free. Both sword and bar skittered away into the dark.

Instantly Teel threw herself on Morgan, her hands closing about his throat. She was incredibly strong. He had only a moment to act as he fell backward. His hand closed on the dagger at his waist, and he shoved it into her stomach. She drew back, surprised. He kicked at her, thrusting her back, drew the dagger in his boot and jammed it into her side, ripping upward.

She backhanded him so hard that he was knocked off his feet. He landed with a grunt, jarred so that the breath was knocked from his body. Spots danced before his eyes, but he gasped air into his lungs and scrambled up.

Teel was standing where he had left her, the daggers still embedded in her body. She reached down and calmly pulled them free, tossing them away.

She knows I can't hurt her, he thought in despair. *She knows I haven't anything that can stop her.*

She seemed unhurt as she advanced on him. There was blood on her clothing, but not much. There was no expression to be seen behind the mask, nothing in her eyes or on her mouth, just an emptiness that was as chilling as ice. Morgan edged away from her, searching the cavern floor for any kind of weapon at all. He caught sight of the iron bar and desperately snatched it up.

Teel seemed unworried. There was a shimmer of movement all about her body, a darkness that seemed to lift slightly and settle back again — as if the thing that lived within her was readying itself.

462

Morgan backed away, maneuvering toward the crevice. Could he somehow manage to lure this thing close enough to the drop to shove it over? Would that kill it? He didn't know. He knew only that he was the only one left to stop it, to prevent it from betraying the entire Jut, all those men, to the Federation. If he failed, they would die.

But I'm not strong enough — not without the magic!

He was only a few feet from the crevice edge. Teel closed the gap that separated them, moving swiftly. He swung at her with the iron bar, but she caught the bar in her hand, broke his grip on it, and flung it away.

Then she was on him, her hands at his throat, choking off his air, strangling him. He couldn't breathe. He fought to break free, but she was far too strong. His eyes squeezed shut against the pain, and there was a coppery taste in his mouth.

A huge weight dropped across him.

'Teel, don't!' he heard someone cry — a disembodied voice choked with pain and fatigue.

Steff!

The hands loosened marginally, and his eyes cleared enough so that he could see the Dwarf atop Teel, arms locked about her, hauling back. There was blood streaking his face. A gaping wound had been opened at the top of his head.

Morgan's right hand groped at his belt and found the handle of the Sword of Leah.

Teel ripped free of Steff, turned and pulled him about. There was a fury in her eyes, in the way the cords of her throat went taut, that even the mask could not conceal. Yanking Steff's dagger from its sheath, she buried it deep in his chest. Steff toppled backward, gasping.

Teel turned back then to finish Morgan, half-raised over him, and he thrust the broken blade of his sword into her stomach.

Back she reared, screaming so that Morgan arched away from her in spite of himself. But he kept his hands fastened on the handle of the sword. Then something strange began to happen. The Sword of Leah grew warm and flared with light. He could feel it stir and come to life.

The magic! Oh, Shades — it was the magic!

Power surged through the blade, linking them together, flowing into Teel. Then crimson fire exploded through her. Her hands tore at the blade, at her body, at her face, and the mask came free. Morgan Leah would never forget what lay beneath, a countenance born of the blackest pits of the netherworld, ravaged and twisted and alive with demons that he had only imagined might exist. Teel seemed to disappear entirely, and there was only the Shadowen behind the face, a thing of blackness and no substance, an emptiness that blocked and swallowed the light.

Invisible hands fought to thrust Morgan away, to strip him of his weapon and of his soul.

'Leah! Leah!' He sounded the battle cry of his ancestors, of the Kings and Princes of his land for a thousand years, and that single word became the talisman to which he clung.

The Shadowen's scream became a shriek. Then it collapsed, the darkness that sustained it crumbling and fading away. Teel returned, a frail, limp bundle, empty of life and being. She fell forward atop him, dead.

It took several minutes for Morgan to find the strength to push Teel away. He lay there in the wetness of his own sweat and blood, listening to the sudden silence, exhausted, pinned to the cavern floor by the dead girl's weight. His only thought was that he had survived.

Then slowly his pulse quickened. It was the magic that had saved him. It was the magic of the Sword of Leah. Shades, it wasn't gone after all! At least some part of it still lived, and if part of it lived then there was a chance that it could be completely restored, that the blade could be made whole again, the magic preserved, the power ...

His ruminations scattered uncontrollably in their frantic passing and disappeared. He gulped air into his lungs, mustered his strength and pushed Teel's body aside. She was suprisingly light. He looked down at her as he rolled onto his hands and knees. She was all shrunken in, as if something had dissolved her bones. Her face was twisted and scarred, but the demons he had seen there were gone.

Then he heard Steff gasp. Unable to rise, he crawled to his friend. Steff lay on his back, the dagger still protruding from his chest. Morgan started to remove it, then slowly drew back. He knew at a glance that it was too late to make any difference. Gently, he touched his friend's shoulder.

Steff's eyes blinked open and shifted to find him. 'Teel?' he asked softly.

'She's dead,' Morgan whispered back.

The Dwarf's scarred face tightened with pain, then relaxed. He coughed blood. 'I'm sorry, Morgan. Sorry ... I was blind, so this had to happen.'

'It wasn't only you.'

'I should have seen ... the truth. Should have recognized it. I just ... didn't want to, I guess.'

'Steff, you saved our lives. If you hadn't awakened me ...'

'Listen to me. Listen, Highlander. You are my closest friend. I want you ... to do something.' He coughed again, then tried to steady his voice. 'I want you to go back to Culhaven and make certain ... that Granny Elise and Auntie Jilt are all right.' His eyes squeezed shut and opened again. 'You understand me, Morgan? They will be in danger because Teel ...'

'I understand,' Morgan cut him short.

'They are all I have left,' Steff whispered, reaching out to fasten his hand on Morgan's arm. 'Promise me.'

Morgan nodded wordlessly, then said, 'I promise.'

Steff sighed, and the words he spoke were little more than a whisper. 'I loved her, Morgan.'

Then his hand slid away, and he died.

*

465

Everything that happened after that was something of a blur to Morgan Leah. He stayed at Steff's side for a time, so dazed that he could think of doing nothing else. Then he remembered Padishar Creel. He forced himself to his feet and went over to check on the big man. Padishar was still alive, but unconscious, his left arm broken from warding off the blows struck by the iron bar, his head bleeding from a deep gash. Morgan wrapped the head injury to stop the blood loss, but left the arm alone. There was no time to set it now.

The machinery that operated the bridge was smashed and there was no way that he could repair it. If the Federation was sending an attack force into the tunnels tonight — and Morgan had to assume they were — then the bridge could not be raised to prevent their advance. It was only a few hours until dawn. That meant that Federation soldiers were probably already on their way. Even without Teel to guide them they would have little trouble following the tunnel to the Jut.

He found himself wondering what had become of Chandos and the men he was supposed to bring with him. They should have arrived by now.

He decided he couldn't risk waiting for them. He had to get out of there. He would have to carry Padishar since his efforts to waken the other had failed. Steff would have to be left behind.

It took him several minutes to decide what was needed. First he salvaged the Sword of Leah, slipping it carefully back into its makeshift sheath. Then he carried Teel and afterward Steff to the edge of the crevice and dropped them over. He wasn't sure it was something he could do until after it was done. It left him feeling sick and empty inside.

He was incredibly tired by then, so weak that he did not think he could make it back through the tunnels by himself, let alone carrying Padishar. But somehow he managed to get the other across his shoulders and, with one of the torches to guide him, he started out.

He walked for what seemed like hours, seeing nothing,

hearing only the sound of his own boots as they scraped across the stone. Where was Chandos, he asked himself over and over again? Why hadn't he come? He stumbled and fell so many times that he lost count, tripped up by the tunnel's rock and by his own weariness. His knees and hands were torn and bloodied, and his body began to grow numb. He found himself thinking of curious things, of his boyhood and his family, of the adventures he had shared growing up with Par and Coll, of the steady, reliable Steff and the Dwarves of Culhaven. He cried some of the time, thinking of what had become of them all, of how much of the past had been lost. He talked to Padishar when he felt himself on the verge of collapse, but Padishar slept on

He walked, it seemed, forever.

Yet when Chandos finally did appear, accompanied by a swarm of outlaws and Axhind and his Trolls, Morgan was no longer walking at all. He had collapsed in the tunnel, exhausted.

He was carried with Padishar the rest of the way, and he tried to explain what had happened. He was never certain exactly what he said. He knew that he rambled, sometimes incoherently. He remembered Chandos saying something about a new Federation assault, that the assault had prevented him coming as quickly as he had wanted. He remembered the strength of the other's gnarled hand as it held his own.

It was still dark when they regained the bluff, and the Jut was indeed under attack. Another diversion, perhaps, to draw attention away from the soldiers sneaking through the tunnels, but one that required dealing with nevertheless. Arrows and spears flew from below, and the siege towers had been hauled forward. Numerous attempts at scaling the heights had already been repelled. Preparations for making an escape, however, were complete. The wounded were set to move out, those that could walk risen to their feet, those that couldn't placed on litters. Morgan went with the latter group as they were carried back into the caves to where the tunnels began.

467

Chandos appeared, his fierce, black-bearded face hovering close to Morgan as he spoke.

'All is well, Highlander,' Morgan would remember the other man saying, his voice a faint buzz. 'There's Federation soldiers in the hidden tunnel already, but the rope bridges have been cut. That will slow them a bit — long enough for us to be safely away. We'll be going into these other tunnels. There's a way out through them as well, you see, one that only Padishar knows. It's rougher going, a good number of twists and turns and a few tricky choices to be made. But Padishar knows what to do. Never leaves anything to chance. He's awake again, bringing the rest of them down, making sure everyone's out. He's a tough one, old Padishar. But no tougher than you. You saved his life, you did. You got him out of there just in time. Rest now, while you can. You won't have long.'

Morgan closed his eyes and drifted off to sleep. He slept poorly, brought awake time and again by the jostling of the litter on which he lay and by the sounds of the men who were crowded about him, whispering and crying out in pain. Darkness cloaked the tunnels, a hazy black that even torchlight could not cut through entirely. Faces and bodies passed in and out of view, but his lasting impression was of impenetrable night.

Once or twice, he thought he heard fighting, the clash of weapons, the grunts of men. But there was no sense of urgency in those about him, no indication that anything threatened, and he decided after a time that he must be dreaming.

He forced himself awake finally, not wishing to sleep any longer, afraid to sleep when he was not certain what was happening. Nothing around him appeared to have changed. It seemed that he could not have been asleep for more than a few moments.

He tried lifting his head, and pain stabbed down the back of his neck. He lay back again, thinking suddenly of Steff and Teel and of the thinness of the line that separated life and death.

Padishar Creel came up beside him. He was heavily bandaged about the head, and his arm was splinted and strapped to his side. 'So, lad,' he greeted quietly.

Morgan nodded, closed his eyes and opened them again.

'We're getting out now,' the other said. 'All of us, thanks to you. And to Steff. Chandos told me the story. He had great courage, that one.' The rough face looked away. 'Well, the Jut's lost, but that's a small price to pay for our lives.'

Morgan found that he didn't want to talk about the price of lives. 'Help me up, Padishar,' he said quietly. 'I want to walk out of here.'

The outlaw chief smiled. 'Don't we all, lad,' he whispered.

He reached out his good hand and pulled Morgan to his feet.

CHAPTER

32

I T WAS A NIGHTMARISH WORLD where Par and Coll Ohmsford walked. The silence was intense and endless, a cloak of emptiness that stretched further than time itself. There were no sounds, no cries of birds or buzzings of insects, no small skitterings or scrapes, not even the rustle of the wind through the trees to give evidence of life. The trees rose skyward like statues of stone carved by some ancient civilization and left in mute testament to the futility of man's works. They had a gray and wintry look to them, and even the leaves that should have softened and colored their bones bore the look of a scarecrow's rags. Scrub brush and saw grass rubbed up against their trunks like stray children, and bramble bushes twisted together in a desperate effort to protect against life's sorrows.

The mist was there as well, of course. The mist was there first, last and always, a deep and pervasive sea of gray that shut everything vibrant away. It hung limp in the air, unmoving as it smothered trees and brush, rocks and earth, and life of any kind or sort, a screen that blocked away the sun's light and warmth. There was an inconsistency to it, for in some places it was thin and watery and merely gave a fuzzy appearance to what it sought to cloak, while in others it was as impenetrable as ink. It brushed at the skin with a cold, damp insistence that whispered of dead things.

Par and Coll moved slowly, cautiously through their waking dream, fighting back against feeling that they had become disembodied. Their eyes darted from shadow to shadow, searching for movement, finding only stillness. The world they had entered seemed lifeless, as if the Shadowen they knew to be hidden there were not in fact there at all but were simply a lie of the dream that their senses could not reveal.

They moved quickly to the rubble of the Bridge of Sendic so that they could follow its broken trail to the vault. Their footsteps were soundless in the tall grasses and the damp, yielding earth. At times their boots disappeared entirely in the carpet of mist. Far glanced back to the door they had come through. It was nowhere to be seen.

In seconds, the cliff face itself, the whole of what remained of the palace of the Kings of Tyrsis, had vanished as well.

As if it had never been, Par thought darkly.

He felt cold and empty inside, but hot where sweat made the skin beneath his clothing feel prickly and damp. The emotions that churned inside would not be sorted out or dispersed; they screamed with voices that were garbled and confused, each desperate to be heard, each mindless. He could feel his heart pounding within his chest, his pulse racing in response, and he sensed the imminency of his own death with every step he took. He wished again that he could summon for just a moment the magic, even in its most rudimentary form, so that he could be reassured that he possessed some measure of power to defend himself. But use of the magic would alert whatever lived within the Pit, and he wanted to believe that as yet that had not happened.

Coll brushed his arm, pointing to where the earth had opened before them in a wicked-looking crack that disappeared into blackness. They would have to go around. Par nodded, leading the way. Coll's presence was reassuring to him, as if the simple fact of his being there might somehow deter the evil that threatened. Coll — his large, blocky form like a rock at Par's back, his rough face so determined that it seemed his strength of will alone would see them through. Par was glad beyond anything words could express that his brother had come. It was a selfish reaction, he knew, but an honest one. Coll's courage in this business was to a large extent the source of his own.

They skirted the pitfall and worked their way back to the tumbled remains of the bridge. Everything about them was unchanged, silent and unmoving, empty of life.

But then something shimmered darkly in the mists ahead, a squarish shape that lifted out of the rubble.

Par took a deep steadying breath. It was the vault.

They moved toward it hurriedly, Par in the lead, Coll just a step behind. The stone-block walls came sharply into focus, losing the surreal haziness in which the mists had cloaked it. Brush grew up against its walls, vines looped over its sloped roof, and moss colored its foundation in shadings of rust and dark green. The vault was larger than Par had imagined, a good fifty feet across and as much as twenty feet high at its peak. It had the look and feel of a crypt.

The Valemen reached its nearest wall and edged their way cautiously around the corner to the front. They found writing carved there in the pitted stone, an ancient scroll ravaged by time and weather, many of its words nearly erased. They stopped, breathless, and read:

Herein lies the heart and soul of the nations.
Their right to be free men,
Their desire to live in peace,
Their courage to seek out truth.
Herein lies the Sword of Shannara.

Just beyond, a massive stone door stood ajar. The brothers glanced at each other wordlessly, then started forward. When they reached the door, they peered inside. There was a wall that formed a corridor leading left; the corridor disappeared into darkness.

Par frowned. He hadn't expected the vault to be a complex structure; he had thought it would be nothing more than a single chamber with the Sword of Sharnara at its center. This suggested something else.

He looked at Coll. His brother was clearly upset, peering about anxiously, studying first the entry, then the dark tangle of the forest surrounding them. Coll reached out and pulled on the door. It moved easily at his touch.

He bent close. 'This looks like a trap,' he whispered so softly that Par could barely hear him.

Par was thinking the same thing. A door to a vault that was three hundred years old and had been subjected to the climate of the Pit should not give way so readily. It would be a simple matter for someone to shut it again once he was inside.

And yet he knew he would go in anyway. He had already made up his mind to do so. He had come through too much to turn back now. He raised his eyebrows and gave Coll a questioning look. What was Coll suggesting, the look asked?

Coll's mouth tightened, knowing that Par was determined to continue, that the risks no longer made any difference. It took a supreme effort for him to speak the words. 'All right. You go after the Sword; I'll stand guard out here.' One big hand grasped Par's shoulder. 'But hurry!'

Par nodded, smiled triumphantly, and clutched his brother back.

Then he was through the door, moving swiftly down the passageway into the dark. He went as far as he could with the faint light of the outside world to guide him, but it soon faded. He felt along the walls for the corridor's end, but couldn't find it. He remembered then that he still carried the stone Damson had given him. He reached into his pocket, took it out, clasped it momentarily between his hands to warm it, and held it out before him. Silver light flooded the darkness. His smile grew fierce. Again, he started forward, listening to the silence, watching the shadows.

473

He wound along the passageway, descended a set of stairs, and entered a second corridor. He traveled much further than he would have thought possible, and for the first time he began to grow uneasy. He was no longer in the vault, but somewhere deep underground. How could that be?

Then the passageway ended. He stepped into the room with a vaulted ceiling and walls carved with images and runes, and he caught his breath with a suddenness that hurt.

There, at the very center of the room, blade downward in a block of red marble, was the Sword of Shannara.

He blinked to make certain that he was not mistaking what he saw, then moved forward until he stood before it. The blade was smooth and unmarked, a flawless piece of workmanship. The handle was carved with the image of a hand thrusting a torch skyward. The talisman glistened like new metal in the soft light, faintly blue in color.

Par felt his throat tighten. It was indeed the Sword.

A sharp rush of elation surged through him. He could hardly keep himself from calling out to Coll, from shouting aloud to him what he was feeling. A wave of relief swept over him. He had gambled everything on what had amounted to little more than a hunch — and his hunch had been right. Shades, it had been right all along! The Sword of Shannara had indeed been down in the Pit, concealed by its tangle of trees and brush, by the mist and night, by the Shadowen ...!

He shoved aside his elation abruptly. Thinking of the Shadowen reminded him in no uncertain terms how precarious his position was. There would be time to congratulate himself later, when Coll and he were safely out of this rat hole.

There were stairs cut in a stone base on which rested the block of marble and the Sword embedded in it, and he started for them. But he had taken only a single step when something detached itself from the darkness of the wall beyond. Instantly, he froze, terror welling up in his throat.

474

A single word screamed out in his mind.

Shadowen!

But he saw at once that he was mistaken. It wasn't a Shadowen. It was a man dressed all in black, cloaked and hooded, the insigne of a wolf's head sewn on his chest.

Par's fear did not lessen when he realized who the other was. The man approaching him was Rimmer Dall.

At the entrance to the vault, Coll waited impatiently. He stood with his back against the stone, just to one side of the opening, his eyes searching the mist. Nothing moved. No sound reached him. He was alone, it seemed; yet he did not feel that way. The dawn's light filtered down through the canopy of the trees, washing him in its cold, gray haze.

Par had been gone too long already, he thought. It shouldn't be taking him this much time.

He glanced quickly over his shoulder at the vault's black opening. He would wait another five minutes; then he was going in himself.

Rimmer Dall came to a stop a dozen feet away from Par, reached up casually and pulled back the hood of his cloak. His craggy face was unmasked, yet in the half-light of the vault it was so streaked with shadows as to be practically unrecognizable. It made no difference. Par would have known him anywhere. Their one and only meeting that night so many weeks ago at the Blue Whisker was not something he would ever forget. He had hoped it would never be repeated; yet here they were, face to face once more. Rimmer Dall, First Seeker of the Federation, the man who had tracked him across the length and breadth of Callahorn and had nearly had him so many times, had caught up with him at last.

The door through which Par had entered remained open behind him, a haven that beckoned. The Valeman poised to flee.

'Wait, Par Ohmsford,' the other said, almost as if reading his thoughts. 'Are you so quick to run? Do you frighten so easily?'

Par hesitated. Rimmer Dall was a huge, rangy man; his red-bearded face might have been chiseled out of stone, so hard and menacing did it appear. Yet his voice — and Par had not forgotten it either — was soft and compelling.

'Shouldn't you hear what I have to say to you first?' the big man continued. 'What harm can it do? I have been waiting here to talk to you for a very long time.'

Par stared. 'Waiting?'

'Certainly. This is where you had to come sooner or later once you made up your mind about the Sword of Shannara. You have come for the Sword, haven't you? Of course, you have. Well, then, I was right to wait, wasn't I? We have much to discuss.'

'I wouldn't think so.' Par's mind raced. 'You tried to arrest Coll and me in Varfleet. You imprisoned my parents in Shady Vale and occupied the village. You have been chasing after me and those with me for weeks.'

Rimmer Dall folded his arms. Par noticed again how the left was gloved to the elbow. 'Suppose I stand here and you stand there,' the big man offered. 'That way you can leave any time you choose. I won't do anything to prevent it.'

Par took a deep breath and stepped back. 'I don't trust you.'

The big man shrugged. 'Why should you? However, do you want the Sword of Shannara or don't you? If you want it, you must first listen to me. After you've done so, you can take it with you if you wish. Fair enough?'

Par felt the hairs on the back of his neck prickle in warning. 'Why should you make a bargain like that after all you've done to keep me from getting the Sword?'

'Keep you from getting the Sword?' The other laughed, a low, pleasant chuckle. 'Par Ohmsford. Did you once think to ask for the Sword? Did you ever consider the possibility that I might simply give it to you? Wouldn't that have been easier than sneaking about the city and trying to steal it like a common thief?' Rimmer Dall shook his head slowly. 'There is so much that you don't know. Why not let me tell it to you?'

Par glanced about uncertainly, not willing to believe that this wasn't some sort of trick to put him off his guard. The vault was a maze of shadows that whispered of other things lurking there, hidden and waiting. Par rubbed briskly the stone that Damson had given him to brighten its light.

'Ah, you think I have others concealed in the darkness with me, is that it?' Rimmer Dall whispered, the words coming from somewhere deep down inside his chest to rumble through the silence. 'Well, here then!'

He raised his gloved hand, made a quick motion with it, and the room was flooded with light. Par gasped in surprise and took another step back.

'Do you think, Par Ohmsford, that you are the only one who has use of magic?' Rimmer Dall asked quietly. 'Well, you aren't. As a matter of fact, I have magic at my command that is much greater than yours, greater perhaps than that of the Druids of old. There are others like me, too. There are many in the Four Lands who possess the magic of the old world, of the world before the Four Lands and the Great Wars and man himself.'

Par stared at him wordlessly.

'Would you listen to me now, Valeman? While you still can?'

Par shook his head, not in response to the question he had been asked, but in disbelief. 'You are a Seeker,' he said finally. 'You hunt those who use magic. Any use — even by you — is forbidden!'

Rimmer Dall smiled. 'So the Federation has decreed. But has that stopped you from using your magic, Par? Or your uncle Walker Boh? Or anyone who possesses it? It is, in fact, a foolish decree, one that could never be enforced except against those who don't care about it in the first place. The Federation dreams of conquest and empire-building, of uniting the lands and the Races under its rule. The Coalition Council schemes and plans, a remnant of a world that has already destroyed itself once in the wars of power. It thinks itself chosen to govern because the Councils of the Races are no more and the Druids gone. It sees the disappearance of the Elves as a blessing. It seizes the provinces of the Southland, threatens Callahorn until it submits, and destroys the wilful Dwarves simply because it can. It sees all this as evidence of its mandate to rule. It believes itself omniscient! In a final gesture of arrogance it outlaws magic! It doesn't once bother asking what purpose magic serves in the scheme of things — it simply denies it!'

The dark figure hunched forward, the arms unfolding. 'The fact of the matter is that the Federation is a collection of fools that understand nothing of what the magic means, Valeman. It was magic that brought our world to pass, the world in which we live, in which the Federation believes itself supreme. Magic creates everything, makes everything possible. And the Federation would dismiss such power as if it were meaningless?'

Rimmer Dall straightened, looming up against the strange light he had created, a dark form that seemed only vaguely human.

'Look at me, Par Ohmsford,' he whispered.

His body began to shimmer, then to separate. Par watched in horror as a dark shape rose up against the shadows and half-light, its eyes flaring with crimson fire.

'Do you see, Valeman?' Rimmer Dall's disembodied voice whispered with a hiss of satisfaction. 'I am the very thing the Federation would destroy, and they haven't the faintest idea of it!'

The irony was wasted on Par, who saw nothing beyond the fact that he had placed himself in the worst possible danger. He shrank from the man who called himself Rimmer Dall, the creature who wasn't in fact a man at all, but was a Shadowen. He edged backward, determined to flee. Then he remembered the Sword of Shannara, and abruptly, recklessly, changed his mind. If he could get to the Sword, he thought fiercely, he would have a weapon with which to destroy Rimmer Dall.

But the Shadowen seemed unconcerned. Slowly the dark shape settled back into Rimmer Dall's body and the big man's voice returned. 'You have been lied to, Valeman. Repeatedly. You have been told that the Shadowen are evil things, that they are parasites who invade the bodies of men to subvert them to their cause. No, don't bother to deny it or to ask how I know,' he said quickly, cutting short Par's exclamation of surprise. 'I know everything about you, about your journey to Culhaven, the Wilderun, the Hadeshorn, and beyond. I know of your meeting with the shade of Allanon. I know of the lies he told you. Lies, Par Ohmsford — and they begin with the Druids! They tell you what you must do if the Shadowen are to be destroyed, if the world is to be made safe again! You are to seek the Sword, Wren the Elves, and Walker Boh vanished Paranor — I know!'

The craggy face twisted in anger. 'But listen now to what you were not told! The Shadowen are not an aberration that has come to pass in the absence of the Druids! We are their successors! We are what evolved out of the magic with their passing! And we are not monsters invading men, Valeman — we are men ourselves!'

Par shook his head to deny what he was hearing, but Rimmer Dall brought up his gloved hand quickly, pointing to the Valeman. 'There is magic in men now as there was once magic in the creatures of fairie. In the Elves, before they took themselves away. In the Druids later.' His voice had gone soft and insistent. 'I am a man like any other except that I possess the magic. Like you, Par. Somehow I inherited it over the generations of my family that lived before me in a world in which use of magic was commonplace. The magic scattered and seeded itself — not within the ground, but within the bodies of the men and women of the Races. It took hold and grew in some of us, and now we have the power that was once the province of the Druids alone.'

He nodded slowly, his eyes fixed on Par. 'You have such power. You cannot deny it. Now you must understand the truth of what having that power means.'

He paused, waiting for Par to respond. But Par had gone cold to the bone as he sensed what was coming, and he could only howl silently in denial.

'I can see in your eyes that you understand,' Rimmer Dall said, his voice softer still. 'It means, Par Ohmsford, that you are a Shadowen, too.'

Coll counted the seconds in his mind, stretching the process out for as long as he could, thinking as he numbered each that Par must surely appear. But there was no sign of his brother.

The Valeman shook his head in despair. He paced away from the craggy wall of the vault and back again. Five minutes was up. He couldn't wait any longer. He had to go in. It frightened him that in doing so he would be leaving their backs unprotected, but he had no choice. He had to discover what had happened to Par.

He took a deep breath to steady himself as he prepared to enter.

That was when the hands seized him from behind and dragged him down.

'You're lying!' Par shouted at Rimmer Dall, forgetting his fear, taking a step forward threateningly.

'There is nothing wrong with being a Shadowen,' the other answered sharply. 'It is only a word that others have used to label something they don't fully understand. If you can forget the lies you have been told and think of the possibilities, you will be better able to understand what I am telling you. Suppose for a moment that I am right. If the Shadowen are simply men who are meant to be successors to the Druids, then wielding the magic is not only their right, it is their responsibility. The magic is a trust — wasn't that what Allanon told Brin Ohmsford when he died and marked her with his blood? The magic is a tool that must be used for the betterment of the Races and the Four Lands. What is so difficult to accept about that? The problem is not with myself or with you or with the others like us. The problem is with fools like those who govern the Federation and think that anything they cannot control must be suppressed! They see anyone different from themselves as an enemy!'

The strong face tightened. 'But who is it that seeks domination over the Four Lands and its people? Who drives the Elves from the Westland, enslaves the Dwarves in the East, besieges the Trolls in the North, and claims all of the Four Lands as its own? Why is it, do you think, that the Four Lands begin to wither and die? Who causes that? You have seen the poor creatures who live in the Pit. Shadowen, you think them, don't you? Well, they are — but their condition is brought about by their keepers. They are men like you and me. The Federation locks them away because they show evidence of possessing magic and are thought dangerous. They become what they are thought to be. They are starved of the life the magic could feed them and they grow mad! That child on Toffer Ridge — what happened to her that caused her to become what she is? She was starved of the magic she needed, of the use of it, and of everything that would have kept her sane. She was driven into exile. Valeman, it is the Federation that causes disruption in the Four Lands with its foolish, blind decrees and its crushing rule! It is the Shadowen who have a chance to set things right!

'As for Allanon, he is first and always a Druid with a Druid's mind and ways. What he seeks is known only to him and likely to remain that way. But you are well advised to be cautious of accepting too readily what he tells you.'

He spoke with such conviction that for the first time Par Ohmsford began to doubt. What if the shade of Allanon had lied? Wasn't it true that the Druids had always played games with those from whom they wanted something? Walker had warned him that this was so, that it was a mistake to accept what Allanon was telling them. Something in what Rimmer Dall was saying seemed to whisper that it was true in this instance as well. It was possible, he thought in despair, that he had been misled completely.

The tall, cloaked form before him straightened. 'You belong with us, Par Ohmsford,' he said quietly.

Par shook his head quickly. 'No.'

'You are one of us, Valeman. You can deny it as long and as loudly as you like, but the fact remains. We are the same, you and I — possessors of the magic, successors to the Druids, keepers of the trust.' He paused, considering. 'You still fear me, don't you? A Shadowen. Even the name frightens you. It is the unavoidable result of having accepted as truth the lies you have been told. You think of me as an enemy rather than as kindred.'

Par said nothing.

'Let us see who lies and who tells the truth. There.' He pointed suddenly to the Sword. 'Remove it from its stone, Valeman. It belongs to you; it is your bloodright as heir to the Elven house of Shannara. Pick it up. Touch me with it. If I am the black creature you have been warned against, then the Sword will destroy me. If I am an evil that hides within a lie, the Sword will reveal it. Take it in your hands, then. Use it.'

Par remained motionless for a long moment, then bounded up the steps to the block of red marble, seized the Sword of Shannara in both hands, and pulled it forth. It slid free unhindered, gleaming and smooth. He turned quickly and faced Rimmer Dall.

'Come close, Par,' the other whispered. 'Touch me.'

Memories whirled madly in Par's mind, bits and pieces of the songs he had sung, of the stories he had told. What he held now was the Sword of Shannara, the Elven talisman of truth against which no lie could stand.

He came down off the steps, the carved hilt with its burning torch pressed into his palms, the blade held cautiously before him. Rimmer Dall stood waiting. When Par was within striking distance, he stretched out the blade of the talisman and laid it firmly against the other's body.

Nothing happened.

Keeping his eyes riveted on the other, he held the blade steady and willed that the truth be revealed. Still nothing happened. Par waited for as long as he could stand it, then lowered the blade in despair and stepped away.

'Now you know. There is no lie about me,' Rimmer Dall said. 'The lie is in what you have been told.'

Par found that he was shaking. 'But why would Allanon lie? What purpose could that possibly serve?'

'Think for a moment on what you have been asked to do.' The big man was relaxed, his voice calm and reassuring. 'You have been asked to bring back the Druids, to restore to them their talismans, to seek our destruction. The Druids want to regain what was lost to them, the power of life and magic. Is that any different, Par, from what the Warlock Lord sought to do ten centuries ago?'

'But you hunted us!'

'To talk to you, to explain.'

'You imprisoned my parents!'

'I kept them safe from harm. The Federation knew of you and would have used them to find you, if I hadn't gone to them first.'

Par caught his breath, his arguments momentarily exhausted. Was what he was being told true? Shades, was everything the lie that Rimmer Dall claimed it to be? He could not believe it. yet he could not bring himself to disbelieve it either. His confusion wrapped him like a blanket and left him feeling small and vulnerable.

'I have to think,' he said wearily.

'Then come with me and do so,' Rimmer Dall responded at once. 'Come with me and we shall talk more of this. You have many questions that require answers, and I can give them to you. There is much you need to know about how the magic can be used. Come, Valeman. Put aside you fears and misgivings. No harm shall come to you — never to one whose magic is so promising.'

He spoke reassuringly, compellingly, and for an instant Par was almost persuaded. It would have been so easy to

483

agree. He was tired, and he wanted this odyssey to end. It would be comforting to have someone to talk to about the frustrations of possessing the magic. Rimmer Dall would surely know, having experienced them himself. As much as he hated to admit it, he no longer felt threatened by the man. There seemed to be no reason to deny what he was asking.

But he did nevertheless. He did without really understanding why. 'No,' he said quietly.

'Think of what we can share if you come with me,' the other persisted. 'We have so much in common! Surely you have longed to talk of your magic, the magic you have been forced to conceal. There has never been anyone for you to do that with before me. I can feel the need in you; I can sense it! Come with me! Valeman, you have . . .'

'No.'

Par stepped away. Something ugly whispered suddenly in his mind, some memory that did not yet have a face, but whose voice he clearly recognized.

Rimmer Dall watched him, his craggy features gone suddenly hard. 'This is foolish, Valeman.'

'I am leaving,' Par said quietly, tense now, back on his guard. What was it that bothered him so? 'And I am taking the Sword.'

The black-cloaked form became another shadow in the half-light. 'Stay, Valeman. There are dark secrets kept from you, things that would be better learned from me. Stay and hear them.'

Par edged toward the passageway that had brought him in.

'The door is directly behind you,' Rimmer Dall said suddenly, his voice sharp. 'There are no passageways, no stairs. That was all illusion, my magic invoked to closet you long enough so that we might talk. But if you leave now, something precious will be destroyed. Truth waits for you, Valeman — and there is horror in its face. You cannot withstand it. Stay, and listen to me! You need me!'

Par shook his head. 'You sounded for a moment, Rimmer Dall, like those others, those Shadowen who look

484

nothing like you outwardly, yet speak with your need. Like them, you would possess me.'

Rimmer Dall stood silently before him, not moving, simply watching as he backed away. The light the First Seeker had produced faded, and the chamber slid rapidly into darkness.

Par Ohmsford grasped the Sword of Shannara in both hands and bolted for freedom.

Rimmer Dall had been right about the passageways and stairs. There were none. It was all illusion, a magic Par should have recognized at once. He burst from the blackness of the vault directly into the gray half-light of the Pit. The damp and the mist closed about him instantly. He blinked and whirled about, searching.

Coll.

Where was Coll?

He stripped the cloak from his back and wrapped it hurriedly about the Sword of Shannara. Allanon had said he would need it — if Allanon was still to be believed. At the moment, he didn't know. But the Sword should be cared for; it must have purpose. Unless it had lost its magic. Could it have lost its magic?

'Par.'

The Valeman jumped, startled by the voice. It was right behind him, so close that it might have been a whisper in his ear if not for the harshness of its sound. He whirled.

And there was Coll.

Or what had once been Coll.

His brother's face was barely recognizable, ravaged by some inner torment that he could only begin to imagine, a twisting that had distorted the familiar features and left them slack and lifeless. His body was misshapen as well, all pulled out of joint and hunched over as if the bones had been rearranged. There were marks on his skin, tears and lesions, and the eyes burned with a fever he recognized immediately.

'They took me,' Coll whispered despairingly. 'They made me. Please, Par, I need you. Hug me? Please?'

Par cried out, howling as if he would never stop, willing the thing before him to go away, to disappear from his sight and mind. Chills shook him, and the emptiness that opened inside threatened to collapse him completely.

'Coll!' he sobbed.

His brother stumbled and jerked toward him, arms outstretched. Rimmer Dall's warning whispered in Par's mind — the truth, the truth, the horror of it! Coll was a Shadowen, had somehow become one, a creature like the others in the Pit that Rimmer Dall claimed the Federation had destroyed! How? Par had been gone only minutes, it seemed. What had been done to his brother?

He stood there, stunned and shaking, as the thing before him caught hold of him with its fingers, then with its arms, enfolding him, whispering all the time, 'Hug me, hug me,' as if it were a litany that would set it free. Par wished he were dead, that he had never been born, that he could somehow disappear from the earth and leave all that was happening behind. He wished a million impossible things — anything that could save him. The Sword of Shannara dropped from his nerveless fingers, and he felt as if everything he had known and believed in had in a single instant been betrayed.

Coll's hands began to rip at him.

'Coll, no!' he screamed.

Then something happened deep inside, something that he struggled against for only an instant's time before it overpowered him. A burning surged within his chest and spread outward through his body like a fire out of control. It was the magic — not the magic of the wishsong, the magic of harmless images and pretended things, but the other. It was the magic that had belonged once to the Elfstones, the magic that Allanon had given to Shea Ohmsford all those years ago, that had seeded itself in Wil Ohmsford and passed through generations of his family to him, changing, evolving, a constant mystery. It was alive in him, a magic greater than the wishsong, hard and unyielding.

It rushed through him and exploded forth. He screamed to Coll to let go of him, to get away, but his brother did not seem to hear. Coll, a ruined creature, a caricature of the blood and flesh human Par had loved, was consumed with his own inner madness, the Shadowen that he had become needing only to feed. There was no response beyond his frantic effort to do so. The magic took him, enveloped him, and in an instant turned him to ash.

Par watched in horror as his brother disintegrated before his eyes. Stunned, speechless, he collapsed to his knees, feeling his own life disappear with Coll's.

Then other hands were reaching for him, grappling with him, pulling him down. A whirl of twisted, ravaged faces and bodies pressed into him. The Shadowen of the Pit had come for him as well. There were scores of them, their hands grasping for him, their fingers ripping and tearing as if to shred him. He felt himself coming apart, breaking beneath the weight of their bodies.

And then the magic returned, exploding forth once more, and they were flung away like deadwood.

The magic took form this time, an unbidden thought brought to life. It coalesced in his hands, a jagged shard of blue fire, the flames as cool and hard as iron. He did not understand it yet, did not comprehend its source or being — yet he understood instinctively its purpose. Power radiated through him. Crying out in fury he swung his newfound weapon in a deadly arc, cutting through the creatures about him as if they were made of paper. They collapsed instantly, their voices unintelligible and remote as they died. He lost himself in the haze of his killing, striking out like a madman, giving sweet release to the fury and despair that had been born with the death of his brother.

The death he had caused!

The Shadowen fell back from him, those he did not destroy, staggering and shambling like stringed puppets.

Bellowing at them still, gripping the shard of magic fire in one hand, Par reached down and snatched up the fallen Sword of Shannara.

He felt it burn him, searing his hand, the pain harsh and shocking.

Instantly his own magic flared and died. He jerked back in surprise, tried to invoke it anew and found he could not. The Shadowen started for him at once. He hesitated, then ran. Down the line of bridge rubble he raced, tripping and sliding on the dampened earth, gasping in rage and frustration. He could not tell how close the creatures of the Pit were to him. He ran without looking back, desperate to escape, fleeing as much from the horror of what had befallen him as from the Shadowen in pursuit.

He was almost to the wall of the cliff when he heard Damson call. He ran for her, his mind shriveled so that he could think of nothing but the need to get free. The Sword of Shannara was clutched tightly to his chest, the burning gone now, just a simple blade wrapped within his muddied cloak. He went down, sprawling on his face, sobbing. He heard Damson again, calling out, and he shouted back in answer.

Then she had him in her arms, hauling him back to his feet, pulling him away, asking, 'Par, Par, what's wrong with you? Par, what's happened?'

And he, replying in gasps and sobs, 'He's dead, Damson! Coll's dead! I've killed him!'

The door into the cliff wall stood open ahead, a black aperture with a small, furry, wide-eyed creature framed in the opening. With Damson supporting him, he stumbled through and heard the door slam shut behind him.

Then everything and everyone disappeared in the white sound of his scream.

CHAPTER

33

1 T WAS RAINING IN THE DRAGON'S TEETH, a cold, gray, insistent drizzle that masked the skyline from horizon to horizon. Morgan Leah stood at the edge of a trailside precipice and stared out from beneath the hood of his cloak. South, the foothills appeared as low, rolling shadows against the haze. The Mermidon could not be seen at all. The world beyond where he stood was a vague and distant place, and he had an unpleasant sense of not being able to fit back into it again.

He blinked away the flurry of drops that blew into his eyes, shielding himself with his hands. His reddish hair was plastered against his forehead, and his face was cold. Beneath his sodden clothing, his body was scraped and sore. He shivered, listening to the sounds around him. The wind whipped across the cliffs and through the trees, its howl rising momentarily above the thunder that rumbled far to the north. Flood streams cascaded through the rocks behind him, rushing and splashing, the water building on itself as it tumbled downward into the mist.

It was a day for rethinking one's life, Morgan decided grimly. It was a day for beginning anew.

Padishar Creel came up behind him, a cloaked, bulky form. Rain streaked his hard face, and his clothing, like Morgan's, was soaked through.

'Time to be going?' he asked quietly.

Morgan nodded.

'Are you ready, lad?'

'Yes.'

Padishar looked away into the rain and sighed. 'It's not turned out as we expected, has it?' he said quietly. 'Not a bit of it.'

Morgan thought a minute, then replied, 'I don't know, Padishar. Maybe it has.'

Under Padishar's guidance, the outlaws had emerged from the tunnels below the Jut early that morning and made their way east and north into the mountains. The trails they followed were narrow and steep and made dangerously slick by the rain, but Padishar felt it was safer to travel them than to try to slip through the Kennon Pass, which would surely be watched. The weather, bad as it was, was more help than hindrance. The rain washed away their footprints, erasing any trace of where they had been or where they were going. They had seen nothing of the Federation army since their flight began. Any pursuit was either bogged down or confused. The Jut might be lost, but the outlaws had escaped to fight another day.

It was now midafternoon, and the ragtag band had worked its way to a point somewhere above the juncture of the Mermidon where it branched south to the Rainbow Lake and east to the Rabb Plains. On a bluff where the mountain trails diverged in all directions, they had paused to rest before parting company. The Trolls would turn north for the Charnals and home. The outlaws would regroup at Firerim Reach, another of their redoubts. Padishar would return to Tyrsis in search of Damson and the missing Valeman. Morgan would go east to Culhaven and keep his promise to Steff. In four weeks' time, they would all meet again at Jannisson Pass. Hopefully by then the Troll army would be fully mobilized and the Movement would have consolidated its splintered groups. It would be time to begin mapping out a specific strategy for use in the continuing struggle against the Federation.

If any of them were still alive to do the mapping,

Morgan thought dismally. He wasn't convinced any longer that they would be. What had happened with Teel had left him angry and doubting. He knew now how easy it was for the Shadowen — and therefore their Federation allies — to infiltrate those who stood against them. Anyone could be the enemy; there was no way to tell. Betrayal could come from any quarter and likely would. What were they to do to protect themselves when they could never be certain whom to trust?

It was bothering Padishar as well, Morgan knew — though the outlaw chief would be the last to admit it. Morgan had been watching him closely since their escape, and the big man was seeing ghosts at every turn.

But, then, so was he.

He felt a dark resignation chill him as if seeking to turn him to ice. It might be best for both of them to be alone for a while.

'Will it be safe for you to try going back to Tyrsis so soon?' he asked abruptly, wanting to make some sort of conversation, to hear the other's voice, but unable to think of anything better to say.

Padishar shrugged. 'As safe as it ever is for me. I'll be disguised in any case.' He looked over, dipping his head briefly against a gust of wind and rain. 'Don't be worrying, Highlander. The Valemen will be all right. I'll make certain of it.'

'It bothers me that I'm not going with you.' Morgan could not keep the bitterness from his voice. 'I was the one who talked Par and Coll into coming here in the first place — or at least I had a lot to do with it. I abandoned them once already in Tyrsis, and here I am abandoning them again.' He shook his head wearily. 'But I don't know what else I can do. I have to do what Steff asked of me. I can't just ignore ...'

What he was going to say caught sharply in his throat as the memory of his dying friend flashed through his mind and the pain of his loss returned, sharp and poignant. He thought momentarily that there might be tears, but there weren't. Perhaps he had cried them all out.

Padishar reached out and put a hand on his shoulder. 'Highlander, you must keep your promise. You owe him that. When it's finished, come back. The Valeman and I will be waiting, and we'll all begin again.'

Morgan nodded, still unable to speak. He tasted the rain on his lips and licked it away.

Padishar's strong face bent close, blocking out everything else for just an instant. 'We do what we must in this struggle, Morgan Leah. All of us. We are free-born as the rally cry says — Men, Dwarves, Trolls, all of us. There is no separate war to fight; it's a war that we all share. So you go to Culhaven and help those who need it there, and I'll go to Tyrsis and do the same. But we won't forget about each other, will we?'

Morgan shook his head. 'No, we won't, Padishar.'

The big man stepped back. 'Well, then. Take this.' He handed Morgan his ring with the hawk emblem. 'When you need to find me again, show this to Matty Roh at the Whistledown in Varfleet. I'll see to it that she knows the way to where I'll be. Don't worry. It served the purpose once; it will serve it twice. Now, be on your way. And good luck to you.'

He extended his hand and Morgan took it with a firm grasp. 'Luck to you as well, Padishar.'

Padishar Creel laughed. 'Always, lad. Always.'

He walked back across the bluff to a grove of towering fir where the outlaws and Trolls waited. Everyone who could came to their feet. Words of parting were spoken, distant and faint through the rain. Chandos was hugging Padishar, others were clapping him on the back, a few from their stretchers lifted their hands for him to take.

Even after all that's happened, he's still the only leader they want, Morgan thought in admiration.

He watched the Trolls begin to move north into the rocks, the huge, lumbering figures quickly becoming indistinguishable from the landscape through which they passed.

Padishar was looking at him now. He lifted his arm and waved in farewell.

He turned east into the foothills. The rain lashed at him, and he kept his head bent low to protect his face. His eyes focused on the path before him. When he thought to look back again, to see those he had fought beside and traveled with one final time, they had disappeared.

It occurred to him then that he had said nothing to Padishar about the magic that still lingered in the broken Sword of Leah, the magic that had saved both their lives. He had never told the other how he had defeated Teel, how it was that he had managed to overcome the Shadowen. There had been no time to talk of it. He supposed that there had been no real reason. It was something he didn't yet fully understand. Why there was still magic in the blade, he didn't know. Why he had been able to summon it, he wasn't certain. He had thought it all used up before. Was it all used up now? Or was there enough left to save him one more time if the need should arise?

He found himself wondering how long it would be before he had to find out.

Moving cautiously down the mountainside, he faded away into the rain.

Par Ohmsford drifted.

He did not sleep, for in sleeping he would dream and his dreams haunted him. Nor did he wake, for in waking he would find the reality that he was so desperate to escape.

He simply drifted, half in and half out of any recognizable existence, tucked somewhere back in the gray in between of what is and what isn't, where his mind could not focus and his memories remained scattered, where he was warm and secure from the past and future both, curled up deep inside. There was a madness upon him, he knew. But the madness was welcome, and he let it claim him without a struggle. It made him disoriented and distorted his perceptions and his thoughts. It gave him shelter. It cloaked him in a shroud of nonbeing that kept everything walled away — and that was what he needed.

Yet even walls have chinks and cracks that let through the light, and so it was with his madness. He sensed things — whispers of life from the world he was trying so hard to hide from. He felt the blankets that wrapped him and the bed on which he lay. He saw candles burning softly through a liquid haze, pinpricks of yellow brightness like islands on a dark sea. Strange beasts looked down at him from cabinets, shelves, boxes, and dressers, and their faces were formed of cloth and fur with button eyes and sewn noses, with ears that drooped and tipped, and with studied, watchful poses that never changed. He listened as words were spoken, floating through the air as if they were motes of dust on streamers from the sun.

'He's very sick, lovely Damson,' he heard one voice say.

And the other replied, 'He's protecting himself, Mole.'

Damson and Mole. He knew who they were, although he couldn't quite place them. He knew as well that they were talking about him. He didn't mind. What they were saying didn't make any difference.

Sometimes he saw their faces through the chinks and cracks.

The Mole was a creature with round, furry features and large, questioning eyes who stood above him, looking thoughtful. Sometimes he brought the strange beasts to sit close by. He looked very much the same as the beasts, Par thought. He called them by name. He spoke with them. But the beasts never answered back.

The girl fed him sometimes. Damson. She spooned soup into his mouth and made him drink, and he did so without argument. There was something perplexing about her, something that fascinated him, and he tried talking to her once or twice before giving up. Whatever it was he wished to say refused to show itself. The words ran away and hid. His thoughts faded. He watched her face fade with them.

She kept coming back, though. She sat beside him and

held his hand. He could feel it from where he hid inside himself. She spoke softly, touched his face with her fingers, let him feel her presence even when she was doing nothing. It was her presence more than anything that kept him from drifting away altogether. He would have liked it better if she had let him go. He thought that it would happen that way eventually, that he would drift far enough that everything would disappear. But she prevented that, and, while it frustrated and even angered him at times, it also interested him. Why was she doing this? Was she anxious to keep him with her, or did she simply want to be taken along?

He began to listen more intently when she spoke. Her words seemed to grow clearer.

'It wasn't your fault,' was what she told him most often. She told him that over and over, and for the longest time he didn't know why.

'That creature was no longer Coll.' She told him that, too. 'You had to destroy it.'

She said these things, and once in a while he thought he almost understood. But fierce, dark shadows cloaked his understanding, and he was quick to hide from them.

But one day she spoke the words and he understood immediately. The drifting stopped, the walls broke apart, and everything rushed in with the cold fury of a winter ice storm. He began screaming, and he could not seem to stop. The memories returned, sweeping aside everything he had so carefully constructed to keep them out, and his rage and anguish were boundless. He screamed, and the Mole shrank from him, the strange beasts tumbled from his bedside, he could see the candles flickering through the tears he cried, and the shadows danced with glee.

It was the girl who saved him. She fought past the rage and anguish, ignored the screams, and held him to her. She held him as if the drifting might begin anew, as if he were in danger of being swept away completely, and she refused to let go. When his screams finally stopped, he found that he was holding her back.

He slept then, a deep and dreamless sleep that

submerged him completely and let him rest. The madness was gone when he awoke, the drifting ended, and the gray half-sleep washed away. He knew himself again; he knew his surroundings and the faces of Damson Rhee and the Mole as they passed beside him. They bathed him and gave him fresh clothes, fed him and let him sleep some more. They did not speak to him. Perhaps they understood that he could not yet respond.

When he woke this time, the memories from which he had hidden surfaced in the forefront of his mind like creatures seeking air. They were no longer so loathsome to look upon, though they made him sad and confused and left him feeling empty. He faced them one by one, and allowed them to speak. When they had done so, he took their words and framed them in windows of light that revealed them clearly.

What they meant, he decided, was that the world had been turned upside down.

The Sword of Shannara lay on the bed beside him. He wasn't sure if it had been there all along or if Damson had placed it there after he had come back to himself. What he did know was that it was useless. It was supposed to provide a means to destroy the Shadowen, and it had been totally ineffective against Rimmer Dall. He had risked everything to gain the Sword, and it appeared that the risk had been pointless. He still did not possess the talisman he had been promised.

Of lies and truth there were more than enough and no way to separate one from the other. Rimmer Dall was lying surely — he could sense that much. But he had also spoken the truth. Allanon had spoken the truth — but he had been lying as well. Neither of them was entirely what he pretended to be. Nothing was completely as either portrayed it. Even he might be something other than what he believed, his magic the two-edged sword about which his uncle Walker had always warned him.

But the harshest and most bitter of the memories he faced was of Coll. Coll was dead. His brother had been changed into a Shadowen while trying to protect him, made a creature of the Pit, and Par had killed him for it. He hadn't meant to, certainly hadn't wanted to, but the magic had come forth unbidden and destroyed him. Probably there hadn't been anything he could have done to stop it, but such rationalization offered little in the way of solace or forgiveness. Coll's death was his fault. His brother had come on this journey because of him. He had gone down into the Pit because of him. Everything he had done had been because of Par.

Because Coll loved him.

He thought suddenly of their meeting with the shade of Allanon where so much had been entrusted to all of the Ohmsfords but Coll. Had Allanon known then that Coll was going to die? Was that why no mention had been made of him, why no charge had been given to him?

The possibility enraged Par.

His brother's face hovered in the air before him, changing, running through the gamut of moods he remembered so well. He could hear Coll's voice, the nuances of its rough intensity, the mix of its tones. He replayed in his mind all the adventures they had shared while growing up, the times they had gone against their parents' wishes, the places they had traveled to and seen, the people they had met and of whom they had talked. He retraced the events of the past few weeks, beginning with their flight from Varfleet. Much of it was tinged with his own sense of guilt, his need to assign himself blame. But most of it was free of everything but the wish to remember what his brother Coll had been like.

Coll, who was dead.

He lay for hours thinking of it, holding up the fact of it to the light of his understanding, in the silence of his thoughts, trying to find a way to make it real. It wasn't real, though — not yet. It was too awful to be real, and the pain and despair were too intense to be given release. Some part of him refused to admit that Coll was gone. He knew it was so, and yet he could not banish entirely that small, hopelessly absurd denial. In the end, he gave up trying.

His world compressed. He ate and he rested. He spoke sparingly with Damson. He lay in the Mole's dark underground lair amid the refuse of the upper world, himself a discard, only a little more alive than the toy animals that kept watch over him.

Yet all the while his mind was at work. Eventually he would grow strong again, he promised himself. When he did, someone would answer for what had been done to Coll.

CHAPTER

34

THE PRISONER CAME AWAKE, easing out of the drug-induced sleep that had kept him paralyzed almost from the moment he was taken. He lay on a sleeping mat in a darkened room. The ropes that had bound his hands and feet had been removed, and the cloths with which he had been gagged and blindfolded were gone. He was free to move about.

He sat up slowly, fighting to overcome a sudden rush of dizziness. His eyes adjusted to the dark, and he was able to make out the shape and dimensions of his jail. The room was large, more than twenty feet square. There was the mat, a wooden bench, a small table, and two chairs pushed into it. There was a window with metal shutters and a metal door. Both were closed.

He reached out experimentally and touched the wall. It was constructed of stone blocks and mortar. It would take a lot of digging to get through.

The dizziness passed finally, and he rose to his feet. There was a tray with bread and water on the table, and he sat down and ate the bread and drank the water. There was no reason not to; if they had wanted him dead, he would be so by now. He retained faint impressions of the journey that had brought him there — the sounds of the wagon in which he rode and the horses that pulled it, the low voices of the men, the rough grasp of the hands that held him when he was being fed and bedded, and the ache that he felt whenever he was awake long enough to feel anything.

He could still taste the bitterness of the drugs they had forced down his throat, the mix of crushed herbs and medicines that had burned through him and left him unconscious, drifting in a world of dreams that lacked any semblance to reality.

He finished his meal and came back to his feet. Where had they brought him, he wondered?

Taking his time, for he was still very weak, he made his way over to the shuttered window. The shutters did not fit tightly, and there were cracks in the fittings. Cautiously, he peered out.

He was a long way up. The summer sunlight brightened a countryside of forests and grassy knolls that stretched away to the edge of a huge lake that shimmered like liquid silver. Birds flew across the lake, soaring and diving, their calls ringing out in the stillness. High overhead, the faint traces of a vast, brightly colored rainbow canopied the lake from shoreline to shoreline.

The prisoner caught his breath in surprise. It was Rainbow Lake.

He shifted his gaze hurriedly to the outer walls of his prison. He could just catch a glimpse of them as the window well opened up and dropped away.

They were formed of black granite.

This time his revelation stunned him. For a moment, he could not believe it. He was inside Southwatch.

Inside.

But who were his jailors — the Federation, the Shadowen, or someone else altogether? And why Southwatch? Why was he here? Why was he even still alive for that matter?

His frustration overcame him for a moment, and he lowered his head against the window ledge and closed his eyes. So many questions once again. It seemed that the questions would never end.

What had become of Par?

Coll Ohmsford straightened, and his eyes slipped

open. He pressed his face back against the shutters, peered into the distant countryside, and wondered what fate his captors had planned for him.

That night Cogline dreamed. He lay in the shelter of the forest trees that ringed the barren heights on which ancient Paranor had once stood, tossing beneath the thin covering of his robes, beset by visions that chilled him more surely than any night wind. When he came awake, it was with a start. He was shaking with fear.

He had dreamed that the Shannara children were all dead.

For a moment he was convinced that it must be so. Then fear gave way to nervous irritation and that in turn to anger. He realized that what he had experienced was more probably a premonition of what might be than a vision of what was.

Steadying himself, he built a small fire, let it burn awhile to warm him, then took a pinch of silver powder from a pouch at his waist and dropped it into the flames. Smoke rose, filling the air before him with images that shimmered with iridescent light. He waited, letting them play themselves out, watching them closely until they had faded away.

Then he grunted in satisfaction, kicked out the fire, rolled himself back into his robes and lay down again. The images told him only a little, but a little was all he needed to know. He was reassured. The dream was only a dream. The Shannara children lived. There were dangers that threatened them, of course — just as there had been from the beginning. He had sensed them in the images, monstrous and frightening, dark wraiths of possibility.

But that was as it must be.

The old man closed his eyes and his breathing slowed. There was nothing to be done about it this night.

Everything, he repeated, was as it must be.

Then he slept.

*

Here ends Book One of *The Heritage of Shannara*. Book Two, *The Druid of Shannara*, will reveal more of Cogline, who calls himself a failed Druid, and of the troubles of the children of Shannara.

ABOUT THE AUTHOR

Terry Brooks was born in Illinois in 1944. He received his undergraduate degree from Hamilton College, Clinton, New York, where he majored in English Literature, and his graduate degree from the School of Law at Washington & Lee University, Lexington, Virginia. He was a practising attorney until recently; he has now retired to become a full-time author.

A writer since high school, he published his first novel, *The Sword of Shannara*, in 1977 and the sequels *The Elfstones of Shannara* in 1982 and *The Wishsong of Shannara* in 1985. *Magic Kingdom for Sale — Sold!* began a best-selling new series for him in 1986; Brooks presently lives in the Northwest.

interzone

SCIENCE FICTION AND FANTASY

Monthly   £1.95

- *Interzone* is the leading British magazine which specializes in SF and new fantastic writing. We have published:

BRIAN ALDISS	GARRY KILWORTH
J.G. BALLARD	DAVID LANGFORD
IAIN BANKS	MICHAEL MOORCOCK
BARRINGTON BAYLEY	RACHEL POLLACK
GREGORY BENFORD	KEITH ROBERTS
MICHAEL BISHOP	GEOFF RYMAN
DAVID BRIN	JOSEPHINE SAXTON
RAMSEY CAMPBELL	BOB SHAW
ANGELA CARTER	JOHN SHIRLEY
RICHARD COWPER	JOHN SLADEK
JOHN CROWLEY	BRIAN STABLEFORD
PHILIP K. DICK	BRUCE STERLING
THOMAS M. DISCH	LISA TUTTLE
MARY GENTLE	IAN WATSON
WILLIAM GIBSON	CHERRY WILDER
M. JOHN HARRISON	GENE WOLFE

- *Interzone* has also published many excellent new writers; illustrations, articles, interviews, film and book reviews, news, etc.

- *Interzone* is available from good bookshops, or by subscription. For six issues, send £12 (outside UK, £13). For twelve issues send £23, (outside UK, £25). Single copies: £2.30 inc p&p (outside UK, £2.50).

- American subscribers may send $22 ($26 if you want delivery by air mail) for six issues; or $40 ($48 air mail) for twelve issues. Single copies: $4 ($5 air mail).

To: **interzone** 124 Osborne Road, Brighton, BN1 6LU, UK.

Please send me six/twelve issues of *Interzone*, beginning with the current issue. I enclose a cheque / p.o. / international money order, made payable to *Interzone* (Delete as applicable.)

Name _____

Address _____

_____